TURKEY SHOOT

To Can & Clíodhna—
You haven't really
experienced Turkey
if you haven't done
it like these people
did! Cheers!

Geoffrey Dutton

TURKEY SHOOT

He might not be the terrorist
you expected

GEOFFREY DUTTON

What you don't know can hurt you.

Turkey Shoot: He might not be the terrorist you expected

Published by Perfidy Press

Copyright © 2018 by Geoffrey Dutton

ISBN: 9781642372953
eISBN: 9781642372960

Printed in the United States of America

Dedicated to the people of Iraq and Syria who, through little fault of their own, have been subjected to barbarous rulers and foreign meddlers that have caused them enormous, unnecessary, and cruel losses and suffering. Their manifold tragedies must not go unnoticed or unredeemed.

FOREWORD

Y OU PROBABLY REMEMBER seeing them on nightly news clips. Rickety boats crammed with displaced people desperately floating to southern Europe, a flood of dispossessed humanity that has yet to abate. Seeking safety and succor, they keep coming, hundreds of thousands of them. Many hand over their life's savings to human traffickers to escape from war-torn Eritrea, Southern Sudan, Niger, Libya, and of course Afghanistan, Syria and Iraq. Extreme poverty and drought force some to abandon their homelands, but most flee tyrants, sectarian violence, ethnic cleansing, or unending war. Thousands have perished at sea, and many of those who made landfall huddle in makeshift camps in Greece and Italy with or without travel documents. Some receive sanctuary as political exiles but most not. Those that are able just keep walking, bicycling, hitchhiking, or pack into buses and trains, traversing arteries into the heart of Europe.

Lightly sprinkled and folded into these hordes are unknown numbers of committed extremists on the move, intent on infiltrating the nations of Europe. They and groups that sponsored them, such as ISIS, Al Qaeda, Hezbollah, and Hamas, held the decadent and hegemonic West responsible for the subjugation of Muslim lands and the debasing of all that is holy to them. Seeking Sharia and a Caliphate at home and revenge abroad, they establish themselves in Europe to recruit aimless and disaffected Muslim youths and radicalize their consciousness. Some they route into conflict zones to take up arms against infidels and apostates. Others form terror cells to target mayhem, such as London, Paris, Brussels, Madrid, and Munich have suffered. The jihadists' logic is that slaughtering infidels will provoke overreactions from the West that in turn will radicalize more Muslims, or at least that's what "national security experts" tend to say before Islamophobic politicians go on to overreact. It seems to be working for all of them: The experts get paid, politicians get votes, militaries and spy agencies get more money to meddle, and terrorist groups get recruits. Only the people and the martyrs lose.

As a whole, the public in the West seems to accept the narrative that Islamic radicals are the product of fanatical civilization-hating mullahs who preach death to infidels and urge young men to martyr themselves to seek salvation and purify the world according to Allah's will. Little is said or known of the life experiences that drive individuals to become jihadists, but it has to take more than a preacher's exhortations to motivate someone to follow a path of destruction to eternity. Happy people don't blow up random strangers, themselves along with them. So what accounts for salafists' agendas? Hatred of secular institutions and lifestyles? A need to submit to a greater cause? Commitment to political liberation? Personal revenge? Western news media rarely bother to uncover backstories or untangle motivations, instead fixating on consequences and suppression of terrorism rather than its causes and dynamics, helping no one understand how terrorists are manufactured not just by mullahs, but by actions of countries like the US, Saudi Arabia, Pakistan, and Turkey.

This book tells the story of one such jihadi, a twenty-something Sunni Muslim, devout but no fundamentalist fanatic. What radicalized him was not the secular stench of Western civilization, even though he had strong doses of it as a youngster in Iraq. His own path to salvation is personal, as jihad is supposed to be, and motivated by revenge, as not all are. What put him on it was the unnecessary and inept invasion of his country by the US that turned his family into internal refugees, ultimately leading to the slaughter of his parents at the hands of an ISIS militia. Mahmoud is on the warpath not because some Imam brainwashed him but because his life was ruined. Secure in his own faith, he despises those who twist Islam to justify despotic atrocities and is willing to find common cause with anyone with the courage to stop them.

Kurdish partisans help him flee ISIS to Syria and hand him over to an international fighting force made up of socialists, communists, and anarchists who infiltrated into northeastern Syria to join forces with the Kurdish resistance to eject ISIS from their ancestral lands. This part of Mahmoud's backstory isn't purely fictional. Such a group of Western radicals is assembled in Syrian Kurdistan and did actually help Kurdish YPG-YPJ (People's Protection Units and Women's Protection Units, the armed wings of the PYD Party) forces drive ISIS out of the strategic border town of Tal Aybad and, more famously, incredibly broke its siege of Kobanê. They patterned the International Freedom Brigade, as they called themselves, after those left-wing partisans who converged on Catalonia in the late 1930s to combat the Fascist takeover of Spain. Within its ranks are women and men, both Muslim and infidel from the Caucuses, Europe, Asia, and the Americas. Some are ex-soldiers while others have never seen combat, but all are drawn to Syria by the depravities of Assad and Islamic statists, collectivist and anti-imperialist impulses, and their own special demons.

They come to Kurdistan to resist fascism and to do whatever they can to help the Kurds to establish a new kind of participatory democracy that is being built in Northern Syria from the bottom up on socialist and egalitarian principles, a place called Rojava (rebranded in 2016 as the Democratic Federation of Northern Syria). Three cantons, Kobanî, Jazira, and Afrin, now constitute this ungoverned multi cultural, non-theocratic enclave—ungoverned in the sense that its residents directly administer their affairs with no reliance on the Syrian or any other state. Rojavans and their supporters aim to incubate participatory confederations throughout Kurdistan and beyond, and are leading by example. Time will tell if their solidarity will prevail against the many forces arrayed against them.

Although rooted in real places and events, this book is a work of fiction. None of its protagonists represent actual people. Certain characters without speaking parts, however, are or are modeled after them. These include public figures, some prominent, others obscure. Certain organizations, institutions, and establishments are mentioned that are also real, some with fictitious names. The story takes place during a month or two in the fall of 2015 and incorporates actual events, some of which occurred before and some after that time frame, compressing time for the sake of a good yarn.

And although some might see it that way, Turkey Shoot is not a radical manifesto or a call to arms. Beyond providing reading pleasure, its purpose is to broaden conceptions of political oppression and reactions to it by vividly transporting readers into a radical subculture made up of real people, not caricatures of "evildoers," having hopes and fears, longings, and relationships not unlike their own. Hopefully, their odds-against struggle to find relevance in a world well on its way to dystopia will find some sympathy. And perhaps that sympathy will engender a bit of empathy, which perhaps might motivate more of us take firmer stands against discrimination, authoritarianism, and militarism..

When a volcano smothers, an earthquake shatters, or a cyclone swamps human communities, people everywhere open their hearts and wallets to help the afflicted. But victims of unnatural disasters such as war, oppression, gang violence, or economic collapse tend not to be seen as equally needy, even those that have no place to live, nowhere to go, and no money to start over with after they bury their dead. Perhaps we think such people are somehow culpable for their fate by not doing enough to get a leg up and to work within or improve whatever system has brought them misery. We tend to blame politicians for not doing enough too, but perhaps they just reflect our own complacency. If landlocked Kurds hemmed in by enemies and a few contingents of foreign supporters can build strong, democratic, egalitarian, and just communities in the middle of a war zone, what's to stop those of us who live in more comfortable circumstances from striving for a better world for us and our less fortunate compatriots?

I. SEEKING REFUGE

We have awoken, and all of creation has awoken, for Allah, Lord of all the Worlds. Allah, I ask You for the best the day has to offer, victory, support, light, blessings and guidance; and I seek refuge in You from the evil in it, and the evil to come after it

Salat al-Fajr

CHAPTER ONE

SUMMER IN ATHENS just wouldn't be the same without mass protests culminating in police riots, and a nice one was shaping up in Syntagma Square. Everyone present knew the well-practiced script: a shield- and baton-bearing phalanx of helmeted men in blue confronts a defiant, boisterous mob outside some ministry, and at some flashpoint proceeds to harshly discipline the protesters.

The Hellenic Ministers—in this case of Finance—were nowhere to be seen, having fled the flood of trade unionists and assorted radicals surging into their sanctum. Behind lowered shutters and barricaded doors, the occupiers rifled through documents, ferreting out content that might incriminate the spineless functionaries who had once again sold out fair Hellas to her predatory creditors.

Knots of policemen passively looked on as Greek nationalist shock troops waded into the crowd to do their dirty work, provoking fights with protesters that typically went their way. But today, it seemed, they would not prevail. Already outnumbered by socialist, communist and anarchist austerity antagonists, nationalist cadres were soon overwhelmed by an arriving column of hundreds of militant unionists. Chanting for a general strike, the communist workers fanned out to surround the rank of riot police guarding the building, generating a human pressure wave that dispersed the rightists.

Careening away from the enemy influx, a stocky nationalist in a black Metallica t-shirt burst from the mob's periphery, colliding with a taller man whose shirt was branded with a raised red fist crumpling a black dollar sign. The impact flung the collidee against a nylon tent with a duct-taped red cross, caving the insubstantial structure. The victim scrambled to his feet, shouting in German-accented Greek that rightists should leave the first aid station alone in case they might need it. He turned to attend to the damages, only to have the offended nationalist yank him to the ground by his blond ponytail and, muttering "*Fae skata, vrómikos kommounistís,*" launch a series of kicks at his midriff

Observing the one-sided altercation, a man trying to right the tent rushed the assailant wielding a tent pole like a rapier, angrily shouting "*Párte to, Skatofatsa!*" Taller, leaner, and decidedly buff, the swordsman jabbed with a fencer's fancy footwork, quickly getting the upper hand. As the nationalist tried in vain to parry his assailant, a pair of policemen materialized. Without ado, they proceeded to separate the combatants and drag the socialist's defender away, meeting his protestations with baton blows to his orange-tinted coiffure. The nationalist issued one last expletive and kick to his victim before running off.

Groaning, the man struggled up with the aid of the spent tent pole. Brushing away tears, he tossed it to a fair-haired woman with wire-rimmed glasses outfitted in a fatigue jacket accessorized with a Red Cross armband. "They got Kosta," he panted in German. "I must get him released."

Passing the pole to a cohort, she asked what had happened. Her response to his description of the assault and his partner's unjust detention for coming to his aid was "Those goddamn Golden Dawn hooligans never get nabbed. What will they do with Kosta?"

"He could be sent away," he gasped, holding his aching side. "I'll try to bail him out tomorrow. It's too chaotic now and I have to warn the others they could be attacked."

"You might have broken ribs," she cautioned. "Go lie down. Tent's almost back up."

He shook his head. "Not yet. Look, there's Spyros. I need to brief him."

Duty-bound, he hobbled away just as the concerned medic's phone sounded the Marseillaise. She greeted her caller in Greek, also with a German overlay. "Salut, Penelope. What's up, girl?" It was a concerned confederate, a ministry occupier seeking awareness of the law enforcement situation outside.

She retrieved a campstool to gingerly perch upon. Brushing away a blond bang, she squinted at the ministry headquarters and advised, "Looks like police are prying open the building's shutters to invade your space. Finish your business and try to make a rear exit. Call me if you get hauled off. Good luck."

Hoping the fate of the occupiers wouldn't be her problem, she clicked off and ducked into the resurrected tent to see who else might be hurting. Finding no one in need of urgent care, she pressed her two remaining volunteers to pack up quickly, warning that the next assault on their outpost might not be so inadvertent. Ten minutes hence, their frail facility was bundled up and ready to go.

Hoisting a backpack and gripping a hamper of medical supplies in one hand and a canister of pepper spray in the other, she wove with practiced situational awareness through throngs of protesters and counter-protesters toward the Metro station. Strangers would assume she was an MD or nurse, not the radical activist the harsh politics of her adopted land had molded her into.

Across Syntagma Square, bullhorns blared as cops dragged bodies away, live ones she hoped. Mass actions like this were necessary but hardly sufficient, she knew, to bring about the stateless society she had come to envision. For that, less confrontation and more dialogs would be needed, plus strategies, allies, resources, and courage she had yet to gather in sufficient quantity. She wasn't about to give up the struggle, but for now, wearied by the seeming futility of it all, she just wanted to get home and curl up with a book and a glass of wine. When liberation isn't happening, a libation can help.

CHAPTER TWO

A S IF TO remind him he had forgotten something important, a seabird swooped past him with a sharp *shree*. Without ado, then and there, in a chill October mist that obscured all but the blue-dawning sky, Mahmoud Al Ramadi lowered himself to his knees facing the sea. As he had still been afloat at the appointed hour of devotion, he now offered *Fajr ṣalāh*, the dawn prayer. The soothing ritual, while it lasted, obliterated the keening and nattering from across the pebbly strand where he and dozens of others had disembarked. He recited his two *rak'ahs*, adjusted his cap, and slowly arose to survey the human specters huddling nearby. Most of these ghosts, he assumed, were displaced, dispossessed beings like himself seeking salvation from grisly circumstances. He shared their aspirations for better days abroad, but while almost all would make long, fraught pilgrimages north, his odyssey would pause several hundred kilometers to the west, or so he hoped.

Through lifting fog he spied a Jeep and two white vans approaching along a two-lane road—security personnel or relief workers, he assumed. Having been cautioned not to get caught up in rescue operations, he took his leave, picking his way along the shoreline, avoiding migrants, cast-off life preservers, and the sorry flotsam of improvised exigency: Plastic bottles and bags. A shoe, a scarf, even a pair of eyeglasses. A man with no complexion, reposed on his side, half-submerged, someone he remembered seeing before. Mahmoud hauled him onto the beach by the armpits and squatted beside him, ear pressed to chest. No breath or heartbeat, only the racing of his own blood. He pumped on breastbone until no more water spat out, then clamped onto purple lips to breathe life back into the luckless middle-aged man, without success. *So close after traveling so far for so long. Such a shame.*

The man's right hand still clutched the strap of an oblong canvas bag. Mahmoud worked it from his fingers, dragged it away, and unzipped it. Inside were sneakers, clothing, packaged food, a Qur'an, a cell phone, and a half-soaked leather purse tied with a drawstring attached to a lanyard. The phone wouldn't turn on but might, he surmised, when it dried out. As willing to reach out to the decedent's relatives as he was, he knew he ought not to, and so returned the instrument to the victim's duffle bag. A glance up and down the beach brought him to his feet with the purse stuffed inside his jacket. "Your misfortune grieves me," he murmured to his mute benefactor before walking on. "May Allah be with you in paradise." His unfeigned remorse for robbing a corpse was soon tempered by the thought *Allah has provided this not for me, but for his work.*

At the berm of the beach he crossed the road and strode uphill, heading north. When he'd lost sight of the shore he stopped to examine his salvage. The purloined purse held a roll of worthless Syrian dinars, but also pieces of gold and silver jewelry, some with precious stones. Mahmoud smiled and gave silent thanks for his ticket to Piraeus.

The road veered from the coast and wound through scattered houses and vineyards to a more barren landscape. Cresting a hill, he spied the harbor he'd noted from his overburdened Zodiac that sheltered several sailboats and fishing boats. Squinting revealed movement on one of them and he hastened downhill, stopping at a weathered store squatting behind two rust-pocked gas pumps. The slam of the screen door behind him roused the old woman at the counter to follow his rummaging with anxious eyes. Seizing a red plastic ten-liter gas can, he mimed to the matron his desire for some petrol, offering a fistful of dead-man dinars. She held one of the bills up to a dusty window, shrugged, wrinkled her nose, and tossed it back, muttering something he was glad he could not understand. Mahmoud scooped it up and in its stead presented a tarnished silver bracelet set with cerulean lapis. Her eyes glinted and her expression softened. She fingered the piece for a moment, tucked it in her tunic, and waved him out to take the fuel and be gone.

He topped off his canister with diesel and sloshed down the hill. Half way on, he set down the canister and from the lining of his jacket extracted a zippered bag of US currency, spoils of war his commander had provided to secure passage. Finding nearly five hundred remained, he pocketed fifty and then inspected the purse he had taken. From its modest collection he selected a gold ring with several small diamonds and another with what might be an emerald before continuing his descent. At the *limáni*, one boat was occupied by a man stretched out on a pile of fishing nets with his feet on the gunwales, chewing a cigar. Waving the fifty, Mahmoud hailed the boat's occupant, shouting "Athens! Piraeus!"

The fisherman had most likely been laying about that morning considering how he could profit from the frantic castaways beaching themselves down the coast, and now one had come to him. He struggled up to sniff the fuel and inspect the money and with a sly smile presented his palm. Aware he was at a disadvantage, Mahmoud reluctantly proffered the rings and waved "enough."

His enticements worked. The captain motioned him aboard his vessel and cast off from the stone pier. Mahmoud followed him to the wheelhouse. As the wooden boat puttered past the jetty, the captain unrolled a coastal chart. Locating the port labeled Piraeus, Mahmoud traced a line to it and received an affirmative nod.

The Aegean shimmered blue under a soft offshore breeze that barely ruffled its swells. Mahmoud perched himself on the foredeck, back to the wales, grimly recalling how his commander had urged him to dispatch whomever ferried him and toss him overboard before entering port, lest he tell tales. But unwilling to betray the mariner who would shepherd him through strange waters, he decided the order was moot. *Let the captain tell whom he will; no one would think twice about his helping a refugee move on.*

Twenty minutes out to sea, a small ship, a coast guard vessel perhaps, broke the horizon. Deciding he needed a hiding place, Mahmoud found he was sitting on one, a hatch cover. He shoved it away and jumped in to hunker in bilge in the company of rotting fish carcasses, nauseously rocking in the wake of the passing ship. When the sloshing stopped, he warily boosted himself up, replaced the cover, and lay on it. When he judged it was noon, he faced the stern and made two *rak'ahs* of *Zhur*, the noonday prayer. He recited prayers as often as he could. He didn't swear, smoke, or fornicate, and had rarely tasted alcohol. He had come to feel his prayers sometimes were heard. Considering all the perils he had recently negotiated, were he a blasphemer, he would have called himself damned lucky.

As daylight dimmed, Piraeus approached. The sturdy old boat puttered past high-rises perched on the shadowed cliffs of Piraiki. In the gathering dusk Mahmoud gestured at a quiet cove, away from the busy harbor. His pilot obliged and nosed in as far as he dared. The thankful Iraqi tipped him with a fifty-dollar bill for more fuel and waded ashore. On the continent at last, on a patch of sand under a high embankment, queasy, half-soaked, he offered evening prayer and then reposed with his head propped on his backpack.

He had a right to be tired. His revolutionary path, which he had been assured would be righteous and glorious, now stretched across three thousand kilometers. To reward him for saving his life, his commander at the Eastern front had tapped him to be a key player in a special operation in Greece, disclosing nothing of its nature. Whatever it might be, it wasn't about to animate the corpses of his parents in Mosul, and that was the point. Some serious avenging needed to be done.

Most of what jihad had entailed so far he could have done without: His battalion's bitter retreat into Turkey after dodging ISIS bullets in Tal Aybah, only to be impressed to lurch across Anatolia in a lorry crammed with Kurds, whom he had to pretend were his saviors and was now glad to be rid of. Then, at the edge of Asia Minor, having to trust his fate to seedy smugglers who relieved him of most of his money for the privilege of rafting to Chios, crammed this time against mothers anxiously stroking wailing children and furiously bailing fathers. Having survived all these and other miracles, here he was in Europe. Feeling ill prepared yet thankful, hands clasped behind his head, he stared into the darkening sky, telling himself *I can do, must do this which was meant to be. For Allah. For Iraq. For my parents and my brother. For liberation. For salvation.*

His eyes soon closed and he slept fitfully until dawn. Vivid dreams, borne by disorientation and pangs of hunger, soothed his slumbering brain. He was in a small orchard on a verdant, sunlit mountain slope. Comely maidens were plucking apples from the trees, laughing and smiling as they filled their baskets with ripe, red fruit, their breasts gyrating their flowing gossamer robes. In the distance, atop a hill, a flag fluttered on a tall pole. "No virgins for you yet," a voice told him. "You must first climb that hill."

CHAPTER THREE

YAWPING SEABIRDS AND grey glimmers of light extinguished his dream, leaving him with hunger, a headache, and a hard-on. He struggled up and gazed up the rocky escarpment he would have to climb to reach the promised flag. But first, he knelt to the rising sun to offer *Fajr ṣalāh*, after which he relieved himself in the bay, stripped away his salt-stiffened clothes, donned khaki pants and a blue polo shirt from his backpack, and interred the foul garments he had worn for weeks under sand and rocks. He drained his canteen into his parched mouth, scrambled up the steep slope, and boosted himself onto asphalt. There, on an esplanade that curved along the bay, he surveyed his surroundings, a stretch of tall, balcony-laden buildings. At the next corner he came upon a sidewalk café he would have entered were it not shuttered. Soon the street diverged from the bay into the shadows of apartment blocks. He trudged through the canyon hoping to be greeted by a place to eat.

His quest was rewarded at a large intersection with a small café, open for business. Hunger drove him inside to gulp down a half-liter of water and tear into a square of *spanakopita*, bread, olives, tomatoes, and refreshing tea for an eagerly accepted ten-dollar bill. Spreading his fingers into the universal phone gesture, he asked the proprietor "Telephone?" and was waved down a cross street.

A brisk five-minute walk brought him to a bus stop and close by, a pay phone. Hoping that it worked, he inserted the phone card he carried and punched in his contact's number from memory, praying that he had gotten it right and that the call would go through without interception.

Anxiety swelled as the number started to ring. His contact's code name had slipped from his mind. He managed to retrieve it along with his own *nom de guerre* just as a gruff voice spoke in Turkish:

"*Efendim!*"

"George, is that you?" Mahmoud replied in accented Turkish.

"Who is this?"

"It's Peter," breathed Mahmoud. "I am here, praise Allah."

"I've been waiting, Peter. I have heard good things about you. We have much to do. You came alone, I hope."

"Yes. I paid a man to take me here from Chios. A fisherman. Now what should I do?"

"Your host awaits you. Do you know where to find him?"

Mahmoud suppressed a snort. "Of course not. I don't even know where I am or what day this is."

George's voice lowered and hissed, "It's Saturday. No one gave you his address?"

"No. I would have remembered it," Mahmoud told him, adding "I thought you would board me."

"Not me. Where are you? Describe it."

"On a long street at a bus stop. It's spelled X-A-T-Z-H-K-something. Behind me is a wall around what looks like a campus or park. I see water way down the street."

"What direction are you walking?"

"Looks like the street goes north," Mahmoud said, noticing the morning sun at his right. "It's very straight."

George told him to hold on while he consulted his city map. Mahmoud stood nervously, his back turned to traffic, until George picked up and told him "I know where you are. It's called Marias Chatzikiriakou Street. Keep walking north. The street will end near some cruise terminals at a boulevard called Akti Miaouli. When you get there, go to the nearest bus stop and pretend you're waiting for a bus. Our comrade will meet you there and take you to his place."

"How will he know me?"

"Tell me what you look like."

Mahmoud described himself: 180 centimeters tall, ragged black beard, dark brown eyes, blue shirt, khaki trousers, grimy tan windbreaker, baseball cap, and a black backpack. George said "Be there in half an hour and stay put until he comes. His name is Andreas and he will know you as Peter. Do not use your actual name, whatever it is. Nobody needs to know." George clicked off before Mahmoud could ask him what Andreas looked like.

Marias Chatzikiriakou Street sloped down before him, long and straight, ending at a patch of dark blue-green water. He walked toward it at a brisk pace, chanting *Andreas, Peter; Andreas, Peter.* Sooner than he'd expected, the street ended at the edge of a circular parking area overlooking several cruise terminals. Next to him was what looked like a church, with a cross atop a tower. No activity, only a scattering of city buses occupied the divided road that ran by it. *It should be easy for Andreas to see me here.*

At the empty bus stop in front of the church he paced the sidewalk. Feeling too conspicuous there, he retreated to the corner of the church to impatiently loiter. About ten minutes had passed when a police car prowled down Marias Chatzikiriakou and stopped at the intersection. Its driver eyeballed him from behind his shades before turning right and slouching down the boulevard. A few fidgety minutes later, a police car, possibly the same one, approached from that direction. It passed by, doubled back, and stopped in front of him. Mahmoud stood warily erect, his mouth suddenly dry as the driver got out and approached. Yes, it was the same cop.

He was used to having strangers—Kurds, Turks, Syrians, superiors—take his measure, but being profiled by the Greek police wasn't part of that repertoire. *What can I do? I can't speak Greek, and if he finds I'm here illegally I'll be detained for sure.* Unwelcome visions of rotting in a filthy jail cell and deportation flashed before his eyes as the officer verbally assailed him in Greek. Instinctively, Mahmoud waved his hands in bewilderment. The cop gave him the once-over, followed by another indecipherable question or command. Mahmoud unconsciously clenched and unclenched his fingers, causing him to think *Maybe I can convince him I'm deaf.* He started gesturing as if he were signing, voicing grunts and mumbles for effect. The cop seemed to get it, because he started speaking louder and more slowly.

Emanating frustration with Mahmoud's impromptu miming, the officer pointed to his backpack, gesturing for him to remove it. Out of options, Mahmoud shrugged and was about to obey the order when he heard a voice from his right calling, "Peter! Peter!" and turned to see a man running toward them up the sidewalk, blond ponytail flapping. The man sprinted up and hugged him as the officer looked on. With his hand firmly attached to Mahmoud's shoulder, he spoke in Greek to the officer, who now began questioning the stranger. *Could this be Andreas?*

It seemed to Mahmoud much longer, but probably only a minute passed before the officer turned and went back to his car. "Andreas?" Mahmoud hissed. His new friend nodded, and draping his arm around Mahmoud's shoulder, started piloting him along the boulevard. Soon he stopped, stepped back, and started to mime sign language at Mahmoud, whispering "Keep waggling your fingers!" Mahmoud complied and they pantomimed as the police car overtook them and sped away.

CHAPTER FOUR

FTER RESCUING THE man he knew only as Peter from the policeman, Andreas steered him along the boulevard hissing "Sprechen die Deutsch? English?"

"English. Some Turkish. No Deutsch. You speak Arabic?"

"Sorry, Peter. Anyway, I was walking to meet you and saw someone matching your description gesturing at a policeman. It looked like you were trying to sign to him, so I thanked him for helping you and told him you're my wife's relative visiting from his village in Thessaly, and you can't hear. He must have believed me, but let's keep moving. Our bus stop is two blocks ahead."

"That was smart of you. So where you taking me?"

"To my place in Keratsini district, other side of town. Half an hour from here if buses run on time."

They boarded an 843 bus loitering at its terminus. Andreas paid their fares and they settled in the back. Mahmoud said "Thank you, Andreas. Praise Allah that you appeared or it would be all over for me. I would have failed before even starting."

Andreas patted his knee. "You will not fail, Peter. We will see to it. You must have had a long, hard journey. How are you?"

As the bus rumbled uptown, Mahmoud told him he felt pretty well despite sleeping outside and hitching rides over several thousand kilometers across Turkey and then at sea. Andreas listened attentively and seemed genuinely pleased to see him. Mahmoud judged him to be no more than thirty years old and taller than himself by at least five centimeters. He was clean-shaven, with sandy blonde hair gathered behind his temples into a thin braid. In his black t-shirt he looked thin but quite fit.

"Incredible story!" Andreas said. "I'm impressed. George will be too, I think. Oh look, we're passing his neighborhood."

"Are we going to stop and see him?"

"Not now. He wants to have a meeting tonight with everybody. Are you up for that?"

"Sure. You mean our team, right? How many is it?"

"Five of us here, now that we have you. Full up!"

Before Mahmoud could ask more about the team Andreas changed the subject, pointing out neighborhoods, shops, reading signs for him. On Dimokratias Avenue, Andreas nudged him from his seat. They disembarked and walked several blocks down a side street to a square where five streets converged near some shops, a café, and a cinema. They turned right and then right again onto a narrow street of small semi-detached residences reposing in semi-repair. Halfway down the block sat a low building, a shop with a sign reading *Radically Chic* in English, and beneath in Greek Ριζική chic. Andreas unlocked the door and they went in.

By the front door, a bulbous black telephone occupied a small shelf next to an equally venerable answering machine. The sparsely furnished dingy white room featured a mirrored wall to their right fronted by a narrow a counter strewn with shears, combs, and bottles capped with spouts. Two barber chairs with overstuffed green vinyl cushions crisscrossed by plastic tape were bolted to the linoleum, a beehive-like hair dryer menacing one of them. Opposite, reflected in the mirrored wall was a low table scattered with old magazines and four tubular chrome chairs with posterior-dimpled orange vinyl cushions.

Grandly gesturing, Andreas proudly told him "This is my salon. When I'm not out organizing I'm a hairdresser here and live upstairs. You'll stay with me there until you leave on your mission."

Mahmoud took in the unpretentious premises and asked his

unlikely host "What did George tell you about me and what I'm supposed to do?"

"Not too much. All I know is that you fought beside one of his old comrades who sent you on to him. Did you volunteer?"

"Not really, but I wanted to get out of that place, so I agreed. But he didn't tell me what it was about. Do you know?"

"All I know is that within a month you will head back to Turkey with a comrade. George hasn't told me the details and I don't need to know. I just take care of things on this end."

"I see. Andreas, how did you get involved and why are you doing this?"

"Come upstairs," said Andreas. "You must be tired. I'll give you lunch and tea." He unlocked a door in the rear of the salon. Mahmoud followed him into a small storage room with boxes on shelves, a counter with a hot plate and kettle, and bottles of water. Off to the left was a water closet next to a bicycle that leaned by the back entrance. Saying "Follow me," Andreas unlocked a door to reveal a stairway.

At the top, Mahmoud found himself in a cheerful kitchen with light lavender walls. An oasis of potted plants almost occluded the view a large window commanded of a stucco wall across an alley, featureless but for its peeling paint. Four polychromed wooden chairs surrounded a round pedestal table graced by a vase of small sunflowers. Andreas motioned his guest to sit down and went to fill a teakettle. He nodded at a doorway opposite the window. "You can sleep on the couch, in my living room. it isn't very comfortable, I'm afraid."

As the kettle heated, Andreas retrieved a ceramic teapot in the shape of a cat with a tail for a handle. Mahmoud repeated his question. "So, can you tell me what brought you to George? Please start at the beginning."

Andreas filled the pot and brought it to the table along with a box of tea bags and two mugs with 2004 Athens Olympiad logos. He sat down and said "Peter, I will tell you. But the less you know, the safer we all will be. You understand, no?"

Mahmoud nodded. They each dunked bags as his host continued.

"Andreas is not my real name, but no matter. I assume Peter isn't yours either. I come from Austria to Athens two years ago to protest against austerity. I connected with other expatriates and local radicals to organize workers and unemployed people we meet at rallies."

"Then you're a Marxist-Leninist, like people in my party?"

"I don't like to label myself. Others can call me what they want. There are many groups in Greece working for change. Piraeus is full of them. I support almost all—even anarchists, but not the nationalist reactionaries of course."

"Do the different groups get along?"

"Sort of. They mostly agree who their enemies are but they're not used to working together. I see them as threads in the fabric of resistance to greed, exploitation and corruption, to be woven together into garments of liberation, and myself as sort of a tailor."

"I think I understand. I myself don't follow any political doctrine. My faith tells me how to live, not some authority or ideology. And *kismet* brought me to Marxist-Leninists comrades who wanted the same things I did, so I joined them. Facing brutal enemies left no time for politics."

"It seems kismet has brought you to us too."

"Can I ask who is 'us'?"

"Besides the five of us, there are several abroad I don't know."

Mahmoud arched an eyebrow. "How do you communicate? Everything is overheard these days."

"We mostly exchange encrypted text messages on customized prepaid phones. Sometimes pictures that get deleted after viewing."

Mahmoud shoved his purple and orange chair back and wandered to the kitchen window. Fingering a frond of palm, he asked "What else?"

"We avoid emails and visit Web sites anonymously. We use secure chat rooms but mostly gather in person. We use code words. You will learn them."

"What kind of code words?" Mahmoud asked, peering down into the alley.

"For people and places, for the operation, and for tasks. The operation is called 'carnival.' If a day goes by when one of us is out of touch, he is supposed to signify all is okay by texting 'It is humid.' If there's a problem, the code is 'It is hot.' When George calls a meeting, he texts 'c u at cinema.' Come, I show you."

Andreas led him into a homey living room. To his left he noticed a bedroom and a bathroom, a well-stocked bookcase rising between them. The furnishings were mostly modern, lived-in but stylish. Two windows overlooked the street from behind a daybed covered in yellow-green plaid facing a coffee table littered with books and newspapers. Three tubular lounge chairs like those in the salon surrounded a television atop a credenza, completing the radical chic look of the place.

From the bookcase, Andreas retrieved a worn copy of *Is Paris Burning?* He thumbed through it to extract a folded-up sheet of yellow paper that he handed to Mahmoud. "This is our codebook. I keep it here. Your first task is to memorize it. You should not carry it about."

The page had about twenty handwritten words and phrases with terse descriptions. Several had been crossed out and replaced with others. Mahmoud scanned the list. "I'll do this today, but I have no telephone and it seems I need one."

"That's in the works. Later we will meet up with our comrade Ottovio who we like to call the Greek Geek. He's preparing one for you." He crossed to the front of the room and lowered the window shades. "Keep them down. Nobody should see you in here."

"That cell phone, can I use it . . ."

"To call people you know? It will make calls to other countries, but you must ask me or George before doing that, understand? Mostly you will receive texts. Reply to the first one with the code for things are okay. Do you remember me telling you what that is?"

"It is—I think—'it is hot.' Is that right?"

"No, Peter it is not," Andreas admonished. "That would alarm everyone."

Mahmoud forced a smile. "I think it's getting very humid in here."

"Expect many muggy days, my friend. The heat wave is just beginning."

CHAPTER FIVE

WONDERING IF IT was time for noon prayer, Mahmoud consulted the electric clock on the credenza.

"Andreas, is it really only nine-thirty? I thought it was later than that."

Andreas checked his phone. "You're right, it is. It's half past eleven. The electricity must have cut out again while I was out. I'll set the time."

Mahmoud expressed surprise; this was, after all, Europe, not Iraq with its incessant blackouts. Andreas explained that outages weren't unusual these days, given Greece's precarious economy and iffy infrastructure, but usually only lasted an hour or so. Mahmoud shrugged, picked up the yellow sheet, and took a seat on the couch to peruse the codes. Some were place names in Piraeus and in Turkey, others mostly questions or responses to them.

"You study," Andreas suggested and went back to the kitchen. "I'll fix some lunch."

From his barely frigid fridge he took out a head of lettuce, a red onion, a cucumber and a green pepper and distractedly sliced them into a wooden salad bowl. Anticipating that his boarder would get around to asking him how an Austrian radical came to be a hairdresser here, he decided not to recount meeting Kosta at a protest rally, hooking up, and eventually moving in with him over his salon. He would simply couch it as learning to cut hair from his friend who was taken to jail after being arrested at a police riot. Kosta's rugged face flickered before him with its dark eyes and orange-accented coiffure. He put down the onion and dabbed his eyes, trying not to think how many times his lover might have been beaten or raped by now.

He placed the salad bowl on the table with olives, slices of sheep cheese, and wedges of pita bread and announced lunch. As he poured tea, a text came to his phone. He smiled. "George must have lit a fire under our Greek Geek, who says your phone is ready. We'll meet him at a café not far from here after we eat."

After their quiet repast, Mahmoud returned to the living room to recite his noonday prayer as Andreas cleaned up. When it was time to rendezvous, they left through the back door, went around the side of the house, and retraced their steps to the square with the little cinema, with Andreas warning his companion to always be alert for idlers and people walking in one's shadow.

Their destination, a funky, nondescript *kafeneío,* was devoid of customers but at least had electricity. Seven beaten-up wooden tables were scattered about, small ones along the side walls, one ensconced behind the front window, and two larger ones in the middle. Andreas took them to the one in back, saying that Ottovio would show up at some point, but time was somewhat elastic for him.

When the waiter drifted by, Andreas ordered *ravani* cakes for three and a pot of tea. "By the way," he inquired, "have you any money?" Mahmoud described the stake in US dollars his commander had given him, but after paying for his various passages only four hundred remained. "Give me a hundred," Andreas recommended. "I'll change it to Euros for you and buy a transit card so you can ride buses and the Metro."

Mahmoud looked up from counting bills to see a chubby young man with deep-set eyes framed by a shock of curly black hair and a pubic beard trudging toward them. "Salut Andreas," the man said, and to Mahmoud "*Chairetísmata*" in a vaguely friendly way before heaving himself into a chair and barking at the waiter for coffee. He helped himself to *ravani* as he pawed out a black Galaxy cell phone from his wrinkled field jacket and placed it on the table. Speaking in Greek, he told Andreas "This is for our friend here. It's unlocked and will work in a number of countries. It's charged up with 120 prepaid minutes and a thousand texts. If they run out, go to a *pantopoleío*, buy refill card, scratch off, and text code to carrier." Andreas repeated his instructions in English.

Mahmoud responded that he'd owned several cell phones but never such an advanced one and asked what functions he should and shouldn't use. In Greek, Ottovio replied, "Only text and call numbers you are given, Reply to texts only if necessary. It shows maps if you need them, but keep GPS off. No email either." Andreas translated and Mahmoud nodded.

Mahmoud's companions continued to converse in Greek, which Andreas did not translate. He picked up his new phone and started exploring its screens, finding an empty address book and only one recent call.

Ottovio finished his coffee and pushed away from the table, excusing himself until later with "τα λέμε αργότερα." Placing a charger for the phone on the table, he said in English "You also need this for when you have electricity."

"So he can speak English," Mahmoud said after Ottovio had lumbered out.

"Oh yes, just not fluently. But he understands it pretty well." He downed his tea and said, "Peter, wait for me here while I change your money. Should only take about twenty minutes."

"Don't you want me to come with you?" Mahmoud asked, his dark eyes darting around the room.

"Your company's fine, Peter. I just think you should keep a low profile. Have some tea and cakes while you're waiting."

As Andreas beckoned the waiter, a young woman entering the café hailed him. She smiled and approached their table. Dressed in black jeans and a navy blue pullover, she was slim, no more than thirty, with honey-blond hair that fell in loose curls around her neck. Wire-rimmed glasses framed her light blue eyes, giving her an intellectual look.

"Salut Andreas," she said, and in German asked "Are you okay? Every time I go by your shop for a haircut it's been closed."

Before Andreas could answer, her gaze flicked to Mahmoud leaning back in his chair, arms folded. "Oh excuse, me, I see you are occupied. Maybe I should check in another time," she said, just as Mahmoud rose and offered her the empty chair. Accepting it with "*Vielen Danke*" she asked Andreas "*Wer ist Ihr sehr höflich Freund?*"

Andreas surveyed the room through narrowed eyes and replied in German "Salut Katrina. My polite friend is Peter, recently escaped from Iraq, trying to connect with his family. He's staying with me before moving on."

The only words Mahmoud could understand were "Peter" and "Iraq." He greeted the woman with "*Inni mushtaaqun ilaykii*" and then asked Andreas "Does your friend know any language besides German?"

With a smile dimpling her cheeks, her gaze lingering, Katrina replied in English "Yes—English, French, some Italian, and Greek. And I hope to learn Arabic. Perhaps you could teach me if you have nothing better to do."

Andreas got up, saying, "Sit tight, Katrina, keep Peter company. I have brief errand. Back in a few minutes," He motioned Mahmoud to follow him to the door, where he told him the story he had given Katrina. It was okay to sit with her, he said. "She's one of my customers and an ally in the resistance. But she's not aware of our group, so keep the talk light." Mahmoud nodded and said he would simply socialize with her until Andreas returned from the bourse. He returned to the table to find Katrina toying with his new phone. "Is this yours?" she asked. "Very nice. My phone is really old."

He told her he'd just gotten it and wasn't sure what it could do. She volunteered to explore its features with him, but soon set it down and asked him what brought him to Piraeus.

He related his more or less veridical but unpracticed cover story: Fleeing to Syrian Kurdistan from ISIS; living with a family there until fighting drove them away, ending up in a Turkish refugee camp; hitching a ride to western Turkey; buying passage on a rubber boat to Chios. Getting put on a ferry to Piraeus by international aid workers who didn't want single men mixing with families in their camp, mentioning he had a cousin in Germany he was trying to reach. She understood his situation, she replied, having been an international aid worker. Mahmoud took the opportunity to prompt her for her backstory.

She was Swiss, she began, from Basel, went to University there, and then signed on with a Geneva-based NGO that provisioned health care in developing nations. When their mission in Senegal needed an assistant, bored and sick of office politics, she jumped at it. With little to prepare her, she was told to organize logistics for public health campaigns like immunizations and malaria prevention. Then, when Ebola emerged, they tasked her to set up supply chains for field hospitals that were often attacked by Muslim insurgents. A few months of that were enough for her. She bailed.

Mahmoud asked if she left Africa because of Ebola or insurgent activity.

"Not really. I simply couldn't take the graft, corruption and predation any more. Local officials were lifting supplies to sell on the black market, pocketing funds, and constantly hitting on me. Our leadership was lazy and incompetent. The top people were overpaid and took holidays on the organization's tab. So I quit, but I never made it back Geneva. When I had to lay over in Athens I got caught up in the resistance to austerity and the sell-out Greek government, and I'm still here."

"I see. So how do you know Andreas?"

First as a customer, she said, but in their inevitably political discussions in the salon, they discovered that they were both fighting the same enemies. Even though he was a committed socialist and she kept the company of anarchists, they mostly agreed on what should be done and sometimes did it together.

"So what have you done with him?" he asked, ears growing warm thinking she might consider his question improper.

Apparently not. "We help each other organize protest rallies and politicize frustrated workers and unemployed youth," she responded. "Besides being very dedicated, he's a wonderful man. I'm glad he's helping you out. Anyway, enough about me. Tell me more about what you've been through. It must have been very tough."

Mahmoud leaned back, searching for words, just as Andreas returned, flourishing an envelope onto the table. "Here's your euros and transit card. How are you two doing?" Not waiting for an answer, he said, "I must go to my shop now. Peter, why don't you come with me? Katrina, we'll get together another time."

Mahmoud hastily complied, telling Katrina "I'm sorry but I must leave. It was nice to meet you."

"Same here, Peter. Don't forget I want you to teach me Arabic," she said with a smile, thrusting at him a napkin on which she had written her phone number.

CHAPTER SIX

FOR AN EARLY supper Andreas fixed an omelet with crusty bread and sliced tomatoes. They ate in the rosy glow of the late afternoon sunlight that filtered through the oasis by the window, speaking little. Mahmoud made himself useful cleaning up their dishes.

"I got you some underwear and socks," Andreas said to his back, "also some pajamas of mine you can wear," not admitting they belonged to Kosta. "You need new shoes. Yours look like they won't last much longer. Why don't you take a shower and make yourself comfortable. When was the last time you were able to bathe?"

"Yesterday, actually, in the Aegean. Everybody got pretty wet."

"That doesn't count, my friend. Please go and enjoy feeling fresh water pour over your body."

Mahmoud followed the advice and lavished in the shower until the water ran tepid. Scrubbing away the salt, sand, and filth from his journey, he reflected that everything seems to be on track so far. He took pride in having executed his instructions flawlessly. But as risky as all that had been, what was ahead could be worse. All he knew was that his mission would take him back to Turkey. According to commander TigerPaw, what George was planning could made headlines around the world.

Toweling off, he replayed his family's many hardships—fleeing Ramadi when he was ten, his brother seven, fleeing the brutal aftermath of the US invasion, struggling to start over again in Mosul.

His father's erratic paychecks from the Ministry of Electricity kept them afloat. And then, three years into his studies in mechanical engineering at the University of Mosul, a plague of locusts descended to chew up their lives. One day while he was at school, ISIS militiamen came to his house. He arrived to find his father's bullet-ridden body slumped in the kitchen near the half-naked corpse of his mother, her throat slit. No sign of little Akhmed—most likely abducted to be turned into an ISIS martyr, and all in the name of what? A brutal power grab by primitive creatures—twisted zealots who despised modernity, civility, justice, learning, and as far as he was concerned, Allah as well.

All thanks to American and European lust for power and petroleum, he fumed, setting Iraq aflame, kindling ancient smoldering hatreds, unleashing one vendetta after another, leveling marketplaces and whole neighborhoods. Then, having crippled his country, the Americans left, oil contracts in hand, handing Iraq over to Iranian stooges, the venal and incompetent Al Maliki government. *No*, he thought, *someone has to pay for creating such misery. We will see to it.*

He emerged from the bathroom, grim but presentable. Andreas, lounging with a book, said over his shoulder "While you were in there your phone jingled. It seems you received your first text."

Gingerly, Mahmoud picked up the device. Indeed there was a text from a number he recognized as George's that simply read: **8 PM at mothers**

"Who—what is 'mothers'?" Mahmoud asked.

"That's a code. Look it up to find out. As I told you, you must memorize them all."

Mahmoud scanned the piece of yellow paper he'd left on the coffee table. "Yes, I see it's a street address, 5 Doganis, number 3. Do you know where it is?"

Andreas described George's safe house, a nondescript flat George shared with a Turkish comrade. He went there now and then to coordinate and make various arrangements. He had found the pad through a local activist he knew whose sister had lived there before moving abroad and was happy to have it occupied.

"You can get there on the 833 or 875 bus," Andreas said. "The 833 stops two blocks from here. The closest stop to Doganis is Astynomia. There's a police station nearby, but don't worry. Cops aren't very vigilant around their station houses unless one was recently firebombed."

Mahmoud recalled his brush with the law. "Can't you take me there this time?" he pleaded. "If I miss my stop or get lost it could be disastrous."

An hour later, on a bus slouching down Anapafseos Street, Mahmoud was pumping Andreas. "So I finally get to meet George. What's he like? What do you think will happen tonight?"

Andreas was half listening, thinking about Kosta and how miserable he must be in his lockup, missing his smile, his laughter, his touch. "I know a few things about him," he eventually replied. "But best to let him tell you. He plays his cards close to his chest and can be very unpleasant if he thinks you know or talk too much."

"Okay, fine. I won't ask personal questions. But tell me why did I have to come here, only to return to Turkey? Wouldn't it make more sense to make our plans there?"

"I don't know. As I told you, my role is to coordinate, house you, and keep you out of trouble. I know George only because one of his Turkish comrades—someone I met at an international youth conference in Macedonia—called and asked me to help him get established here. My guess is that George started this operation in Turkey and came here to escape being busted."

"Why were they after him?"

"Can't say. George never talks about it. After he made his way to Piraeus he called me looking for shelter. He stayed on my couch for a week before I located the place we're heading to now. Until we got better acquainted he was quite close-lipped. Still is."

Why, Mahmoud asked was an Austrian radical helping a Turk on the run?

"It's what I do—organizing, logistics, helping comrades. Once

George decided I could keep my mouth shut, he asked me help him, but I have nothing to do with the Turkish side of things. George and his roommate Michael are in the MLKP, the Marxist-Leninist Communist Party of Turkey. I assume you are too, but of course I'm not."

The bus rattled to a stop at Astynomia and the two got out. On Andreas's instruction they separated before meeting again on the next block. Mahmoud shivered as he passed the police station and picked up his pace. After they reunited, Andreas said "Relax Peter, you will be very welcome here. I won't stay for the meeting. After I speak with George about something I'll leave. To return to my place, retrace your steps and wait for the 833 bus across the street to come home. Last bus comes around eleven." He handed Mahmoud a key to his flat and pressed a button labeled 3. The intercom crackled and squawked "Who is it?"

"Andreas. I have found your cat." A pause, then the buzzer sounded. They ascended the stairs as the front door slammed shut behind them. The higher they climbed, the darker it got.

CHAPTER SEVEN

A T THE THIRD floor, a cracked-open door dimly spilled yellow rays of light onto dusty concrete. Andreas pushed open the door, silhouetting a compact man with long, straight black hair who waved them in. "*Merhaba Peter! Gelin lütfen!*"

"Peter, Meet George," said Andreas, beckoning Mahmoud in.

"*Sağol. Tamam,*" Mahmoud casually replied as he entered, nervously scanning his surroundings. The room was sparsely furnished with a sagging couch, an ottoman, a television on a low table, and half a dozen cane chairs surrounding a Formica-topped table. Two of the chairs were occupied.

"*Hoşgeldin comradim!*" announced George, grasping Mahmoud's shoulders and ceremoniously kissing him on both cheeks.

In Turkish, Mahmoud praised God for his safe arrival and asked George how he was doing.

George grinned. "I don't praise God, but I am well and very pleased that you are here. But I'll be even happier once you are gone!" He stepped back to inspect his catch. "You look fit. I hope you are prepared to change the world. Our plans are almost complete, but some things are taking time. Anyway, meet our team. There are four of us here and several more in Turkey."

One of the sitting figures turned toward them. It was the Greek Geek Ottovio. "Good I see you another time," he said. "Does new phone work?"

Mahmoud withdrew the Galaxy from his trousers. "So far. I like it. I see it does many things."

"Yes, and can do many things *to you* if you are careless. Remember I say keep GPS off? Check each day. If is on, someone may be tracking you. Come, I show you setting."

"You can show Peter later," said George. "Let's finish introductions. Michael, meet Peter. Peter, meet Michael. You two will be comrades in arms in Antalya."

The other man at the table rose and approached. He was a bit shorter than Mahmoud and not as lean, with wiry black hair, and seemed older, perhaps because of his narrow glasses and streaks of silver in his black goatee and mustache.

With a hug and a kiss to each cheek, he greeted Mahmoud. "*Merhaba! Tanıştığıma memnun oldum.*" Mahmoud echoed it was good to meet him too.

Andreas waved "Hello again, Michael, Ottovio. George, unless you have further use for me here, I'll be on my way."

"Okay," said George. "Keep Peter out of trouble and take care in leaving, as always. See you."

George sat on the sofa, spread his arms on the backrest and crossed his legs. "Peter, why don't you start by telling us about yourself and how you got here."

Mahmoud ran down his escape from Anbar Province, his years in Mosul, the coming of ISIS and the loss of his family. He said he had no reason to stay but nowhere to go. "To make a long story short," he told them, "Some Kurds from school helped me escape to Syria, where I was adopted into a YPG militia. They trained me in combat, but since I'm not Kurdish they handed me over to IFB. You know them, right?"

Michael nodded. "Sure," George said. Comrade TigerPaw, your leader, helped organize the International Freedom Brigade."

"Soon," Mahmoud continued, "we joined up with another YPG unit preparing to take on ISIS. We attacked a border town called Tal Abyad. A lot of smuggling went through there to and from Turkey. I think the YPG wanted control of that."

"And they got it. Then kicked you guys out, right?" said Michael.

"Yes. We fought along with YPG comrades for ten days and won. ISIS retreated and the Kurdish commander took control. He wanted to absorb our battalion, but TigerPaw refused and took us across the border to plan our next move. Before long, he picked me to work with George and sent me across Turkey to float to Greece with Syrian refugees."

George shook his head wearily. "It shouldn't be that hard to work with Kurds against a common enemy, but it often is. I'm glad we don't need their help for this project. OK, Michael, you go."

In a quiet voice that grew more emphatic, Michael told his story. He came from a liberal secular family. He was in graduate school studying literature and history when his father, a newspaper journalist, was thrown into prison on trumped-up charges of defaming the government of Turkey, along with dozens of other writers. He dropped out of school to help his mother try to win his father's release, but to no avail. Michael thought it no coincidence that soon he was called up for military duty. As he couldn't afford paying a hefty fee to avoid service, he ended up a conscript at a base near the Syrian frontier.

At the eastern front, he saw how National Police gendarmes were mistreating Kurdish citizens. Local government officials demanded bribes and kickbacks only to do their jobs badly. Then his unit was ordered to transport supplies destined for ISIS fighters the military was secretly moving along the border to Kurdish areas just inside Syria so that they and the Kurdish resistance could kill each other off. Adding to his depression, one day his aunt called to tell him his mother's cancer had spread and he was needed at home. He got furloughed to attend to her, but when he got to Izmir he found her on her deathbed.

Michael's voice came close to cracking. "Burying my mother with my father in prison and then having to return to duty left me in bad shape. My aunt helped settle affairs and used insurance money to pay off the government to release me from the army, bless her."

Mahmoud told Michael he identified with his situation and asked "So what took you from there to here?"

"I returned to school, but my resentments only grew. A fellow student was an MLK Party activist who encouraged me to write an exposé of the military's support of ISIS based on what I witnessed. We set up a blog and put out three articles before the government got it shut down. We assumed we'd be arrested if they found out who we were."

"And then?"

"So my friend and I went underground. Went to live at an MLKP safe house outside Izmir that already had three cadres living there. One of them knew George and had heard that he was looking for help with an operation in Greece. I wanted to keep moving, so I volunteered. I didn't know what was involved any more than you probably do."

"So is Turkey looking for you now?"

"Not that I know of, but they don't advertise their arrest lists. If they know who wrote those articles, I'm sure I'm on one."

George had gone into the kitchen while Michael was talking and returned with a bottle of wine and some tumblers. Setting them down, he addressed the matter Mahmoud had been warned not to ask about. "As for myself, I am of course Turkish, born in Bursa but have moved many times. Like yours, my real name does not matter. My parents were bourgeois leftists who exposed me to socialist discourse, but after seeing them and their kind persecuted and marginalized too many times I concluded that intellectualism didn't work, only direct action. I started working with like-minded people in the MLKP to take down the corrupt capitalist system by whatever means possible. We are the vanguard of revolution and have shown we can strike anywhere. That the party is outlawed proves we have been effective."

When Mahmoud mentioned that he did not drink alcohol, George sent Michael to the kitchen to fix tea for him and continued talking, relating that he'd entered Greece through Thessaloniki and traveled by bus to Athens, where he connected with Andreas. He observed that the turmoil in Greece was predictably producing revolutionaries faster than they could be arrested and hoped for the same in Turkey. Exactly why he had exiled himself, however, he didn't go into and Mahmoud thought it best not to ask.

"But enough about me. Let's get on with it, comrades." George removed a folder from a messenger bag on the floor and extracted a map—a Turkish topographic map, not easy to come by as the military controls their distribution. They lifted their glasses to let him spread it out, revealing part of Antalya province near the Mediterranean coast. He pointed to a location out in the countryside labeled Aspendos.

"You may know that a G-20 summit will take place in Antalya next month. High-level officials from many nations along with bankers and CEOs will assemble to hammer out arrangements for fitting Turkey and other emerging economies into the imperialist world order. First on their agenda is a welcoming ceremony under the stars. A convoy of buses will take the delegates to Aspendos, a big Roman amphitheater that still hosts many events, located here, twenty kilometers east of Antalya city. The event will take place starting at 1730 on November fifteenth and will last two or three hours."

"You're sure of that?" said Mahmoud.

Ottovio piped up. "You want to see delegates' program I skimmed off G-20 Web site? They didn't do a very good job securing it."

George showed them a photograph of the imposing stone amphitheater. "This is the venue. Delegations will bring security details and Turkish soldiers will patrol the area. They will probably sweep for explosives and wireless devices, so we can't use any of those. And of course we can't just charge in there, blasting away. There will be more security forces than delegates"

"Could we use a truck bomb?" asked Mahmoud.

George dismissed the idea. "See that massive front wall? That could hardly dent it. Couldn't even get near it. So no bombs, no guns. Instead, we'll set up a doom machine and be long gone when it goes off."

"So, you want to kill them all without explosives or any of us nearby?" Mahmoud asked. "How?"

"With *this* . . ." George said, pulling from his bag a short length of white plastic tubing about two centimeters across, "and a few other things." He handed it to Mahmoud.

"As for any other event at Aspendos, a wood platform for speakers and entertainers will be set up. It's about a meter high and stretches across that big front wall. In front they'll lay a carpeted floor for the delegates. The platform consists of twenty-two modules that bolt together. Each module is numbered according to its location."

"How did you find that out?" Mahmoud asked.

"Our comrade in Antalya has a contact who works there who can provide a key to the shed where the modules are stored." George took another photo out and laid it down. "Here's the underside of the platform. Our guy snuck under it and shot these pictures during a rock concert there. He identified stage sections where our stuff should go."

"And what stuff is that?"

"In several weeks, you two will go into that building and fasten two wooden boxes under platform units that go at the front the stage. Inside, the boxes look like this." He ripped a page out a notebook and drew a square containing two rounded cylinders. From each he sketched a hose that connected to a T-joint, from which another hose extended. Over the tee he drew a small rectangle. "That's a quartz clock timer we can pre-set for any date and time we choose. At that moment, it opens two solenoid valves to release compressed gas from those cylinders. The two components mix and react to flow out through the tube going out the top."

"I see," said Mahmoud, "and the tube pipes the gas out onto the stage."

"Correct, through two small holes facing the front of the stage at either end, shooting gas into the crowd. The devices will be ticking away, programmed to go off about half a minute apart, without making a sound."

"And those bottles contain . . ."

"Sarin, an odorless, tasteless aerosol. Inhaling a tiny amount can kill a man within a minute."

CHAPTER EIGHT

MAHMOUD SANK INTO the couch cushions as George continued to outline his plan.

"...We have procured two rounds of Sarin—also called GB—in Nylon bottles, which will not trigger a metal detector. They came out of Syria and weren't easy to get. Sarin doesn't have a very long shelf life, so it's usually deployed as a binary weapon—two nonpoisonous liquids that are mixed just before release."

"That's the kind we have, right?"

"Yes. That's why there are two cylinders per box. Much safer to transport that way, but it complicates our task. Building the release mechanisms is taking longer than we expected."

"My job almost done," Ottovio proudly announced. "I make two smart watches with quartz oscillator, some chips, display and keys I take from old cell phones. You set and forget."

"No GPS, I hope," Mahmoud said.

George ignored the wisecrack and went on. "The bottles are small—about a liter each, mostly propellant. The timer opens both bottles at the same time. The two components squirt into a small chamber, mix into sarin that will vaporize when it hits the air."

Mahmoud leaned forward. "So how do we install the devices? Seems it could take a long time."

"It should go fast. You only need two tools. You guys will go in at night with headlamps and knapsacks. You will have armed the boxes and sealed them beforehand. Ottovio will show you how. The top of each box will be covered with Velcro, with a short tube sticking out. You'll have a stapler, a manual drill with a wood bit, and two squares of Velcro, each with a pre-cut hole. First you locate the platform module numbered 1-A."

"Hope it will be easy to find" said Mahmoud.

"You may have to move some around. Be sure to put them back as they were. If you can't locate it, use 2-A or 3-A. It must be row A. Staple a Velcro pad at a front corner of the module, many times."

Michael interrupted. "How will we know which side goes in front?"

"Good question. The modules bolt together, so the front is the side with no holes in it."

"Okay."

"Then drill a hole in the platform through the hole in the Velcro pad for the emission tube. Align the tube with the hole, press the box onto the pad, and clean up your droppings. Repeat with the other box in section 11-A, 10-A or 9-A, and you're good to go. The only tricky thing will be finding the right platform sections. But they're all numbered, and you'll have plenty of time."

Michael followed up "What time should we set the timers for?"

"The program says the event will begin at 1800. It should last at least two hours, so even if it's delayed our window is quite big. I would set them for about 1900."

Mahmoud rose to his feet and went over to George. "What if something changes and the event is moved or cancelled? It won't be possible to disarm the things, so what then?"

"No problem," George calmly responded. "By then you'll be long gone and we'll just let it happen. The real intent of the attack will be clear to everyone. Yes, it will be disappointing, and bystanders may die. But when we crow about it as ISIS on social media people will be furious. Killing innocents is their thing, no?"

Mahmoud didn't reply. Ottovio played with his phone. Michael sat motionless, gazing at the floor. George took a sip of wine and said "So we trade a few tourists for tens of thousands of innocents killed by imperialist aggression. Yes, that would be unfortunate, but look, when will you ever have the chance to decimate so many power structures, all at once? And we won't stop there, no matter what happens. I have more plans. We'll bomb a police station. Take down a power transmission line. Steal and reveal state secrets. Everything we do, we will generously credit to ISIS."

Ottovio offered details. "Yes, we'll hack government networks. Deface state Web sites. Grab secret documents and emails, reveal on Wikileaks."

From his bag George extracted a handwritten sheet of paper and handed it to Mahmoud. "This is an English draft of the statement we'll release on social media after the operation. Peter, I want you to translate it into Arabic, edit to make it sound like ISIS, and then translate it back into English. You'll be videotaped in disguise narrating both versions before you go. After your attack, Ottovio will add news footage and push it out on the net."

Mahmoud accepted the document with a nod. He looked it over, folded it carefully, and put it in his breast pocket. He sipped his tea, now cold, and turned to his new partner. "Let's get some water, Michael," he said, and led him into the sparsely equipped, unkempt kitchen. He filled two glasses in the sink and handed one to Michael, who accepted with "Sağ olun."

"So how do you feel about all this?" Mahmoud asked.

"Naturally I'm a little nervous. You must be too, hearing about it for the first time. But you will get into it."

"Maybe. I need to think about it more."

"You heard George. It's an amazing opportunity to launch a revolution. We're lucky to be part of it."

"Yes, it could be. We all have our reasons to be here," Mahmoud asked. "What are yours?"

"It's not just my father being in jail or because it's a great target shoot. It could save Turkey from becoming a religious dictatorship. The governing party can't have it both ways."

"What do you mean?"

"They can't on one hand brag to fundamentalists that they safeguard the flame of Islam, and on the other tell the princes of globalization

Turkey is the model Muslim secular state while dismantling it, bit by bit. They try to hide that contradiction by suppressing criticism of their religious agenda and how they help ISIS kill Kurds and Arabs. It's totally cynical."

"For my part," said Mahmoud, "I too despise how Turkey is acting, but that is not my main concern. I can't bring my parents back to life or rescue my brother, but I'll do whatever I can to defeat the ISIS criminals. Since we can't strike them directly, we might as well strike out at imperialists to discredit Turkey and put heat on ISIS. But still, I'm not sure that George's plan will go smoothly. Are you?"

Michael glanced down at his shoes. "George is very smart. He has been in the vanguard for a long time. He says key party members are committed to this operation. It's been planned in detail. It's going to happen. Who are we to say it cannot work?"

"I don't know. I have to think about it."

"OK do that, but don't think yourself out of the mission. You're past the point of no return."

"What is that supposed to mean?"

Michael clenched his comrade's shoulder with a word to the wise. "George owns this operation, and now that you know about it he owns you too. Don't even think about getting out."

Mahmoud's stiffened and his eyes narrowed. "Umm, just suppose I walked away."

Michael's voice went from sand to gravel. "I heard about one of his comrades who backed out of an earlier operation and went off with his own plan. They had a confrontation that led to a scuffle and George pitching him out a window. Please don't cause trouble. We need you."

Mahmoud wandered over to the kitchen window. In the darkness all he could see was the top of the fire escape silhouetted by a window across the ally that had its blinds drawn. He turned to meet Michael's eyes. "I'm not saying the mission won't work, just wondering what could go wrong. I'm an engineer. That's what we're trained to do."

"So go back in there and tell George you want to look for holes in the plan. See what he says."

"No, Michael, not now. I'm tired and need to leave. Andreas said the last bus leaves the station at eleven. It's almost that now."

"No problem. You've been through a lot. Get some rest."

Mahmoud returned to the front room. Mahmoud told George he had to catch a bus and asked if was it all right to leave. George nodded and said to Ottovio, "You should probably go with Peter. I think you both are on the same route."

Looking more bored than tired, Ottovio said, "Okay. We go now."

The two bearded men, one thin and the other not, clomped five floors down the dim stairway, out to the street, past the police station to the bus stop. A policeman getting out of his patrol car didn't seem to notice the two men as he went into the station.

Within two minutes the 833 bus pulled up. Only three other passengers were aboard; two older women burdened with bags and a punked-out teenaged girl with orange hair and plentiful eye shadow in a black jumpsuit punching her phone.

The two men felt safe to sit together and took a seat near the back, not talking shop or anything else, Mahmoud exploring his phone as Ottovio interrogated his. After a while, Mahmoud asked, "Can you remind me what the bus stop closest to where Andreas lives is called?"

"I don't know where he lives" came the helpful reply.

Mahmoud described Andreas' neighborhood as best he could noting he lives two or three blocks from the café where they first met. That should be Vyronos, Ottovio told him, about six stops beyond where he would get off. "Is big street. Shops on corners." Then he got up and pushed the call button. "Ciao," he told Mahmoud. "I get off now."

The bus chugged to a stop and Ottovio plodded into the night. Mahmoud noticed the stop was named Platenos, and tried to decipher bus stop names as the bus gathered speed. He made his way to the front and said to the driver, "Vyronos? Vyronos stop please?" The driver said something in Greek. Mahmoud shrugged and said "Sorry." But the driver seemed to get it and gave him the high sign.

Less than two minutes later the driver called out "Vyronos!" and pulled to the curb. Even though it hadn't seemed like six stops to him, Mahmoud got out. As the bus rumbled away, he surveyed his surroundings, nondescript apartment houses and a few shuttered shops. Under the sodium glare of street lights nothing looked familiar.

He jiggled his phone in his hand, considering turning on GPS, despite Ottovio's warning. *No, let me call Andreas to come get me.* But instantly he realized he didn't have his host's number. His phone held only one, George's. He considered texting, but decided that would make him look stupid.

Afraid to wander away, he suddenly remembered that he had another phone number, the one Katrina had slipped to him. He ran through his pockets and was relieved to find it. *Should I call her? She's not one of us and I know little about her. But if she's a good friend of Andreas, I should be able to trust her to help me get home.* Deciding it wouldn't hurt to text her, he hesitantly he typed: this is peter we meet today in cafe & i need some help. He hit Send, exhaled, and sat down in the bus shelter.

His mind drifted back to the meeting on Doganis and his mission. He hadn't bargained on a high-profile target involving massive security and multiple national leaders. But George's deep investment and Michael's enthusiasm somewhat offset his qualms. This was his kismet, and he had to see it through. For solidarity. For revolution. For payback. Not to mention the wrath of George.

His phone buzzed away his reverie with the words whatsup peter. Katrina had answered!

Feverishly he typed: i got of bus at rong stnp canu help go hom and leaned back. A minute later came a call and he blurted "Katrina, hello. I am lost!" Calmly, she asked if he was okay and told him not to worry—she could help him find his way. He told her he got off at the Vyronos stop, but it looked completely unfamiliar.

As soon as he started to describe his environs, she said she understood. To his relief, she told him to stay right there and she would come.

They clicked off. He sat down again, massaging his temples, wondering if he had done the right thing. But there it was. He would handle it as best he could.

CHAPTER NINE

B Y HIS PHONE it was now 11:40. Several cars passed by. He hoped a patrol car wouldn't be next and that Katrina had gotten his location right. Ten dreadful minutes later, a small blue-white light caught his peripheral vision. The light bobbed closer until the cone of a street lamp limned a bicyclist.

Katrina rode up and dismounted. "Salut, Peter. I came as fast as I could. Are you okay?"

"Feeling better, thanks," he said, rising.

"When you said you got off at Vyronos and were confused, I knew what had happened," she explained. "There are two stops with that name, almost a kilometer apart. You got off at the first but should have waited for the second one."

Why didn't Ottovio tell me that? he thought, irritation infusing relief, but only said "Praise God you came. I could have slept with rats in an alley. I wanted to call Andreas but I don't have his number."

She said "I'll give it to you. But let's get out of here. We'll go to my house. It's much closer. Sit behind me on the luggage carrier. Come on, it's mostly downhill from here."

He started to protest, but she was already mounting her steed. He slid behind her, lightly wrapping his arms around her waist, and they wobbled off into the humid night. She navigated through narrow streets, swerving around potholes and casually parked cars as the night breeze tousled his hair. When the bike bounced on a loose cobble Mahmoud tightened his grip around her waist but slacked off as the heat of her body passed to his.

The two-headed two-wheeler rattled down a cobbled street and skidded to a halt at a two-story stucco apartment house numbered 37. He followed her down an alley and around to a back door.

"Some of my anarchist friends helped me liberate this little house," Katrina said as she chained up her bike. "I share it with the woman upstairs. It's a cozy space to retreat to at the end of the day." She unlocked the door and flicked on a light. "Please come in," she urged.

He removed his shoes before crossing the threshold to a large white-walled kitchen with cookware, dinnerware and pottery on unpainted wooden shelves. A drop-leaf table took up the center of the room. "Let's call Andreas," he was glad to hear her say. "But first, are you thirsty? I have wine, San Pellegrino, coffee, tea, and orange juice. What would you like?"

He explained that he did not drink alcohol, but would welcome some coffee. "I'll fix us some espresso, then." She switched on her coffee maker and dialed her phone.

In German, she said "Salut, Andreas. I call this late to let you know that Peter is here with me. Why? Well, he got lost coming home. Said he didn't have a number for you. Fortunately I was able to find him. We are at my house." They briefly conversed and she extended her phone to Mahmoud. "Peter, he wants to speak with you."

"Peter," said Andreas, "Glad you're safe and not wandering the streets. We think you should stay where you are. In the morning she'll take you to meet me. Are you okay with that?"

He would rather go to his house, Mahmoud said, but staying where he was made sense. Andreas reassured him. "You'll be fine there. Katrina is a good person. I trust her to help you, but as I told you, do not discuss any of our work with her. Do you understand?"

Mahmoud gave him his word. Andreas said he would meet them tomorrow at a nearby taverna, and would bring a city map to avoid future confusion. They rang off.

"So," Mahmoud told her, "I guess you're stuck with me."

Katrina smiled as she placed a glass of white cubes on the table. "It's no trouble, Peter, really. Here's your coffee and some sugar."

He dropped two cubes into his cup and suppressed a yawn.

"You can sleep on the floor in here, she said. "I sleep in the other room. I'm sorry, but that's all I can offer."

"This is fine," he said. "I've slept in many worse places."

She sipped her coffee and went on. "I'm kind of a night owl. When you texted I was reading a really interesting memoir about a terrorist bombing at a university in Israel. True story. The author's wife was badly hurt in the attack and several of her friends died. He decided to track down the terrorist who did it and confront him. I think he eventually does, but I haven't got that far yet."

Mahmoud looked up from his cup. "Really? Does he want to kill the attacker?"

"No, I don't believe so. He had decided that more violence would only make things worse for everyone in Israel and Palestine. He hoped to be a peacemaker." She got up and returned with a paperback with a black cover littered with fragments of charred paper, each with one word. Together they spelled out *What Do You Buy the Children of the Terrorist Who Tried to Kill Your Wife?*

"I would like to kill the terrorists who murdered my parents," Mahmoud muttered. "Instead I killed a man who was shooting at one of my comrades."

Katrina's eyes widened behind her spectacles. "Really! Where was that?"

"Fighting ISIS in Syria, but the shooter could have been from anywhere."

"And then what happened?"

"They outnumbered us but we beat them. I don't know how. I was told about forty of them died. Four of our battalion did not survive. Then the commander of the Kurds we fought beside took over the town and ordered us to disband and join their force. Our leader wouldn't allow our brigade to be absorbed by YPG, and so led us across the border to Turkey to fight somewhere else."

"Did you fight again?" she asked, leaning closer.

Mahmoud sensed he'd said more than he should have. "No. But what about you? Have you killed anyone?"

She frowned. "No, but sometimes I've wanted to."

"Like who?"

"In Africa I was not far from villages where assassins called Boku Haram slaughtered men, raped women, abducted children. We aided some who escaped. Some were little kids, orphans. I wanted those criminals to be tortured and killed. Sometimes still do. But you said your family was wiped out. It must have completely changed your world. All I lost was innocence."

He put down his cup with a sigh. "Life has a way of flaking away one's illusions."

Katrina scowled. "And making others just as fast. I thought the people I worked with at the NGO were part of the solution, but their good will masked a selfish mentality. They said they'd come to help but were mostly in it for themselves. It took my hope away. I quit."

"And so why are you here now?" asked Mahmoud, capitalizing on their role reversal.

"As I told you in the café, I was returning to Geneva by way of Athens. Lots of chaos when I got there. My flight got cancelled. Demonstrations. Strikes. Riots. Police brutality. Corruption and austerity. The third world all over again. I found a hostel where I met other foreigners who had come to resist the capitalist octopus and decided to stay to see what I could do. That was nearly two years ago and I'm still here. Hopefully without illusions this time."

"So what illusions have you lost?"

"That people who say that they are here to help really mean it. That charities are altruistic. That political leaders are trustworthy. I fell in with so-called anarchists who are really community organizers and bridge-builders. In small groups we experiment with new models for organizing work, new forms of cooperation that can build strong communities out of broken people. It might as well start here, where all institutions seem to be failing."

Not that he believed Katrina would take up a gun, he could almost envision her in his old battalion helping cadres sort out their differences. He found himself saying, "Yes, we must overcome selfishness and mistrust to slay the monsters that want to devour us."

"I feel the same, Peter."

Again he wondered if he'd said too much, hoping she hadn't taken his words as an implicit invitation to collaborate. "I'm half asleep now," he said. "The floor is fine. I have slept on the ground many times."

She got up and rummaged in a closet. "This air mattress will help. It pumps up quickly by foot. And here's the sleeping bag I used it in Africa. Don't worry, there's no Ebola on it. Good night, Peter. Sleep well."

"Thank you, Katrina. You too. Good night."

She entered her bedroom and closed the door. Mahmoud stripped to his shorts, switched off the light, climbed into the sleeping bag, and closed his eyes. It had been a long, fraught first day in a new land. And now it was ending in an anarchist's kitchen.

In her room, she changed into her nightgown, slid into bed, and took her journal and pen from her nightstand. She paused, pen to lips, and then started writing.

2 October: That handsome Iraqi man who boards with Andreas called tonight, lost at the wrong bus stop. I brought him home, we sat and talked about ourselves and I put him to bed. Perhaps next time, if there is one, I will take him to bed. He seems quite shy, but resolute, and doesn't say what he's up to with Andreas. Why do I want to know more? Why do I care? Maybe I'm a sucker for attractive, militant, wounded men. Watch out girl.

CHAPTER TEN

WHITE CURTAINS BILLOWED in pale light, animating dim shadows on Mahmoud as he sat up with a start, awakened by a staccato rattling. Who might be banging on the kitchen door at such an early hour? *Police like to do that*, he thought, squirming from the sleeping bag. He tiptoed to Katrina's bedroom door and knocked softly, just as the sound stopped. "Katrina! Come!" he whispered hoarsely.

Shortly the sound of padding footsteps and Katrina in a nightgown. "What is it, Peter?" she asked, her voice husky with sleep.

"It woke me up. Maybe someone banging on your back door, but now all is quiet."

"I'm glad you're here," she whispered as she walked across the room. "Let's listen." She slid open a drawer and armed herself a long rolling pin.

"Stand behind the door," she breathed, and took a position across from him with arm raised. They stood as statues for almost a minute. Then more stuttering thuds. Mahmoud stiffened, but Katrina smiled and lowered the rolling pin. "It's from the window. A shutter banging against the house in the wind." She pulled aside the window curtain, revealing the twilit alley. Sure enough, small bits of trash gyrated past as the shutter flapped. "Happened before," she said. "I should secure it."

She returned the rolling pin to its nest and rubbed her eyes. "First thing in the morning I make coffee," she announced. "Would you like some?"

"Please, Katrina."

She turned away. Mahmoud quickly dressed and sat at the table watching her tamp dark brown powder into the brewing cup and switching on the machine. As she lazily crossed the room it occurred to him he had been staring at this woman in her negligee. Realizing he liked what he saw, he averted his eyes.

She set down two steaming espressos and brought some pastries and a dish of butter. "I love croissants," she said, setting out four. "The Swiss way to start the morning. I couldn't get them in Africa, so I'm making up for lost time."

Mahmoud said he'd heard of them but had never tasted one. "Here, try it. Put butter and jam on, if you like," sliding over a pot of marmalade. "I bet you never had marmalade either."

Mahmoud admitted he hadn't, and bit into his croissant. It reminded him of baklava, without its cloying sweetness. "It's good," he said, taking another bite, realizing how hungry he was.

"Want to know why they're crescent-shaped?" She asked, tearing one apart and buttering one half. He nodded, assuming she would have told him anyway.

"Everyone thinks they're a French invention, but the story goes that they were first baked in Vienna after breaking the Ottoman siege. Turks were tunneling into the city. Some bakers working late at night heard digging sounds and raised the alarm. Not long after, their army was driven back. Vienna was saved, and to celebrate, some baker created pastries shaped like the Turkish crescent. True story, or perhaps just a legend."

He took another bite, leaving flakes on his beard.

"Oh, they called them *kipferli*," she added, "Marie Antoinette—who was actually an Austrian Princess—introduced them to King Louis' table. Eventually they were named an official French pastry. Who knew the French had official pastries, but isn't that just like them?"

"I would never attack that way," he said. "No digging for me. Tight spaces make me nervous. I want room to move around."

"Attack what?" Katrina said, and then cast down her eyes. "I'm sorry. Withdraw the question. None of my damn business."

It startled him. Something like the embarrassment of a boy whose mother finds a nude pin-up in his underwear drawer flushed his face. He looked into his cup, wondering why she was curious, almost wishing that it were her business. Aware of Andreas' admonitions, he let the wish wither, but had no ready reply, realizing he had a story to explain his past, but not his future intentions.

"As I told you," he managed to say, forcing himself to look at her, "I have unfinished business with ISIS." The gaze she returned was steady, luminous, bespeaking curiosity.

He started spinning. "Last year, m-my cousin Walid fled to Germany. If I can find him, I will tell him what happened to my family and learn what happened to his. I'll try to convince him to return to Ramadi to look for relatives to join us, and when the time is right go to liberate Mosul." The spinning stopped. He hoped she would be satisfied and change the subject.

She reached across the table to wipe the crumbs off his beard, saying, "I understand. You have scores to settle." She put the napkin down and dabbed butter on her croissant. "But I can't imagine anything much more difficult and dangerous."

She finished her croissant in silence, staring into the middle distance. Mahmoud quietly got up and took his cup and plate over to the sink. Katrina brought her plate and asked "Peter, do you mind cleaning up here while I get dressed? Then we'll go to meet Andreas at the taverna on Dimokratias."

Wiping crumbs from the table, regretful of his imprudent revelations and improvisations, he resolved to be more circumspect. He bundled the sleeping bag, deflated the mattress, and returned to his seat. His mind was in Mosul when she exited her bedroom, dressed in blue jeans and a green pullover under a field jacket that looked like military surplus. A rolled-up black bandanna encircled her head, slightly askew, like the halo of a fallen angel. He could almost see her in the field, by his side. He shook his head to let it go.

"We can go now," she said, massaging in hand cream.

He placed the bedding in the closet and said, "Okay, I'm ready," unsure of what that meant. The way she smiled when he said that looked like she might be wondering too.

Past shops cluttered with whatnot, skirting idlers, shoppers and their conveyances, the Iraqi warrior and his infidel escort threaded their way along teeming Dimokratias Avenue. Mahmoud stopped walking and opened his phone. "Katrina, can you show me how to find the GPS? I was told to keep it off."

She took a look and found all its location services turned off, explaining how pesky busybodies use them. She laid the phone on his palm then snatched it back. "Oh yes, let me add Andreas' number to your phone book. I see mine there, but only one more. Looks like you could use more friends."

After passing an auto repair shop and a Domino's Pizza, she said, "This is the place where Andreas said to meet." The modest establishment was open to the street with tables laying claim to the sidewalk. Its hard-to-miss sign announced ΤΑΒΕΡΝΑ ΟΜΦΑΛΟΣ in big blue letters. She read out the sign as *Taverna Omphalos*, adding that omphalos roughly translates to 'navel of the world,' in Greek mythology.

The popular restaurant wasn't as crowded as it would be in a few hours. She led him inside to a table with wooden chairs with tattered cane seats. The navel of the world, he observed after looking around the shabby interior, seemed to have picked up some lint.

"What would you like, Katrina?" he asked. "I will pay. You have been very kind to me."

She thanked him said she's like some coffee while they waited. Mahmoud asked her to order it and some tea for him and inquired if she would stay after Andreas arrives.

"Only if he invites me to. I doubt he will, but that's okay. Oh here, let me see your phone again." He handed it to her and she pointed at an icon in the corner of the screen. "See, that means there's Wi-Fi nearby, and it is not protected, so you could be automatically connected to the Internet. It might be from the restaurant, someone living nearby, or even a laptop trying to lure you to connect. I doubt anyone around here wants to mess with your phone, but let's turn off your Wi-Fi until you need it."

Mahmoud's eyes shifted warily. "How do you know all these things, Katrina?"

"My dumb old phone doesn't have all these features, but my friends worry about it all the time. We're pretty sure movement people's phones and computers have been hacked. So now we take care to minimize our footprints, you know?"

The waiter hadn't yet brought their order when a battered red motor scooter pulled up in front. Its driver dismounted and hurried in. It was Andreas.

Breathlessly he said "Salut. It is good to see you both. Thank you, Katrina, for helping him out. I hope you had a good rest, Peter." He slapped a folded-up map on the table. "Here is a city map for you, Peter. It has street names, bus and metro stops, everything you need to not get lost again. Take it wherever you go." His eyes narrowed as he sat and leaned forward, jiggling his knee. Katrina started to say she was leaving, but Andreas cut her off, declaring that he and Peter needed to head downtown to Drapetsona. Mahmoud opened his new map and Katrina pointed out where the neighborhood was. He recognized it as the area he had visited last night.

"Why, Andreas," he asked. "Is there trouble?"

"I'll tell you on the way, Peter. Katrina, I'll catch up with you when I can. It may be a day or two before I'm able to cut your hair."

No problem she assured him, and followed them outside. She watched them mount the Vespa. Its motor chugged, growled, and whined as they bounced onto the pavement. Katrina called after them, "Good luck! Call me if you need any help!"

The men's sudden departure puzzled Katrina but didn't worry her. She added *find out what Andreas is up to* to her mental to-do list, which already included pick up mail, go food shopping, and catch up on correspondence, and went about her day. The post office involved the biggest detour, so she went there first. The first several months in Piraeus she'd moved around a bit and had rented a mailbox as a way to receive official correspondence and letters from abroad. After taking possession of the building she and a female comrade had liberated, and considering her line of work, she decided she should keep her letter drop.

Since she'd last checked for mail, all that lay in wait was a bill from the electric authority, a bank statement from Switzerland, a couple of circulars, and what looked like a personal letter bearing no return address, postmarked Piraeus, addressed in Greek to Katrina Kunt. *How nice*, she thought, *I'll save this to read with tea and chocolate this evening, and stuffed the lot in her handbag.*

Her errands accomplished, she trekked home with a baguette and a sack of potatoes, cabbage, beets and soup bones for borscht. Once home, she laid her mail on her lampstand and went to make soup. After cutting up beets and placing them and the bones in the oven to roast—as her grandmother had taught her—she couldn't stand the suspense and retreated to her reading place to rip open her secret admirer's letter. It was unsigned, brief, and to the point:

Your next insult to Hellenes will be your last, filthy foreign anarkist kunt.

She settled back in her overstuffed armchair wishing she had a cigarette, but having kicked nicotine a year ago resisted the urge. It could have been her tweets, her blog, or both that had brought her unwanted attention from an online mouthpiece for the Golden Dawn Party, an ultra-nationalist entity calling himself SuperPlato. At first, he seemed to be gratified when she retweeted some of his posts, hoping his militant disdain for the political class and international capital could convince leftists and nationalists that they had common enemies. Of course, she didn't retweet the anti-Semitic and racist slurs that SuperPlato vomited out, and said as much on her own blog.

She abandoned her armchair to retrieve her laptop from her nightstand drawer. Cradling it cross-legged on her bed, she reviewed her latest post called *Who's an Alien?* to find it had garnered fifteen responses. She read it over:

Listen nationalists, there's no such thing as a Greek or even a white race unless you believe ancient Greek origin myths are real. If you go back far enough, no one is racially pure. If you believe the Bible, everyone came from the Middle East. If you believe science, everyone came from Africa via the Middle East. Greeks arose from bush babies, just like everyone else. So stop looking down your semi-Semitic noses at Jews, Muslims, blacks, and foreigners. You're mongrels too. Get over it.

All but three of the comments she read were supportive. Of the rest, the ones in all caps must have been deposited by nationalist trolls. Among other provocations, they instructed her to go back to whatever shithole of a country she came from, because defending immigrants is a betrayal of all the Hellenic Republic stands for. *A special place in Hell is reserved for all internationalist scum*, one wrote. She'd expected blowback, but the online graffiti was unnerving, the hate mail more so. How did SuperPlato latch on to her P.O. box number? Did the Hellenic Police have a hand in it? Whatever, clearly she had to watch her back from now on. Pensively, she closed her computer, somersaulted from the bed, and sallied forth to fix her grandmother's soup.

Chapter Eleven

Swerving around stationary and moving obstacles, bulling through intersections, Andreas piloted the Vespa down Dimokratias and turned right on Maritiou. Speeding along the broad boulevard oblivious to changing traffic signals—as seemed to Mahmoud to be the local custom—Andreas addressed his clinging comrade over his shoulder.

"We think something has happened to Michael," he shouted over the snarl of the engine. "I just talked to George. He told me that when he awoke this morning Michael was gone."

"What?" Mahmoud yelled back, "He left no note or text or anything?"

"Nothing. George wanted to text him but decided not to risk it. If Michael had been picked up his phone might be in the hands of the police."

"So what did George do?"

"Said he packed up their stuff, wiped down the flat and left as soon as he could."

Mahmoud had to ask. "So why are we going there?"

"To meet George and give him the Vespa. He'll take their things to my place. We'll take the bus back."

The scooter passed by a large cemetery, crested a hill and sped down to turn left onto Sokratous Street. After another left, Andreas slowed down. "Keep your eyes open for police and people who look like they're doing surveillance."

They slowly cruised down Doganis. People were walking and hanging out, all seemingly minding their own business. "Look into parked cars, Peter. Try to see if anyone is inside."

Before Mahmoud could apply his powers of observation they encountered George sitting on a low wall with a black garbage bag at his feet. The Vespa stuttered to a halt and the men dismounted to bracket their comrade. "This is not good," George said. "He has been with me almost constantly. It isn't like him to wander off without checking in. I can't text or call him for obvious reasons. So I left a note on the door saying 'Call your mother.' He'll know what that means."

"If he comes back," said Andreas. "What else can we do?"

"I don't know, Andreas, but I need to stay with you tonight. Everyone I know is out of town or in jail . . . that was a joke."

"Of course," Andreas replied. "Peter, I hope you don't mind. It will be a little crowded but we'll make do. Take the Vespa and Peter's key. Go up and try to relax. We'll take a bus and meet you there."

Mahmoud had been standing watch from the corner of his eye. "I see two policemen leaving that station house," he announced. They all slowly shifted their gaze to the right. The two cops were conversing, their voices inaudible.

"Time to go," George said. "Take care." He straddled the Vespa, balancing the black bag on his crotch.

He kicked the scooter to life and sedately headed down the block, made a right turn and then gunned the engine and sped away as the two policemen continued to chat. As Andreas nervously checked the time, Mahmoud said, "I like that the scooter is red. That's our color."

The next morning, Mahmoud again awoke at an early hour from fitful sleep, this time prompted by rhythmic snorts from the other side of the bed. In times past and in various unkempt quarters, the snores of assorted bunkmates had also interfered with his rest, but not like this. *What makes me think he's gay?* he wondered, watching Andreas peacefully slumber. Quietly, he slipped out of bed. In the next room, George lay on his back on the couch, also snoring. In the kitchen, he looked for something to drink. He settled on a carton of orange juice from the fridge, poured some into a glass and sat at the table staring at the greenery by the window.

It had been a major relief when Michael texted George late in the afternoon to say he was all right. Had he not checked in, they would have bought morning newspapers to see if an incident possibly involving him had been reported. Next, they would check hospitals and then the city morgue. Fortunately, none of that was necessary. Michael's message, mother am ok with a friend c u soon, showed that it was from him, but what friend? That he even *had* a friend upset them. By slipping out late at night without saying anything, Michael had taken unnecessary risks that could have jeopardized their mission. Mahmoud recalled how he had almost been detained when he first arrived. That surely would have been the end of him.

George had been more than upset—he was livid. He texted Michael, emphatically instructing him to return home straightaway and stay there until he returned. Even after the okay came, George didn't calm down for an hour. They suspected Michael's friend might be a woman who had offered him her body, but who? A sex worker? Nobody besides them and Immigration was supposed to know of Michael's presence in the city. It had been a dangerous breach of discipline, and George told them he was prepared to dump Michael if he decided he wasn't fit for the mission. That possibility troubled Mahmoud. He took comfort in having a Turkish partner because he had seen little of that country, spoke its language poorly, and worried George might make him run the operation alone. That possibility also had compromised his evening's rest.

Now that they knew Michael was safe, none of them particularly wanted to deal with him. George had decreed he should spend the night alone in their flat, repenting and worrying what would become of him. There the matter rested, but soon George became restless. He said he was hungry and suggested they go out for air and find something to eat, preferably pizza. The notion met approval, and around five they walked down to the Avenue to find a pizza parlor. Mahmoud suggested the Domino's he'd noticed, but George said he didn't patronize chain restaurants. It wasn't about their food, he explained, it was the principle: You don't feed global capitalism; you eat local. The pizza parlor they ended up at turned out to be run by Bosnians, but their pizza was reasonably palatable if one avoided ethnic toppings like peas and potatoes. They hiked back to the flat in time for Mahmoud to pray and George to watch the news.

Mahmoud was still nursing his orange juice when George wandered into the kitchen in t-shirt and shorts, tousled and cranky, muttering "*Günaydın*" by way of a morning greeting. After gazing out the window for a while, he said he wanted the two of them to return to the Doganis flat to confront Michael, who should have spent the night there. Mahmoud had been looking forward to coffee and breakfast, but George clearly wanted to get moving.

They hurriedly dressed and George messaged Michael: **where r u? mother coming home**. While awaiting a reply, he found a piece of paper and wrote a note for their sleeping host: *Went back. Took Vespa. Will return to you asap.* George tossed Mahmoud his bag and Michael's things and told him to follow. Out in the alley came a terse reply from Michael: **will b there**. Taking that to mean that Michael *wasn't* already there raised George's hackles all over again. "This is too much! If he stayed away another night, he better have a damn good reason."

The Vespa swerved through back streets with Mahmoud precariously perched behind, clutching cargo with one hand and clinging to George with the other. As George maneuvered around a turning bus, Mahmoud remarked, "I didn't even have time to pray this morning."

Over his shoulder George growled, "Then pray now. Pray Michael has not ruined everything. Make sure God is listening."

George slowed down at Doganis Street and seeing no potential spectators parked around the corner. Ascending the dank stairwell,

Mahmoud hoped Michael would find sufficiently contrite words to mollify George, if that were possible. Inside they found Michael sitting on the couch. Instantly he was on his feet, crying "I am sorry! I am very sorry! I know I should have asked you if I could leave, but I was sure you would refuse. Nothing bad happened and nobody observed me."

George scowled "Nobody? You stayed with someone. For two nights. Who is it?"

Mahmoud shivered. He too had stayed with someone the night before, but let that slide.

"I will tell you the truth," Michael said, propelling his body to its full extension.

"And it better be the whole truth," snapped George.

"On the ferry to Piraeus I meet a Greek girl, a college student living with her parents here. We like each other and she gives me her number. Thinking about her drove me crazy, and so other day I call her. She say her parents went to the country and asked me come over. We made love that night and next day I wanted to go but she begged me to stay and I could not resist her beauty. But I told her nothing."

"Sex is one thing, but you must have said something about yourself. What did you tell her?"

"I gave her my cover story. That I am here to research my thesis, study Greek history. She has a little Turkish and English, but we don't talk much. We make love."

"What now?" queried George, coming closer. "Will you see her again?"

"Perhaps—with your permission."

"Wrong answer!" George barked, launching a fist into Michael's stomach. Michael doubled over and George kneed him, sending him sprawling onto the couch.

Between gasps, Michael cried "It wasn't wrong! I was foolish! No harm was done!"

Tugging Michael to his feet by his shirt, George pulled him close. "No, Michael, this is revolution. This is your jihad, not a college seminar. Everything must happen as I say. If I ever decide you are a threat to this mission you will be floating in the harbor."

George let go. Michael fell back on the cushions, sobbing.

Glowering, George turned to Mahmoud. "The same goes for you, my friend. Keep your nose clean and away from crotches."

CHAPTER TWELVE

AFTER GEORGE KNOCKED the hubris out of him, Michael slowly uncoiled. "All right," he rasped, clasping his aching midriff, "I am ready to continue. If the girl calls, I will tell her I had to go home. What do you want me to do?"

George laid out the Antalya map and unlocked a tablet computer that he carried in his bag. "We plan, Michael. We practice. We commit every detail to memory. I have photographs of where you will go." He held up a flash drive. "Our man in Antalya took photos and videos of the place and sent them in an encrypted file I downloaded from a computer at the public library."

Plugging the memory stick into the tablet, he said, "Haven't seen these myself yet. I hope they are nice and sharp." He clicked on an archive file and responded to a prompt for a password. It was refused. He tried again, and then another password, but the file still failed to open. "We had agreed what the password would be," he muttered. "He better not have changed it. Either he did or the file's no good."

"What can you do about it?" asked Mahmoud. "Can he send it again?"

"He can be hard to reach and we need to be online at the same time. Perhaps Ottovio can help. He has crypto tools, he told me." George placed a call, exchanged a few words, and then told Mahmoud to take the Vespa uptown. "He said he'll be waiting for you at the café where you guys first met. If he's able to crack the file, bring it back right away."

"And if he can't?"

"Text me either way. If he fails, I'll go to back to the library to contact Antalya, but I'd rather not go through that. While you're away, Michael and I will script the operation and work out transportation."

"Be happy to, George" Michael said, as if he had a choice.

"You two will take a bus and stop off to pick up the devices on the way to Aspendos. You'll need tools and suitcases to carry it all. We need to make those arrangements. We have a lot to do." He handed the key to the Vespa and the thumb drive to Mahmoud with "Do not lose this, Peter! Now go, and keep out of trouble!"

Downstairs, Mahmoud discreetly peered through the front door and only saw two people waiting at the bus stop. At the Vespa, he studied his map. He vaguely knew how to get back to Keratsini but not exactly where the café was. He decided to head to Andreas' place and navigate from there. If he were still confused, he would check in with him.

The machine chugged to life and bumped off the sidewalk. Mahmoud immediately had to swerve to avoid a car backing into a parking space. Accelerating with a quick backwards glance, he wondered if he'd imagined seeing cops in that car. When he came to Maritiou Boulevard he turned right, knowing it would take him most of the way. Dodging potholes in the uneven pavement brought to mind that he had driven only one vehicle since fleeing Mosul, a jeep under fire in the battle for Tal Abyad.

He was jerked into the present by a van pulling out from a curb that nearly clipped him. He decided its driver wasn't interested in him, but George's paranoia and concern about being tracked had made him edgy. He started wondering how he would feel transporting tanks of deadly poison across Antalya province and rigging a death trap and whether he was considered expendable. He didn't think George would willingly sacrifice him, but the man wasn't easy to read. Although Mahmoud admired his toughness and resolve, he didn't like how he patronized everyone and treated them coldly. They weren't, after all, a military unit; they were comrades who should fully collaborate, not simply act on orders. Thinking there was nothing he could tell George that could shape the mission summoned his slain father and how he had treated him as a youngster, yelling at him, dictating what subjects to study and who not to hang out with. But at least his father had more kind words for his little brother, that skinny kid with bad eyes who was probably already dead. He must have disappointed his ISIS captors—there was no way that Akhmed was militia material.

Approaching his neighborhood, he commiserated with Michael, whose innocent affair with his Greek temptress had caused him as much pain as pleasure. His thoughts turned to the estimable Katrina, who seemed to be fond of him, but an angry motorist's horn after he ran a red light ended his reverie, ejecting her image.

Mahmoud managed to home in on Andreas' building, trying to recall how they had meandered to the café that first day through alleys and streets that converged at odd angles. He killed the engine and was about to head down the alley when he saw that the door to the hair salon was open. Inside, Andreas stood behind a chair that was swiveled away, cutting a customer's hair. No one else seemed to be present, so he spoke up.

"Excuse me, Andreas. Can you give me directions, please?"

Andreas put down his shears and came to the door. "Salut Peter. Directions to where?"

"Remember the café you took me to? I have to meet Ottovio there," motioning him to the scooter, where he opened his map. "It's not far or hard to get there," Andreas advised. "Make a sharp right at the apothecary. From there it's only a block to Dodekanisou. The café is on your left, down the street. So what's up?"

Mahmoud told him about the locked-up file that Ottovio was needed to pry open. Andreas seemed more interested in Michael's fate than the flash drive's, and invited Mahmoud to return for lunch to talk. Mahmoud thanked him and, saying he'd be back, mounted the scooter and found his way to the café, where he spied Ottovio at the back table, sipping coffee and caressing his laptop. Mahmoud ordered tea and handed over the memory stick. Ottovio inspected it and wiggled it into a port. Shortly a list of files to popped up.

"Which one?" Ottovio asked. Mahmoud pointed to a zip archive and handed him the scrap of paper with its supposed password, which obligingly failed for Ottovio too.

"File may be corrupt. If is, maybe I can fix. If no, I try program to crack. But can take long time."

As his companion typed obscure commands, Mahmoud received his tea and savored its astringency. He was curious to get a look at the images of Aspendos just beyond reach, but by the time his cup was dry Ottovio was still furiously typing away, and soon gruffly announced "File structure looks okay. Just wrong password. This machine too slow to crack it. I take home to my little supercomputer."

"How long can it take?" asked Mahmoud.

"Depends on password strength. Maybe ten minutes, maybe ten hours. More even."

"Shall I come too?"

Ottovio snapped the laptop closed and got up. "Sorry. No visitors where I live. I call George when done. He tell you. See you later. You pay coffee please."

Mahmoud didn't feel like leaving. Lunch and a debriefing with Andreas could wait a while. He ordered another tea and gazed out the front window. Just as the waiter deposited his beverage, a familiar female entered the café, waved at him, and came to his table smiling. Tossing her head from side to side, she chimed "Salut, Peter. Fancy meeting you here. How do you like my new haircut?"

"It . . . it is very nice, Katrina," he stammered, eyes pinching. "Shorter hair fits your face and suits you very well."

Unlike their first meeting at this very table, he suspected, this one might not be an accident. Wanting to excuse himself without seeming rude, he reluctantly offered her a seat, which she gladly accepted.

"Andreas was doing my hair when you stopped by," she explained. "I thought you might be here. But you look a bit distressed. Am I intruding? Shall I leave?"

He settled back, trying to compose his features. "No, it's okay, Katrina. There's nothing I have to do right away."

Over her shoulder Katrina ordered coffee. She turned back to Mahmoud, pulled her chair closer and gazed at him. "After you and Andreas zoomed off, I thought about your situation. It must be a hard for you here, and a little lonely. Is there any way I can help?"

Hoping to read her intentions, he replied "Thanks but nothing right now. What kind of help were you thinking about?"

Her reply, "Oh, I don't know. Maybe inquire with relief agencies to locate your cousin in Germany," failed to comfort him.

Shortly after her cup arrived, Mahmoud's phone buzzed in his pocket. It was only the second voice call he had received. It was Andreas, who did not waste time with pleasantries. "Come to my place right away. I'll tell you more when you get here. Where are you?"

Mahmoud explained he was at the café but did not mention Katrina.

"Hurry. Get over here now," Andreas barked and ended the call.

"I'm sorry," he told Katrina, "but I must go now. Maybe we can talk later."

"It's okay. Call me when you get a chance." He appreciated not being quizzed.

Andreas had sounded stressed, urgent. Driving back to his flat, Mahmoud assumed a new problem had come up. It might solve itself, like Michael's disappearance, or it might not, like the encrypted file that Ottovio was working on. Upstairs, Andreas was pacing across the kitchen, fingers locked behind his back, not his usual unflappable self.

"We have big trouble and have to think clearly and act carefully," Andreas said as soon as Mahmoud closed the door.

"Michael called. Not very long after you left, apparently, the Hellenic Police—gendarmes—showed up at Doganis Street and grabbed George as he was leaving. Michael barely managed to escape. I told him to take the bus to Vyronos where I'll meet him."

Mahmoud collapsed into the sofa, stammering "W-w-what does this mean? What will we do now?"

"The police have George but at least not his phone. I know that because Michael told me he had rescued it. But that phone may be bugged. We mustn't let it betray us."

"Why would the police want George?" Mahmoud asked. The man was a cipher to him.

"He kept his background to himself to keep us from telling the wrong people. But the guy who connected us hinted that he's wanted in Turkey on terrorism charges going back a while. He's been living underground here and there for some years, but it looks like they finally closed in on him."

Mahmoud let that sink in. "So, are we next? I am sure nobody knows I'm here, but could they be looking for you?"

"All his contacts are in his phone—that Michael has—or in his head. I don't think they can trace any of us. But they might have his tablet. I think he kept all his files on that flash drive that you just took to Ottovio. So we may be lucky, but for how long I can't say."

Mahmoud wasn't feeling lucky. "So it seems the operation is finished."

"It looks like that. We can't pull it off without George. Even if we could, you might walk into a trap."

Mahmoud leaned back and expelled a sigh. Along with the mission, his confidence was seeping away, replaced by fear of dishonoring his family, forsaking his jihad, being forsaken by God. No longer an avenger, now he was just another displaced casualty of war. He buried his face in his hands, murmuring, "What will we do, what will we do?"

Andreas grasped his shoulder as he'd done when steering him away from the policeman down by the port, telling him "Michael is safe and we still have each other. We must hang together, as they say, or hang apart. But now I must run to get Michael. Wait here. I won't be long. If I'm delayed I'll text you."

Mahmoud nodded and handed him the Vespa key. "Allah be with

you," he told him, not knowing whether that meant anything to his infidel accomplice.

"*Wa 'Alaykum as-Salaam!*" replied Andreas, turning to leave. "See, I picked up a little Arabic. We'll hang together and make new plans." He went down the stairs and outside. The Vespa's engine stuttered, rumbled, and echoed down the ally. Mahmoud stood at the window, looking past the potted plants to the brick wall across the ally, a wall as blank as his future had just become.

Chapter Thirteen

IT WAS MAHMOUD'S turn to pace circles in the kitchen and hyperventilate, trying to expel a throttling dread. Would George betray his comrades under torture? Was he being tracked too? He checked his phone's GPS setting and was relieved to find the battery was dead. But that made him feel equally vulnerable, so found his charger and plugged it in. As much to calm himself as to petition the deity, he prayed, and was back on his feet by the time the two others arrived. He and Michael embraced wordlessly before Michael hobbled to a chair and began describing the unfortunate events.

Fearing that Ottovio wouldn't be able to decrypt the file on his flash drive, George had decided to purchase another one before heading to the library to contact his comrade in Antalya. Michael had been absent-mindedly observing the street from the front window when he noticed three men—two of them in uniform, the other not—emerge from a black car parked across the way. They walked briskly toward George as one of them appeared to hail him. George reacted with a subtle motion with his right arm and walked briskly to the corner and out of sight. The three men briskly followed, and after several minutes returned to the front of the building bracketing George.

When he saw cuffs coming out, Michael grabbed his backpack and stuffed into it the map and photos George had left on the table. He pushed open the kitchen window and stepped onto the rickety fire escape, and hoping that no one was staking out the alley, closed the window. He raced down four flights of rusty stairs, and leaped two meters to the pavement, twisting his ankle. In pain and unable to run, he looked for cover. Close by was a small dumpster, heaped with bags of rotting garbage. Quickly he tossed out a few of them, chucked in his backpack, boosted himself up, and burrowed into the putrid container. Under his blanket of refuse he quietly suffered, fighting suffocation, waiting for his ankle to stop throbbing. When he could endure the rancid stench no longer, he squirmed up and peeked out. All looked quiet, so he shouldered his backpack and gently lowered himself down.

At the end of the ally, he veered and hobbled down the block to the corner of Doganis. Cars and pedestrians were about, but no sign of the three men, their black car, or George. At the spot where it looked like George had dropped something, nothing lay on the ground, but nearby was a basement window behind a well about half a meter deep. Within it, he saw dead leaves, a yellowed page of newspaper, several tattered plastic bags, the molding remains of something, perhaps a half-eaten gyro, and a black object that looked like a cell phone. Heedless of onlookers or that a rat could be snacking down there, he lay down, reached in, and extracted the object between two fingers. Yes, it was George's cell.

He struggled to his feet and lurched across the street to the bus stop bench. Finding the phone was unlocked, he looked up Andreas in the address book. But concerned that the device could be compromised, he decided to shut it down and called with his own phone. To his relief, Andreas answered.

When Michael stopped speaking, Andreas lamented, "I can't bear to think what he must be going through now, or soon enough."

"For sure," Michael agreed. "It will be horrible for him. But he has comrades in Turkey. They should be warned."

"I once heard George speaking to someone in Turkey," Andreas said. "I recall him using the name Erol, most likely a code name. Perhaps the number's in his phonebook."

Michael switched on George's phone to find it was locked. He asked Andreas if Ottovio could crack the code.

"That would be tough, even for someone with his talents," Andreas said. "Let me see . . ." He gazed at the ceiling stroking his chin. "It's just a hunch, but try number 15, then kasim—that's k-a-s-i-m—then number 15 again." Michael keyed it in and the phone woke up.

"How on earth did you know that," Michael asked, noticing that the password was Turkish for a date in November.

"Let's just say it fit a pattern. I'll explain some other time."

Michael found a number for Erol. "Copy it down," said Andreas, handing Michael a small pad. "All of them, in fact. Then shut it down. You're the only Turk here, so perhaps you should call Erol."

"What will you say, Michael?" asked Mahmoud. "That comrade might get suspicious if someone besides George calls him."

"I'll simply tell Erol what I know," replied Michael. "I'll greet him by name and then say that our friend George was detained for questioning in Piraeus and that I thought he should know right away. If he disconnects, at least he will have that information."

"But wait" Mahmoud said. Suppose this Erol is also in custody? You could be talking to a cop. Maybe Erol revealed George, and that's why he was taken."

"Seems sort of unlikely," Andreas responded, "but if they do have Erol's phone, they could easily trace a call from one of ours."

They decided it was not worth the risk. Michael copied down George's contact data and Andreas called Ottovio to give him the bad news. Even from where he stood, Mahmoud could hear swearing in Greek. When Ottovio finally calmed down, Andreas asked him if he could securely contact this Erol person. Send an anonymous text message, Ottovio suggested, per usual. Andreas composed a message for Michael to translate that included "carnival," the operation's code name. Of course, even if Erol received it, he might not signify to an unknown sender.

"That's all we can do for now," Andreas muttered. "So then, what next?"

"Are you talking about the operation?" Mahmoud asked.

"No. Look. They have George. They also have my partner in prison.

They probably have a file on me, independently. I have no idea what it would take for them to connect the dots, but it could happen."

"What are you saying, Andreas?"

"I don't think we should remain here. I'll ask a friend if you can hang out a few days, until we can find some kind of safe house. Then we'll decide if we can go forward."

"Wait," Michael said. "Does your friend know anything about our work?"

"Nothing. She's an anarchist activist who lives nearby. I've worked with her to organize actions here and there. I've told her nothing about us. Peter has already met Katrina, as she is known. She's very discreet and supportive, and I trust her to shelter you and not reveal your presence."

Andreas dialed Katrina and started talking in German. Michael and Mahmoud exchanged worried glances, perhaps for different reasons. Mahmoud tried to reassure his partner, saying if Andreas says she's a committed activist whom he trusts, that was good enough for him. Michael didn't reply.

Andreas closed his phone. "She said she's happy to do it. Both of you—gather your things and walk over to the café. Your hostess will meet you there."

Michael tried to stand up, grimaced, and sat down again. "What are we supposed to tell her about ourselves and why we need her help?" he said under taut eyes.

"What I told her was you're both illegal aliens. She already knows that I've been sheltering Peter, who I said met you in the library the other day. You too were homeless, so Peter asked me to put you up. I did, even though it was a little crowded. But today, I got a tip from a friend that certain bad actors—I wasn't specific—might be targeting me. I said I need to make myself scarce for a while and that you guys should too in case anything goes down. That's your cover story. Got it?"

"Won't she be curious about who those 'bad actors' are?"

"She's likely to assume it's a group of ultra-nationalist thugs.

Could well happen, as she surely knows. Just say you don't know any details and you're just doing what you've been told."

Michael managed to heave himself out of his chair and wobbled about the room, still grimacing. "I guess it's decided, then. So Andreas, where will you go?"

"Don't worry about me—I can take care of myself. I'll shutter my shop and lay low somewhere until I see how this is shaking out."

Although neither man asked what "somewhere" meant, Mahmoud inquired when they would see him again.

Andreas started to pace the room in his edgy way. "How about tomorrow? Let's meet at Taverna Omphalos on Dimokratias, say around noon. Peter, you know where that is, right? Until then, don't call and only text if necessary. Now go. She's waiting at the café."

"Hold on," Michael muttered. "I'm not done copying down George's contacts."

"Sure, Michael. Take that list of contacts with you and keep it safe. I don't want it here. Drop that phone into the first sewer grate you find, but keep the battery and the memory card. Ottovio can use them."

Andreas was still pacing. He seemed in a hurry to leave. "Have a good evening with Katrina," he said. "You'll like her. She's a very interesting and good-hearted person. Now go!"

There was nothing left to say but "good luck." The two refugees hugged their protector. Mahmoud collected their belongings, shouldered both backpacks, and helped Michael down the stairs to make their uncertain rendezvous.

Chapter Fourteen

A S AFTERNOON PALED, Katrina and two young men traipsed into her tidy kitchen, men bereft of a mission of which they could not speak. One of them, whose ankle ached more now, immediately removed his sneakers. The other did as well, as was his habit upon entering a private home.

She reached under her sink for a basin. "I'll give you some warm water with Epsom salts to soak your foot," she told the first man. "It looks like quite a sprain. Did you stumble running?"

The first man glanced at the second, who raised and raised his chin slightly with an almost inaudible *tssk*. "I–I stepped off a high curb," he explained "Wasn't paying attention. Stupid thing to do."

She ran hot water from the tap into the bucket, swirled white crystals into the water with a wooden spoon, and placed it in front of the suffering Turk. "Take off your sock. Keep soaking until the water's cold. The salt will draw out water and reduce the swelling."

She turned to the other man. "You guys are welcome here as long as it takes to find a new home. This kitchen will have to be your bedroom, I'm afraid. There are just two rooms here, although they're large. I know people with more space and who might take you in, if you would rather sleep more comfortably."

"Thank you," said Mahmoud. "But let's ask Andreas before you contact any friends. Not tonight, though. He asked not to be disturbed."

"Sure. We'll take it day by day. But for now, I just realized I don't have much food around. I'll go shopping before the markets close. It'll take about half an hour. Before I go, would you like something to drink? I have milk, orange juice, water and wine. Peter, I know you don't drink wine, but Michael, would you like some?"

Quizzically glancing toward Mahmoud, Michael requested milk. Mahmoud asked for the same. Katrina put a carton of milk and two mugs on the table and stepped out with a shopping bag.

Michael said, "It sounds like you know this woman, Peter, or at least she knows you."

Mahmoud poured milk for them, recalling Michael's escapade and subsequent upbraiding. Choosing his words carefully, he explained "The first day I was in Piraeus, Andreas took me to that café and she came in. I gave her my cover story. We chatted for a while about ourselves. She talked more than I did. I revealed nothing about our work."

Michael demanded more data. What is her background? Why is she in Piraeus? What is she up to? Who are her friends? Mahmoud said he knew nothing of what she did with the anarchist crowd she ran with, only that Andreas thought a lot of her. Still, Michael speculated, authorities could be watching her. How would we know?

Testily, Mahmoud said that was possible, but did Michael have a better plan, like going to his girlfriend's place?

Michael didn't respond and changed the subject: "My phone's dead. I left the charger at the hideout. Can I use yours?"

"*Tamam.*" Mahmoud took the phone and set it charging, then sat at the table, gazing out the window. After a while he said, "So my friend, let's get creative and talk about moving ahead. Now that they have George, we can't hope to attack the G-20, don't you agree?"

Michael wasn't ready to forgo the mission. "Could still happen, I suppose, but we'd need an entirely different strategy."

"Like what?"

"I really don't know, Peter. Maybe we could attack from the air."

"Right, like we borrow an attack helicopter from the Turkish Air Force. Or maybe a missile."

"Um, Actually, I was thinking of a drone."

Mahmoud left Michael's flight of fancy hang. They consumed the milk and eventually turned to trading reasons for why Katrina had been gone so long. When she finally returned from her shopping trip, her dour expression did little to dispel their edginess.

"*Grüse*, my friends. Sorry I'm late. I got some lamb and vegetables to make a nice Swiss stew. I'm afraid it's not Halal meat. Is that okay?"

No problem for him, Michael told her. And while Mahmoud preferred his meat to be blessed, he said it was fine and asked how she would cook it.

"You mean *we*," she responded. She asked the men to pitch in and received no objections. Placing a cutting board on Michael's lap, she tasked him to roughly chop garlic, onions and mushrooms. Mahmoud's job was to peel potatoes and carrots.

She turned to pour olive oil into a Dutch oven, remarking, "As I said, stay here as long as you need to. I'm happy to help. Now I know it's not my business, but are you guys in some sort of trouble?"

Michael's foot twitched involuntarily, sloshing water in the basin. Mahmoud's leg jiggled under the table. "Maybe Andreas is," Michael protested, "but I'm here to research my thesis, that's all. Mahmoud's a refugee trying to move on. We're just temporarily homeless thanks to whatever is going on with Andreas."

"Sorry," she said. "Because you hooked up with Andreas and he's always supporting some action or another, I just assumed . . ."

Michael cut her off. "Well, you assumed wrong."

"Point taken. Anyway, I know some groups here who are planning local actions against, shall we say, the financial sector. If that sort of thing appeals, you two might fit right in."

"Impossible," said Michael. "I'm not Greek, nor an anarchist. Neither is Peter."

Mahmoud was more accommodating. "I'm not an anarchist, but I have nothing against them. If I didn't have to worry about deportation, I might try to help. Fighting the system doesn't require ideological purity."

Michael couldn't resist a rejoinder. "Perhaps, but win or lose, ideologies and interests will clash. There will be internal power struggles. It always seems to happen, especially after victories. Look at the Russian revolution. And today's Turkey for that matter."

Engrossed, Katrina said, "It doesn't have to be that way, Michael. The anarchists I know work in small groups and improvise constantly. When a task is done, some people fade away and new ones show up. Like anyone else, they have disagreements but they struggle for consensus, and once one is reached, they are of one mind and take action. If they fail to agree, they splinter and build new coalitions. There's no repressed minority. That's the very soul of liberation— freedom to take many paths."

Michael pondered the refutation and said "So, suppose by some miracle anarchists were able to smash the state and incapacitate elites. Would they be able to bring order from disorder? How would they avoid bitter—even deadly—conflicts over goals, means, resources?"

Katrina removed her glasses and gazed toward the window. "Anarchists understand that entrenching leaders leads to bad politics. Like socialists, we resist predatory elites, and so the last thing we want to see are anarchist elites telling others what to do. And the key to avoiding that is term limits."

"What's that mean?" snorted Michael.

"Like I just said. You do something for a while and then connect to another group. Nobody stays in a position longer then necessary to get a job done."

Picking up a potato that he'd fumbled, Mahmoud asked "If people keep dropping out and coming in, doesn't that make it harder for work to go on?"

Cubing lamb, Katrina remarked "Sometimes the work doesn't need to go on. Many group objectives can be achieved relatively quickly. But some tasks, like health care or fire protection, have to continue indefinitely. You need both specialists and generalists, but you don't want special interests taking over and you don't need generals running the show."

Michael wasn't convinced. "It sounds like everyone has to know how to do everything. That doesn't seem practical."

"Everyone should be a teacher and a student. Specialists can rotate to where they're needed and generalists can fit in almost anywhere and still be useful. Everyone learns by doing."

Over the sizzle of browning meat, she continued. "Take what we are doing now. I'm teaching you both how to make stew with lamb. We are working as one, and when you leave, you'll be able to make it with beef or chicken and teach that to others. You don't hoard your knowledge, you teach it to others, you know, like chefs do on TV."

She reached for the cutting board on Michael's lap, but he held onto it to make a point. "Cooking is one thing, but we have a complex economy run by companies and governments that don't share their recipes. How would you open that up?"

"By changing what work is. And education. Modern economies make workers either unskilled or overspecialized and vulnerable to disruptions. School curriculums kill curiosity and don't teach critical thinking or practical skills." She reached into her pocket and pulled out a red penknife. "Think of each citizen as something like a Swiss Army knife that keeps on adding tools. Learning new skills keeps their minds agile and gives them multiple stakes in outcomes. Everybody wins except the hegemons."

"What's a hegemon?" Mahmoud asked.

Michael, of course, knew. "That's someone who exercises economic, political, or military power over societies, seeking a monopoly of control. Just because they want to and can. The Ottomans were hegemons by divine right. Today, hegemony is the political consequence of monopoly capital."

"It's what business schools teach their students to be," added Katrina. "Why cooperate when you can gain more by dominating? And now that you know, Peter, tell us the hegemon you most love to hate?"

"Well," he said, eyes wandering, "of course, America is number one. But if you mean a person, I guess I would say Abu Bakr al-Baghdadi, that dog who calls himself Caliph of the Islamic State.

"And why, Peter? Why did you pick them?"

"It's both personal and political, Katrina. Look how many have suffered and died for their ambitions, my family and me included. They have no moral authority. They need to be stopped."

Katrina added the onions to her stewpot and turned, waving her chef's knife at him. "So what will you do about them? What is *your* recipe for hegemon stew?"

Chapter Fifteen

THE THREE FREE radicals supped and bantered by candlelight. Katrina's quip about hegemon stew had led her and Michael to trade ideas for revolutionary memes suitable for t-shirts. Mahmoud let the conversation flow over him as he chewed his meat and on ways to cook up oppressors. His musing was cut short by Michael laying down his fork and bluntly asking Katrina "So how's it going? What have you and your friends done recently to smash the state?" The challenge prompted Mahmoud to shoot Michael a glance that said *Friend, are you ready to answer that question?*

Seemingly taking no offense, Katrina calmly replied "I'd like to think that we played no small part in bringing down the New Democracy technocrats earlier this year. We helped to defeat the austerity referendum that would have punished millions of working and poor Greeks."

"And after that," Michael countered, "Germany kept up the pressure until the Syriza-led government caved in. What has been your strategy in response?"

Now Katrina bristled. "By direct actions we made it clear that the Greek people will not let financial elites decide their fate. We blockaded the German embassy. We took casualties but we demonstrated that Greeks would not submit to their inhumane demands. Social media amplified that message around the world."

Mahmoud wiped his mouth and gazed at Katrina. "I'm afraid

Michael has a point. Revolutionary change takes more than a few demonstrations and a bunch of tweets. But what it takes I can't say."

Michael ran with it. "Yes, there's not much use in marching or tweeting or petitioning hegemons, as long as elites lust for power and money."

Katrina was adamant. "Listen friends, I have nothing against direct actions. I've been involved in a few over the years. If you want to make your mark on the world and have some good ideas for doing it, I'm with you. But whatever you do, try to make it widely viewed as consequential."

"What would make it consequential, Katrina?" asked Mahmoud.

"Taking on an actually or symbolically powerful target to undercut its authority. What you do should inspire masses of people with hope and draw them out of apathy to make the changes they want to see."

"Well," said Mahmoud, "the change I want to see right now is from awake to asleep. I really need a rest after all this."

That plan would have to do for now. Katrina took his cue and got up. "Let's wash dishes and clean up here so you guys can sack out."

Soon a night-shirted Katrina slid into bed with her journal. She described receiving her unexpected boarders and ended her entry with an alarming encounter she had while she was out.

I was almost done shopping today when a rough-looking character in the store stared at me as if he recognized me. A Nationalist, I bet. Could be someone we faced off in Syntagma Square. I was almost home when I noticed he had followed me. I hurried on and went into Christos' clothing store and then ducked out the back door and made it through alleyways home. But now he sort of knows where I live. First the hate mail, now this. Don't like it.

She put her journal away and picked up a book of poems by Rumi, which she hoped would relax her enough to fall asleep. Having two men in the next room helped too.

Mahmoud awoke in morning stillness with morning stiffness. Upon retiring, he had offered Michael the air mattress, volunteering to sleep on the linoleum. Squirming from his sleeping bag and struggling to his feet, the notion of getting a couch for Katrina started to appeal. Michael was still snoozing, as was Katrina, he assumed. He stumbled to the sink, splashed water on his face, and brushed his teeth. After dressing, he sipped orange juice. It clashed with the toothpaste, so he put it down and went out for a walk, taking Katrina's keys from a hook by the door.

The weather seemed a bit muggier than yesterday, he noted as he walked down towards Dimokritias Avenue, bringing to mind their code for signifying A-OK, which clashed with how he was feeling. It wasn't the scent of danger so much as a fetid mix of paranoia and hopelessness that muddled his mood. He worried who might be looking for him and realized how little he could do about it or anything else. The worst of it was the uncertainty—about George's fate, the mission, and his future. Should he stay here, dodging the law, to involve himself with Andreas and Katrina in the struggles going on in this city? Or should he risk going back to rejoin his brigade? But how could he get there or anywhere else?

A garbage truck rumbled by with remains of the days. On the broad avenue, few people were about. Some waited for a bus or hurried to work. One or two ambled distractedly, tugged by dogs. A man exited a bakery along with a refreshing puff of air that pulled him into the present. He stopped and peered through its window at a woman doling pastries into a case that held a tray of croissants. He would get some, he decided. Katrina would appreciate it. When his turn came, he negotiated for half a dozen in sign language and climbed back up the hill, his pockets five Euros lighter and his arm a hundred grams heavier.

In the alley behind her house he nearly collided with someone coming the other way, a woman with a bush of frizzy reddish hair wearing jeans and a Wonder Woman t-shirt over her ample figure. Mahmoud excused himself in Arabic and then in English. The woman exclaimed "Oh sorry, I was in a hurry." Smiling, she asked, "Can I help you?"

"Thanks, but I'm headed here," he replied, pointing to the back door with Katrina's key.

"That's my house. You must be visiting Katrina."

"Um, yes. We're having breakfast together."

"That's nice. Tell her I said 'hi.' It was nice to meet you," she said with an expectant gaze.

Mahmoud only said "I will. Same here."

She shoved a hand at him. "My name is Penelope. I'm a graphic artist. Katrina and I are good friends. We help one another out."

"That's nice," he echoed. "I'm Peter. Well, good to meet you, Penelope."

"Likewise, Peter. I must go. I'm late to teach my drawing class. Maybe catch up with you later."

Much later. Probably harmless, but let's hope she doesn't pop in on us.

Around that time, in the Attalos Hotel in central Athens, in an ivory-hued room with rose curtains and a purple, yellow, and blue Turkish carpet, awakening in a king-sized bed to morning light, Andreas stretched his limbs and rolled over to face at the man sleeping beside him, lightly shifting the arm to cradle his torso. The man opened one eye and then the other to gaze fondly at his old friend, who murmured *"Lieber Ivan, ich bin so glücklich, Sie hier sind."*

Ivan's blue eyes fluttered and beamed. He gently pushed wisps of hair away from Andreas' brow, replying in German "And I'm so glad I was sent to Athens, Jürgen. It's been so long." He propped himself on his elbow. "I can't get over it. You haven't changed a bit. So good you wanted to see me when I called to say hello."

Andreas ran fingers down Ivan's flank. "Since Kosta went to prison I've missed the touch of a lover. Especially yours."

Cradling his chin on the curve of Andreas' neck, Ivan told him "Me too. We are the same that way. Since Kurt's passing last spring, all I've had to occupy me is my work."

"How hard it must be for you. At least I'll get Kosta back before too long."

"I hope it's a joyful reunion," Ivan said. "But at the moment, we're a couple of castaways in a strange land, so let's make of it while we can."

Andreas lifted his head to meet Ivan's eyes. " Absolutely. For as long as you can be here. Any idea how long that'll be?"

"It's looking like the job will take at least a month."

"And the job is . . . ?"

"I'm the project engineer for a new airport terminal. Sounds impressive, but I'm basically clerk of the works, keeping contractors on schedule and under budget." He glanced at the clock radio. "Speaking of that, I hate this to end, but I must get going. I'm meeting my client for breakfast. You're welcome to hang out in my room until I can get away, sometime after three. Then we can go somewhere to have some wine and you can tell me more about what you've been up to."

"Nothing I would like better, Ivan. Right now, I have more challenges than I can manage, and that would be the perfect antidote. So, go do your thing and then we'll drink to one another."

Andreas lazed in bed watching Ivan as he showered, shaved, fit a pale yellow shirt over his broad shoulders, and don a steel grey suit that set off the touch of silver on his temples. Picking up his attaché case Ivan said, "Wish me luck, Jürgen. I'm off to tell the Ministry of Infrastructure that their new terminal will again be delayed thanks to their incompetent contractors."

From his pillowed perch, Andreas told his departing friend "Sorry for you, but that's lucky for me. Call me when you get off."

Ivan opened the door, picked up the complementary morning paper that lay in wait and chucked it onto the bed. "Entertain yourself with yesterday's news. Ciao! See you later!"

Andreas ignored the missive. He pulled the comforter over him to luxuriate and doze. Around nine, he roused himself and padded to the bathroom to take a shower whistling *Your Song* as he lathered himself. While drying off, Kurt, his friend too, came to mind, struck down before his prime by a sudden aneurism. And then Kosta, languishing in that provincial prison. He should be writing more often. And he would tell him about Ivan. Kosta should understand. In the weeks before his arrest, he had taken to going out alone at night, sometimes not returning until morning. Though Andreas had let him prowl without bitterness or prompting for details, it made him feel a little less special. But their life and work together was good, and he had learned to live with it.

After he dressed, he brewed a cup of Earl Grey in the room's coffeemaker and sprawled on the bed with the newspaper. The headline said SOUTHERN EUROPE BRACES FOR NEW WAVE OF REFUGEES. "So what else did you expect," he editorialized to the walls, and turned the page. His eyes fell on a news item on page three: TURKISH TERRORISM SUSPECT TAKEN IN PIRAEUS. *What's this?*

The Hellenic Police issued a statement last night that they have detained suspected terrorist, a Turkish citizen identified as Gurcan Bac. Mr. Bac is the alleged mastermind of bombings in Istanbul and Ankara in 2003 that killed 57 people and injured hundreds of others. Al Qaeda was implicated in the truck bombings that demolished two synagogues, a bank, and damaged the British Consulate, killing its chief officer. He is one of a handful of suspects that have eluded capture for a decade or more. The police said he was taken into custody in Piraeus without incident yesterday, but did not say how long he had been in Greece or what activities he was engaged in here. Bac is expected to be extradited to Turkey, where he faces possible life imprisonment.

George? He read it again. *Who else could it be?* He'd never known George's real name or history. Now he understood why George ran such a tight ship. *This is a catastrophe! What do they know about the rest of us? Nothing, I hope, as long as George doesn't talk. None of us have police records, but Peter is here illegally and Michael is in exile.*

As he often did in when his superego nagged, he stroked his chin. *The men are safe with Katrina but what shall I do with them?* He decided they must be told in person. He texted Mahmoud that he was on his way over, stuffed the newspaper into his backpack, and headed to the Metro. On the way, he stopped at a bank booth. His wallet held two debit cards, one of them entrusted to him by George along with his PIN with instructions to empty his bank account if told to or should he get into trouble with authorities. The code he entered was the one he'd correctly surmised was also the password for George's cell phone. He took five hundred euros, the most allowed, and would keep withdrawing until the account was empty. Where that money had come from was a mystery. That guy was full of surprises. Curious George.

Chapter Sixteen

MAHMOUD LET HIMSELF into Katrina's flat to find Michael grunting out pushups from the floor. "Way to go, comrade!" Mahmoud exhorted. "You set a good example." Holding open his paper sack, he said, "Here's your reward. I took a walk and found this bakery. Katrina likes croissants for breakfast so I got two each."

From his prone position, Michael said "Really? She told you that?"

Loath to admit he had breakfasted there, he improvised. "When I met her in that café, that's what she was eating. I had a bite and decided I liked them."

When she presented herself, Katrina saw the croissants and asked where they'd come from. Mahmoud described chancing upon them and then her outgoing neighbor. "Penelope's that and more," Katrina answered. "Did she grill you?"

"Not really, she just said to say hi to you after checking me out."

"Penelope's a good soul but she has a nose for news, so be careful with her. If you run into her again and she asks about you, just say you're a friend who's teaching me to speak Arabic. I'd like that anyway, you know."

As Michael stood up, Mahmoud noticed his guarded countenance and quickly changed the subject. "Let's make coffee and have these, okay"

Shortly after breakfast, Mahmoud's phone chimed with a text from Andreas: sad news about our friend—CU in an hour. For

Katrina's benefit, Mahmoud elided the sad news part. "Andreas said he's coming over soon."

"Before he gets here, I need some quiet time to work on a blog post," Katrina said. "If you don't mind, please straighten up the kitchen." To nodding assent, Katrina took her demitasse into her bedroom, closing the door behind her.

Andreas arrived to find his comrades wanly discussing what they could or should do. "Where's Katrina?" he inquired.

"In there," Michael said, pointing over his shoulder. "Writing a blog. Hope it's not about us."

"Let her stay," he said, laying down the newspaper and pointing to the article about nabbing George. "See here. They say he's a fugitive terrorist."

Mahmoud scanned the article, frowning. "Will they really hand him over to Turkey?"

"That'll be the end of him if they do," lamented Michael. "Us too, probably."

"His interrogation will be tough," Andreas said, "but somehow I doubt George will reveal much."

Neither man replied. Andreas broke through the cloud to ask about their evening.

"We helped Katrina fix dinner while she gave us a recipe for anarchism," said Michael. "It was . . . interesting."

"She also said she might be able to find a bigger place for us," added Mahmoud. "Should we take her up on that?"

"Let's hold off on that," Andreas told him. "Something better might come up. Stay put and give me a day or two to explore some options. Right now I'm more worried about George than about you guys."

It was only 9:30 and Ivan was already having a no good, terrible day. At breakfast, the Ministry of Infrastructure functionary informed him of multiple problems with the new air terminal—both its design and its realization. For one thing, certain steel struts the plan called for were too complicated for the fabricator, who was asking for an extra fifty thousand euros to do the job. With a straight face he suggested that the money would have to come out of Ivan's firm's fee. *And into whose pockets*, wondered Ivan.

For another thing, the material specified for curtain walls was too expensive. That contractor wanted to substitute a cheaper type of slab. *Nice of them to tell us before they did it.*

"Oh, and the stonemasons are on strike, and it looks like welders will be next."

"How about the plate glass people?" Ivan asked. "What do they want?" The reply came, "Nothing, except an extra month to deliver."

"Well," said Ivan, somewhat diplomatically, "things happen more slowly in Southern Europe, I guess," and arose from the table. "I'll review contract documents and will refer these issues to my manager. Then I'll go to lunch. Expect a call this afternoon."

He spent the next hour at his computer wading through contracts, invoices, and memos, taking notes that he attached to an email message. He folded his laptop and trudged downstairs. Outside, he opened his phone and dialed Andreas.

At Katrina's, Andreas was making plans for the three of them to meet up with Ottovio to brainstorm when the call came. "Hi Jürgen," Ivan chirped. "What are you doing?"

"We're thinking," Andreas replied.

"Who is we? Are you still in my hotel room?"

"I went back to Piraeus to confer with some people I work with. What's up?"

"Well, my meeting ended early and I'm thinking about lunch. Interested?"

"I might be. We aren't likely to get much done in the next couple of hours."

"I really need a break. Let's find a pleasant place to eat. Got any ideas?"

They arranged to rendezvous in Piraeus at a cheerful dockside restaurant. Andreas clicked off and told the men "I'm afraid I can't join you at Taverna Omphalos, but why don't you two guys go and hang out with Ottovio. Ask him what he thinks we can do about George. He can be very insightful when he's in a good mood. I'll come back here after three and we can take it from there."

"Where is this place?" Michael asked. "The streets around here confuse me."

Katrina emerged from her bedroom sporting an uncharacteristically sour countenance, muttering to herself. "Oh hi, Katrina," Andreas said. "You look a bit vexed. What's up?"

"Salut. I'll say. As soon as I post something, trolls are shitting all over it."

Mahmoud was confused. "Who are you talking about, Katrina?"

"Ugly little creatures who spew out hateful comments wherever they lurk, in my case ultranationalist shitheads trashing my ideas, derailing discussions, calling me an anarchist bitch. Ugh."

Andreas identified. "Those punks are our nemesis. But at least they're only attacking your words. They have done much worse."

"Tell me about it," Katrina replied. She didn't mention SuperPlato's poison pen letter or being spooked by a stalker.

"I'm sorry it keeps happening," Andreas said, touching her arm, "but I need another favor. Can I ask you to you take the guys over to Taverna Omphalos in half an hour to meet my friend for lunch?"

"Might as well" she replied. "Where are you going?"

"An old friend from Vienna is in town, an engineer supervising a big construction job. Wonderful man. I'm meeting him for lunch to catch up."

"Sounds like a nice break," she said, "and you deserve one. Don't worry, I'll take good care of your boys."

From the street, Andreas phoned Ottovio to invite him to the taverna and relay the account in the morning paper. After Ottovio had calmed down, Andreas advised that the men would be with a friend who was temporarily boarding them, a radical whom he implicitly trusted but wasn't clued in. He asked the hacker to treat her cordially and try to divine her intentions. After she leaves, get the men to focus on the future and how we can help George. Ottovio said he'd be there and reluctantly consented to check the woman out.

Andreas motored to the Metro terminus on the Vespa to pick up Ivan, an inelegant mode of transport that nonetheless had its charms. Café Santorini sported dated decor, and while its kitchen turned out unremarkable versions of grilled meat, fish and side dishes, its overview of the picturesque yacht basin somewhat compensated.

Over their wine, Ivan unloaded. The job was insane. He was going insane. He recounted this morning's meeting with the Greek official.

"That would drive me crazy too," Andreas said, emptying his glass and refilling.

More venting. "I'm dealing with grifters and village idiots. How am I supposed to schedule construction tasks for shady contractors in league with venal bureaucrats? When workers aren't striking, management complains that they can't meet our specs and pressures the government to issue change orders. I have to cost each one out and send it to my boss for approval. I might as well have studied accounting."

With a consoling gaze, Andreas reached for Ivan's hand across the table. "I didn't realize how much I missed you these two years," he told him. "From my selfish point of view, having you here with time on your hands is a blessing. It gives us a chance to enjoy each other's company. I hope you feel that way too."

"Of course I do. After Kurt was taken from me, I focused on my career and became blind to life. Waking up with you this morning brought that home. Now here I am, perhaps for several months without a lot to do. You can stay with me as long as you want to and show me the city. We can hang out in cafés, visit museums, and go dancing at night."

Andreas squeezed his hand. "Here's an idea. For what you spend in a week for that fancy hotel room, you could rent a nice little pied-à-terre in Piraeus for several months. It would save your firm money, and my friends and I could help you furnish it. It shouldn't be hard to find a nice place. The economy is terrible and there are many vacancies these days for those that can afford them."

"But you have a flat," Ivan replied, "and Kosta's not around. Couldn't I bring my things and stay with you there?"

Andreas glanced furtively around the room and leaned forward. "As you probably remember, not all of my activities are strictly legal. No drugs or stealing—nothing like that. It's the politics of the people I associate with." In a conspiratorial whisper, he added "And recently I received a tip that the authorities may want to detain me. Until that blows over I need to lay low somewhere."

"That's quite dramatic. Tell me more,"

"There's another thing. There's no room for you in my flat right now because I'm sheltering two men who are in Greece illegally. They need a safer place to live until they can move on. They're well-spoken, considerate people, not criminals, but would face persecution if deported. Why not rent a flat where we all could stay for a couple of months?"

"Are they Syrians? Wouldn't surprise me. They're all over the place."

"Nope. One's Turkish, the other Iraqi. Neither can return home. Politics. War."

"I see," said Ivan, staring into his wine. "So it won't exactly be our love nest."

The waiter brought a tray of grilled octopus and a salad for Ivan, stuffed grape leaves and spanakopita for Andreas. Ivan picked up his fork and set it down again. "I'm sorry Jürgen. That sounded selfish. You know, part of why I fell in love with you was your beautiful idealism and commitment to building a better world. And here you are in this dysfunctional country, still at it. I'm afraid I gave up my dreams for social justice a long time ago. How is it you can still love a corporate sell-out like me?"

"You're not a sell-out, Ivan. You just chose a path to save the world by building things that people need. Yes, your job keeps you secure and well fed, but that's not a cause for shame."

"Well, some of our clients and managers can be a cause for shame. Sometimes I feel I'm in the wrong profession."

Andreas dipped a wedge of pita in herbed olive oil and handed it to Ivan. "So why not enjoy ourselves together while you're here and keep my boys safe in a pleasant home that your company will pay for? What do you say?"

In his gentle, crafty way, Andreas could be very persuasive. By the end of the meal, helped along by more wine and draughts of ouzo, Ivan had agreed—with enthusiasm—for Andreas to rent a flat in Piraeus. He would pay up front and get reimbursed by his firm.

Andreas insisted on paying the bill. He drove Ivan to the Metro and walked him to the entrance, arm draped on his shoulder. "It'll be great. Everything about your being here makes me happy. I'll start looking for a place right away. Could happen within a week. Tell me, what kind of place would you like?"

They reached the turnstiles. "Let's see . . ." Ivan began. His faced crinkled into a grin. "Well, I want a big bed, a view of the sea, and modern decor. Cream-colored walls with rose curtains, like my room at the hotel would be nice. What else . . . of course, cable or satellite TV. Oh, and there must be two bathrooms. I hate having to wait to take a shower."

Andreas beamed back and they hugged goodbye. "Your wish is my command. I'll talk to an estate agent today and tell you what I find when I return tonight. Ciao!"

Chapter Seventeen

E VANGELINE VYROS RAN her fingers through a jumble of white-tagged keys on a large ring and pushed one into the lock of a plate glass door, saying, "I think you will like this place. It has a guest room, an office, and even views of the harbor." She twisted the lock open and waved Andreas to follow her up the stairwell of the nondescript apartment house on Marias Kiouri street. She led him to a door on the third floor, which, after some fumbling she managed to unlock.

"Oh," Andreas exclaimed, "I see it's fully furnished. That's a nice surprise. Very tasteful, Evangeline." He toured the cheerful, modern living room with contemporary furnishings and windows overlooking a tree-lined avenue, shooting photos as he went.

Andreas hadn't met the middle-aged estate agent before. She came to him through her son Spyros, an apprentice pharmacist and a fellow traveller with whom he'd worked to marshal democracy demonstrations. Evangeline had been eager to help when he called. Her trickle of clients weren't particularly clamoring for apartments in Keratsini these days.

"The owners of this condo live here for seven years," she told him. "This season they visit relatives in America and rent it out. If you want it, I'll need to see the lessee's identification and bank information. You said he's a friend. Where is he from?"

"He's a single man from Vienna. We were classmates there. Now he's a civil engineer at a big company stationed in Athens for some time and would like a two-month lease. I'm sure he has sufficient financial resources."

The front of the apartment had an open plan. The living room flowed into a dining area, separated from the kitchen by a counter with chrome and leather stools. The updated kitchen had gleaming steel appliances and marbled counter tops. A corridor ran past the kitchen to three bedrooms, one with windows overlooking Dimokritias Avenue, and beyond that the shipping harbor and a giant parking lot full of automobiles arrayed like a company of sailors. The master bedroom had the same view, plus sliding doors leading to a balcony. The third bedroom, halfway down the hall, was smaller and overlooked the apartment house next door. It was set up as an office, with a teakwood desk and bookshelves, a tan leather couch and a matching swivel chair.

"There's a half-bath opposite the kitchen," Evangeline advertised. "The main bathroom is between the two bedrooms and has a Jacuzzi."

"And how much does all this luxury cost?" Andreas asked, snapping more pictures.

"For the two months, three thousand euros, plus one thousand security deposit, all in advance. It is expensive for Keratsini, but well worth the price, I'd say. For you, I charge half my fee, and you can pay it whenever you want."

"You are very kind, Evangeline," he responded, "but you will get your full fee. He can afford it. So, if there's no charge for the graffiti on the wall across the street, I think we'll take it."

On the way out Andreas remarked, "The family who lives here appears to be quite prosperous. What kind of work do they do?"

He did not expect Evangeline's' answer. "I believe the gentleman is a retired police detective. As for his wife, I don't know."

Lured into the taverna by odors of charring eggplant, frying fish, and roasting Souvlaki the trio found the room already fully occupied. Mahmoud claimed a sidewalk table, where the desultory overtaxed waitress might or might not notice them. Having

expected Katrina to move on, he became uneasy when she asked
to sit with them until their friend shows up. Despite wanting her
to buzz off, Mahmoud consented as Michael mimed disapproval.

She settled in and leaned in on forearms. "I want you to know that
I'm very sorry you've lost your comrade. What that means for you I
don't know, but for me it means you might be camped with me for
a while. I'm happy to have you, and the least I can do is buy another
air mattress so one of you doesn't have to sleep on the floor. I'll do
that today."

Mahmoud took his time replying "Thanks, Katrina." Michael
didn't offer thanks. Instead, he asked her to explain what made her
think they were at a loss for a comrade.

Her mouth pursed as her eyes leveled on Michael. "A couple of
things," she exhaled. "First, out of the blue, Andreas begs me to house
you guys. Second, there's this." From her handbag she withdrew the
newspaper that Andreas had left in her kitchen and pointed to the
account of the alleged terrorist's detention. "They cuff this guy and
Andreas turns paranoid. If he's someone you know, I'd say that you
two could use more friends and he could use a good lawyer."

Michael's eyes darted between her and the newspaper. He removed
his spectacles and flipped them around by one stem, saying "Never
heard of that guy. Don't know who spooked Andreas either. It's good
of you to take us in, but please don't . . ." just as Ottovio lumbered up
carrying a computer bag.

Ottovio's initial anger over George's arrest had subsided, and
today was in a relatively benign mood. One reason was that his efforts
to decrypt George's flash drive had succeeded, not that it mattered
much now, but he was a proud master of his craft. He scudded up
a chair, addressing Katrina with predictable indiscretion. "You look
sort of familiar. I am Ottovio. And you are . . . ?"

Her cheeks dimpled as she offered her hand. "My name is Katrina,
"I'm an old friend of Andreas. He helped me organize street actions
and now I repay him by taking care of his homeless boys."

Ottovio only nodded. She asked him if he was Greek "*Eíste Éllines,
sostá?*"

When "*Kalí mantepsiá*," good guess, he replied, she switched to his language.

"I'm sorry that your comrade was taken away," she said. "I don't know what you were doing with him and I don't care to know. I'd like to help you guys, but if you don't want me around, I'll leave."

Greek back at her. "Why do you care? What kind of help are you talking about?"

Katrina spoke in English for the others' benefit. "I'm helping your buddies because someone's on Andreas' tail, maybe theirs too. I work with anarchists mainly, but often find common cause with socialists like Andreas. All of them find me a reliable ally. I help them with opposition research, spotting strategic opportunities, and coordinating responses. Do you want to see my résumé?"

Her guests chuckled but fell silent when Ottovio said a little too loudly "No! I want to see your police record!"

He took out his laptop, inserted a flash drive, and proceeded to open a file. Switching back to Greek, he said with evident pride, "I have here the master criminal database we hacked from a Hellenic Police server about two months ago."

"I see," She said in Greek. "Very interesting. Might I ask what you are doing with it?"

"I do opposition research too. My friends and I map the social networks of politicians. Also police, judges, and their relatives and associates. Some of these characters have criminal connections. Some of them *are* criminals. Anyway, I'll ask the questions if you don't mind. You say your name is Katrina. What is your address, please?"

She hesitated, shrugged, and told him. He typed a query. A few seconds later he said "Two records for that address. One is Alexiou, Penelope. Other is Burmeister, Anna. Is one of them you?"

"The latter," Katrina admitted, her eyes widening. "The other woman lives upstairs."

"Okay then. It says Anna is a Swiss citizen and legal resident since 2013. No arrests, but suspected to be involved in violent protests. May go by 'Katrina.' Also that you blog on an anarchist website."

All she could say was "Someone they detained at a rally or one of their informants may have told them that, but I've never been arrested."

"Many activists end up in this database. Some they watch or use as informant. Your record doesn't say you are one. Very lucky for you."

Mahmoud and Michael shifted in their seats, waiting to be clued in.

Still in Greek, Katrina huffed "So, do I pass your test? Am I suitable for your company?"

"For now," he said, closing his computer. He addressed the two men in English. "This woman is okay to stay with. But you should find your own place in case police go see her."

Mahmoud said, "Agreed. I think Andreas is working on it."

"Here you go," said Ottovio, holding up his phone for them to see a recent message from Andreas: **tell guys housing on way. all meet her place @ 4.**

Katrina got up from the table. "Nice to meet you, Ottovio. I enjoyed our interrogation. Now please excuse me. I need to buy an air mattress."

The men had finished eating when Katrina returned a half hour later. Two were drinking beer, one lemonade. Depositing a box she'd purchased at a discount store, she said she'd also like a beer and was offered her old seat. The men had been puzzling over what to do about George but at her arrival Michael steered discussion to general social conditions, and proceeded to quiz the Swiss miss about her political proclivities. She described some of her anarchist friends' projects and how she had helped. Then she changed the subject.

"So what about your buddy, most likely a guest in the fabulous Korydallos Prison. Are you gonna help him?"

"In what way" Michael guardedly responded.

"I know people who have been there, done that, and lived to tell tales. You might want to talk to them."

"I'll pass that on to Andreas," said Mahmoud dryly. "But let's drop this for now."

Katrina could take a hint. As they self-lubricated with another round of beer and lemonade, she provided commentary on the fucked-upness of the Greek state. This devolved to her and Ottovio trading war stories to the others' incredulity, which went on until Mahmoud reminded them that Andreas would return soon. They divvied up the tab and Katrina led the bunch to her flat, where she excused herself and retired to her room, leaving the men to ruminate in the kitchen until Andreas showed up sporting a bottle of sparkling wine and an impish smile.

"I hope you guys had a good day," he said. "I certainly have. So tell me, what did you do with yourselves? Was Katrina with you?"

"She was," Michael reported. "And I couldn't believe it when Ottovio pulled up her police record and read it out. He seems to have them all. Told us he thought she's okay to stay with but we should move on."

Katrina had just entered the kitchen. "Sure, I'm okay to be with, but what about you guys?"

Michael bristled. "What's that supposed to mean?"

"Perhaps we should see what the Hellenic Police think. So, mister cyberhacker, have you gotten readouts on these guys?"

Ottovio said he'd done due diligence. Leaving out himself, he reported "I find you there, Andreas. Nothing exciting. For these guys, no names, no data."

Andreas stroked his unshaven chin. "Hmm . . . tell me more later. Anyway, want to hear what I learned today?"

He didn't wait before announcing with evident glee that he had located an apartment that would more than meet their needs, a twenty minute walk from here on Marias Kiouri Street, offering a slide show for their approval. Oohs and ahs followed his phone around the room.

"Renting a pad like that must be expensive," Katrina said, "unless you know somebody."

"Well it is, and I do." Andreas. "Last night I found an angel." He told them of his old friend's coming to town and his work situation. "I convinced him that renting a flat would be more fun than the swank hotel he's at and a lot cheaper. He's happy to share it with Michael, Peter, and me, and we can move in as soon as Ivan pays and signs the lease, maybe this weekend."

Michael looked distressed. "You told him about us?"

"Sure. You're part of why he's doing this. To give refugees a place to live. He's very compassionate."

"Uh, how well do you know this person?" Mahmoud inquired.

His hand forced, Andreas casually leaned against the wall pressing thumbs together as he told them of his bond with Ivan in college, what their reunion meant to him, and how renting this unit solved several pressing problems at once.

"I'm not sure," Mahmoud said dryly. "Your friend might talk to people about his roommates."

"Yes, Peter, I understand your concern, but Ivan knows I'm an activist, and he admires me for it. He was too, when we were students. I told him you are both undocumented. He appreciates your need to keep low profiles."

Even so, Mahmoud was sure that Ivan would hear of things he shouldn't, but he wasn't about to bring that up. Not in front of Katrina. Here was another plan he felt powerless to affect. He sighed.

Andreas kept on marketing. "Look, Ivan won't be around during the day. And when he is, he'll pitch in. He's into good food and likes to cook and even clean house. You'll like him. He's very goodhearted and fun company."

Silence resounded to his spiel. Andreas broke it. "So, are you guys on board or not?"

After a while, Michael said, "You know this guy. We don't. It's your call."

"Peter?"

"At this point, I don't have much to lose," Mahmoud said, "except maybe my name."

"What do you mean?" asked Andreas.

"Peter isn't my real name. I want to stop using it."

"Why?"

"It's too Christian. Your friend won't believe it. Nobody outside this room knows I'm here. Peter can go away." He didn't mention the possibility that George might give him up under duress.

"So what should we call you?" asked Katrina.

"My real name is Mahmoud. Mahmoud Al-Ramadi. As that sounds, my family is of Ramadi, but I lived mostly in Mosul. Please call me Mahmoud."

Andreas stroked his chin again. "I can't see how that could hurt. Mahmoud it is then."

"All right then," said Michael. "I don't want to hide under an assumed name either. I am Kaan, k-a-a-n, Kaan Sultanoğlu. My father was never afraid to denounce oppressors under his byline. Why shouldn't I?"

"Gee," Katrina said. "Who knew?"

"Maybe police," suggested Ottovio, peering over his laptop, affixing a flash drive. "I check my database. Spell please."

Letters were listed. Keys were tapped. No other sound save breathing until Ottovio declared, "Okay, no records for those names."

"All right then," Andreas said, holding up his bottle. "Let's break out glasses and toast to our new life together."

Not to be left out, Mahmoud made an exception and took a sip and sneezed when bubbles tickled his nose. All chortled and drank up.

Chapter Eighteen

I T TOOK JUST two days to exchange paperwork for the apartment on Marias Kiouri, time sufficient for Katrina's guests to appreciate her new air mattress. Evangeline expedited by entrusting a key to Andreas in advance. Unable to forget that the owner was a former police detective, and suspecting that a lot of these guys never really retire, Andreas decided that a security check was in order and summoned a bemused Ottovio to join him at the condo around sunset.

When the Greek arrived with his kit bag, he told Andreas that he wouldn't enter the building if it had security cameras. He handed the Austrian a masked flashlight and a spray can of WD-40 oil, instructing him to surreptitiously anoint the lenses of any cameras he found, and retreated to the shadows across the street.

Andreas hurried past the security camera in the cramped lobby, stalked up to the third floor, and let himself into the flat. Seeing the nearby security pad blinking green, he punched in the code Evangeline had given him. When the blinking stopped, he exhaled and played the flashlight across the ceiling, disclosing a round housing looking to him like a motion sensor mounted above the front door and a smoke detector on the kitchen ceiling. Aside from another smoke alarm down the hall, nothing else looked like a security device. He descended to the lobby, occluded the security camera with a spritz of oil, and let Ottovio in.

On their way up Ottovio asked, "What makes you think place might be bugged?"

"Just being diligent, I suppose," Andreas replied nonchalantly. "I'm told the owner's a retired police detective."

"*Skata!*" Ottovio hissed. "You would have to rent from a cop! This better not be a set-up!"

"Evangeline wouldn't do that," Andreas insisted. "No way this could be a trap. Anyway, who would want to monitor Ivan? It's his rental, remember?"

At the door he told Ottovio what he'd found. "Motion sensor is no problem if that's what it is," Ottovio advised as he cracked open the door. "Keep lights off. I look around first. Only whisper if you must speak."

The motion detector checked out. It was likely hooked to the alarm system that Andreas had disarmed and which Ottovio now put to sleep. Switching on the kitchen lights, Ottovio placed his kit bag on the counter and took out a small device with buttons, a knob and LED readout. Andreas asked what it was.

"Whisper!" he hissed. "Is RF spectrum analyzer. Detects ambient radio waves. Frequencies and strengths. Cheap but good enough. Now we check for audio bugs. When I point, follow finger and clap hands once." He signaled Andreas to go to the kitchen. "Now!" he hissed. Andreas clapped. "Again!" Another clap.

"No signal. Good. Okay, we go other rooms."

Neither in the hall, bedrooms, nor bathrooms did Ottovio's needle jump. Still *sotto voce*, he pronounced the premises free of eavesdropping. "So, unless hard-wired," he said, "no audio bugs here. Let's keep working."

Andreas followed him into the little office. On the desk was a dock for a laptop and a small printer. The dock was plugged into the wall and had a cable that went under the desk. Ottovio followed it to its destination and said, "There's the router. Connects to TV cable. Let's see if it's working." He took his laptop out of its bag and woke it up. After starting a program, he unplugged the cable from the dock and clicked it into his computer. "Let's see who we talk to. IP

address assigned . . . has signature of home network . . . connecting
to Net . . . okay, we're on."

"Could your traffic be intercepted?" Andreas asked with furrowed
brow.

"Always possible. Only way to prevent is to assign different IP
address. That's what proxy servers are for."

"Whatever. But what about the wireless signal—couldn't someone
tap into that?"

"Lucky for us router is behind times. No Wi-Fi."

Andreas gave a shrug. "I guess we can do without. Are we done?"

"All set. We can go eat now."

"Good idea. It's on me. You earned it."

Outside, cooling night air had gathered the humidity and smog into
a noxious drizzle. Ottovio said he was in the mood for Chinese, but
the place he had in mind wasn't nearby. At a bus stop on the Avenue
they sheltered under a nearby tree. Ten minutes into watching the
haloed lights of freighters in the harbor, Ottovio said "Too many
connections from here. Too wet. We take taxi."

Yet damper after a three-block walk, they managed to bag a cab.
Ottovio directed the driver to downtown Athens. "You'll really like
this place, Andreas."

"Where are you taking us?"

"Name is East Asia. Great selection, pretty authentic, not too
expensive. Sushi too. Near Syntagma Square."

Andreas was more focused on the location than the food. It was
there that Kosta had been arrested in a police riot, and near there
Ivan was situated and might be about to head out for dinner. Judging
it useful to get Ottovio's take on Ivan, he asked, "Would you like to
meet Ivan? He might be able to join us. Shall I check?"

"Might as well. Does he like Chinese?"

Ivan picked up the call just as he was heading out for a drink and a
solo supper, and appreciated being included. When Ivan jumped in at
the Attalos Hotel, Andreas introduced Ottovio as the ur-technologist

who had remanufactured his cell phone. A quiet five-minute drive brought them to the little restaurant tucked away on Apollonos Street. Even on a rainy Thursday night, the East Asia was a popular hangout. Titillating whiffs of seafood, pork fat, soy, ginger, and garlic goaded their appetites as they queued in the tiny lobby, so near and yet so far from repast.

The wait turned out to be worth it. Service was swift and attentive and the kitchen efficiently pumped out appetizing platters. They shared spring rolls, octopus salad, and fried dumpling starters and sampled Ottovio's hot and sour soup. For main courses, Ivan chose fried noodles with duck, Andreas got shrimp with ginger and green onion, and Ottovio went for one of his faves, curiously translated as "the onion explodes the pork."

"They should branch out to Piraeus," Ottovio said between slurps of soup. "I'll tell the manager. I would like it on Facebook, if I used it." When his bowl was empty he asked Ivan how he liked Athens so far.

"It's an exciting city," Ivan said. "Bigger than Vienna, certainly a lot more turbulent. And the way things are going, I should have more than enough time to get to know it. I'll be living in Piraeus. What's it like there?"

Ottovio described the funky diversity of the port city and its ruins, museums, seedy shops, its bars and clubs, mostly in and around its waterfront districts. "I took you to lunch in that area the other day," said Andreas.

"Yeah, I liked it there," Ivan told him. "Lots going on."

As the house hacker and the structural engineer chatted, Andreas poured tea and leaned back. Ottovio told of dropping out of technical school once he figured out he already knew most of what was being offered and going into business for himself. Mostly this involved database programming and computer security, but on the side he reconditioned cell phones to make them as secure as possible, as he'd done for Andreas when he needed a trustworthy instrument for conducting antifascist actions.

Ottovio's patter was interrupted by their waiter brandishing their entrees, which he ceremoniously deposited and unveiled, bowing as he retreated. "You can tell he proud of food," Ottovio said. "They do good job here."

Ivan asked how soon they could move in. "Your call," Andreas said. "I've got the keys now. We can move in as soon you get the three thousand euros and Evangeline's fee to her."

"Is tomorrow morning soon enough? I can't wait to see it."

"Assuming that works for Evangeline, we can probably take possession anytime after. Good enough?"

"Perfect, Jürgen. So lets go back to the hotel after dinner and take advantage of the gym and sauna while we can."

And the privacy, Andreas thought. *We won't have much of that soon.*

Chapter Nineteen

AS WHEN ENTERING parenthood, moving into a new home furnishes one with a new lease on life, pregnant with possibilities. And so to the contemporary decor of 156 Marias Kiouri, along with their scant belongings, each of the four men brought hopes for fecund fellowship. Ivan seemed especially gratified. It cheered him to come home to the exotic company of Mahmoud and Kaan, whom he immediately dubbed the Levantine Brothers. It pleased him to share the king-sized bed-with-a-view with Andreas. The brothers bunked in the second bedroom, which luckily came with twin beds.

They luxuriated in the Jacuzzi and viewed football matches on the widescreen TV in the living room. Ivan was an enthusiastic chef and partial to Mediterranean cuisine. On days when he came home from work early, he would orchestrate repasts in the high-tech kitchen, with the brothers doing prep and Andreas usually on salad detail. While Mahmoud sometimes pined for Iraqi comfort foods like *ful medames*, he regularly praised his maker for delivering him from the rude cookery of war zones and refugee camps garnished by filth, stench, and lice.

That first day, Andreas and Ivan strolled to the big supermarket nearby to stock up on groceries subsidized by Ivan's *per diem*. Ivan wanted their first meal together to be a housewarming part of sorts. Lacking friends in town, he asked Andreas to invite his. And so, Ottovio and Katrina were asked to join them for *kakkavi—*

Greek seafood chowder, plus tortellini with puttanesca sauce and a radicchio-arugula-tomato salad with lemon-dill vinaigrette, rounded out by baklava and espresso. Over the first course, for Ivan's benefit, Andreas turned the conversation toward Mahmoud and Kaan, whom he had told to polish their patter.

Mahmoud's story also didn't deviate from the truth by much: He described fleeing Iraq through Syria into Turkey—eliding the bit about fighting in the International Brigade and then being sent on a mission. After being smuggled to Kos, he said, rescue workers put him on a ferry and sent to Piraeus. The smugglers had snatched his passport, he lied, making it impossible to move on. As for how he ended up in present company, he said he struck up a conversation with Andreas at a taverna and got taken in.

Kaan's narrative was also relatively straightforward and nearly true: He was a graduate student from Izmir visiting Greece to research his thesis on social structures of ancient Greek city-states. When he first arrived, he had stayed in a couple's apartment found through AirBnB, but when relatives came to visit he had to leave. As luck would have it, he happened to encounter Mahmoud at the library and asked him if he knew of any place he could stay, which led to Andreas offering to board him. It all sounded perfectly probable.

Their cover stories weren't just for Ivan's benefit. He easily accepted his new roommates, but the authorities might be less credulous. Mahmoud's situation was complicated by having no entry stamp, not that it was so unusual for his sort to lack one, but it limited his options. And returning to Turkey could put Kaan under surveillance, if not arrest.

They dug into steaming bowls of fish stew. After complimenting Ivan's cooking, Katrina ungraciously started grilling him. "Here we have Mahmoud, displaced by war from his homeland. How has Austria responded to the flood of refugees?"

"Austria is trying to cope, like Germany, he answered. "I suppose we could do more, but look; Hungary dumped busloads of refugees at our frontier and then erected a fence. We haven't done that."

Kaan interjected. "Germany and Austria and Greece are overwhelmed. This should never have happened. There's a root cause for all this chaos, and it's spelled U-S-A."

Ivan challenged. "Are you saying it's all America's fault for invading Iraq?"

"That and Afghanistan, and setting Iran up for revolution before that. They pushed the dominos, and they fell on millions of innocent people."

Katrina amplified. "There's blood on many hands, of course, especially men like Assad, Putin, Paşa, and most of all Obama, who fronts for those who want to rule the world or at least own most of it."

Ivan bit. "Like who?"

"The list is long. Oil and gas companies. Mining and heavy industry. International finance. Drug companies. Defense contractors. Then there's the secretive TPP, the so-called trade agreement that extends monopoly power across the Pacific Rim. Obama is all for it."

Kaan seconded. "Yes, that's how imperialism has always worked, but these days they colonize economies instead of countries. Monopoly capitalists don't care who needs to die to satisfy their greed. War is a profit center for them."

All the radical rhetoric made Andreas uneasy. Ivan mustn't get the idea they had an agenda. But before he could change the channel, Ottovio came on:

"War also goes on in cyberspace. Spying on dissidents. Social media propaganda. Data hacking and sabotage. All countries do it and also are vulnerable. Networks are not secure. Too easy to compromise user credentials. Governments try to keep lid on, but the worms crawl in and come out with state secrets and corporate data."

Katrina nodded. "It sort of levels the playing field, don't you think?"

"Definitely," the hacker responded. "The Net lets people unmask power. Governments are losing their edge. Companies too."

"My company was hacked," said Ivan. "We lost project plans client lists, emails and probably more, and still don't know whether government spies, a competitor, or a data pirate did it."

"Your files could be for sale," suggested Ottovio, "on some black site."

"What's that?"

"We call it Dark Web. You want corporate data, personal credentials, state secrets? Whatever, is there. You just need to know how and how to take care. Some sites even let buyers rate sellers, like eBay."

Ivan couldn't get over it. "That's incredible, Ottovio! How do you know all that?"

"You go to hacking school. You learn by mimicking the masters."

Andreas hurriedly ran to the kitchen to get the tortellini just as Kaan went at it again: "No offense, Ottovio, but the geeks won't inherit the earth any time soon. That's because the super-rich already own most of it and want the rest."

"What makes you think so?" Ivan asked him.

"It's in capitalism's DNA. Look, economic elites aren't stupid or uninformed. They see things falling apart everywhere, but what do they do? Instead of using their vast resources to improve matters, they double down, looting and punishing the planet."

"You really think so?"

"Absolutely. Then, when they've impoverished everyone else, they'll jet to their palaces and private islands with their mercenaries. They have constructed, my friend, an engine of apocalypse, and if the rest of us are to survive, we must throw sand in its gears."

"That sounds a lot like class warfare if you ask me," observed Ivan.

Kaan smiled. "Ah yes, but they only call it class warfare when we fight back."

Andreas rushed in with the next course and a forced smile. "Ivan, you must taste this *tortellini puttanesca*. It's just divine!"

Katrina and Ottovio took their leave of the émigré salon around 11 as the Levantine Brothers did dishes and traded war stories. Andreas and Ivan had retired to their bedroom. In contrast to the faux Bauhaus look of the front rooms, its furniture was vaguely Italianate and overly ornate, like the quarters of a courtier on the make, but the fluffy expanse of the bed made up for it. They stripped to their shorts and went out on the balcony to enjoy the night air, lightly perfumed with a mixture of Bougainvillea and petroleum distillates. Leaning against the wrought iron railing, Ivan said, "Kaan seems quite radical. Is Mahmoud like that too?"

"Not that I know of. He's very pious, though. Prays a lot. Fortunately there's a mosque within earshot to tell him when. He wanted to go there but I told him that's impossible. A police informant could easily finger him."

"Why should he care? He's not doing anything illegal."

"Mahmoud isn't *doing* anything illegal; he *is* illegal. If someone tells the police he's suspicious of him, he may be questioned, put into a camp, and maybe deported."

"I feel sorry for him. Why can't he simply apply for a new passport?"

Andreas played along. "I suppose he could. I'll tell him to visit the Iraqi embassy to see what it takes."

Ivan threw him a look. "Want to take a Jacuzzi with me?"

"I would, but I'm tired now and really need some sleep. Do you mind?"

"C'mon, Jürgen, it'll do you good."

Enervated, Andreas could only respond, "Probably would, but I'd just fall asleep there and drown."

"I'll miss you in the tub. I've been looking forward to relaxing there all day. But it's fine. See you later. Don't snore."

They kissed. Soon the rumble of the hot tub was lulling Andreas as he snuggled under the comforter, first pondering how to keep Ivan unaware of what they were up to and what that might ever be. No answers came before Ivan slid beside him to make him forget the questions.

The Brothers were putting dishes away, also pondering game plans.

"I've been thinking," Kaan said, "what we could do. We could still strike some significant target in Turkey and lay it to ISIS. Remember the other day I said it would be cool to attack the G-20 meeting from the air?"

"Yes, I think so," Mahmoud said, yawning.

"Well if it can't be the G-20 in the Aspendos arena, maybe we could attack another place by air."

"You have a pilot's license?"

"No pilot necessary, at least on board. We use a drone."

"We could get a drone? Like the US uses?"

"No, of course not. I mean a little one. They're not hard to find."

"Like how big? How much could it carry?" the engineer inquired.

"I think they come in all sizes, but big ones must be expensive."

"The target would have to be outdoors, right?"

Kaan nodded. "Probably. It should be a gathering of important people, don't you think?"

Mahmoud stretched his arms and yawned again. "I guess so. I'll think about it."

Agreeing it was time to unwind, they took the last of the tea and sat down in front of the television. Kaan clicked to a news program. A photo came up of a toddler lying on a rough beach, the sea lapping at his little limbs. It was, the narrator said, that of a Syrian boy washed up on Turkish shores after the overloaded boat he was on with his parents foundered. The image had gone viral and was being talked about all around the world.

Mahmoud pointed to the screen. "Look at that. Do you think all that talk will stir any action to help refugees?"

"For a while. More aid might be raised and more refugees will turn up to claim it. And no doubt, politicians will find ways to create more of them."

Kaan switched off the TV. Mahmoud went to wash up and then to pray in the living room. When he climbed into his bed, Kaan was lightly snoring. He lay on his back, eyes open, hands clasped behind his head. The image of the dead child drifted before him. He thanked Allah for not meting the same fate out to him. Presently George's visage materialized and he prayed for him. His gratitude turned to

Andreas, who always seemed to be saving the day, and then to the supportive Katrina.

He rolled over toward the slumbering silhouette of Kaan, still feeling appreciation. He thanked Allah for him and for the splendid shelter they enjoyed before his eyes fluttered and closed. Behind them, Katrina's face, a nice way to end the day.

Chapter Twenty

I VAN AWOKE AT seven with Andreas hugging his back. He rolled over to kiss the sleeper's brow before reluctantly slipping out of bed to dress. Today there would be another "progress" meeting with the idiot functionary that he did not look forward to. He fastened his watch, put his laptop in his attaché case, and hurried down the hall, intent on grabbing a latte and a croissant at a nearby café he had discovered. At the door, he encountered Mahmoud at morning prayer in the living room before hastening on.

After *Fajr ṣalāh*, back in his room, a text message awaited. It was from Katrina: **want 2 come for breakfast?** Unsure of her meaning, he responded: **all or just me?** He was combing his hair when she answered: **just u whenever u can get here.**

Again he wondered why she had latched on to him, what she had in mind. He wanted to go, wanted to know, couldn't decide. His comrades were unavailable for comment, but why ask them? He tore a page from a notepad on the counter and wrote *I take early walk. Back in 1 or 2 hours. M.* Then he messaged Katrina: **will come 20 min.** Pocketing his phone and city map, he went forth into the expectant dawn. Down the street, he overtook a man in a business suit walking a small dog deftly detouring around a feral cat with flattened ears perched on a doorstop. At Dimokratias Avenue he turned left. Up at the Taverna Omphalos he retraced the steps the gang taken to get to her place the other day.

When he announced himself, he found her preparing a frittata and toast. With a welcoming hug she instructed, "Sit at the table. I'll serve you" and started by pouring him black tea, saying, "Last night was pretty intense. I felt a bit uncomfortable discussing our views in front of Ivan."

"I think it was okay. Andreas said he was political once too." He spooned sugar into his tea and stirred it a while.

"Still, do you think he got the idea we might want to do something about those evils?"

Ignoring her use of the first person, he said, "I doubt it. Ivan probably thinks we are just a bunch of idealistic leftists and a crazy hacker. Anyway, we aren't up to anything. Are you?"

Katrina turned off the burner, put a lid on the frittata, and sat down across from him. "That's one of the things I wanted to talk about," she said, her eyes rising to meet his.

"You mean doing something?"

"That's right. With you and your buddies."

"What's that supposed to mean? Like I said, we aren't doing anything."

"What you're doing is hunkering down, licking your wounds. Is that your idea of radical action?"

He shifted in his seat, crossed his arms. His mouth felt dry. He took a sip of tea and stared at her across his cup. "So what's your idea?"

"I have lots of ideas and I've made some of them happen. I don't want all that fierce rhetoric I heard last night go to waste. I know I could help take it to the next stage."

He put his cup down, rattling the saucer. "I'm not sure what you mean, Katrina."

"For one thing, Andreas is a trusted friend who knows how to get things done. I'd follow him anywhere."

"He's a good man. I owe a lot to him, but I'm not sure he wants your help."

"But mostly it's *you*. I admire you for your courage, commitment, and your quiet fierceness. I think you're a beautiful man and I want to work by your side. There. I've said it."

Mahmoud helped himself to more tea. He stirred in a lump of sugar at length, staring at the table, avoiding her expectant gaze, aware of warmth coming to his cheeks. "I-I enjoy your company too and I'm grateful for your help." He cleared his throat. "But let's not make things complicated."

She sat back and crossed her arms. Voice rising, she said, "Things already are. Your leader is in jail. You're here illegally. You need a plan. Let me help you, for God's sake."

He gazed at the window, seeing light and shade intimately swirling in the sun-dappled curtains. Piercing him with blue steel eyes she said, "I just told you I wanted to be with you. So tell me, do you at all want that?"

"There are other people involved. It isn't for me to decide."

She leaned toward him, her forearms extended. "Of course, Mahmoud—I like that name so much better than Peter—but how do *you* feel about it, about me?" He became aware he was tapping his cup on its saucer. He put it down and cupped her hands in his palms.

Her hands turned to squeeze his, her grasp fast. "I – I like you very much," he said. "I admire you, and I am grateful to you, and . . ."

"And might even love me?"

She pulled his arms toward her in a gentle tug-of-war, leaning in until their lips brushed with the scent of tea. Through slitted eyes she murmured "You are really special and I don't want to lose you."

He became aware of how tight his grasp was and relaxed his grip to settle back in his chair, waiting for words more coherent than his thoughts and desires to come.

Hers came first. "Does my saying that make you uncomfortable?" He lifted his chin with a quick *tssk* and lowered it. Her lips pursed in a half smile, again she inquired. "Tell me, then, tell me did you ever kiss a woman before? Did you have a girlfriend you left behind? Tell me, because I have no wish to cause you to be unfaithful."

He drew a deep breath and expelled "In college there was a girl I liked," and released her hands. "We would go to cinema and hold hands and steal kisses. Sometimes we would go to restaurants, usually with her brother, at her father's bidding. Her family was Shia and mine Sunni, and that was a problem. And then, when the occupiers pulled out, they moved to Basra, very far away. She went to work in a bank. We exchanged letters for a while, and then she stopped writing. I don't know why."

"Do you miss her? Would you like to find her again?"

"I think about her sometimes, but my life has changed so much since then and my future is so uncertain I see no possibility of reuniting."

She refolded her arms. "I had a boyfriend my last year at university. He asked to marry me, but I had other plans and didn't want to settle down. After that, I was pretty celibate. The guys at the NGO were either creeps or wimps, and the African men who weren't rapists were serial adulterers. Then I came here, but none of the movement men have attracted me—except Andreas, and we both know that's not going to work."

"Perhaps it's not a good idea to get involved with men you work with," he said. "It can cause problems. You could lose the path you need to follow."

Her arms unfolded, her fingers found his and twined. "Look at me. We are not so different. Do you not see someone committed to human liberation, who follows a path like yours and your comrades'? Why can't we follow it together? I understand your fears. I have them too, but I am ready. I have never been more ready."

He felt caution retreating like an arc of sea foam on a beach, in its wake scattering pebbles that formed Arabic letters conjuring up a poem. "I only know this in Arabic—something like your task is not to seek for love, but just to tear down the barriers within yourself that you have built against it. Rumi said that."

She smiled and gazed upward. "I take it to mean that love is not opposing my path, it is a path of its own. I love Rumi too. Is not one of his lines 'Love is fearless in the midst of the sea of fear'?"

"It sounds familiar. I am sure love can sustain courage. Perhaps it is its only source," he said, flashing on the time of war and how his love for his lost family helped him face and attack the enemy. He squeezed her hands again. "I – my heart tells me to voyage with you on that sea of fear. But we could capsize and lose everything. You said you are ready, but ready enough for that?"

As her lips parted to speak, his phone buzzed. He wanted to ignore it but it might be urgent. He let go of her hands. The phone displayed a text: **RU OK**

Just a check-in from Andreas. He coded a positive response: **it is humid. Very humid.**

A reply came: **good. c u at cinema soon.** It seemed a meeting was being called.

"I am sorry but I must leave," he said halfheartedly. It was too abrupt.

"I understand," she answered. "The two paths. But you can't go before we eat. Let me serve you a frittata with love and tea to fortify you for your day."

She slipped away to the stove. As she sectioned the frittata, Mahmoud came to her from behind to encircle her waist. He felt her warmth, restraining an urge to cup her breasts. Chin on her shoulder, mouth to her ear, he breathed "You are beautiful, Katrina, and strong. Perhaps we could be comrades and more. I don't know. I must think about it. But one thing I do know is that after I go, and probably forever, I will remember this moment."

She half-turned and put two fingertips to her lips and then to his, saying "If you mean remember forever and not go forever, then I will let you go."

"I did not mean that I would never see you again. I will return when I can."

"You may return tonight or whenever. If it's without barriers, you won't need to sleep in the kitchen."

II. Kindness of Strangers

Those that have embraced the Faith and fled their homes, and fought for the cause of God with their wealth and with their persons, and those that sheltered and helped them, shall be as friends to each other.

The Holy Qur'an 8:70

Chapter Twenty-One

NOT UNLIKE A morning staff meeting almost anywhere, Team Andreas assembled at nine with coffee, tea, and pastries, with Mahmoud, Kaan and Ottovio in attendance, reluctant leader *pro tem* Andreas presiding. Putting down his tea and clearing his throat, Andreas called them to order.

"Salut, team. Let's figure out what we're doing. But first, any old business?" Kaan said he thought they should review the list of George's contacts he had copied from the cell phone that was now swimming with the fishes. He passed the paper around. Aside from Erol's none of the code names rang a bell with anyone. Andreas still wanted those comrades to know George was in stir, but Ottovio pointed out that any of those people might be under surveillance or even custody.

"Maybe George wouldn't want some of them to know," Mahmoud added. "I would wait."

"Okay," Andreas said. "I agree, George should signify, if he can. Trying to save him is old business too, but let's hold off talking about that for now. So Kaan, what have you been up to?"

Kaan related the idea that he and Mahmoud had talked about, attacking a person or a group with some sort of drone, and chuckled "Wouldn't you love to show the world that imperialists don't have a monopoly on lethal drones?"

Andreas thought it was a sweet idea but hardly practical and somewhat premature. But just in case one might come in handy, he advised Ottovio to find out what he could about small drones.

He continued barking orders. "Kaan I want you to come up with a list of potential targets and dates for the operation. Mahmoud, look into payloads and how much of a punch different kinds can pack."

"Sure, Andreas," Mahmoud responded wearily. "And what about you? What's your task?"

"My job is George. Need to find out what name he was using that he hid from us. Once we know that, we can look for legal help."

"You have no clue?" asked Mahmoud.

"He never told us. It was always George—no last name. Hardly discussed his past. I'm sure he's been insisting to interrogators that he is not Bac, but some other dude. But what dude is that?"

"If police have his alias," Ottovio said, "it's in his dossier. I crack database again to liberate his record."

"Thanks," Andreas said. "And once you have it, maybe you can erase it."

Ottovio tugged at a curl of beard. "Sorry. Files are protected. Can't change or delete anything. But that would screw them up royally." He escorted his computer into the study to plug into the Net.

Andreas stood up, hands behind his head, telling the other two. "Okay, let's get busy." Then he went to the kitchen to refill the teakettle with water.

All morning, Mahmoud had been quietly preoccupied with Katrina's proposition—two of them, actually—fearing that any mention of her comradely and carnal desires would threaten the brotherhood they were building. Convinced that she would keep popping up, he wanted closure. Part of him, the part he had just discovered in her kitchen, found her worthy of desire. The other part was more complicated. He wasn't looking for a fling in the hay or martyrdom with virgins, not that he assumed she was one. He had other expectations, which didn't exclude taking a wife. He had lived and fought alongside females—strong, confident, resolute women, most quite exotic to him. Some of them took lovers, but the cross-comrade affairs he'd observed rarely ended well and usually eroded morale. And now that a compelling woman with warrior qualities had presented herself to him, he was torn. He believed she cared for him, her zeal was real, and what she said about herself was true, but what hadn't she told him? Might she just be looking for protection from something or somebody?

He doubted that she could be some kind of double agent. Clearly, Andreas trusted her, but could he vouch for everyone she was involved with? And what about the enemies she had mentioned? Would they become his? He wasn't sure he wanted to become her support system, not that he was afraid to protect her, but his own seemed rather tenuous. After being orphaned and fleeing the country, he had found a sense of security in his brigade he was starting to miss. But just as he was getting comfortable with his new comrades, he was ordered away. With George probably gone for good he needed a new a network, and Katrina already had one.

She had correctly concluded that he and his buddies were cluelessly adrift. He had come to admire her dedication, perspective, and activism. She's well connected. He wondered if he should take Andreas aside and ask if he'd let Katrina become a confidant. He could frame it as a business proposition that could benefit everyone, one he was sure Andreas would at least listen to and consider. But what if he said forget it and told him to avoid her? Even if he agreed to let her in, hiding their budding relationship would be impossible. No, it wouldn't work to cajole Andreas to ease her in and then reveal their involvement. Nor was seeing her on the sly an option. Either she was all in or all out. Everyone should know everything, and it was up to him to be up front and make it work. If Andreas went along, Kaan and Ottovio would almost certainly fall in line. And if George ever returned, it would be a *fait accompli* he would have to accept.

He watched Andreas brew tea in the kitchen and asked him for some. It took two cups to decide what to do. He texted Katrina: can u meet @ that taverna @ noon?

Before long he received the anticipated reply: sure.

He bussed his mug to the kitchen and mentioned to Andreas that he was heading out to meet Katrina at the taverna to pick her brain about ex-prisoners from Korydallos. Andreas seemed wary and suggested coming along, as he'd expected he might.

They arrived at the omphalos to find her already inside the eatery reading a book. She beamed a smile that faded when she noticed Andreas in tow.

Mahmoud was all business. "We just learned that a friend of ours is in Korydallos prison and want to help him. You told us you know people who were held there who might be good to talk to."

Her brow crinkled. "I think I know who you're talking about. Please go on."

Andreas did. "We need to tell him we're on his case, and find out if he's been mistreated. Do you know anyone who might have inside information or could suggest a good lawyer for him?"

Katrina lowered her gaze, muttering, "I know more people who have been in that hellhole than I wish to count. And I happen to know a recent inmate who might be just the person to talk to."

"Who might that be?" asked Andreas.

"Her name is Eleni Yannatou. She was released a couple months ago from unjust confinement after going on a three-week hunger strike that got a lot of attention."

"What was she in for?" Mahmoud asked.

"For no crime, just an act of conscience. She refused to sign a so-called 'certificate of social conscience' disowning her jailed husband, Stavros Gianopulos. And even though she was locked up in the women's wing a few dozen meters away from him, they wouldn't let her see him. I would blow a hole in that place if I could."

"Do you know Eleni?" asked Andreas.

"Sure. She's great. Such fire and defiance she has. More than anyone I know except maybe you, Mahmoud," she said, finally lifting her eyes.

"I want to talk to her," urged Andreas. "Can you introduce us?"

"No problem, She's probably pretty busy, but I'll try to run her down."

"Thanks. Sounds like a good start. Give me a ring as soon as you can."

"Sure," she said. "Anything else I can do for you?"

Arising and motioning to Mahmoud, Andreas replied "Not that I can think of. We'll see you later."

"Wait," said Mahmoud. "There's one more thing, if you don't mind." He reached for Katrina's hands across the table, as earlier in her kitchen.

Andreas noticed the gesture and repaired to his seat. He leaned back, stroking his chin. "What's up, Mahmoud?"

Mahmoud looked intently at her, then at him. "Andreas, may I have your permission to marry this woman?"

Andreas stopped stroking his chin to let his left eye twitch. "Would you repeat that please? I don't think I heard you correctly."

Mahmoud rephrased his proposition. "Katrina and I are in love and want to marry, I said, but only if you give your blessing. What say you?"

Andreas was in denial. "Are you serious?"

"Totally," Mahmoud said, eyeing Andreas like a sniper. "We talked it through and it's what we both want." He glanced at Katrina. She squeezed his hands.

Already, Andreas had entered the second stage of grief, victimization. "This is what I get for asking Katrina for help. Something like this could tear us apart."

If Mahmoud's proposal had put Katrina off balance, she didn't show it. She disengaged their moist hands and said, "It won't ruin your conspiracy. It will make it stronger. Promise. And whatever you're up to, if it's big and bold it could inspire more resistance and change than any street march or vigil."

Tilting back his chair, Andreas inquired "Mahmoud, what have you said to her?"

"Nothing, Andreas. I told her I have no plan. Do you?"

Aside from trying to free George from prison, which he had thought this meeting was to advance, Andreas had nothing either. He swiftly entered the third stage, that feeling of impotence. Casting his eyes downward, he murmured, "Everything's falling apart. I can't seem to stop it."

"No it's not," Mahmoud shot back. "And you aren't alone. We have work to do. I didn't come this far to give up, even after such a setback. I thought you would welcome Katrina's energy and ideas."

"Yes and no. I know Katrina for over a year and have nothing but respect for her. I know she's good at inspiring and organizing people, but that's the last thing we should do. And as far as I know, she has never used a weapon."

Mahmoud turned to her. "What do you say, Katrina?"

Arms folded, eyes smoldering, she spat back "So my background's not right? You don't go to school to become a revolutionary. How am I any less qualified for the vanguard than you guys?"

"Of course you're not, Katrina," Andreas said with pleading eyes. "But it's hard to see what you would add to the equation."

"To an equation that so far equals zero, a lot. To paraphrase an American hegemon, you go to war with the life you've got, and I'm at war with any and all oppressors. It's time they got a dose of their own destructiveness. I'm ready to do that."

"To do what?"

"To make a big splash that will stir the disaffected to take action. To break out of apathy, cynicism, and hopelessness, because they'll see fighting back works."

"And turn them into anarchists?"

She rolled her eyes. "Get real. Political activists need to climb out of their ideological boxes if they hope to change the world. Who can predict what that change might amount to, but it could take fire anywhere and everywhere. And I'm not about to sit around and serve Mahmoud supper when he comes home from the revolution. I want to be by his side—and by yours—to create it. Does that help?" She dropped her arms to her lap and folded her hands.

Andreas was gazing at the cracks in the ceiling, fingering his stubble. She'd said nothing that he disagreed with and was already helping them, but getting her more involved, especially as Mahmoud's girlfriend, would complicate risk. According to Ottovio, her police record was no more worrisome than his own. But a careless aside to one of her many acquaintances could still compromise them, as could loose lips around Ivan. And then there was George. Were he to learn of these foreign bodies it would surely blow his cork.

The equation that equaled zero had too many unknowns. Katrina already knew some of its terms, but not the full expression. Now it seemed she would have to. His eyes drifted down. She was still glaring at him. With a sigh, he entered stage four, inconsolable bargaining with the inevitable. "Think about it, Katrina. This is a big deal. Having a relationship with this man will change ours too, and those you have with everyone else."

"I suppose so. I believe I can handle that."

"Sooner rather than later you'll have to break ties with people you associate with. You will be isolated. You might even need to change your identity. Make sure that's what you want because there's no going back. Your days as a free agent will be over."

It was her turn to sigh. "If that's true, I suppose I'd have to stop blogging too," she said. "Maybe it's just as well. Nationalist trolls have been poisoning my postings. It drives me crazy but I can't stop it. I don't need that shit."

Recalling how skinhead recently attacked an anarchist meeting nearby and how the police just stood by watching, Andreas took pity. "I'm sorry, Katrina. It must be tough. Are you afraid of what they might do to you?"

"To be honest, yes. I could use some backup. Look, I want to get on with my life. I'd gladly sacrifice blogging to join forces. You're right to point out that following your path will change my life, and I'm ready for that. Together we'll be stronger, you'll see."

Mahmoud put his hand on her shoulder. "I think it will be good for all of us, even though it might be difficult at first." She cupped his hand and squeezed.

"I can see I'm outnumbered here," Andreas replied, "but I don't want hormones making a decision that affects all of us. Both of you need to take some time to think this over."

"I'm sure it's what I want," she responded, "but I'd like to talk it over with Mahmoud. Tonight, if that's all right with you."

"If you have a serious discussion, it's okay with me," Andreas replied, "but Mahmoud's absence will be noted."

Mahmoud replied, "I will say that I am going out because I need some time to myself. No explanation needed."

The final stage, acceptance of sorts. "This could be a new beginning or the beginning of the end. Please think very carefully . . . no matter how much fun you're having."

CHAPTER TWENTY-TWO

THE EVERYDAY EXIGENCIES of managing a multinational conspiracy were taking a toll on Andreas. Playing quartermaster, taskmaster, and now marriage counselor consumed his days and Ivan's attentions his nights. Today's therapy session had put him even further off-kilter. After the couple left the taverna he treated himself to a falafel gyro and a glass of wine to unwind. It was early afternoon and there was nothing he needed to do until Katrina put him in touch with the ex-inmate Eleni on behalf of their current one.

The food fortified and the wine emboldened him. Tired of coping with the conundrum that was Katrina, he decided to visit his residence to see if everything was okay there. Ever since George's nabbing he'd avoided the place, but now wanted to see if anyone had searched, bugged, or staked out the premises. He also wanted to resume styling hair, not that he had much time for it, but it was his only regular income and he hated to see it wither.

At the corner of his street he peered down the block. Two people from the neighborhood chatted in a doorway, but no one else loitered. He ambled down the opposite side looking for lurkers in parked cars. Seeing none, he crossed the street and went to the door of his shop and found it was still locked, as was the door around back that led to his flat. He let himself in and checked for signs of entry. The storage room seemed undisturbed, but he found the rear door to his salon was unlocked. Had he left it that way? He couldn't be sure. Within, it was just as he'd urgently left it: used towels tossed on a chair, tufts of hair—probably Katrina's—on the floor, and a half-finished cup of tea. He drained it into the washbasin wondering if he would ever work there again.

The answering machine by the telephone was blinking. That phone, registered by Kosta under the shop's name, was his only landline. He used it only for business purposes, thinking it could have been tapped after Kosta's arrest. He decided to play the messages later and retreated to the back room. The deadbolt to his flat was still secured. He unlocked it and ascended to the kitchen, where dishes still beckoned from the sink. Everything in the living room looked normal, also in the bedroom. Feeling thankful that his effects weren't strewn about amid upside-down drawers, he grabbed his old rucksack and stuffed some clothes into it. In the living room, he took his copy of *Is Paris Burning?* from the bookshelf, verified that it still held the list of secret code words, and packed it along with his potentially incriminating daily agenda. Leaving the mess in the kitchen, he went back downstairs, locking the door behind him.

His bicycle still leaned in the corner of the storage room. He was about to wheel it out when he remembered his messages, which he expected to be from customers needing urgent haircuts. Three of them awaited his attention. The first was from a female customer asking for an appointment. Also the second, from a male client wondering if he had closed the shop. The most recent one had come that morning, and it was from George. His voice sounded scratchy, stressed and, as usual, he was terse.

"They have me in Korydallos in a small cell with three other aliens. They tell me I will be extradited. When I demanded a hearing they were most unpleasant and told me to get a lawyer. Your job is to get a good one over here to defend me. Tell him they have the wrong guy. Hope you get this message soon. It's now Tuesday, around 9 AM I think. The carnival is over. Good luck and get me out of here."

He had given George that number for emergency use only. This call clearly qualified, but now the police would likely take a renewed interest in this location. They could already had paid a visit, even though he saw no evidence of that, except perhaps for the unlocked inside door.

George sounded dreadful, but at least he had managed to call. Andreas replayed the message and then deleted all of them. He decided he should remove himself lest any cops show up, and a way to discern that came to mind. He went into the restroom and ripped off four sheets of toilet paper. Neatly folding one a few times, he inserted the wad in the crack of the front door, just above the latch. Then he retreated, folding up little wads, wedging them in doorways before locking them.

Out in the ally, he rigged the back door and pedaled off to the condo. About half way there his phone went off. He pulled over to find a text from Katrina: eleni says talk 2 mikos. u cn meet him @ our cafe @ 3. look 4 beard & blue striped shirt. It was almost three already. He wanted to alert the men to George's message, but this was more important, and so texted back ok tell m go 2 condo by 4, u 2. Then he messaged Ottovio to tell him to join them.

He turned the bike around and headed to the café to meet Mikos, whoever he was, and took his own street to get there. Approaching his building, he noticed a black car that he was sure hadn't been parked there when he left, or at least hadn't been occupied by two men, and turned aside as he cycled by. Quite possibly Hellenic Police detectives, not a good sign. But as he rode on, he realized that if they got in they would find no useful evidence. If they pulled fingerprints, he thought, they might find Mahmoud's and maybe Michael's, but only his own might be identifiable. But then he recalled George had spent the night there too and felt stupid for not wiping the place down.

Before pedaling to his rendezvous he made a detour to his bank and withdrew five hundred euros of his funds for a retainer and unforeseeable expenses. His bank account could easily absorb it. Not long ago, his meager income from cutting hair had been supplemented by an inheritance from his grandfather, a well-known Viennese clockmaker who had worked almost every day until he died at 94. At first, he had felt the bequest mocked his revolutionary values, but the semi-employed activist came to appreciate the lifeline and had made peace with himself by spreading some of it around.

He settled into the café with a cup of tea to wait for Mikos, eventually spying a young man with a scraggly beard wearing a blue-and-white striped shirt. Andreas hailed him and offered to get whatever refreshments he wanted, it was on him. Guardedly obliging, Mikos ordered a pastry and coffee and fell silent. After Andreas had reeled off enough of his radical credentials, Mikos opened up and they conversed for half an hour. It turned out that he had been in Korydallos for three weeks—not long by most prisoners' standards—and got out just last Sunday, the day after George was detained. Yes, he had heard rumors that a Turkish terrorist had been locked up in a special cellblock for Very Important Prisoners. From his cell, he said, he sometimes heard echoing screams, possibly from that section. Rather than dwell on George, Andreas asked Mikos how he was treated in jail.

Mikos shrugged. "I was beaten with a hose by one guard for some petty thing, but generally they don't torture protestors unless they think they are organizers. But that place is full of animals. If the germs don't kill you, some bad-ass convict might for looking at him the wrong way."

The younger man felt lucky to have survived. "Just being there can kill you. Tuberculosis and hepatitis are rampant. The TB has become so durable that it can't be limited or treated by medications. From midday onwards, there's only one doctor and a nurse to treat us. If more than two people have a serious problem at the same time, they're as good as dead."

"Any escapes that you know of?"

"Not for some time. Tunnels have been dug, but they were always found out. Aside from the notorious Vassilis Palaiokostas and his frequent flier miles, no jailbreaks that I know of."

When Andreas asked how prisoners manage to communicate to the outside, he was informed that each cellblock had one or two pay phones, but only the first call was free. Cell phones are routinely smuggled in, but anyone wanting to use them needed to pay its owner up to ten euros for the privilege of making a call.

Did Mikos know of any lawyers who had fought extradition cases? One he kept hearing about comes from a national organization of human rights activists. He has sued the government over illegal detentions and inhumane treatment. Andreas took down his name and thanked Mikos for the information. As they rose from their table, he asked Mikos why he'd been incarcerated.

"It was ridiculous. My friends and I stitched two bed sheets together to make a big banner calling for a demo to oppose the EU bailout. We hung it on a wall in front of the Acropolis and started making noise. Police showed up and busted us for defacing public property, of all things. I guess they didn't want the view of the symbol of Greek democracy polluted by free speech."

In parting, Andreas he slipped Mikos twenty euros as a courtesy. He mounted his bike and cycled to the condo, vowing he would get George out one way or another. But then what?

Chapter Twenty-Three

ANDREAS SKIDDED UP to the condo minutes before Mahmoud and Katrina materialized. Her unexpected arrival brought to Kaan's countenance a puzzlement that morphed into a frown when Andreas thanked her for connecting him with Mikos. His apparent distress prompted Andreas to take him aside. They repaired to the little office to talk.

Stridently he demanded "Why is Katrina involved in George's case? How much does she know?"

"Lower your voice!" hissed Andreas. "Calm down."

"Sorry. So why is she here?"

"So far, all she knows is that one of our friends was arrested. I asked her to network to find legal help."

"Um, does she know why they took George?"

"She read the newspaper report too, so yes. You were there, remember?"

"Are you sure you want her here? She'll certainly want to know more."

Taking a deep breath, Andreas lowered himself into the desk chair and swiveled forth. "We have a situation. I have decided to enlist her in our group."

"What? Why?"

"Several reasons. First, like us, she has dedicated her life to liberation. Second, she's well organized and very resourceful. Third, we can use someone who can make inquiries and travel freely without raising suspicions. And finally, she and Mahmoud are in love. They told me today."

Kaan sucked in a gasp. "Are you serious?"

"Afraid so. I have already talked to them about what that implies. I instructed her that it will require total dedication and could entail grave dangers. After listening to both of them, I'm satisfied that she will commit herself to our goals."

"They're lovers? Since when? How can you permit this?"

"I know it seems unfair," said Andreas, gently touching his hand. "But look, you hooked up with a random stranger. George was right to call it off before it got complicated, but this is very different."

"Katrina will complicate things even more, I'm afraid."

"Perhaps, but she'll be an asset, not a liability. I know her well and am sure of that. And given their closeness and apparent commitment, we couldn't allow her to remain outside. This way, we can keep tabs on her."

"But suppose she decides to drop out? Think of what she will know. It scares me, frankly."

"She will not drop out, I will see to it. She will continue to live in her flat and visit us as needed. She said she'll even stop blogging. And having her around as Mahmoud's new girlfriend will help keep Ivan from thinking we're up to anything."

"I guess it's decided, then. I like her too, but something tells me she spells danger."

"So, look," Andreas said, easing from his chair, "if you suspect she is compromising us, let me know immediately. But right now, I want you to welcome and cooperate with her fully. Deal?"

"I don't think I have any choice but to agree. I want us to move ahead. Katrina is very smart, but she needs to be very discrete and fully dedicate herself."

"I'm sure she will. And since there's no operation to talk about there's little to lose at this point."

"That will change, you know. I hope you know what you're doing, Andreas."

"This will be a good thing," said Andreas, embracing his comrade, pressing his thumbs together to wish himself luck. "You'll see."

In the living room they found Ottovio, who immediately pulled Andreas down the hallway, croaking, "What is *she* doing here? This isn't a social gathering." Andreas pushed him into the office and reiterated his speech to Kaan, reminding him that he'd already agreed she was clean after viewing her police record.

"Whatever," Ottovio protested. "She's an extra degree of freedom that could take ours away."

"Okay, let's consider that," Andreas obliged. "Ottovio, do *you* have a girlfriend?"

"I sometimes spend the night with a woman I have known for years. What of it?"

"Does she know what you do?"

"She knows I hack for freedom. So does she, actually, but we don't discuss our work."

"Then what do you do together, if I might ask?"

"We like to sit around, drink wine, do competitive Sudoku, play video games. Things like that."

"I see. Always the geek. What else do you do together, like professionally?"

"Sometimes we study cool hacks to learn new techniques. But I keep my private life totally separate from my work. Even she doesn't know about the police files hack."

"You felt free to tell Katrina about it. Didn't seem to think that was risky."

"Okay, I see your point. She doesn't necessarily mean bad news—but it's up to you to keep her in line."

"That's what I'm doing. So are you on board?"

"For now. I want to see her in action."

"Then equip her with a phone so you can keep tabs, okay?"

"I suppose."

"Okay then, be nice to her. We need her help to get a lawyer for George."

They found the others snacking from the fridge and toking tea that Mahmoud had fixed. Andreas cleared his throat and said, "First off, as you all now know, Katrina has joined our team. I want you guys to give her a warm welcome. She has deep movement experience and knows, as she says, how to get things done and not get caught. Come to the living room. it's time to talk shop."

"Wait," said Kaan. "First, I think we should vote on bringing Katrina into the team. Let's make it official."

"I suppose," Andreas said, fingering his stubble. "Okay, all in favor of Katrina joining the team raise your hand. Katrina, I am afraid you can't vote on this."

Mahmoud raised his hand, and then Andreas.

"All opposed?"

Kaan's hand went up. Ottovio didn't move.

"Do you abstain, Ottovio?"

"I just work here. I accept majority decision."

"So Katrina, you are in. Congratulations." Andreas turned toward Kaan. "You seem to have issues. We'll talk about that later."

"Thanks," Katrina said. "I'm really excited to be here."

"*Chairetísmata*," said Ottovio. "Looks like I'll need to issue another cell phone"

"Isn't there a secret handshake or something?" Katrina asked.

"That's just in the movies," Ottovio told her. "The real secret is knowing how to avoid handcuffs."

Over by the front window, Andreas stood rocking on his feet, hands in pockets. "All right, then," he said. "Here's my report. I took an ex-prisoner to lunch, a young activist named Mikos. Was in Korydallos when George came there. Heard rumor that some fugitive terrorist had showed up. I asked if he knew a good lawyer, and he gave me a name." He dug a slip of paper from his pocket and read.

"It's Demitrios Karras." He handed it to Katrina. "Katrina, I want you to look him up. See if he'll take the case."

Katrina licked her lips and brushed her bangs back. "Hmm. What am I supposed to say? That some guy whose real name I don't know is in Korydallos and needs his services? And, how should I couch my relationship to George and why I'm up to this? I mean, who are we to want to spring a terrorist from jail?"

Andreas begged to differ. "Well, first of all, who says George is that terrorist? He himself denied it in the message he left on my answering machine. His identity may be something a lawyer could contest. We know him by his code name, but he assumed a new identity years ago and I assume has fake papers to prove it."

"He does, BTW," Ottovio put in, "Turkish passport under Yilmaz Turgut."

"Are you sure?" Kaan asked. "What's your source?"

Ottovio ingested the last of his coffee. "You know police database I download last month? This is version from yesterday," he said, holding up a flash drive. "Was delicate procedure."

"You left no fingerprints, I hope?" Kaan asked.

"Used proxy server. At most they see time file last accessed. Had no name to go on, so I use date of arrest. And there is Yilmaz Turgut with note they ask Turkey if valid passport exists. No answer on that."

"Yilmaz Turgut? That name's new to me," said Andreas. "Any other information about him?"

"Of course. They assume they have Gurcan Bac. They note 2011 Interpol alert saying Bac may have entered Greece."

"Anything else?" Andreas asked.

"You bet. An informant, a woman, Dolores Cardozo, a Spanish national, identified as MLK Party cadre. I find her record too. She was detained two weeks before George. May still be in jail, also in Korydallos. Both records say she fingered him."

"How curious. Do you suppose . . ."

Kaan cut in. "It sounds like George had a relationship with this woman. But I was with him for almost a month and saw no sign of it."

Andreas scowled. "When you two lived at Doganis, did George, say, take any nights off?"

"Actually yes. Once he told me he was going out of town overnight. I didn't ask about it, of course. But why would he hook up like that? He knew the risk."

"We are all human beings," Katrina reminded them, looking at each man in turn, all of whom had recently entangled themselves in outside relationships. "We all have drives and want to be loved."

Andreas was forced to agree. "Yes, and love drove George right into the arms of the Hellenic Police."

Katrina continued. "I'm curious, Ottovio. Could you expunge George's record?"

"No. I logged in as employee with read-only privilege. But I wouldn't kill it."

"Why not?"

"Would look fishy. Set off alarms. At most would delay things. Maybe as last resort."

Andreas' impatient arms met in a clap. "Let's focus on a legal strategy. If we hand over George's record to his lawyer, he'll want to know where it came from. What do we tell him?"

Mahmoud broke his pensive silence. "Just say you can't reveal your sources. But what could he do with it?"

"Maybe not much" Katrina said. "But suppose we removed the incriminating stuff and replaced it with our version of history. Ottovio, can that be arranged?"

"In theory. Would need to edit record and update police file. Tricky but not impossible."

Andreas seems to unwind "Not a bad idea. I like it. See what's possible, Ottovio. Now let's move on. Kaan, have you found any tentative targets?"

"I tell you," Kaan said, hands pressed on the breakfast bar as if it were a lectern. "I focused on Turkey, knowing it as well as I do. And while Turkey has plenty of problems with bad actors, the buck always seems to stop with one of them, Osman Paşa, President of the Turkish Republic. He bends state power to turn public high schools into religious academies. He aids and abets ISIS, attacks Kurds, represses free speech, and has jailed opposition figures and even top military officers. He himself alludes to establishing an Islamic state that would absorb Kurdistan and at least some of Syria. Thinks he should be Sultan. He's subverted the republic. Thirteen years of this is way too much. He must be stopped."

"That was quite a brief, Kaan," Andreas said. "Supposing he's our target. How can we get near him?"

"His official itinerary is sketchy. He will, of course, attend the G-20 summit in Antalya, but that's not an option for us. But Paşa also visits religious schools, headline party events, and shows up to officiate here and there."

"How many of those events might be accessible?" asked Andreas.

"Can't say, but he always seems to be cutting ribbons and breaking ground for construction projects from malls to mosques. He is salting the country with new mosques and somehow diverts government funds to build them, even though that's unconstitutional. His religious base loves it."

"Any such events likely to happen over the next one to three months?"

"Possibly. I'll set up phone alerts for news items and notifications about him from the official Andalou press agency. But we won't have much lead time, so we'll need to be ready to act."

"All right," Andreas announced, "let's take a poll. Should we target the Turkish President at a public event?"

"Am I allowed to vote?" asked Katrina.

"Sure. All in favor of doing that, signify now."

Everyone but Ottovio raised a hand. "Abstain," he said. "Want clearer game plan."

"Okay, I should have said *provisionally* targeting. But, for now, President Paşa must go!" Andreas proclaimed to raised fists. "So Kaan, dig deep. Compile a list of where and when our target will appear in public. Maybe Ottovio can help, but for now he should concentrate on hacking George's record. Without leaving fingerprints."

"Already know how," Ottovio responded. "Just need right credentials to make changes. Could take time."

"Well then, keep at it. Mahmoud, research weapons, anything that could strike from a distance. Keep it simple."

Mahmoud looked at his shoes. "Sure Andreas."

"What about me?" asked Katrina.

"I already told you. Now that we have George's assumed name, you can contact Attorney Karras. Make up a convincing story about whom he's dealing with and why they want to get him released. Got it?"

With a salute and a smile came "Aye-aye sir!"

"All right, then," Andreas said impatiently. "Let's get busy and gather here tomorrow afternoon for progress reports."

From behind the breakfast bar Kaan blankly observed, "Tomorrow is Saturday. Ivan will probably be around."

"Right, Kaan. I had forgotten. So instead, let's meet at Katrina's place. With your permission of course, Katrina"

"No problem, Andreas. Afterwards, we'll make a meal. So what will you be doing?"

"I'll spend the first part of the day with Ivan—I promised him we'd visit museums and go to lunch. He'll probably want to hit a club with me at night, so I'll just skip out after we eat. Are you okay with that?"

"Sure," she said. "I'll supply the food, you guys the labor. Oh yeah, I'm out of wine. Ottovio, would you please bring a couple of bottles?"

"My pleasure, comrade Katrina." It seemed she had made at least one new friend.

Kaan stood with crossed arms, his face all but expressionless. Andreas took him into the study, where he demanded to know why the Turk had voted nay for the Swiss. Only because, Kaan insisted, she has no clue how to conduct herself in a stealth operation. The slightest remark, text, or call about their activities could be overheard and passed on. Andreas agreed that she needed to be indoctrinated and they rejoined the others. "Everyone gather 'round!" Andreas announced. "It's time to review our operating rules. Pay attention, because Terrorism 101 is now in session. There will be a quiz after class. No note-taking please."

Chapter Twenty-Four

For the next quarter hour, Andreas lectured on security precautions, Ottovio assisting, Katrina questioning, and Kaan interjecting, as Mahmoud sat quietly by, until a metallic rattle startled them to silence. The front door opened to reveal Ivan, home from work early, briefcase and a bottle of wine in hand.

"Salut all," he said with a smile. "It's good to be home. Nice to see you again, Ottovio and Katrina. How is everyone?"

"Doing well," responded Andreas. "How was your day, Ivan?"

"It could have been worse. At least my bureaucrat said he pushed back on some contractors who were pumping up costs. But not much will change unless they learn how to manage things in a proper sequence."

"Nice to see you, Ivan," Katrina said. "Ottovio and I were just leaving. I hope you have a relaxing evening." Catching the hint, Ottovio closed his laptop and slid off his stool. "Yes we should be going."

After the door closed behind them, Ivan asked Andreas "They were here last night too. Are they lovers?"

"I sincerely doubt it," Andreas responded. "Just part of my circle of local radicals."

"So what did you do today, Jürgen?" inquired Ivan, preferring to use his old friend's given name, strangely the Germanic cognate for George.

Andreas took up the stool that Ottovio had warmed. "In the

morning, I spoke with some people about organizing a protest in behalf of political prisoners the police are holding and refuse to charge or release. I'm sure you've sensed how fragile the state of democracy in Greece is, not to mention the economy.

"Oh yes," Ivan said. "There seems to be plenty to protest here. What else did you do?"

"Let's see . . . later on, my friends came over to plan a surprise party for someone we know. I never did that before. It takes a surprising amount of work to pull that off."

"Well, let me know if I can help. I love surprise parties."

"Thank you, Ivan, but you have already done more than enough to help."

Mahmoud's outward calm belied his irritation at Kaan for voting down Katrina. He wanted to slam the impudent Turk around, but knew that wouldn't help and had no wish to play the bully. His sulking ire brought to mind his overbearing father punishing him over small matters like losing track of possessions, imperfect test scores, and wanting to hang out with friends. Rather than arguing with his hotheaded baba, he coped with passive-aggressive noncooperation. To avoid recapitulating that behavior, he chose to remove himself, slipping out of the condo while Andreas and Ivan were talking in their bedroom and Kaan was in the bathroom.

After their awkward confessional with Andreas, Katrina had invited him over for dinner, hinting at a special dish he'd never had before. He had equivocated and let it hang, but now texted her to say he would come for supper after all. Her response was swift and encouraging: **fabulous**, she wrote.

On his way up Marias Kiouri street, he fired off a text to Andreas: **taking night off. u know y & where 2 find me.** He dawdled along, killing time, looking into shop windows, watching men argue about politics in cafés and refugees panhandling at bus stops, nostrils flaring from the sour stench of uncollected refuse, trying to decipher store signs that shouted at him in capital letters, observing laundry flapping on balconies where black-clad grandmothers sweetly dozed when they weren't spying on neighbors across the way. Along the way, he stopped at a little *manáviko* and bought some bread, cheese, dolma, and fruit. A few blocks on, he patronized a sidewalk florist and walked away with a bouquet of petit sunflowers. Expectantly burdened, he strolled on to her apartment with a spring in his uncertain step.

He was greeted by Katrina in a blue silk sheath dress with a white and yellow floral accents that fit alluringly, complemented by a lapis and silver necklace and hints of jasmine and musk. He put down his purchases to wrap her in his arms, taking in her scent, murmuring, "How lovely you look. Are you taking me out on the town?"

"Only if you insist, but I was hoping to have a quieter time. I see you came prepared, so you probably do too." They kissed, at first tenderly, then with growing ardor, compelling him to release her to quell his mounting desire.

"It was quite a day," he said breathlessly. "I cannot believe all that happened."

"It certainly has been, and it's not over. Must you go home tonight?"

"Only if I'm told to, but somehow I don't expect that."

He presented the bouquet he had bought. She smiled and hugged him. "*Sonnenblumen* we call these, Aren't they so cheerful? They remind me of home. Thank you!"

She arranged the blooms in a blue ceramic vase and, set it on the table and inspected his other offerings. "These are nice appetizers. For dinner, I'm cooking you Swiss comfort food."

"And what is that?"

"It's vegetarian. We call it *Rösti* and *Rotkohl*. Rösti is a pancake of grated potatoes fried in butter until nice and crisp. Rotkohl is braised red cabbage; I sauté it in onions and butter, vinegar, red wine, sugar and spices. Don't worry. The alcohol evaporates during cooking. I'll put out the things you brought, and then you can help me cook while we nibble." She put up a pot of water on the stove to boil and handed him a kitchen blade. "Get six medium potatoes from that cupboard, wash them in the sink, cut them in half and drop them in this water.

When they're halfway done, grate them right into the skillet. While the boil, take that red cabbage out of the fridge. Quarter it and cut away the hard core. Then slice it crossways into thin strips. I'll slice the onions."

Tears came to both of them, Katrina's from hovering over onions, Mahmoud's from memories of helping his mother cook when he was a boy and life was slowly normalizing after the American occupation, before ISIS came to call. It had been nearly a year since he'd lost them, but a sorrowful rage that he couldn't or wouldn't shake abided.

Katrina finished her slicing and wiped her eyes. "What is it, love?" she asked, noticing his tears.

"Cooking made me think of home and then of what my family suffered, but I weep not just for them. There are millions of other victims whose needless misery the Americans and their allies created. It is inexcusable."

She dabbed his eyes with a dish towel, murmuring "And for that, my dear, fierce man, we shall make them pay dearly."

Over candlelight and small talk, the sweet and sour succulence of the rotkohl complemented the crunchy, buttery richness of the rösti, new combinations of familiar ingredients that made Mahmoud request seconds. Katrina tidied up while Mahmoud brewed tea that they sipped at the table eating the strawberries and grapes he had brought. He told her how peaceful he felt. "I was angry with Kaan for voting against you. I still resent that, I guess, but it's his problem. He needs to get over it."

"It surprised me too. I think it upset Andreas more than me, because he took Kaan aside to talk. Then Andreas gave us the spy craft talk, probably because Kaan told him I'm a security threat. But it wasn't a bad idea at all. I didn't know you guys used codes and custom cell phones to communicate."

"Well, Kaan doesn't know you as well as Andreas and I do. He may not trust you, but I think he's also a little jealous. George actually beat him for visiting a girl he had met and made him call it off. Seeing us together must feel unfair to him."

She took his hand across the table. "I think he's basically a reasonable person. It might be a good idea for you to have a talk with him soon to smooth things over. We need solidarity, not suspicion and resentment."

Mahmoud squeezed her hand and let go. "Maybe you should speak with him too, or at least show support for some of his ideas."

"You mean like taking out Paşa? It's just a pipe dream, but it it's worth considering."

"Yeah, it seems totally beyond us."

They sat for a while quietly picking at their fruit as one candle after another consumed itself. Mahmoud cleared his throat but no words followed. She studied his countenance as she plucked a grape from the fruit bowl and popped it into a wisp of a smile.

"Give us a kiss, love," she said, stretching forward. Mahmoud leaned in, closing his eyes as their lips connected, pressing, opening, lingering. With arching eyebrows, he consumed the surprisingly sensual offering her tongue delivered, then reached for one himself, arose and went around to her. She stood to receive the orb and hold him close. They kissed, longer this time, pressed together while candle wax dribbled onto the tablecloth. Katrina puffed out the flame and murmured to him "Come to the bedroom, love. I want to show you something."

She tugged him through the door into a room flickering with candlelight and pulsing with a techno beat from a small stereo that masked the beating of his heart. He let her guide him to an overstuffed wingback chair with rose upholstery. Saying "Make yourself comfortable. I'll be right back," she entered her bathroom and shut the door.

He seated himself and stroked the chair's well-worn arms, taking in her sanctum. Beside him was a round mahogany table with a candle in a bowl and several books. He imagined her curled up there, reading while sipping wine or tea, and examined their titles—a German or Swiss cookbook. *Homage to Catalonia. A Perfect Spy.* More books lined the shelves under the sound system. On a small desk in a corner her laptop swirled with colorful patterns. His inquisitive gaze wandered to her queen bed fluffed with a white comforter, passing on to a Victorian dresser, its top bare except for a few bottles of cosmetics, a little book that lay open, and another half-consumed candle.

He stood up, contemplating whether to stay, immediately doubting it would dismiss his jitters, and paced about, coming to rest at the dresser. An ornate mirror behind it reflected a brow pinched with puzzlement that he tried to cancel with a smile. As his face softened, his beard raggedly pronounced itself to be insufficiently presentable. His gaze dropped to the slim volume on the dresser-top, *Love Poems of Mewlana Jalaluddin Rumi*, a text the Iraqi knew well in its original script. It was splayed open to a page with a verse that began:

Let go of your worries
and be completely clear-hearted,
like the face of a mirror
that contains no images.

He raised his eyes, noticing he was still smiling, then lowered them and read it again. Had she left it there for him?

His back was turned when she re-entered the bedroom. "Do you like it?" he heard her say.

"Oh yes, it's beautiful," he told her, fingering the book. "Rumi has this simple way . . ."

He looked up to see her reflection behind his and turned to face her. She twirled on her toes for him, billowing her dusky red negligee and approached, lips parted in a half smile.

"You look so . . . ," was all he managed to say before her arms encircled his accepting shoulders and pulled him close. He kissed her, lingering, desire swelling, until she released her embrace and slipped away to toss at him something lying on the bed, a set of blue and white striped pajamas.

A wink and a nod urged him toward the bathroom. "I thought you should be comfortable when you came to me. I wanted red ones with a little hammers and sickles but they seem not available. Go in and try them on."

Haltingly, he obliged, ceremoniously marching into the bathroom holding the folded garments like a pillow bearing jewels by an actor exiting a scene he hadn't rehearsed. Just big enough to turn around in, the room enveloped him with her lingering fragrance. He took his time to undress, obsessively folding his clothes and underwear, ritually washing his hands and face, and dried them with a fresh towel she had left for him. And then, still not ready for his life to change, he donned his flannel costume and walked back onstage to wing his lines.

She was lying in bed, the comforter pulled up to her chin. "You look so handsome, love. Come." Her voice quavered, revealing a hint of shyness that somehow emboldened him to grasp the comforter and snap it to the floor. He slid beside her, letting her arms pull him to her, inhaling her musky scent, nestling in the firmness of her breasts as they came together, belly to belly.

His stage fright soon joined the comforter on the floor. He proved an attentive student, shy yet eager, but not learning so fast as to spot her nighty. She softly instructed him, showing and telling the spots that pleasured her most, including her ear when he breathed into it. And breathe he did.

Chapter Twenty-Five

ARLIER IN THE morning than Mahmoud would have liked,
Katrina roused him with steaming coffee, insisting that he suit
up to go shopping. To complement his meager wardrobe—
salt-stained sneakers and two changes of clothing plus the underwear
Andreas had given him—she wanted them to hasten to the boisterous
flea market squeezed between the harbor and the Metro terminus,
promising bargains galore. Half an hour later the early birds were
chuffing down Anapafseos Avenue in a nearly empty 833 bus.

"I can't believe this," Mahmoud exclaimed as he took in the
swath of vendors lined up on Zaimi Street as far as his eye could
see. Some had sizable stalls, covered in tarps to entice buyers out
of the hot sun. Others just sat on the sidewalk behind piles of stuff,
much of which looked like so much refuse save for price stickers.
Sellers wandered about with items in shopping carts or tacked onto
poles they carried high, some topped with fluttering flags. One
pole was entirely festooned with flags and pennants for assorted
nations, sports teams, political parties, and schools. They ambled
through a cacophony of vendors crying "*Ella! Ella!*"—Come! Come!
Bargaining with customers, yelling, crescendoing as they reached
consummation. Boom boxes screeching. Hands slapping on tables.
Off to the side, the occasional passionate orator making political
points semi-coherently. Snaking through the action brought him
back to the big bazaar in Mosul, equally chaotic but postwar lacking
the diverse offerings found here.

At the vast clothing area Katrina's instruction was to wander all the way through before buying. Take your time. Note what you like and where it is. She needn't have bothered. Tactics like walking away from a deal and then returning to fetch a better discount were embedded in his Iraqi DNA.

He found some shirts he liked—a work shirt, a light blue dress shirt, a black pullover, and several t-shirts. At one stall, she had him try on a white sports coat and pronounced the effect manly. He also got the nod for some jeans and khakis he selected, and was urged to acquire a pair of black trousers to complement the jacket, 007 style. He followed suit, but a quest for the requisite black bow tie came up double zero. From a pile of random apparel he brought up a black windbreaker featuring a bold white "FBI" on its backside that he coveted. Katrina nixed it, advising that it would make him stand out. He settled for a military-style jacket with lots of pockets that she insisted was just what a busy radical on the move needed. Later, at a somewhat fashionable *katástima papoutsión*, he shopped for footwear, settling on sturdy athletic shoes. At her urging, he picked up a pair of black dress shoes to complement his evening attire.

Mission accomplished, the couple trundled toward the bus station, squeezing through knots of pedestrians, skirting inching cars that seemed oblivious of each other, dodging meandering motor scooters and teetering bicyclists. Riding uptown, Katrina nestled her head on his shoulder. His arm snaked over her shoulders only to withdraw as he cautioned himself about public displays of affection.

At her place, they arrayed his purchases on her bed. She prompted Mahmoud to model them to see how well they fit. Eventually his garments occupied her armchair and they the bed. She lay by his side, stroking his chest. "You look great no matter what you're wearing, but I like you best this way."

Pleasurable sensations led to peaceful drowsiness. Feeling hunger, Katrina slipped away and dressed as Mahmoud dozed and went to fix lunch. A tin of sardines came to light, which she served up with farmer's cheese, tomatoes, red onion and a baguette, a quick meal she used to make in her student days. After arousing him with kisses she told him to dress up. When he emerged in his new khaki trousers and a navy blue t-shirt with *Red Sox* on the back she approved. "Nice outfit. Good cover too. Even with the beard, you could pass for an American."

Saying he didn't want to fritter the day away, Mahmoud insisted they educate themselves about weaponry. Katrina was all for it, and they settled at the kitchen table with her laptop to explore the mechanics of malfeasance or, as the engineer put it, ways and means to fell a body from a distance. She took the opportunity to check her inbox, only to mutter "Oh crap!"

"What is it?"

"That nationalist asshole is harassing me again. Third time in two months."

Mahmoud peered over her shoulder at the one-line message written in Greek. "What did he say?"

"This email just pleasantly says *Any day expect your throat slit bitch.* Nice. He never threatened death before."

"That's really creepy. Shouldn't you report it?"

"Don't make me laugh. The police won't help. Too many of them are nationalists themselves."

"Sounds like bad news for leftists."

"Absolutely. After cops tip them off, thugs come to break up our rallies and bust heads. A couple of months back some stormed into our collective's workshop, pushed people around, and then trashed the place. When the police finally showed up, they shooed away the skinheads and arrested some of our guys for protecting themselves. How's that for criminal justice?"

"Disgusting. Sounds like extremists in my country, except ours have machine guns. Have they gone after you or Andreas?"

"Just once. When one of them barged in at a rally and started attacking Andreas, his partner Kosta fended the skinhead off. Then some cops broke it up. They beat Kosta and hauled him away, and that's why he's serving time. Andreas took it very hard. I think it made him more militant and drove him to get involved with George."

He put his hand on her shoulder. "I'm sorry for them both. But now I worry for your safety. I want to take care of this creep. Any idea who he is?"

"Probably one of the goddamn Golden-Dawners who troll my blog. Might be the same prick who sent me hate mail the other day. Might be the one known as SuperPlato. Or else one of his miserable minions."

"Really? What did that say?"

She got up and came back with the poison pen letter. "It says '*Your next insult to Hellenes will be your last, anarkist kunt.*' Apparently he didn't like the reaction I posted in my blog to a rude comment."

Mahmoud recalled his rude wakening to the banging of a shutter. Next time, it could be for real. "Katrina, this is serious! He could come after you any time. If he knows your mailbox and your email address, he might know where you live."

"Yeah I know. But what am I supposed to do? Barricade my house?"

"That would be a good start. Let's go get one of those pole things for your door."

"I'm glad you're here, love. We can do that, but let's get on with our homework."

Reluctantly, he agreed to drop the subject and they started browsing weapons. Curiously, despite the planet having many deadly devices per capita, they found their choices were limited. He found a .22 stealth pistol for sale, made without metal parts. A handsome instrument but unfortunately out of their price range. They found even stealthier weapons that pretended to be pens, phones, or cigarette lighters. Not all were expensive but doubts arose over their power and accuracy.

"Say," he said, "look at this. It's quiet, accurate at up to thirty meters, and made of plastic." It was a target pistol powered by a CO_2 cartridge that shot small pellets, an air gun, one of many kinds, he told her, mostly legal most everywhere. The pistol looked like a real gun and wasn't expensive, less than fifty euros. She asked him what it shoots.

"Little steel balls. A dozen or more rounds without reloading. It seems they can shoot darts too."

"It looks cool," she replied, "but you'd need quite a lucky shot to kill a person unless the balls are radioactive or something. And you might have only one shot."

"Yeah, and I don't like how real it looks. I'd rather carry a weapon that doesn't look like a gun."

"What do you mean? Like a bow and arrow or a spear?"

"Hardly," he sniffed. "I might as well wear a loincloth and war paint."

"Say, that gives me an idea. Indigenous people in tropical forests still hunt game with blowpipes that shoot darts soaked in poison. They make the pipes by hollowing out saplings and bamboo. Let's look."

Soon she found pictures of blowpipes, some ancient, some modern, most around a meter or so in length. Further search located ones for sale, made of aluminum or carbon fiber. She asked him what he thought about it.

"I think it would take a lot of practice," he said. "How far can those darts travel?"

"This vendor says they can be accurate up to twenty meters, depending on the kind of dart and that wildlife managers use their products to tranquilize big game with hypodermic syringes. Seriously."

"We should get one to try," Mahmoud said. "That's the only way we'll ever know if it would work."

She shut the laptop saying "Oh yeah, I volunteered for dinner duty," and started scribbling a shopping list. After she finished she told him "While I'm out, why don't you go see your Turkish buddy? Make an effort to patch things up."

Avidly as a schoolboy summoned to homework, Mahmoud messaged Kaan he was coming to the condo to work on delivery systems, specified as toys, which the Turk tersely acknowledged.

Assuming a defensive posture, Mahmoud made wary way to the third floor to be greeted by a dispirited *Merhaba* from a taciturn Kaan loitering in the kitchen. Sensing his roommate's dejection, Mahmoud mentally quivered his arrows and embraced the Turk, kissing his cheeks in comradely affection. Promptly he expressed contrition. "I apologize for being away so much and for upsetting you. That was rude of me. *Tamama?*"

Kaan's deadpan livened up a little. "*Bir şey değil.* I'm sorry if I overreacted. Everything feels so unsettled, so unsafe right now."

"*Size katılıyorum,*" Mahmoud agreed, and quickly changed the subject. "This morning Katrina and I went down to the *pazar* to buy clothes and shoes I really needed."

"I see," said Kaan, stepping back. "The American look. I could use new clothes. Tell me about it, but first, let me tell you about my research."

"Into Paşa's activities?"

"Yes. It's not going well. He's been running around the country quite a lot, but we only get told where he went afterward."

"Probably to avoid being ambushed. Where have you been looking?"

"The Andalou Agency, of course. Online newspapers. Gossip columns."

"Well, wherever he goes, somebody there has to know ahead of time. Have you been looking for local news stories?"

"I've tried, but you know, it's a big country."

"Well, just keep at it. Maybe Ottovio can help. He's pretty good at turning up hidden information."

They startled when Ivan, who had been with Andreas in their bedroom, popped into the kitchen.

"Hi guys!" he grinned. "What's up? How are plans for the surprise party coming?"

Chapter Twenty-Six

S TEPPING OUT WITH shopping bag in hand, Katrina realized she needed two more chairs for dinner that evening. Recalling that her upstairs neighbor had a few, she went climbed up to housemate Penelope's pad. The two of them liked to say they had "liberated" the building they now occupied, but it hadn't come free. After its owner kept shrugging off his property taxes, the city threatened to take it over. The two women had struck a deal to live there rent-free by paying off the tax bill over time. Her bond with the forty-ish Greek woman had solidified during Penelope's occupation of the Finance Ministry with fellow anarchists, who merrily rifled through files, smashed computers, and smeared walls with pig's blood. Penelope was among those fortunate to elude police. Katrina herself hadn't herself been an occupier. From an improvised command post, she had helped advised her comrade of police activity. In that and past direct actions, her predilection for peripheral engagement had kept her from harm's way.

As usual, Penelope welcomed her warmly. Katrina told her she needed two extra chairs to seat some dinner guests.

"My pleasure, Katrina. Take these chairs right here. I won't need them anytime soon. Are your guests movement people?"

"Not really. A small group of friends. And some refugees they are helping."

"Well, I'd love to meet them," chirped Penelope, inviting herself. "I always like to round out my circle of radicals."

Katrina didn't like where this was going. "Can I give you a rain check, Penelope? One of the refugees is in mourning and we're gathering to lift his spirits. Nothing personal. We'll get together another time."

Penelope smiled under a crinkled nose. "I understand. Not a problem. Take the chairs and enjoy yourselves."

Katrina did so and then went shopping. She had decided to throw together a plate of antipasto, a Greek salad, and, with Andreas in mind, fix *Wiener schnitzel* and noodles. But as Mahmoud didn't eat pork, she instead bought chicken cutlets. Dessert would be the refugees' problem.

After she'd prepped her food, Katrina went to relax in her rose-colored chair with her book about the Israelis and the Palestinian terrorist. Three chapters and a half-hour doze later, Kaan and Mahmoud arrived to end her reverie. Kaan, not much of a cook, presented a box of baklava and a tub of ice cream from the supermarket in a flourish of amicability. Ottovio soon followed, toting three bottles of wine, two red and one white.

"Oh, this is for you too." He handed Katrina a Galaxy phone and a charger. "I hope you remember what I say. As little data as possible. Absolutely no personal use. You have a phone for that. If it has any team numbers, delete them. And no GPS on either phone." Katrina said she understood and would scrub her flip phone.

Andreas showed up in time to toast to their endeavor and finish the white. Katrina deployed candles as they dug into the starter plate. Exuding the urgency of a man late for a date, Andreas quizzed each of them about what they'd done since yesterday. Ottovio reported he wasn't able to manipulate files on the police server. He'd started phishing for access points but had no ETA.

"Any luck with tracking the President?" Andreas asked Kaan. "Find any leads?"

"Afraid not, Kaan admitted. "But I've broadened my search to some provincial towns with construction projects."

"How about weaponry, Mahmoud?"

"Katrina and I did some research. We need to do more."

Neither the schnitzel surprise nor anything he'd heard seemed to buoy Andreas' deflating spirits. "Wish we could pick Ivan's brain," he said wistfully. "He's a clever engineer who would love this kind of challenge."

"We don't need Ivan," Mahmoud insisted. "As an engineer myself, I can imagine how he would approach it."

"Yes, Peter—um, Mahmoud," Andreas answered. "Go on."

"Well, first you need to define the problem, which basically is to deliver a certain payload to a fixed location, hopefully undetected, within a fairly small time frame. George's plan to attack the G-20 event had space and time under control. We control neither. Until we know what, where and when, setting a trap with Ottovio's timing devices won't be possible."

"That's a shame. He must have worked hard on them."

"You want the simplest solution that can do the job," he continued, "to minimize what could go wrong. So, let's start over. What are the simplest methods of assassination we can think of?"

"Suicide bomber," Ottovio said matter-of-factly.

"Projectile bomb," suggested Kaan. "Some sort of mortar."

"Sniper," Andreas offered.

"Lets talk about sniping," Katrina put in. "Mahmoud and I came up with an idea we wanted to tell you about."

"Shoot," said Andreas gamely, his libations having unwound him a bit.

"Hold on," said Katrina. She fetched her computer from her bedroom and set it on the counter. One of three browser windows displayed images of aboriginal people and westerners using blowpipes. Another had a catalog of blowpipes of various lengths and construction. The third held nothing but darts. Some were sticks tied with feathers, but most were higher-tech, including a variety of syringe tranquilizer darts.

"Guys in the jungle have been nailing large game over decent distances for centuries," she said. "Pygmies, even. Does the trick. Silent and deadly."

"Blowpipes are cheap," Mahmoud added. "Darts too. What do you think?"

"Intriguing," Andreas said, "but risky. Our marksman would need to shoot with great accuracy."

Eyes fell on Mahmoud, the only one in the room who had ever shot and killed someone. Not as a sniper, but as a grunt in urban warfare. No matter, that qualified him as a hit man in their eyes.

An awkward silence ensued that Katrina filled, announcing, "I want to look into this. Besides the pipe and darts, we'd need poison—a powerful one too."

Impatient to leave, Andreas instructed "Then let's get some answers. Ottovio, work with Kaan to find a creative way to learn where the President plans to travel."

Ottovio grunted assent. Kaan looked relieved.

"And you, happy couple—do some *discreet* research to see what you can blow that's lethal. Get a blowgun and see what it can do."

"Glad to, chief," Katrina obliged.

Donning his coat, Andreas urged "Keep at it, everyone. We need answers. Enjoy the rest of the evening. I'm going clubbing with Ivan."

Katrina giggled. Have fun. "Club a nationalist for me while you're at it."

After Andreas let himself out, they could overhear him talking in the back hall and pressed an ear to the door. Looking perturbed, in a hoarse whisper Katrina urged "All of you, into the bedroom! Shut the door and keep still." The men scrambled out as she collected the dinnerware into the sink, just as three sharp raps issued from the back door. Composing herself, she spoke through the door. "Who's there?"

"It's Penelope," came the muffled response. Katrina cracked open the door.

"Hi, Penelope. Did you come for your chairs?"

"No, you can just keep them until tomorrow. Just saying hello and good night."

"Thanks," Katrina advised. "I'd invite you in for tea, but I'm on my way to bed now."

"No problem. That was a nice man I just ran into. I think I've seen him around. One of your dinner companions?"

"Yes. You probably saw him at a rally at some point. He's an organizer."

"Oh yes. I remember the ponytail. Anyway, I won't detain you. Have a good evening."

"Thanks. You, too." Katrina smiled and shut the door.

When she heard the second floor door close, Katrina entered the bedroom, finding it unoccupied. "You can come out now," she told the bathroom door. "All clear."

"Who was that?" inquired Kaan as the three men filed out.

"Just my neighbor, interrogating Andreas. She's okay but has no need to know. She thinks I'm alone, so perhaps you should leave now."

In nodding agreement, they returned to the kitchen, where Ottovio scooped up his laptop and took his leave. Katrina took Mahmoud aside to tell him "I think you should go home with Kaan. We'll have other nights."

With a wistful "Okay," Mahmoud kissed her cheek and the Brothers took to the night.

CHAPTER TWENTY-SEVEN

THE LEVANTINE BROTHERS returned to the Terrorist Ranch, as Katrina liked to call their condo. As she'd intended, ejecting Mahmoud helped to keep his fragile peace with Kaan. They entered to find Andreas and Ivan idling in the living room. Ivan was pouring cordials as the latecomers entered.

Slightly tipsily, Ivan greeted them. "Salut, my friends. Care for a drink?"

Noncommittally, Kaan replied. "I thought you guys would still be dancing or something. Is everything okay?"

"We didn't like the music in the club," Andreas said. "And the crowd was so *young*! But it was fun for a while."

Ivan seems undeterred. "There must clubs in this town we'd like better. I'll see what people are saying on Facebook."

Andreas graciously offered to make tea and Mahmoud accepted. Kaan accepted a shot of Drambuie from Ivan and they went to lounge on the couch. Kaan pulled out his phone and started paging through alerts he'd requested about the president's activities. Then he put it away, took a hit of cordial, and announced "Word from Turkey has it that if his party gets a majority in Parliament this coming election, Paşa will force through a law to let himself stay in office indefinitely. Disgusting!"

"I thought only third world despots did that sort of thing," Ivan replied. "That's so tacky."

"Didn't Putin do something like that?" Andreas wondered aloud.

Omer settled back in the couch, eyes and mouth tightening. "As wannabe despots go, Osman Paşa surely rivals Putin." He glanced toward Mahmoud. "Your ISIS nemesis, Al-Baghdadi may be more brutal, but he and his cadres emerged from brutal circumstances to spread a primitive theology that Paşa seems very comfortable with."

Kaan seemed ready to rant. Andreas' brow started to scrunch.

"Paşa achieves the same result by cowing the press and subverting state and civil institutions, one office-holder, law, and edict after another, until nobody can challenge his authority without being struck down. Al-Baghdadi is considered an outlaw by most of the civilized world. Paşa is considered an esteemed head of state. But they are both plagues upon the planet and tyrants who must be stopped."

He took another gulp and settled back. Looking up from his drink, Ivan said "Kaan, I understand you are bitter because your father is in jail. You told me he's a newspaper journalist. What did he do to deserve that fate?"

Ivan clearly had poked a hot button. Andreas paled as Kaan took the floor. "I can tell you, but like all politics in Turkey, is complicated. In 2010 national police arrested hundreds of military officers for an alleged coup plot, code name Sledgehammer. Most of the general staff was sent to jail plus others, maybe 250 people in all. Their lawyers said the prosecutor had presented forged documents. The accusations were never followed up. Legal procedures were not followed. All but maybe thirty-five defendants were convicted and sent to prison for fifteen to twenty year terms. Journalists, including my father, and others who wrote that evidence had been fabricated were arrested for defaming the Turkish State."

"And are they still in jail?" Ivan asked.

"Not the officers, just the journalists and intellectuals. Last year, the Constitutional Court overturned the Sledgehammer verdicts and the officers were released. But my father was not."

Mahmoud queried their resident expert whether the military might intervene.

Unlikely, Kaan opined, now that the top brass has been shuffled out and replaced by party loyalists. "However," he added, "there is the matter of the "Parallel State," as Paşa has been calling it."

"Sounds like a spy thriller," Ivan observed.

"It's better than that. Behind the scenes, a power struggle has broken out between Paşa's Party and exiled power broker Mehmed Davacı and his worldwide, supposedly peaceful and charitable religious organization. Paşa and Davacı were allies until recently, and Davacists were appointed to many government positions. Now they are embedded in the government and the military, with conflicting loyalties. If Paşa tries to purge them and things get rough, they could end up purging him."

"That would be great," Mahmoud said, "but what do the Davacists want that's so different than what Paşa wants?"

Kaan was more than happy to explain. "Mehmed Davacı is a shady character. He runs his organization like a godfather from out of sight, abroad. His people infiltrate rather than confront. He's an Islamlist who talks to other religious figures, even the Pope. His organization—they call it *Hareket*—has been worming its way into Turkish institutions. People believe Hareket was behind Sledgehammer, that their plan was to frame the military to eliminate its old-line secularists. It's really hard to know what they would do if they ran the country."

Commiserating with the pickle that Kaan's father had gotten into, Andreas lamented that the Official Story is becoming the Only Story in more and more countries, not just in Turkey. "Both on the Internet and off, journalists and bloggers who expose authoritarian trends are let go or persecuted. Even teenage kids get hauled away for blowing off politically incorrect steam. The fascist shoe fits many nations. Turkey is just one of many to wear it."

"What do you mean by fascist, Andreas?" Mahmoud asked.

Andreas got up and went over to the bar to refill his glass. "Basically, a cancerous symbiosis of corporate and state power that is inherently acquisitive, aggressive, power-hungry, demanding total allegiance, and inevitably corrupt."

"Yes," Kaan added, "private and public interests combine into an authoritarian, corrupt political system run by unaccountable elites. Some of them may be elected, but they don't serve or answer to the people."

Ivan wasn't too inebriated to connect theory and practice. "I can see how it works in my world," he said. "Contractors bribe people at the Ministry of Infrastructure—my company's client—to get favorable contracts or overlook poor performance. If I escalate an issue with a contractor, someone up at the Ministry asks them for a consideration to disappear my complaint. What's the solution to all this corruption?"

Kaan answered with a marine metaphor. "It's built deeply into the system. There's a saying, 'a fish rots from the head,' but what we're talking about is more like an octopus. That's what made George's plan so brilliant. Decapitate the octopus to free the people from its tentacles so they can rise up in revolt."

His words hung in suddenly still air until Ivan asked the inevitable question: "Who is George?"

Andreas quickly interjected, "He's someone I told my friends about who was planning a stealth attack against some VIPs. Fortunately for them, he was prevented from putting his plan into action."

"His plan sounds quite ambitious," Ivan replied. "Was he going after, like, heads of state, bankers, and such?"

With a flip of his ponytail, Andreas replied, "I don't know who might have been the targets. Some high-level officials from several countries at an important meeting, but the police stopped him and the plan fell apart—at least that's my understanding."

Kaan withdrew, announcing, "I'm very tired. Good night everyone."

Mahmoud echoed, "Yes, look how late it's gotten. Good night Andreas. Good night Ivan," and followed Kaan into the bedroom.

Mahmoud shut the door and glared at Kaan. "You were lucky that Andreas covered for you. I hope what he said satisfied Ivan."

"Me too, Mahmoud. I'm sorry. I'll be more careful. But you know, that plan's over and we really don't have one to reveal anyway. We know *who*. We know *why*. But we don't know *where, when,* or *how*. It depresses me."

Mahmoud unbuttoned his shirt and hung it in the closet. "We can do this, Kaan. I know we can. But it sounds like your heart may not be in it anymore."

"Not true! Of course I'm committed to an operation. I just wish we knew what it was."

"Then go figure out *when* and *where* and I'll take care of *how*."

Mahmoud went to the study to pray and returned to find lights out. He stood contemplatively by the window watching the restless silver-dabbed chop on the harbor, his face pallid in the moonlight. There was, he realized, more than one *how*, not just the means he'd use to dispatch the target, but how to get in and get out. Then there was how to handle Katrina if she made noises about joining him, and how that would play out. He stripped of his clothes and slipped into bed. *Good night moon, shining on us all.*

Midmorning, a hung-over Andreas took a text from Katrina: OK to visit? He told her to give him half an hour, jumped into the shower to decompress, and was fixing tea when she arrived.

"Good news, I think," she told him. "I rang up Karras and he picked up, even on a Sunday. I told him I was calling for a friend who is trying to free one Yilmaz Turgut from Korydallos. Karras said he'd heard about the case and asked to hear my take."

Rocking on his heels, hands in pockets, Andreas asked "So what did you tell him about yourself or why you care about George/Yilmaz/Gurcan?"

"I identified myself simply as 'Artemis' and told him a version of what you said happened. Said I didn't actually know Yilmaz but had a friend who moved away whose apartment he was subletting and was inquiring on her behalf."

"Say anything else?"

"Well, to make it sound more credible, I told him I thought they were lovers before she went abroad. But Karras seemed motivated already. He said that he's represented many people in deportation hearings and won quite a few."

Andreas' rocking slowed. "That's good."

"However, this isn't a normal case because George is alleged to be a terrorist fugitive from justice in Turkey."

"Did Karras say how he would handle that?"

She shrugged. "He said it would depend on what evidence they have and are willing to present."

"Why would they withhold their evidence?"

"To keep their sources and methods secret. If they won't reveal how they fingered George the judge could dismiss. If he doesn't, Karras said he would appeal to buy time."

Andreas stared at the floor. "Well, at least that's something."

"So do you think you'll hire him?"

"Sure. I want George out. I'll pay for the lawyer and the court fees, as long as it takes, even if it consumes my inheritance. My grandfather wouldn't mind. He hid Jews from the Nazis in World War Two and helped some escape to Greece."

Katrina smiled. "That's very kind of you. Karras seems to be very obliging, so don't be too generous."

Andreas stopped rocking. "I guess that's the best we can do short of breaking him out of prison."

"No joke", Katrina responded. "It's been done. But it would put Solicitor Karras in the hot seat if George escaped."

"Right," he said. "I'll just move over and invite him to sit down."

Chapter Twenty-Eight

LATER IN THE day at Katrina's, Mahmoud started obsessing over pipes and darts. Before long, he said he'd come up with something and needed her help. This involved traveling to a local hardware store, which they exited with a one-meter length of 20-millimeter PVC pipe, a bag of flathead nails, and a roll of duct tape. On the ride home, Katrina said, "We need a mouthpiece. I don't think duct tape would do it. Let's see, what else could we use . . . Hey I know!"

She hustled them into an apothecary that also sold supplies for invalids. Inside, they found rubber ferrules for canes and walkers and selected a couple that snugly fit the pipe. With its end bored out, she believed, a cane cap would make a fine mouthpiece.

Immediately upon return, Mahmoud took to tinkering. With Katrina's Swiss knife, he excised the flat end of a ferrule, paring and smoothing the opening he'd made. Then he wrapped the heads of half a dozen nails with strips of duct tape, trimming them into little conical skirts. Turning one over in his hands, he said, "These darts won't work very well but at least we'll get an idea. I'm going out back to see how they work."

Don't, she advised, not so close to home, and suggested using the small park near his condo to practice, a place nobody hung around except for the homeless men who sometimes slept there. Soon they were on their way, with Katrina repeatedly admonishing her hit man not to twirl his weapon like a drum major's baton. As they had hoped, the triangular plot of land was unoccupied. For a target, Mahmoud chose the stoutest tree in the lot, backed off ten paces, and raised his weapon.

"Hold on," she said. "You need a target." She picked up a stray page of newspaper from the ground, crumpled and flattened it, and pinned it to the tree with one of the darts. "Okay," she said backing away, "go for it."

Mahmoud stuffed a dart into back end of the tube, aimed, breathed in deeply, and blew. Lazily, the dart wobbled into the dirt next to the tree.

"Pretty wimpy," Katrina remarked. "You can do better than that, can't you?"

"Bad mouth contact," he said sheepishly, "or maybe just a bad dart." Taking another dart from his shirt pocket, he huffed harder. With a slight pop the dart flew past the tree to end up under a tall shrub about ten meters away.

"Much better," she said, "except for your aim. Here, give me a try."

Mahmoud handed over his weaponry. Raising the pipe, she inhaled deeply and pressed her mouth tightly against the rubber. Her shot pinioned the projectile to the tree two hands below her target. Mahmoud pulled the dart out, surprised how far it had penetrated. "I guess that wood isn't as hard as I thought," he said, to which Katrina stuck out her tongue.

They continued to compete, managing to strike the tree from ten meters back roughly half the time but always missing the paper target, which he kept blaming on the sloppy aerodynamics of his improvised projectiles. Intent on making his mark, he raised the tube to his mouth just as a voice behind them barked "HEY! WHAT'S GOING ON HERE?"

Quickly lowering his pipe, Mahmoud turned to see Andreas approaching, two sacks in hand, apparently on his way home from the supermarket. Relieved that it was only his comrade, Mahmoud said casually, "Oh hi, Andreas."

"Cops regularly patrol this park," said Andreas. "How would you explain what you are doing?"

"I guess I'd say 'Just a little target practice, officer,' offered Mahmoud."

"Or maybe," Katrina added, "We have a rat infestation. This is how we'll get rid of them."

Officiously, Andreas intoned, "May I see your identification, please?"

"I see what you mean," said Mahmoud sheepishly.

Sternly, Andreas said "Well, let that be a lesson. Now hand over that thing before it gets you into trouble. I want to try it."

Having hit the tree two out of five tries, Andreas gave up and led the couple home to find a moody Kaan. Such was his funk that he took no note of the slim tubular object Mahmoud carried.

"Is everything okay, Kaan?" Katrina asked, touching his shoulder. "You look sort of down."

He let tell of his existential despair that their target would ever emerge into the open from his palace lair.

"No luck, eh?" Andreas chimed in. "Maybe you should look for more sources."

"I doubt it'll help, but I'll try." His eyes left the floor. "Hey Mahmoud, what's that thing?"

Mahmoud gave him a rundown of his simple tool. Kaan precipitated from his fog of futility to examine the thing from various angles before submitting several obvious questions. What could it shoot that was deadly enough? How far? How accurately?

Mahmoud recounted what he'd read on the subject but had to admit that his prototype wasn't so great.

Katrina elucidated. "These silly darts are just a hack. What we want are tranquilizer darts—flying syringes. Just find the right kind of juice for them and you have a mean machine. Jungle hunters have been killing large animals that way like forever."

Andreas expressed doubt. "Maybe you can bring down animals that way, but a man could pull out the dart before it could hurt him."

"Maybe so," she replied. "Need to think about that."

"Here's something else I'll bet you didn't think about," Andreas said.

"What's that?"

"What do you think your target might be wearing?"

"A suit," she said.

"And what else, aside from shirt, tie, socks, and shoes?"

"Underwear?"

"Sort of, except it's probably not made out of cotton."

"Ooh," she exclaimed, "a bulletproof vest!"

"Expect that," he warned. "Do you think a dart can make it through one?"

Mahmoud agreed he had a point. "Let's assume that whenever the President is out in public he's wearing protective clothing. So, he may only be vulnerable in his face and neck, maybe his shoulders and arms."

"And that means you must shoot with extreme accuracy," insisted Andreas. "So, either perfect your blowgun or buy a better one, and then practice, practice, practice with darts you intend to use. Only then will we know what it can do."

"Besides that," Kaan interjected, "we need to know the venue and the setup. The target can't be too far away."

"That's your Job, Kaan," Andreas reminded him. "So keep that in mind."

"Great," Kaan muttered. "Now I'm supposed to analyze the layout of all the events I find."

"Like I said, Kaan, that's your job. First, find an event that's open to the public. Try to put yourself there. Get a feel for the space."

"All right. I'll focus on the more intimate events like school and mosque dedications. But we may only learn a few days ahead if he'll show up."

Katrina observed "People who work for Paşa must keep track of where he's headed. We need to know what they know. Isn't that the kind of secret information Ottovio specializes in scooping up?"

Mahmoud frowned. "Umm, Ottovio doesn't read Turkish."

To which a voice responded, "Ottovio doesn't need Turkish. Servers aren't programmed in Turkish."

It was the hacker himself, emerging from the study where he'd been quietly hacking George.

"Maybe not code," he continued, but server and file names probably Turkish. I might need a little help. Ready, Kaan?"

Kaan nodded and Ottovio took him into the study and closed the door. Ottovio fired up a browser.

"Okay, we start at site Paşa shows public, then see what connects to it."

Kaan put up the official website of the Turkish Presidency. "I see it has page with calendar," Ottovio said, "but only shows two old events, none in future."

"Yes, they don't update it very often. So now what?"

"So, I go to the contact page. See, has a form you can type message and send back. What I send back is code, program big enough to overflow server input buffer into unprotected memory."

Kaan wasn't quite following. "So, what does that get you?"

"Okay, now server runs my code. Installs program that watches for connections to update calendar page and reports IP address. That server I try to crack to find master calendar file and hope it's not encrypted. Can take a while. If that exploit doesn't work, I have others to try."

"How long is a while?"

"Hours to weeks. Depends on when that page updates, how hard server is to crack, how well they protect calendar file."

"So what can I do?"

"You can bring me double espresso and translate pages."

Andreas announced he had been shopping to prepare a special dinner for Ivan to thank him for sheltering his refugee friends. Having lied to Ivan about planning a surprise party, he decided it should be for him. Noting that they had not many hours to put it together before Ivan returned from his workout at an uptown gym, he straightaway dispatched sous chefs.

When Ivan returned, cheerfully radiating endorphins, Andreas broke out a bottle of Bordeaux he'd been hoarding, a gift from Kosta when they'd first moved in together. He ceremoniously poured the purple to those assembled. Mahmoud declined but took a sip of Katrina's after Andreas raised his in toast. "To a true friend and benefactor who has been so kind. We sincerely thank you for everything, Ivan!"

Ivan responded with aw-shucks modesty and went on to make a startling announcement: "I am very sorry to say that I will be leaving my happy family in Piraeus soon."

Katrina lowered her glass. "What happened, Ivan? Nothing bad I hope."

"It wasn't personal. My company say work here is taking too long, and give me a more urgent assignment. But don't worry about your house. It is paid for through the end of next month."

Mahmoud asked when he would leave and was told next weekend. After a few days in Vienna to handle his affairs, he would go to Turkey to oversee a construction project. "I've never been there and I am looking forward to seeing Kaan's country. But I'll miss Athens and your fine company, especially yours, Andreas."

Specifically, Kaan sought to elicit, where in Turkey?

"Bursa. I don't even know where that is."

"About a hundred kilometers due south of Istanbul, across the Marmara Sea," Kaan told him. "It's quite a nice city. It sits on a plain, but is close to mountains. Europeans like to ski there. If you're a skier, you're in luck."

What was the project there, Andreas asked.

"A new cultural center we designed. Work is supposed to last up to a year, but they have barely broken ground. It will take at least a month to excavate and couple more just to set the foundation. It has to go smoothly for my company to get new contracts there."

Separately the conspirators mulled over what Ivan's revelation might signify beyond losing a roommate.

A fecund moment later, Ivan wondered aloud "Turkish seems like a tough language. How hard is it to learn?"

"I could give you a crash course," Kaan offered. "But no way I can get you up to speed before you go. Maybe you should have a personal translator, someone who understands what's really going on."

Ivan said he wasn't sure that would be necessary. Kaan disagreed: "I'll tell you why. Turks can be quite indirect. Don't expect everyone you deal with to say what they really think. You need to infer their agendas and read their body language. Few foreigners are good at that."

Ivan asked for an example, and Kaan obliged by raising his chin with a faint "Tssk." He asked Ivan whether his gesture meant "yes" or "no." When Ivan said he assumed it was affirmative, Kaan replied "Wrong. It means 'no'. You can get into trouble not knowing things like that."

"Kaan, are you volunteering?" Andreas asked, an eyebrow arched.

"Not really. I have to finish my research. But I should to go home to confer with my advisor one of these days. I suppose I could drop in on Ivan for a few weeks to teach Turkish and help him deal with the locals."

"But I thought you couldn't go back to Turkey, Ivan replied. "Isn't it unsafe for you there?"

Kaan hesitated, his eyes flicking to Andreas. "I've . . . been in touch with friends and relatives. None of them reported official inquiries about me. And nobody would expect me to turn up in Bursa. As long as I don't tell anyone and keep out of trouble, I should be fine. I really would like to help you."

The others caught his drift. Andreas was on it. "That's good of you, Kaan. Why shouldn't you give Ivan a hand for a while? You will always be welcome here when you return to Greece."

"In between language lessons you can work on your project," Katrina suggested.

"Yes," added Mahmoud. "I might even visit you, if I am able to travel again."

"Me too, Ivan," Andreas warbled. "I hope they give you a nice big apartment."

CHAPTER TWENTY-NINE

ALMOST A FORTNIGHT hence, crammed into a tram on an unseasonably warm day with forty-odd swaying passengers, sweat-stained and bone tired after sixteen hours in transit, Kaan Sultanoğlu recalled the old proverb: *Hamama giren terler*— "One who enters a Turkish bath sweats." It captured the moist anxiety he'd felt fresh off the ferry, facing the uniformed woman at the immigration booth until she waved him on with a welcoming *Hoşgeldiniz*. Relieved but rumpled from folding himself into an intercity ötöbüs, here he was, plying the streets of Bursa, surrounded by familiar, welcoming sights, smells, shops, signs, and the rough mingling of Turks. The mundane sacredness of it all, its humble, slightly shabby *je ne sais quoi* warmed his austere soul.

Emerging from the Demirtaşpaşa metro stop, he trod west along a busy thoroughfare, savoring its happenstance and bustle. Although he wasn't lost, he accosted a sidewalk *simit* vendor to ask for directions just to converse in his native tongue, trailing crumbs from the sesame-coated circle of dough he walked away with. At his destination, an apartment block on Kemal Bengü Street, he pressed the buzzer to hear the intercom crackle *"Effendim. Kimsiniz?"* and grinned. Already Ivan had picked up enough Turkish to be able to say "Hello, who is there?" So he announced *"Ben Kaan. Aç kapıyı lutfen"*—It is I, Kaan. Please open the door.

"Merhaba!" the intercom squawked. "Fifth floor, flat 502."

Ivan let him into the home they would share. He hugged his reinstated roommate and received a Turkish cheek kiss, a gesture Ivan had picked up but was never quite sure when to use it. Kaan dropped his backpack and valise in the front hall, removed his sneakers, and followed Ivan in. Surveying the well-furnished living room and its expansive front window, he exclaimed, "This apartment rocks! How did you find it?"

Ivan took no credit. "My company rented it for the lead engineer when he got the project underway. Then they sent him to Sweden on a new job and I took it over."

From their perch overlooking Bursa's Osmangazi district, they surveyed the neighborhood. In front of them were the grounds of the Kemberler Mosque, a large green park crisscrossed by walkways. To their left was the site of the cultural center that Ivan's company had designed. The view pleased Ivan. He told Kaan "I love it! I can oversee the project right rom here—in my pajamas, if I want to. I hope you'll like living here. Let me show you your bedroom."

Once again, Kaan would occupy luxurious quarters. As a committed socialist, depending on a big corporation felt a bit shameful, and here was doing it again. But, to his perverse pleasure, his room turned out to be cramped, verging on ascetic. Contradictions of late-stage capitalism thus disposed of, the scholarly and incorruptible Kaan Sultanoğlu sat on his monk's bed considering how best to approach his mission. Without a clue to its whereabouts or whenabouts, he decided to use his time to explore the city when Ivan had no need for his services.

As he—but not Ivan—hoped, soon Mahmoud would join him with a stealth weapon, a simple hollow tube capable of felling someone a dozen meters distant. The possibility that Katrina might tag along fairly terrified him, as he was sure her presence would complicate everything whether or not she came with a separate agenda. He tried to think of a support role that would keep her out of the way. Nothing came to the weary traveler's mind, and so he texted Andreas informing that he had arrived safely, stretched out upon his thin mattress, and drifted into welcome sleep.

While Kaan's message gave Andreas one less thing to worry about, he was far from jocund. George's fate along with that of his moribund business still haunted him. Ivan and Kaan's absence and Mahmoud's home away from home created a keening to re-occupy his own flat, which might or might not be under surveillance. To settle the matter he decided to summon Ottovio to bring his spy gear over there.

They met at the end of his street and casually ambled to his building, eyeballing for possible stakeouts, and went around back to find the rear door was still latched. Advising Ottovio about his toilet tissue alarm system, he unlocked the door and gently pushed it open. Just inside a tiny packet lay on the floor. Ottovio picked it up. "Maybe fell and we didn't see it. No dirt on it. Doesn't look kicked around."

The back room had a lavatory, a door leading to the hair salon, and another to his apartment upstairs. Ottovio pointed at the salon. "See that?" he whispered. On the floor, just to the right of the door, was a similar wad of paper. Andreas shuddered when he found the door unlocked. "Shh! Speak very softly," the Greek hissed. "I check for bugs now."

He turned on his spy-o-matic and scanned the spectrum for active wireless devices. "Like we did at the condo," he whispered. "Clap hands once. Walk around. Clap again when I point." After a round of slow applause, Ottovio muttered, "No signal detected. But this is just the back room. We go into shop and make noise there."

To their dismay, clapping within the salon gave a positive result, after which Ottovio circled the room with his meter, snapping his fingers. The signal peaked near the front wall, by the telephone. Ottovio peered under its shelf, then withdrew a small screwdriver from a vinyl pouch and gingerly unfastened the back plate of the old phone. Taped onto the shell was small black cylinder, from which dangled a wire—clearly a recent addition.

"I see these before," Ottovio whispered. "We call them cock-roaches." With a wire cutter he snipped the antenna to less than half its length. Several claps later he pronounced the bug hard of hearing, and reassembled the phone. "This is transmitter. Must be receiver.

Do you have Wi-Fi?" Andreas shook his head. Ottovio told him the receiver must be somewhere outside, perhaps on a utility pole where it could phone home. That, he said, he could do nothing about, but whoever might be monitoring will just hear mumbles now.

They retreated to check the apartment upstairs. As Andreas unlocked the stairwell door, the wad of paper he had stuck there fell out—propitious news, he hoped. They ascended and carefully unlatched the kitchen door. Everything including the unwashed dishes seemed undisturbed. Ottovio strolled about, fingers popping, but detected no stray signals.

"Looks like they never came up here," he said. "Maybe got called away or got scared off."

"Perhaps they had trouble jimmying the lock" Andreas hypothe-sized. "It sticks even for me."

Andreas started to unwind. Thanking Ottovio for his help, he said he would do some cleaning before returning to the condo. "Let's all meet tonight over there. You and I can talk about what to do with the cops' database."

"Plus one, Mr. Holmes." Ottovio saluted and tromped down the stairs. Andreas washed his food-encrusted dishes, stowed them, and swept the floor. He considered doing his laundry but didn't feel up to it. Instead, he made himself a cup of tea, stretched out on the couch to think about what else needed to be done, and just as Kaan had done some five hundred kilometers away just recently, soon fell into sleep.

Chapter Thirty

DAYLIGHT WAS GIVING up when Andreas roused himself from his unplanned nap on his day bed. He checked the time. Almost six! Hurriedly, he locked up and hastened to the condo where he found Ottovio impatiently waiting.

"Didn't you say be here at six?" the unusually prompt hacker asked.

"Uh-huh. Sorry. Overslept."

"We need to edit George," Ottovio said. "I found how to change his record. Let's do it."

Only then did Andreas remember that he'd dozed off before summoning the couple. Just as well. This was more important.

Feeling a bit peckish, he told Ottovio to wait as he nuked them a bowl of popcorn and set it by the hacker. Stuffing kernels in his mouth, Ottovio said in Greek: "Oh by the way, want to hear something interesting?"

"Sure."

"G-20 is over. They all went home. And that reception at Aspendos we were going to enhance?"

"What about it?"

"Never happened. Wasn't on the final program. Zero reports about it on the web."

"So it was cancelled?"

"That or they never intended to do it in the first place. Bet that event program I phished out was bogus"

"*Scheisse!* The operation would have been a disaster!"

"So maybe good thing George got busted. Anyway, time to let him out."

Ottovio pulled up a black window with white text, George's purloined police record they were about to doctor. The master had cracked the computer of a police clerk who updated the database to somehow purloin his password. Now he was free to alter data *ad lib*, not just copy it. "Phishing for freedom," he called it.

Ottovio snorted. "You know what that idiot's password was? Take a guess."

"It wasn't 'password' was it?"

Almost as bad. It was 'μυστικό'—'secret'—What a tool."

"So, what we are trying to do here?" Andreas asked. "I guess we could delete George's record or anyone else's, or even all of them."

Eyes fixed on his screen, Ottovio demurred. "Would only delete records if we wanted them to notice it."

"Which we don't—at least not yet. That could be either a bargaining chip or a parting shot. But we can edit George's case file to make it say whatever we want."

"Within reason, Andreas. We can't make it too bogus. They have ways of cross-checking, you know."

"Got it. So anyway, let's start. It says that according to his passport, Yilmaz Turgut—George's official alias—is 40 and last lived in Istanbul. Is that true?"

"Age may be right. But George said he grew up in Bursa. And if you look down here," he said scrolling down, "It says Gurcan Bac, who they think he is, was originally from Bursa."

"Okay, let's keep it that way," Andreas advised. "What else does it say?"

"Besides that old Interpol bulletin, only evidence I see comes from an informant. Someone they ID as 137419, female, 33. That Spanish woman we think George was seeing."

"Dolores Cardozo, was that her name? She may still be locked up. Have you found a record for her?"

"I did." He opened a second black window to reveal her dossier.

"Says she cooperated and gave information on Bac couple of weeks ago. But see, her record says they released her five days ago, so she's not in Korydallos any more."

"Hmm. Looks like time off for good behavior—that is, for ratting on George. Does it say where she went?"

"A note says Spain had inquired about her, so maybe she got turned over. Clearly they were watching her. Then George shows up. How convenient for them."

Well," Andreas said, "let's hope they don't find her again, because I want to change her record too."

"How?"

"Have her admit she slept with Yilmaz, not Gurcan. A different person."

"Got it. What else?"

"Make it say that she claimed to have no contact with Bac for last eight years and was transferred to custody of Spanish Marshals on whatever date they let her go."

"Okay." The Greek typed away with the Austrian proofreading as best he could.

"Now go back to George's record. What does it say that she might have told them?"

"She claimed they were lovers. Met in Thessalonica. Didn't George say he came through there?"

"Lovers okay, but scratch meeting in Thessalonica" Andreas instructed. "What else do they have on George?"

"Exhibit A, state evidence item 72468, Acer tablet computer. Contents of memory examined. No browsing history. No readable personal documents. Two downloaded images, owned by user. One encrypted file, source and content unknown."

"George was careful not to save files there, but who knows. Keep the 'no personal documents part, but get rid of the rest. What else is there?"

"Looks like Turkey hasn't yet signified about passport. We can have Turkey say travel document for Yilmaz Turgut is legitimate."

"Beautiful, Ottovio, beautiful," Andreas crooned. "Do that, and

just add a note that Mr. Turgut has been fully cooperative but contin-
ues to deny he is Gurcan Bac, and I think we're done here."

"You maybe, but not me. Tonight, when police are not changing
database I download whole thing again, patch records we changed,
upload it, and reset file timestamps to what they were. At least I have
script to do some of it."

"I appreciate that very much," Andreas said, patting his comrade's
shoulder, "I wish you a wonderful evening, my friend. But first, print
out George's new record. I'll need it when I meet with that attorney
tomorrow."

Demitrios Karras, Esquire, arose to greet the tall pony-tailed man
who approached his table at the sidewalk café. The eatery was
near his office in a bourgeois residential district of Athens that
had seen better days, but the establishment's phalanx of potted
plants and its veneer of fairly fresh whitewash did their best to
keep up appearances. Although Demitrios was dressed neatly
and carried himself with dignity, he too looked like he had seen
better days.

The lawyer extended his hand. "How are you? Good to meet you,
Mister . . ."

"Carnival, Andreas Carnival. Just call me Andreas, please. I'm
here in behalf of my friend Artemis, the woman who contacted you.
She wasn't able to be here today and asked me to meet with you."

"Yes, I remember. She said she was an acquaintance of the
defendant, Mr. Turgut."

"Not quite, Mr. Karras. Artemis has a friend whose apartment Mr.
Turgut was sitting for her and is concerned for him. We hope you will
be able to secure his release, because he was unjustly imprisoned."

"He isn't the only one. Lots of people are detained for no good
reason."

"Tell me about it, Mr. Karras . . ."

"Please call me Demitrios, Andreas. Now, let's have coffee and go
through the case. Do you want to eat?"

Andreas leaned in as the ambient noise level suddenly shot up. "Wanting tweet? Sorry, I didn't get that."

Karras's reply was drowned out by the reverberations of four quickly approaching motorcycles along the narrow street. Two of the drivers wore leather vests with a meander symbol and the letters: Χρυσή Αυγή. The others wore black t-shirts, and one had a meander or possibly a swastika tattooed on his bicep. Karras turned to Andreas and remarked "Nationalists—I should say fascists. Riders of the Golden Dawn party, looking for trouble or just leaving it, no doubt."

Andreas knew them well. "I've had run-ins with golden goons. Many of my friends have too. Somehow they never seem to get in trouble for assaulting leftists."

Karras, too, had been around that block. "True. Everyone who's paying attention knows the police use them as shock troops. Anyway, what can I get for you?"

Andreas just asked for tea and wasted no time outlining his case. Yilmaz was a victim of mistaken identity, he insisted. He wasn't this terrorist who was the target of an international manhunt.

Karras asked how that mistake might have been made.

Andreas stroked his chin, declaiming matter-of-factly "It seems that Turgut was spotted leaving the apartment of a woman whom the police were watching. She and Gurcan Bac, the wanted terrorist, were thought to have been lovers. They nabbed him assuming he was Bac. He's not. They just both happen to be Turkish men who like radical chicks."

"So Mr. Turgut may have consorted with the same woman. Was he acquainted with Mr. Bac, perhaps?"

"Don't know, but it doesn't matter because he isn't Bac, and we have no reason to believe Yilmaz ever violated the law in Greece or Turkey. He's here legally, but his visa might expire if he lingers in prison, so we need to move quickly."

"The police could have evidence you don't know about."

"I'm convinced the police have nothing on him, Demitrios"

"And how can you be so sure?"

"Because I have read his official police dossier. Do you want to see it?" He opened a manila folder, withdrew a copy of the form he and Ottovio had updated, and handed it across the table.

Demitrios scanned the page, eyebrows arching. "This is what their internal records look like. I have seen others. Where did you get it?"

"From another friend whose special skill is peeking into computer systems. He pulled this arrest record from a server at the central police station only yesterday. Take a closer look. Do you see anything to indicate that the man they have is the one they want?"

Momentarily Karras replied, "Nothing. If this is all they have on him, he ought to be freed immediately. You say this is official record? Your friend took nothing away?"

Andreas settled back and gazed upward. "Positive. This is . . . the exact record the police have. So, will you take the case? I can pay you. How much do you want?"

"I will. In cases like this I usually charge five hundred euros as a retainer, and another five hundred when the matter is concluded, plus expenses and fees. Can you afford that?"

Andreas reached for his wallet and counted out three 100-euro notes. "This is all I can give you now. I hope it will do. Likely I can come up with the rest of it by the time Yilmaz walks out of Korydallos."

"That's fine. I have taken such cases before and won most of them. It will require a petition to the court. The judge will ask for the police records, and if this is all they can produce, I am sure the judge will order his release."

"And if the judge doesn't?"

"There are two levels of appeal available, but I doubt we'll need go there."

"Thank you, Demitrios," Andreas said, handing across the money. "This cheers me up. So now, what will you do next?"

"I'll visit Mr. Turgut in prison to request that I represent him and ask him a few questions. May I give him your name?"

"By all means, and also give him this." Andreas took a sheet of paper from his folder and scribbled a message: *Dear Yilmaz, We miss you and hope you are okay. We are well and await your return. Do not fear. The lawyer knows you are not the man they want and the police cannot prove otherwise. Call me when you are released and I will come to get you –Andreas Carnival.*

"I'll tell him just that," Demitrios said, "and get back to you in a day or two."

Andreas offered his hand. "Call me if I can be of further help. Otherwise I will await your call saying Yilmaz will soon be a free man. Thank you so much for your help."

"It pleases me to help people the government abuses," said Demitrios, "especially when a case is as unproblematic as this one seems to be. I'll talk to you shortly."

Demitrios picked up the document Andreas had given him and strode away. Andreas lingered for a while, savoring his hopeful feeling that perhaps the carnival still was in town. His reverie was interrupted by the waiter presenting the check, prompting him to recollect that he'd just given Karras all his cash.

"I'm sorry," he told the waiter, "I'm afraid I can't cover it. Mr. Karras said he'd take care of it."

"No problem," the waiter replied. "Next time he comes we'll just keep him standing until he pays up."

"Thanks. He's a lawyer, so have him stand at the bar."

Chapter Thirty-One

EXCEPT FOR HIS interrogators, it was the first person who had come to see him in the dozen or so desolate days since he'd left the phone message for Andreas. Sallow and faintly bruised, George was escorted to a visitation room littered with candy wrappers and cigarette butts. Sitting on rough concrete benches designed for discomfort, three other inmates talked in hushed tones with their visitors through rusted grills along a long wall. The guard directed him to a soiled bench, where he sat, shifting position, drumming his fingers, wondering who had come to see him. Shortly, a guard on the other side opened a door to usher in a middle-aged man in a blue suit and owlish spectacles carrying a brief case and pointed to George.

"Your name, please," the man asked in Greek, and again English, disclaiming "Sorry, I don't know Turkish."

"I am Yilmaz Turgut," George replied in English. "Who wants to know?"

"My name is Demitrios Karras, Esquire. I will serve as your attorney, if you wish me to represent you. I have come at the request of Andreas Carnival. Do you know such a person?"

"I see," George said, recognizing the secret handshake. "I believe I've met him. So yes, you may represent me. Please inform the court that I am not the person they think I am."

"I will do my best, Mr. Turgut. From what I've seen, yours looks like a case of mistaken identity. I think I can get you released quickly. Unless factors I am unaware of complicate the matter."

"Factors like what?"

"Well, if the police have more evidence than they appear to have, they could convince the court you may have broken some law, even if that charge is unrelated to your detention. Then, they would likely issue formal charges to keep you in custody. But first of all, tell me how have you been treated here?"

George leveled his gaze. "My interrogations weren't pretty, but I suppose they could have been worse. I was beaten on and off for two days to make me admit I am someone named Gurcan Bac and to crimes I allegedly committed, terror attacks in Istanbul many years ago. I told them I know nothing more than what I read in newspapers."

"I see. The allegation that you were beaten could help to convince the judge that an innocent man, the wrong man, was maltreated for no good reason."

When the lawyer summarized the benign police report, George spat "What a joke. As for that woman, whoever she is, we've never met. This is absurd!"

"They did not accuse you of breaking any laws in Greece, then?"

"No. Nothing like that. Please, get me out of this hellhole as soon as possible, Mr. Karras."

"I'll present the court a petition today I have already prepared. The court is set up right here in the prison. I'll inquire every day whether they are moving on it. If they drag their feet, I'll threaten to contact the newspapers to say that the police got it wrong when they trumpeted their arrest of a wanted terrorism suspect. Adverse publicity has helped to speed release in similar cases."

"So how much longer could mine take?"

"A week to a month, I'd say. Very hard to predict. But I shall do everything I can to move the process along."

"I suppose that's as good as I can expect. So go and do your legal wizardry, sir, and keep me and Mr. Carnival informed."

The lawyer passed a pen, a contract, and his business card under the grill separating them. A ten-euro note was wrapped around his card. "This is a contract between us. It will inform the court that you allow me to represent you. Please sign."

George scrawled a practiced signature and handed the document back, receiving in return a folded sheet of paper. Karras told him "This is a greeting from Mr. Carnival. I know it's tough in here. All considered, you seem to be holding up well. Don't do anything to make yourself noticed or disliked, and call me in four days if you don't hear from me first. Use that money to pay for the call."

Karras got up to leave, wishing George well. George called after him to ask who was paying his fee.

"Mr. Carnival, but as you have no further record and seem to have done nothing wrong, concluding the matter shouldn't take much of my time."

George slowly got to his feet. Arching his back, hands on buttocks, he said "Well then, both of you have my deep gratitude. Good luck to you."

"You are most welcome, Mr. Turgut. Take care."

The guard came to guide George down a hallway and through a courtyard to his cellblock. The outside air seemed sweeter than it had going the other way.

As George and Karras conferred in the visitation room about freedom, at the condo Mahmoud and Katrina were updating Andreas on their project. Mahmoud was telling him that a well-made blowgun can send a hollow-needle dart quite far with surprising accuracy.

"Tranquilizer darts come in two diameters and three sizes: fox, deer and elephant. Needles can deliver up to 5 cc's of liquid and have three holes around the tip. Three, in case the dart lodges in bone."

"What about the blowpipes?" Andreas asked. "How long do they need to be?"

"A meter to a meter and a half," he answered. "The professional ones are on the long side, made of carbon fiber or aluminum."

"And what about range?"

"They say fifteen to twenty meters, more than twice the length of the hallway here. No specific claims of accuracy, but they say a trained shooter can be very precise."

Andreas folded his arms. "Hmm. That might do. So, what would your dart deliver?"

"Possibilities include strychnine, cyanide, and metallic salts, maybe even rat poison," Katrina replied. "There are natural toxins too, like frog and snake venom, plant extracts, and quirky chemicals marine creatures excrete. The question is how to get them."

"How about that stuff they use for tranquilizing animals?"

"For large animals, the drug of choice is etorphine. It goes by the trade name M99."

"What does it do to people? We don't want to put him to sleep unless it's forever."

"Here's the thing," she said with a cheery grin. "People are super-sensitive to it. It's a monster opioid ten thousand times stronger than morphine. I read that one drop on the skin can kill a person. So we wouldn't need much."

"Gee, there you go. That sounds perfect. Where do you get it?"

"It's a controlled substance. Only certain veterinarians are allowed to buy it."

"So where do they get it?"

"Don't know. Are there special pharmacies for animal doctors?"

"I suppose a pharmacist could tell you," Andreas said, "And I happen to know one. He's the son of the realtor who rented me this apartment. Spyros has helped me to organize actions."

"Rings a bell," Katrina said. I might have met him. Do you think he could get etorphine?"

"I could ask, but the less he knows or suspects, the better."

"Why don't you say you want to get rid of a pack of wild dogs that has been terrorizing the neighborhood with a blowgun and M99 darts. See what he says."

"Possible. Even if he doesn't believe the dog story, he'll trust that I know what I'm doing. I can give it a try."

"Be careful, Andreas," Mahmoud cautioned. "Make sure he talks to no one."

"Of course," Andreas said, picking up his phone. "So while I'm out, find out where you can get a high-quality blowgun and some syringe darts and figure out how to get it all into Turkey without getting caught."

"No problem, Chief!" chirped Katrina.

"Sure, Andreas . . ." Mahmoud said, staring at the ceiling. "Will do."

CHAPTER THIRTY-TWO

A S KAAN EXPLORED downtown Bursa, wind picked up and splatters of rain blotted his jacket. Assuming it could only get worse, he looked for shelter. The Green Mosque wasn't far away, but he decided he would rather not watch people pray and quickened his pace. Soon he spotted a *lokanta* specializing in döner kebap and sprinted inside.

He sloughed off his coat and seated himself. From the enticements on the menu he ordered a lamb döner roll-up with yogurt sauce, pilaf and salad, and sat back to ruminate. Predicting where the Turkish president might show up in public continued to feel futile. Depressed at having nothing to report to Andreas and the others, he pulled out his phone to check sources again. On it was a text message—no, two of them—from Ottovio that he hadn't noticed on the street.

The first message was unpronounceable and made no sense: **gRz12Aj57**. *A code of some sort, but what kind and what for?* The second one was even shorter and more cryptic: **is.gd**. *Say what?* He let the cryptograms percolate as the waitress brought him his platter. Six bites into his döner, it occurred that is.gd could be a website of some sort. *Is it somehow related to that first string of gibberish?*

He put his sandwich down, suspiciously tapped is.gd into his phone's browser, and sent it out. A page appeared. It had an input box for entering a Web address, which the page offered to shrink to a small number of characters. *I see. The messages could be two parts of URL that redirects somewhere.* Firing off a request for is.gd/gRz12Aj57 rewarded his conjecture. A page popped up on a site identified only with a nine-digit address. All it displayed was a box labeled Password.

So now what? Ottovio didn't give me any passwords before I left.

He picked up his döner and brought it to his lips. *Or did he just do that?* He put it down and proceeded to enter gRz12Aj57 into the password box. The page refreshed to display many lines of raggedly formatted text in Turkish.

He chewed as he tried to make sense of it. Names, dates, places and annotations were scattered about haphazardly, dribbling randomly through white space.

He noticed place names, all but a few of which seemed to be in Turkey, many of them in or around the capital, Ankara. Some vaguely familiar surnames caused him to speculate. *Of course! This must be a raw dump of the President's private agenda! The geek did it!* Starting that night at the condo, Ottovio had bugged the president's public announcement page to lead him to the server with a master calendar file and put its data to this text file. Now he had the key to the kingdom. *That clever fellow*, he thought, also awarding himself credit for deducing all that.

He scooped a few forkfuls of pilaf into his mouth and scrolled through the file, pausing at a mention of Bursa. Soon fragments of text around it congealed in his mind to indicate an appointment in Bursa on the seventh of December at one PM at Mihraplı *Cami*, not the most famous mosque in Bursa, but perhaps the most stately. The event was labeled "Awards to children for Quraanic prowess," and its specific location identified as "Cami courtyard." *Perfect! A ceremony for young scholars. Out in the open! Right here in Bursa!*

His food was cold by the time he had scanned through the file, but no matter. *It's right on the other side of town. No need to travel to some distant city. I gotta go there.* He donned his moist jacket, quickly paid the waitress for his half-eaten lunch, and ran out into the rain, calling "*Taksi! Taksi!*"

The couple had come to an impasse. Pro blowguns and syringe darts seemed widely available but unobtainable locally and couldn't be ordered online without betraying one's identity. After quitting their assignment, one thing led to another and the two ended up lounging on the big sofa in the condo enjoying each other's closeness until Mahmoud's phone interceded. It was Ottovio texting come c u. where r u?

@home he responded. They continued petting until the doorbell sounded. Katrina got up, straightened her clothes, and let Ottovio in.

Breathlessly he huffed "They need an elevator here," then perched on a stool at the counter, flipping open his laptop, requesting coffee.

"After I tell him where I put Paşa's agenda, Mister Kaan text me with URL," he told them. "He find something he like and showed me pictures on a tourist site." The photos he brought up showed an ornate mosque with an elegant attached courtyard rimmed by an arcade. Within it sat a tiled kiosk with an octagonal copper roof.

"Looks like our target will go there. Kaan said 'ceremony courtyard.' Seems he choose this venue."

"Where is this," asked Mahmoud, "and when is it supposed to happen?"

"In Bursa, of all places. He give no date but I can look up."

"Well," Mahmoud said, "I hope it's not very soon. We have a lot to do, and then we have to get there."

A noise from the hallway caused Ottovio to slam his computer shut. The latch clicked and Andreas came in.

"Hey everybody," he chirped. "What's happening?"

Without waiting for an answer, he launched into an account of his visit with his young pharmacist friend. "I went over to where he works and took him to lunch. I gave him Katrina's feral dog story and asked if he could get this M99 animal tranquilizer—what's its real name?"

"Etorphine," Katrina reminded him.

"Oh yeah, etorphine. Anyway, he knew the stuff. Told me right away he could only get it with proper paperwork from a vet. Then, to get it from the vet, the user needs more paperwork that gets filed with authorities."

"Maybe on black market?" Ottovio volunteered.

Andreas shook his head. "Doubtful. I asked Spyros. Not enough illegitimate demand for it, he thinks."

"So that's out," Katrina rued. "Too bad. I'll keep looking."

"So what's happening here?" Andreas asked them. "Any progress on procuring projectiles?"

"Not really," Mahmoud said, "but look at this." He pointed to the pictures on Ottovio's screen. "Kaan sent these. He thinks this is the place—and it's right there in Bursa."

Andreas looked at the pictures, stroking his chin. "Paşa will visit there?" he asked. "When?"

"Kaan didn't say," Mahmoud said. "He only sent a link to the pictures, implying there will be a ceremony in this courtyard."

"Superb!" said Andreas, breaking into a smile. "Kaan really came through!"

"Perhaps with a little help from a friend," growled Ottovio.

Katrina hugged him, saying, "What would we do without you, beautiful geek?"

Agreeing that the mosque seemed as promising a shooting gallery as one could hope for, they refocused on their procurement problems. Katrina excused herself to go home to resume payload research. The men took to discussing how to anonymously purchase darts and blowpipes on the Internet.

"Anyway," Ottovio observed, "need shipping address. Any ideas?"

"Not my flat. And not Katrina's. No way," said Andreas.

"How about this place? Mahmoud asked. "Nobody knows we're here."

"I don't know," Andreas said. "If the investigation—and there will be a big one—leads to Piraeus and they discover things were shipped here Ivan's name could come up."

"Not good," muttered Mahmoud.

"They would track him down to find him in Bursa, of all places.

Who knows what he might say? We can't let him get caught up in that."

"Also," Ottovio reminded them, "owner here is ex-cop."

"I think I can build a blowpipe that will do the job," Mahmoud said. "The one I made is almost good enough. What I need is the right kind of dart."

"Then focus on that," Andreas advised. "Be quick about it. You need to get some and practice constantly. Ottovio, when will that event happen?"

Ottovio scrolled through the file with the ragged itinerary. "December seventh, afternoon."

"Less than three weeks away," Andreas sputtered. "Mahmoud, get moving."

Mahmoud said he would shower and pray and then head to Katrina's to work on missile technology. Knowing the *where* and the *when* of it both motivated and enervated him. In his fraught state, he cherished her company now more than ever.

Straightaway upon returning home, in slippers and black bandanna, Katrina proceeded to sweep up Cinderella style with her witches broom as she obsessed over poison. M99 wasn't in the picture, but other toxins she'd stumbled across had possibilities. She corralled a pile of dust in a corner and went to the bedroom to consult sources.

Hoping to identify toxins lacking antidotes, she meandered through the Net, looking into how victims of poisoning might or might not be resuscitated, which lead her to more forthwith descriptions about doing people in, including murder mysteries. The cozy crimes of Agatha Christie—who had worked as a pharmacist and had literarily deployed dozens of toxic substances—were often cited as being particularly well informed. Katrina considered getting some of her books from the library but kept digging. Then, way down in her search results, she unearthed a hidden gem—a transgressive samizdat handbook that someone had scanned and posted on an obscure website. Its introduction indicated it had circulated within the US black ops community in the 1950s. To her great glee, it was chock full of recipes and best poisoning practices with step-by-step instructions for extracting toxins from things like molds, fungi, leaves, flowers, seeds, and even insects.

Mahmoud's entrance was greeted with "Wow, you can make rather nasty things in your own kitchen with the right ingredients!"

He removed his shoes. "Like what?"

"I'll tell you, but we might need chemicals and equipment that could hard to find. Did you ever study chemistry?"

"I took a year of it and then forgot most of what I learned. What did you find?"

"An old spy manual. Tells you how to make something called ricin that looks like a good bet. Says it has no taste or odor, can't be detected in the body, and it's untreatable. A few milligrams do the trick."

"Interesting. Where does it come from?"

"From seeds of the Castor plant."

"Whatever that is. What do you need to make it?"

"Not much, really. This article says just water, some solvent and salts, and common kitchen equipment. Oh, and castor beans."

She recalled her grandmother kept castor oil in her medicine chest and soon confirmed that oil from the seeds is indeed used for treating constipation and dandruff, among other things. The plant's official name, she told him, is *Ricinus communis*. The specific epithet was quite apt, she said. "Makes me giggle—just append a 't'." She showed him a picture of it.

"Look at those big spreading leaves and weird flowers," she said. "I'm sure I've seen it growing in parks and along roads in Switzerland, so I bet it grows here too."

"Hey, remember when we were practicing in that park?" he asked. "One dart that missed the target landed under a big plant with leaves like those. We should go back and look."

"Definitely. Let's get a sample to identify. While we're down there we can pick up some fish for dinner."

Soon enough they set out with her laptop, shopping bags, and the thrill of the hunt.

CHAPTER THIRTY-THREE

ARLIER THAT DAY in an adjacent time zone, Kaan had exited his taxi at Mihraplı Mosque as a rainstorm was letting up. The tranquil elegance of the multi-domed edifice and its tall, graceful minarets impressed him. He noted that, unlike so many older mosques, it wasn't crammed against other buildings behind a forbidding wall. In contrast, the spacious compound was demarcated by decorative wrought iron railings atop a low masonry wall. In front, a small park shaded by tall pines provided welcome respite. Atop the two-story stone building, a massive square tower supported a sky-blue dome. A fractal cascade of half-domes flanked the tower. Smaller domes, almost too many to count, capped a colonnade that encircled a courtyard. Three minarets, each with three porches, towered behind the structure and a fourth was under construction.

He descended steps to the park where scattered visitors strolled meditatively along the shaded walkway. Three sides of the building were ringed by a driveway, which he decided to circumnavigate. Starting at a wide gate where cars could enter, he ambled down to one of the minarets that towered over the complex. To his right was another compact park with a reflecting pool and tables where a few people had gathered after the rain next to a diminutive teahouse that was open for business. On his left was a broad flight of steps leading up to a courtyard.

He sauntered on and turned left at the next minaret to encounter a second flight of steps ascending to the back of the plaza. To his right, a fenced-off parking lot was piled with stones and other construction material, apparently for a new minaret. Ahead stood an exit with an iron gate. The driveway narrowed and curved around the unfinished minaret, passing by yet another flight of steps up to the west side of the plaza. In all, he counted six entrances—two for vehicles and four for foot traffic—along the compound's scalloped fence. To test emergency egress, when nobody seemed to be watching he boosted himself up on it and swung himself over the railing to the sidewalk.

He re-entered through the nearby auto gate and climbed the broad steps on the west side, passing under the domed arcade through a gap in a hip-high filigreed stone wall. That wall would also be easy to surmount, he reckoned, but as the plaza was almost three meters above the driveway, leaping would entail a hard landing. The peristyle of slim pillars encircled three sides of the expansive courtyard. On its fourth, three massive doorways stood ready to admit the faithful to prayer through the rear of the mosque. Squatting on the plaza near him was an attractive circular kiosk sheltered by an overhanging octagonal copper roof, set atop a blue, white and ochre tiled apron almost seven meters across. Several protruding spigots served to ablute the feet of worshippers before entering to pray.

Playing the tourist, he snapped pictures of the kiosk, the plaza, the rear facade, the arcade and its filigreed wall, and the staircases. He judged the plaza to be at least twenty meters across by thirty long. The nine meters of separation between the arcade and the kiosk, Kaan figured, wasn't too much to prevent a well-positioned shooter from prevailing.

He retraced his steps around the complex, taking pictures of the stairways, gates, teahouse, and construction yard. At the front steps, he sat in the park, scrolled through his photos, and texted a slide show to Andreas, noting: **here is where he will come and go. wish u were here.** He dallied there, contemplating the elegance of the structure and its promise of grace without forgiveness for Paşa Bey. Then he took to the street to find a bus stop and head home to resume educating Ivan in how to negotiate the treacherous terrain of Turkish bureaucracies.

After a welcome soak in the Jacuzzi, Andreas shuffled to the kitchen to find Mahmoud and Katrina busily making preparations. Supper, he presumed until he heard Katrina asking, "Do you think we can use this nail polish remover?" and Mahmoud's reply, "It's probably pure enough. Anyway it gets washed out later."

She was holding up a bottle. Mahmoud seemed to be cracking nuts with a pliers and dropping bits of them in a jar. Both were wearing rubber gloves.

"Should we use all of them?" she asked.

"What does the recipe say?"

"A hundred-twenty-five milliliters. I bet we have at least twice that."

"So let's use half of them."

Andreas stole up to surprise them with "Hi there! What's for dinner?" Katrina startled and Mahmoud dropped the seed he was holding.

"Don't bother us," Mahmoud snapped and picked up the pip. "This is tricky work."

"It's a surprise treat," Katrina said, "for Mr. Paşa. You can't have any."

"What's this sinister-looking plant?" Andreas inquired, pointing to the greenery on the breakfast island. "What are you up to?"

Katrina described the specimen and handed him her cheat sheet. The recipe wasn't very long. "According to our research, ricin is dead easy to make."

"Not only that," Mahmoud cheerily added, "we wouldn't need a syringe to deliver it."

"How so?"

"Our source shows how to make a decent dart from a bamboo skewer stuck into a cork. You roll a small piece of paper around the shaft and fasten it with thread, then soak it in poison. If your target yanks the dart out, the paper stays in to deliver poison."

"That would do the job?"

"It seems so," Katrina responded. "Ricin can take a day or two to work, but just a little does it and there's no antidote."

Andreas contemplated the matter, massaging his chin. "I guess it's worth exploring, but this isn't the place to be cooking up poison. Take this stuff home, Katrina, and continue your experiment there."

Mahmoud obediently screwed on the cap of the jar he was filling with pulp and put the rest of the seed pods in a plastic bag. "Yessir!" barked Katrina. "And by the way, we brought home some fish and summer squash for you to cook for dinner. Okay?"

"Only if you scour the counter and wash everything you touched. That shrub gives me the creeps."

"Will do," she sighed and started wiping. "But stop worrying. We'll take proper precautions."

"You had better, unless you care to join the Dead Terrorists Society."

Katrina and Mahmoud toted their lab supplies back to her place after enjoying the fish that Andreas had fixed and the tempting photos of the mosque that Kaan had relayed from Bursa. They didn't make tea or even conversation, just jumped into bed and enjoyed what came naturally. *Aprés*, Katrina volunteered to give her man a back rub, to which he readily acquiesced.

Stroking and kneading his taut shoulders, she said, "I'm going too, you know."

"Where?"

"To Turkey. It would kill me not to be there with you."

"You mean on the mission itself? There's no place for you, and if I'm captured you would be too, probably. No way I would let that happen."

"Of course there could be a role for me. Should be. Has to be."

"Stop talking nonsense." He propped himself up on an elbow. "Only Kaan will be with me. We already decided that."

"Listen pal," she said, chop-chopping his shoulder, "you need backup. You just don't realize yet."

"There will be chaos. I might lose you," he objected, "and nobody should see us together."

"I can take care of myself," she insisted, pounding harder. "Was a Jujitsu black belt in college. Used it once in Africa. Wrestled away from a cop at a demo. Don't underestimate me."

"Ow! Take it easy! I believe you, but forget about that. What would you do there anyway?"

She stopped pelting him, stretched out next to him, and gazed solemnly into his eyes. "There's lots I could do. If I'm inside, I can create a diversion, like—I don't know—scream that someone stole my purse. Or wait outside with a getaway car."

"I don't know . . ."

"And besides, someone has to video the whole thing or we'll have no credibility. Have you thought about that?"

"Kaan plans to do that."

"Okay, but wouldn't you like a voice in your ear telling you when it's safe to shoot or alerting you if anyone is looking your way, like cops, sentries, and guys with dark glasses and earpieces?"

"I see your point," he admitted. "We haven't talked tactics much. I guess I should stop thinking of myself as the Lone Ranger."

"Who's that?"

"A good guy on an old American TV Western. I watched reruns of it in Arabic when I was a kid. A masked man going from town to town on a white horse helping people get rid of bad guys. But then even he had a helper, an Indian who rode with him named Tonto."

"See?" she said cheerily. "There you go. Call me Tonto."

CHAPTER THIRTY-FOUR

KAAN WAS GETTING edgy and let Andreas know. Cryptic texts burst forth from Bursa with increasing frequency urging swift action. With the big event less than three weeks away, he wanted Mahmoud there with him, properly equipped, with sufficient time to organize the operation, mentioning that he had located an ideal place for the two of them to rehearse.

Besides George's shaky situation, Andreas worried over Mahmoud's readiness and felt compelled to light a fire under him and his helpmeet. They still didn't have a production model or juice for its payload. Ways and means of getting to and escaping from the venue had yet to be identified. First, obtain a better blowpipe. He would give the lovers three options: buy locally, order on the Internet, or improve upon their prototype. Then there was Katrina's witch's brew. He mounted his bicycle and pedaled to her flat for a pop inspection.

In her kitchen, he found them at the table strewn with sticks of wood, wine corks, and assorted implements. Mahmoud proudly presented his handiwork.

"Katrina had some wine corks," he explained, "almost the right size. I shortened and sanded them, drilled a hole in one end, and stuck cut-down bamboo skewers into the holes." He handed one to Andreas to inspect. "See that sleeve near the tip? That's writing paper tied off with sewing thread. So, if our victim pulls out the dart, that paper tube stays behind to keep releasing poison."

Andreas took the artifact and fingered its business end. "Assuming it can fly straight, I like that design. Very . . . sharp. So, how would you transport the little guys safely and unobtrusively?"

"Well," Katrina said, "we'll transport them unarmed and broken down, and hide the shafts, say in a pack of cigarettes, even inside the cigarettes. We can bundle the corks inside socks or clothing. The ricin powder will fit in a tiny container that would be easy to hide. The day of the event, we assemble a dart, give its tip a soak in ricin, secure it in the tube, and head off to work."

Andreas fretted at her use of the first person plural but let it slide. "Just one dart?" he asked, to which Katrina averred he would only have one go. Reloading in haste would be awkward and dangerous, and carrying a second dart puts incriminating evidence on his person. Nevertheless, Mahmoud was preparing many darts for target practice and to perfect their design.

They would, furthermore, disguise the blowpipe as a cane for Mahmoud to lean on as if he had a bad leg. It would sport a removable wooden handle, and its hollowed-out rubber tip would serve as the mouthpiece. A stopper with a nail through it will secure the dart for transport. At the event, Mahmoud will twist off the handle, yank out the stopper, aim, and shoot. He would then replace the handle and limp away.

Hands on swaying hips, Andreas considered their curious improvisation. Simple, assuredly. Effective, possibly. Stealthy, sort of. Chance of success, unknown. Alternative, none. Projecting executive authority as best he could, he exhorted, "So let's get on with it and give Kaan less to worry about. Katrina, fire up your chem lab and make some ricin. Handle it like it was plutonium and seal it in a sturdy container."

He turned to Mahmoud. "Mister assassin, I want you to get a dart board or make a target from cardboard. Find a secluded place to practice and work your way up to twenty meters. You need to hit the bull's eye nine times out of ten to call yourself a marksman. If you can't perform at that level, the plan won't work. Got it?"

Assuring him he would practice like crazy, Mahmoud then brought up another matter. He still had George's video script, supposedly a message from ISIS taking credit for the G-20 attack that he had been told to recite in Arabic and English. "The Antalya script has to be reworked for Bursa. If Kaan is looking for something to do, have him write something I can record before I go."

"Maybe in Turkish," Katrina said. "After all, isn't it supposed to be a call to arms for Turks?"

"Good point. I'll put him on it right away."

Minding the script was one more task impeding his own agenda, freeing George. Hands still on hips, he testily instructed, "Pick up the pace, you two. Make your weapon and your witches brew. Mahmoud needs to get to Bursa as soon as possible to case the venue and work out logistics with Kaan. Zero hour is less than three weeks off."

"Aye, aye, sir!" Katrina barked, saluting.

"After I leave I'll look into getting Mahmoud a ferry ticket. Let's meet tomorrow to see what you have." He turned to exit, but Katrina tugged at his wrist.

She cleared her throat. "Um, there's one more thing."

"What's that?"

She glanced at Mahmoud and back at Andreas. Realizing what she was about to say, Mahmoud went over to her and curled his arm around her waist. "We'll need two ferry tickets, not one," he told Andreas.

Andreas rubbed his forehead in disbelief as they cheerfully faced him like Hummel figurines.

"You mean for her? I don't see any role for Katrina once you leave Greece. She's never been to Turkey. She doesn't speak the language. It complicates things and increases the risk for you and Kaan."

Katrina embellished the pitch she'd given Mahmoud in bed. She could hang back to provide the men with intelligence by voice or text. Maybe create a diversion just before Mahmoud strikes or drive them away afterwards. Posing as a sightseeing couple would dampen suspicions. Most of all, she wanted to be at his side, even if something bad happened.

Andreas remained unconvinced. "Yes, I suppose you could be an asset there. But you would be one more moving body to coordinate and keep safe, because you might need their help too. And what will you do afterward, when the entire Turkish government is hunting you down? If you are captured, you can be sure you'll be tortured to give up the others."

Pacing, arms flapping as Katrina stared at the linoleum, his diatribe continued. "I also worry about what Ivan would tell the police if they were to question him. In fact, Mahmoud, I don't want you to go near him. If your picture is broadcast, a neighbor might recall seeing you around and tell the police."

"Fine," Katrina replied. "I agree about Ivan, and that's another reason they need me. Let me rent a hotel room for us. Ivan won't even know we're in town."

Mahmoud quickly buttressed her: "She has a point, Andreas. Think about it."

"Okay, okay. Just stop nagging." Andreas said, letting his arms droop, lamenting the absence of the man who knew how to get things done, and who had said he'd grown up in Bursa. But even that might have been a lie.

More overwrought than when he'd arrived, Andreas escaped to the street in a tangle of loose ends. He biked to the end of the block, pumping pedals with leaden feet toward the empty condo that no longer charmed him to occupy. He missed Ivan's close companionship, even the testy Kaan, and Mahmoud was rarely there these days. His pedaling slowed and at the next intersection he made a u-turn. *For the first time in two weeks I will spend the night in my own bed.* It didn't matter that his house was under surveillance. As long as he didn't talk to the walls he could just as well be lonely at home.

Motivated by the Austrian's insistent demands, the couple proceeded to compile a list of establishments in greater Athens that might supply the required materials. Beside a dartboard, they needed a length of perfectly round plastic pipe, a cane with a wooden handle, extra rubber tips, cork stoppers, surgical masks and gloves, a reagent or two, a mortar and pestle, canning jars, and some simple tools. Katrina mapped out an itinerary for their expedition, but by then it was after five, too late to embark. Instead, she fried potatoes and chicken cutlets while Mahmoud cleared the table and assembled a salad to sup by candlelight, a romantic ritual they had come to share.

"Seems to me," she said after a while, "you'll need help both inside and outside. Has to be two people. One person inside to divert attention and another to spirit you away."

"Kaan can't make a fuss; he's already got a job."

"Right. He can't call attention to himself. Looks like it's up to me."

"I see what you mean. But we also need a driver."

Katrina nodded. "And a car. It would be risky to rent one. Think Kaan could steal one?"

"I doubt that's in his skill set," he said dismissively, "and I can't see us hailing a taxi or a bus."

Katrina got up and took their plates to the sink. Stretching her arms, she said, "I don't think we're getting anywhere. Let's sleep on it."

He came up behind her and grasped her outstretched arms. His fingers slid along her sleeves to imprison her shoulders, his breath in her ear murmuring "But maybe not right away."

She turned to him, wrapping her arms around his shoulders, feeling the tautness of his body against her, whispering "Of course. First things first."

CHAPTER THIRTY-FIVE

ANDREAS DISMOUNTED IN the alley next to his home sweet bug-infested home and cautiously let himself in. To his relief, his paper-based alarm system revealed no new evidence of intruders. His salon's empty chairs and scattered implements reprimanded him for forsaking clients he gladly would have served had he not unexpectedly been elevated to commander-in-chief. A red light winked fresh messages on his aged answering machine. Customers inquiring whether *Radically Chic* was still in business, he assumed, but that might not be all.

Two messages awaited scrutiny. The first was from one of the men he and Kosta used to hang out with, wanting to get together, a bitter reminder of how his social life had atrophied. He let it go and inhaled the next message. George had issued another typically terse directive: "Karras says court will rule soon on his motion to dismiss. Thinks I'll be freed. Could happen soon. When it does, I'll tell him where to find me. Call him."

He exhaled, replayed the message, erased it and, for perhaps the first time all day, smiled. The weight on his shoulders suddenly seemed bearable, shareable. He wanted to ring the attorney but it was already late afternoon. No matter; Karras would get in touch when it was definite.

He left the salon and crept up to canvas his flat. Satisfied by its apparent normality, he brewed tea and found some stale crackers, gruyere cheese, pickles and olives to nibble on, and brought his refreshments to the living room. Sprawled on the couch, he considered implications of George's return, wondering how he would react when he learned his big operation would have spectacularly failed. His newfound cheer darkened anticipating George's reaction to their half-baked plan and Mahmoud's amateurish weapon. And would he not blow his top when confronted by a clued-in and somewhat impertinent Katrina? Were he to object and jettison her, that would be almost certainly scotch the operation. So then what? Back to marching through the streets of Athens with homemade banners?

Enough damn headaches for one day, he decided. He refreshed his tea and switched on his TV to see what untruths the networks were pandering. As usual, most of the content was either depressing or inconsequential, but then came news seeming to claim that ISIS was being beaten back in Syria and Iraq. NATO countries, even Russia, were said to be fuming that Turkey was playing footsy with ISIS while attacking the West's Kurdish allies. It occurred to him that if Mahmoud managed to eliminate the Turkish hegemon, it could be a huge favor to the great powers. Was that what they really wanted to do? That prospect was more than he could wrap his mind around, but thinking about Turkey summoned images of Ivan, a considerably more gratifying prospect. And so aroused, he picked up his phone and placed a call.

A phone chimed as Ivan and Kaan lounged in their living room absorbing a rather silly Turkish sitcom. They weren't just idling. Kaan claimed watching TV shows was a great way to tutor his roommate in colloquial Turkish. The improvised language lessons seemed to help. Ivan's comprehension seemed to improve day by day.

The incoming call caused them both to reach for their instruments and Ivan won. He answered, replied in German, and went into his bedroom to talk. Assuming it was someone from Ivan's company, Kaan turned back to the antics of a dysfunctional Turkish family only to be treated to a seven-minute commercial break.

Just after the program resumed, Ivan emerged. He muted the jabbering box and handed his phone to Kaan. "It's Andreas. He wants to talk to you." Kaan was pleased. He hadn't heard Andreas' friendly voice since he'd hustled himself out of Greece. He expected the Austrian to be as upbeat as usual, but found his comrade less than chipper.

Kaan excused himself and took the phone to his monk's cell. From Piraeus, Andreas told him he missed him and asked how he was doing. All Kaan had to report beyond catering to Ivan was revisiting the mosque, reviewing updates on Ottovio's obscure server, and looking for a car to beg, borrow or steal, unsuccessfully so far.

"I wanted you to know," Andreas told him, "that I expect George to be free within days. Probably. Don't get too excited, because something could still go wrong. I just wanted you to be prepared."

With a Cheshire Cat smile, Kaan replied, "That's great news! I don't want details. Just tell George that except for transportation everything on this end looks good, assuming my partner shows up soon. But you sound a little down. Are you worrying that George might not get behind our plan?" For a Turk, Kaan could be quite direct.

Andreas sloughed off the mention of his low mood. "I had a long day and I'm tired. As for George's reaction, there's no telling. If he likes what he finds, he'll do anything to make sure you guys are covered. If he doesn't, he could yank you out of there. Be prepared for anything."

"Hopefully, it won't come to that. When is, um . . . Peter coming?

"Hopefully within ten days. He's got a lot to do."

"That's shaving it close. Tell him to hustle. Anything I should do right now?"

"Yes. He can't bunk with you guys, so look for hotel rooms. Don't tell Ivan that he's coming."

"Check."

"Scout out small, cheap hotels near the location. Inquire, but don't rent anything yet. Ask if they take cash and have a convenient back door."

"Okay, I'm on it. Just one room, right?"

"You might need two. In different hotels. Gives us options. I'll let you know as soon as we decide."

"Two rooms? Is someone else is coming?" he asked, brow knitting.

"I said I'll let you know."

"Okay. Anything else?"

"Yes. You say you found a place to practice. I hope it's indoors and very private."

"It is, um, especially on weekends and it's not occupied very often."

"We can't have any spectators. Look for a back-up location. Practicing is very important."

"We'll be fine, but I'll look around if that's what you want."

They signed off. Kaan returned to the living room, where the TV now exhibited a German-language news program with pictures of human carnage in city streets as police in combat gear and paramedics rushed about.

"Where is that?" he asked Ivan. "Baghdad? Cairo?"

"It's Paris. Half a dozen terrorists shot up restaurants and shops and a theater full of people. One blew himself up outside a stadium. It's terrible. At least a hundred dead."

"Do they know who did it?"

"No suspects yet. One dead terrorist. They say ISIS claimed responsibility."

"The bastards," Kaan replied in disgust. "One of their bombs just tore through a crowd of commuters in Ankara. This must stop. They must pay for their barbarism."

"Yes, it must stop. But Syria must also be stopped from savaging its own people. Isn't Turkey trying to topple Assad?"

Kaan chose his words carefully. "Yes, it is, but what Turkey wants is an Islamist client state in Syria to extend its influence in the region and finish off the Kurds. That would be bad news for Syrians and everyone else."

"I wouldn't want to see that myself, but how to make Turkey change its ways? They had an election not long ago and Paşa's party did very well, so Turks must approve of what his government is doing."

"Most Turks don't know about Paşa's double dealing," Kaan spat, "because all dissent is stifled now and news outlets censor themselves. My father is locked up because he investigated official corruption. My country is becoming a fucking evil empire in league with ISIS."

"Well," Ivan told him, "I'm not very political, but I try to follow events and I understand how you must feel. If, as you say, Mr. Paşa is way out of line, I hope somebody does something about it. But only the Turkish people can make that happen."

Kaan nodded. "I hear you. They should." *With a little help.*

For the first time in several weeks, Andreas awoke in his own bed. By nature he was an early riser, but this day he felt like sleeping in. After a second snooze, he went to the kitchen to make tea, wondering if he should stock up on food, even though he wasn't sure how often he would be there in the coming weeks. He was scribbling a list when his phone chimed. The caller's number seemed familiar but not one he knew by heart. He picked up and said hello in Greek.

"Good morning, Mister Carnival. This is Demitrios Karras. How are you today?"

"Oh hi. I'm well, thanks. I received a message from Geor—um Yilmaz that he might be getting out and you would supply the details. Wonderful news."

"It looks like Mr. Turgut will be released. It could happen as soon as tomorrow or as late as next week. The court gave the prosecution a hard time when it could not provide good evidence that Turgut actually is Gurcan Bac. But as a fugitive is involved, they still regard him as a person of interest, given the accusations. Also, he's an alien who doesn't appear to be gainfully employed."

"I guess that's as much as we could expect. Yilmaz said you would let me know where to meet him. Did he tell you?"

"He said he would go to a café in Keratsini around the corner from a cinema. He didn't supply a name or address."

"I think I know which one he means," Andreas replied, "Will you alert me when to expect him?"

"Yes, I was planning to call you when I know. But listen—the police will retain his passport to prevent him from leaving the country."

"Since he's no longer a suspect, why would they, and how and when will he get it back?"

"As I said, he's a person of interest. If he plans to travel abroad, he needs permission from the police until they return his travel documents. Meanwhile, they'll issue him an alien identity card."

"I see."

"But that brings up another issue. They need an address and phone number. He told me he will go back to his apartment, which I recall is on Doganis, but he no longer has a phone. Can you get one for him?"

Andreas told him he would obtain a prepaid cell phone and asked how much was owed for his services. Karras told him that for now the three hundred euros already paid would do. "We can discuss that later. This has not been a very difficult case. Let's hope it remains that way."

Saying he would report back with a phone number, Andreas thanked him again and clicked off. He would buy a simple disposable phone that George could carry when he chose to. As the Doganis flat was likely being watched, he should repair to the condo. Once that lease was up . . . well, one thing at a time.

He texted Ottovio signifying George's imminent release and need for a secure instrument. He dressed to go out for breakfast and buy a decoy phone. On his way, he texted Mahmoud: **finish shopping & start making. expect pop quiz.**

Sitting in the café happily anticipating his omelet, toast, tea, and the prospect of easing of his burden, Andreas congratulated himself. He'd kept the team together and in fact grew it, hatched a plan, launched Kaan, and rescued George. Things weren't so dismal after all.

Chapter Thirty-Six

THE STREETS OF Piraeus glistened in an early seasonal rainstorm, washing summer's dust from pavements and automobiles. Andreas enjoyed moisture scrabbling down his face as he hastened through the downpour under an oversized umbrella, stopping only to drop coins into the cup of a homeless man shielding himself under a leaf of cardboard.

Waterlogged knees down, he furled and ineffectually shook his umbrella as he entered his familiar haunt, where the inclement weather gave him a choice of scruffy tables. Habitually, he commandeered the big round one in the rear and sat facing the door armed with ravani cake and tea.

For the next half-hour he idled, passing time by exploring the prepaid phone he had bought, trying not to worry. He punched in Karras's number. The attorney didn't pick up, so he left word that the number he was calling from was what he'd requested. On his third tea, the door opened to a downbeat of wind and a symphony of splatters, blowing in a short, bedraggled man in black denim jeans and a blue work shirt, with long, dripping black hair framing his stubbly chin, thin lips taut. Dark-rimmed eyes furtively scanned the room.

With mock formality belied by moist eyes, Andreas rose and extended his right hand as the man approached. "What a pleasure to see you again, Mister Turgut!" The man's drawn smile grew teeth as he hauled Andreas in like a mackerel to wrap him in a bear hug and kiss him on both cheeks.

"I have never been so happy to see anyone in my life, my dear Andreas, believe me," he blurted. George was back, turned out from Korydallos prison about an hour ago along with a trash bag containing all his belongings. He deposited the bag on the floor and oozed into a chair as Andreas told him to order whatever he wished. "Something hot and nourishing, but first some tea, also very hot. I haven't had a decent meal since we went out for pizza."

As George excavated a plate of lamb moussaka and salad, Andreas studied his features. The ordeal had left his face drawn, almost cadaverous, the crescents under his eyes darker, the stubble on his left cheek not quite hiding a bruise. "You don't look so great," Andreas confessed. "It seems your spa didn't treat you so well. Do you feel all right?"

"The pain in my ribs will probably go away. But I didn't get sick, like so many of their other customers. Lots of TB around, the nasty kind. I guess I should be grateful for being kept away from the general population. Anyway, how are you and the guys?"

Andreas again congratulated himself, this time out loud. "I managed to keep us together. Found us a nice apartment not too far from here. Rent-free. I'll take you there later so you can get some rest."

"What about staying in your place? Why didn't you do that?"

"Too crowded, and besides, thanks to your phone call, the HP visited and bugged the place."

"So what did you do?" George asked between forkfuls.

"A friend let us use his place when he left town," Andreas said, before changing the subject to the G-20, noting it had taken place last week without incident, adding that no reception ever took place at Aspendos. All their efforts would have been for naught.

"I see," George said, pinched features fusing anger and relief. "We must have been disinformed that the opening event would take place there. They never intended to hold it, I'll bet. Maybe they were just baiting a trap." He looked down, rubbing his brow. "I should have known." It was as close to contrition as Andreas had ever seen George come.

As George consumed dessert, Andreas crafted an account of what his crew had been up to, how they had congressed nearly every day, overcoming despair to evolve an operation, and were on track to do something big a few weeks hence in Turkey. When George forcefully pressed for details, Andreas held his cards, pledging to reveal all that evening. He handed George the decoy cell phone he had bought at the behest of the police, and said he would receive a proper instrument soon. Then he messaged their comrades, directing them to Marias Kiouri at six for another surprise party.

"It seems you've done well, Andreas. I'm incredibly grateful for what you did to get me released. I could only hope you were on my case. When Karras showed up, I knew I hadn't been abandoned. I was pretty low by then. I won't horrify you with my treatment there, but I will say it improved once I had a lawyer."

Andreas paid the waiter and they took to the street. The rain had almost ended and people were emerging from shelter. Umbrella and bag in hand, alert for miscellaneous minders, they trod down the long block toward Dimokratias Avenue and on to George's new and improved quarters.

The bourgeois luxury of the flat on Marias Kiouri, with its plate glass windows and balcony overlooking the harbor, its comfortable modern furniture and sleek kitchen by equal parts impressed and distressed George. He was tactfully informed that an old friend from Austria had taken it for a few months and then had to leave, rent prepaid. Andreas conducted him to the Brothers' bedroom and instructed him to take a long, hot soak in the Jacuzzi.

As he stripped off his sodden clothes, George asked where Michael and Peter were at. "They're out," he was told. "By the way, they go by their real names now. Shall we call you Yilmaz now?"

"No. George. It's better that way."

"That's fine. You'll always be George to me anyway. Go relax now. I'm going out for groceries. We'll all get together in a few hours."

When Andreas returned from the supermarket, he found George asleep on Kaan's bed in a bathrobe and quietly covered him. He gathered wet clothing and put it in the washer, started a big pot of water for spaghetti, and prepped a carbonara sauce, reflecting on how to tell George about Ivan and Katrina. Ivan could wait. Katrina soon would be on display, and that presented a problem. He considered instructing Mahmoud to leave her behind, but then decided he had to confront the issue. As he minced garlic, he rehearsed his introduction.

Katrina was good friend from the anti-austerity movement, he would say. She boarded the men for several days when we all had to scatter. Even though they kept your plan to themselves, she sensed their desperation and offered to help in any way she could. We all told her she was doing more than enough, and that would have been the end of it but for her romantic interest in the Iraqi. She had met him his first day here and took a liking to him right away, though initially he didn't seem attracted to her. I told him I trusted her but to avoid confiding in her. He kept to his cover story, but just a week after your arrest they told me they were in love.

George would want to know how I allowed that to happen, and I would admit it blindsided me. Of course I disapproved and said so, but at that point we had no plan and were close to giving up. Their liaison forced me to bring her under my supervision by incorporating this smart, dedicated woman into our team. She agreed to all my stipulations and so far hasn't disappointed. Proving to be a great asset to the group, actually. Yes, that's how he would put it.

He turned from worrying what George would think of Katrina to wondering how she would react to him. George's authoritarian style might not sit with such free spirit. He hoped she would be smart enough not to remind George how involvement with a female comrade had brought him down. Deciding it would help to show George Katrina's rather ordinary police dossier, he texted Ottovio to bring his laptop along with some wine, and started fixing a salad. Spinning lettuce, he continued to fret that the self-possessed Swiss might come across as too flippant. To motivate good behavior, he texted Mahmoud: **come @ 630. tell her to defer to the boss.** To underscore his concern he added **no smartass remarks**, hit Send, and pinched his fingers for good luck.

Katrina and Mahmoud wound up their peripatetic shopping expedition shortly after one. Laden with assassination paraphernalia and rainwater, they repaired to her kitchen for coffee before settling down to work. After sanding the ends of his new pipe down to velvet smoothness, Mahmoud undid the wooden handle of the invalid's cane they had bought, whittling and sanding it to snugly fit his tube. Boring out and shaping the cane's bottom ferrule into a mouthpiece took a bit longer, as the stiff rubber was prone to chip. Lastly, he set about transforming his collection of stoppers and skewers into a cupid's quiver of satanic arrows.

Katrina didn't think castor seeds were hazardous to handle but nevertheless donned surgical gloves before prying open seeds and depositing the pips in a canning jar to soak overnight. "Tomorrow I'll do the extraction," she told him. "Oh yeah, it sounded like you got a text message a while ago. What was it?"

"Oh," Mahmoud replied, not looking up, "that was Andreas telling us to come at six-thirty."

He continued fashioning darts, at length querying, "Are you prepared to meet George? Would you like to know more about him?"

"Sure. None of you ever said much about him. All I know is that he was your capo and got popped after some dame ratted him out. Never knew what he was up to. What's he like?"

"I know little about him personally. He's complicated, hard to read, pretty demanding. Very methodical and determined to bring down the system. He came to Greece to run his own show, we think, after a series of bombings in Istanbul."

Katrina pulled her latex gloves to scratch her ear. "So what did he want you to do?"

"I thought you knew—disrupt the G-20 summit in Turkey with sort of a time bomb."

"Tell me more."

"Not now. George might, but please don't press him about it. It doesn't matter anyway. We're done with that."

"Whatever" she sniffed. "I won't ask."

"He may not be expecting you, so wait to be introduced. Be polite and charming, even if he grills you. Don't argue with him or make wisecracks."

Scowling, fists on hips, Katrina exclaimed, "Look, I've had to deal with plenty of alpha males. You make it sound like I was planning to be obnoxious or can't handle myself. "

Mahmoud slumped back. "No love, I don't think that, not at all. Put yourself in his shoes. He's a professional assassin on the run. Is super careful, trusts nobody but his closest comrades, but still got captured after a lover gave him up. Andreas got him off, but think how he must feel about comrades getting involved with outsiders? Got it?"

Her indignation gave way to contrition. "Got it. I'm sorry I yelled at you. Guess I assumed he was like Kaan, just more intense. He has a right to be suspicious, but please don't worry. I'll do my best not to provoke him."

She came to the table and bent down to cradle his face and kiss him. "Love you, really do. Now keep working. I want you to give him a demo."

CHAPTER THIRTY-SEVEN

A S SOON AS he saw him, Ottovio flashed a big grin, hugged George and told him how happy it made him to have him back, a major show of affection for that matter-of-fact man. Pouring wine, Andreas said, "Later, Ottovio will show you what he did with your police file. Your lawyer doesn't know it, but tampering with your official record is one reason you were freed."

Shaggy eyebrows arched, George said, "You can do that? Amazing."

Offhandedly, Andreas allowed, "Ottovio can also show you the police record he dug out for our new comrade," quickly continuing before George could interrupt. "It's no more damning than mine. Never been detained. No known police involvement. Smart, dedicated, and very discreet. She is also Mahmoud's girlfriend."

George sank into the sofa, blinking at his bug-eyed reflection in his wine glass. Looking up, he said "I hope you know what you're doing, This doesn't feel good, but I'll reserve judgment until I meet her and see what you all are up to."

Andreas reeled off the backgrounder he'd worked up, emphasizing the necessity for admitting Katrina into their circle. After his spiel, George sedately replied, "I see. So what does she know about me and other cadres? As little as possible, I hope."

"About people you have worked with, nothing. For that matter, nobody here does. About the G-20 thing, only that you planned an operation that got abandoned. About you, she knows what we know:

your alias, what we think might be your real name, and why they took you." Andreas opened his agenda book and handed George the news clipping about his arrest. "I'm not saying you're that guy, but that's what they thought. And by the way, it was Katrina who located your lawyer for us."

George scanned the article, poker-faced. "Nope. I'm not him. I got a lot of questions about that and told them I'd heard about the bombings he allegedly planned, but I was in Izmir at the time. In the end, there was no evidence and they had to let me go. Or was there?"

Andreas and Ottovio exchanged knowing glances. Andreas replied with a sigh and "Well, so it goes. It would be cool if you were him, but we love you just the way you are."

"Anyway, that doesn't matter because we ate their homework." Ottovio said. He logged into his laptop and popped up George's police record, the real one. "See," he said, "they linked you to this Spanish woman. Did they ask you about her?"

"More than once. I told them I never knew her and she must be lying to save her skin."

Behind them, Andreas rolled his eyes.

"So here is her original record. It says she said she was involved with you and helped you escape after the Istanbul synagogue was bombed."

"That's either a total fabrication or a mix-up."

"Whatever," Ottovio told him, bringing up two new windows, "now they think different."

"Or at least the judge does," Andreas avowed, "and that's what counts."

George scanned the doctored data. "I like your fabrications much better than the Spanish woman's. I don't know how you did that and I really don't want to know, but thank you."

A hesitant knock on the door. "That would be our happy couple," Andreas announced. "I hope this will be the start of a wonderful friendship."

As Andreas approached the door, George asked "So where's my man Michael? I thought he lived here."

"In Bursa. We'll explain later."

Mahmoud entered first. He saw George on the sofa and hobbled over to greet him, leaning on a cane. George smiled but didn't rise from his seat. "*Merhaba*, Peter. It is very good to see you. I see you brought a friend. You look quite fit, so why a cane? Did you hurt yourself?"

"Welcome back George. You can call me by my real name, Mahmoud. There's no need for Peter any more. And no, I'm not injured. You'll see." He waved in a somewhat bedraggled Katrina, still in the old clothes she'd worn to shell her sinister seeds.

Licking a dimpled smile, she approached George with arm extended. "Hello," she said, My name is Katrina. It's very good to meet you, George."

George stood to accept her handshake, giving no reply. She went on. "It's wonderful you are free. I thought it would never happen. Please excuse my appearance. I was still working when we had to go."

"That's all right," George told her, not letting go. "Nice to meet you too. So what kind of work do you do?"

Katrina stammered "M-Mostly I plan and coordinate direct actions." She glanced at the other men, their faces expressionless. "But today I was fixing a cocktail to serve to Mister Paşa."

George released her hand, settled on the sofa again and crossed his legs. He sipped his wine and said, "Let me guess. He's coming for dinner."

"No, he's too busy building a caliphate. I'm afraid we'll have to visit him to deliver our delectable injectable."

Mahmoud had hobbled into the hallway and now extended his right foot like a tap dancer and twirled his cane. Andreas smirked. Ottovio giggled. George's eyes flashed around the room. "Okay, what's going on?"

"Show him your moves," said Katrina, stepping back with a flourish to indicate a pillow on the sofa. Mahmoud twisted off the cane's handle, deposited it on the breakfast counter and took a step back, plucking at the end of the cane as he leveled it at the sofa. George nervously leaned away as Mahmoud crouched, put the tube to his lips and puffed with a soft plop. George looked down to see a rubber stopper protruding from a pillow next to him.

"Go ahead," Mahmoud told him. "Pull it out. It won't hurt you."

George gripped the cork and slowly withdrew it to reveal its bamboo business end. He held it up and turned it in his fingers. "This is the weapon that will bring down the Turkish Government?"

"It's silent," said Mahmoud, reassembling his cane.

"It's deadly," said Katrina.

"It's doable," said Andreas.

"And if he doesn't show up at the party," Ottovio added, "We'll get together somewhere else."

Before, during, and after dinner, George peppered them with questions as Andreas laid out the plan. Mahmoud and Katrina had developed it after the team settled on a sniper attack on President Paşa, a strategy that had bubbled from Kaan's brain. The method was Mahmoud and Katrina's idea. They had fixed upon it because of its stealth qualities and because the materials could be discretely acquired, the weapon was easy to make, and the poison was hard to trace.

"Clever and resourceful," George responded, "but step back and tell me what you expect to accomplish."

"Best case scenario," Andreas told him: "Paşa will be stopped from becoming dictator for life. Presently, Turks are losing hope as they see their republic slip away. The assassination will create a power vacuum and enough turmoil for democratic movements to rise up. And, after we put out messages from ISIS saying they did it, Turkey may stop supporting and trading with them."

George tried to interrupt, but Andreas kept talking. "Worst case scenario," he continued, "it precipitates a coup by an antidemocratic military. Also, if not enough Turks act to reject Islamification and continued authoritarianism, we fail. But it could still break ties with ISIS."

"Wrong!" George exclaimed, springing up to pace the room, hands in pockets. "Worst case is you miss him or he recovers. The shooter is captured and the team is pursued and rounded up. Emergency rule is decreed and we're back to square zero."

"Your plan had risk factors too," Andreas reminded him. "And now we know for sure it would have failed, and retribution would have followed too. What's different now?"

George stopped pacing to rock back and forth. "It's getting in, eliminating the target, getting out, and not getting killed, or worse, caught. My plan had no risk factors at the tail end. Without knowing more about your setup and the situation Peter will go into, I can't say how likely to work or risky it is."

Katrina broke in to say, "May I say something?" and didn't wait for permission. "I think George is spot on. Success depends on how well we plan and coordinate our movements plus a bit of luck. Suppose Mahmoud and Kaan manage to get into the ceremony. Kaan's job is to record what happens. Hopefully Mahmoud can position himself well. If he can't, we wait for another opportunity. If he can shoot, assuming nobody spots him puffing on his pipe, he'll need an escape plan, but that hasn't been worked out. So George, how do we get him out of there in one piece?"

George's rocking slowed and then stopped. "Can't say. Need to know all we can about the security setup, where guards and exits will be, what areas are open to movement, and so forth. A car and driver should be stationed nearby. Michael won't be able to protect Peter and needs to get out himself. And if Peter is fingered he'll either die or talk, if not both. You tell me how he can avoid detection."

"He'll employ psychology to appear harmless by limping in, leaning on his cane," Andreas offered.

George gazed at the ceiling, rocking again. "That could help, I suppose, to avoid suspicion. Our assassin should think like a magician and must not appear capable of causing harm. Even those who observe him shoot should doubt what they saw. So, perhaps, instead of acting lame, he could wear dark glasses and tap his cane. People will assume he is blind. Wouldn't that be better cover?" They had, it seemed, captured the mastermind's imagination.

"Great idea, George," Katrina said. "Mahmoud, let's give it a try."

"Yes, Peter," George said, approaching him. "Do that. Become a blind man. Practice walking around in dark glasses with your eyes closed. Learn to speak with people without following their movements."

Mahmoud cast an apprehensive glance to Katrina and got a wink in return. Their song-and-dance had gone over well. Despite his doubts about outcomes, it seemed that George just might climb aboard their slow boat to Bursa.

CHAPTER THIRTY-EIGHT

GEORGE'S IMPLICIT SUPPORT for the plan with certain reservations instilled in Mahmoud a heightened pressure to perform and focused Katrina on her tasks. They fell into a training regimen. Arising at five, Mahmoud grunted out fifty push-ups and sit-ups before a half-hour run with Katrina up and down steep streets to build stamina. After breakfast, off to a quiet alley two blocks away to refine his technique. Sitting, standing, eyes sometimes shut, besides accuracy he focused on speed, fluidity, and wind drift, blunting missiles that bounced off the wall. Noticing that some darts flew better than others, he triaged and studied them to understand why, reshaping and weighting some with carpet tacks to improve their aerodynamics. He noted that darts made from rubber stoppers penetrated more deeply than cork ones did, but had shorter ranges. He favored rubber, but ultimately the choice would depend on how close to his live target he could get, so he continued to perfect both kinds.

Together, they studied geography on her laptop. Panning and zooming maps of Bursa, they imprinted the cityscape on their neurons—its landmarks and street network, especially about and around the Mihraplı mosque—noting access points, one-way streets, parking, and possible hiding spots.

In a surgical mufti, Katrina processed a batch of seeds, filtering out residues to make a concentrate of what she hoped was pure ricin, but after evaporating the liquid no solids remained. So she reread the recipe and started over with her remaining pods. It occurred to her that they wouldn't know if she had the real thing without chemical analysis, which neither of them knew how to do. Mahmoud suggested shooting one of the many feral cats that roamed the city as a test, but Katrina was sure the wounded animal would run off not to be found again.

Her second distillation managed to precipitate some whitish clumps, which she carefully set out to dry away from breezes on tinfoil under a paper tent. Mahmoud peered at the granules from a safe distance and asked whether they would be enough.

"Well, let's say we have just a quarter of a gram, two-hundred fifty milligrams. From toxicology reports I found, if this is pure ricin it would be enough to kill about a hundred adult humans."

"That's pretty scary," he said, backing off. "Please don't sneeze."

When her substance had dried, in new mask and gloves, she gently ground it in a mortar and scraped the powder with a plastic spoon into a tiny vial, and screwed on the lid, sealing it with tape. She nestled it in a small cosmetics jar padded with cotton balls, screwed it closed, and let him know he was free to breathe.

After methodically mopping up with disposable wipes, all the leftovers went into a trash bag that she tied up inside another. On their way over to the condo, she heaved the bag into a dumpster behind an auto repair shop when Mahmoud told her nobody was looking.

George had received a cell phone from Ottovio and his list of contacts from Andreas in an envelope that also held eleven hundred euros. "That's your life savings, George. I withdrew all of it except for fifty euros I thought I should leave behind. Your debit card's in there too."

George didn't even look in the envelope before making his first call, cutting off Kaan's gushing to issue orders to identify escape routes from the mosque complex by car, transit, and foot. Look for a vehicle but not a rental. Try to anticipate what security will be like. He signed off with admonishments to maintain his roommate's ignorance and to stay away from women.

A little later, his phone buzzed unexpectedly. His new phone was dark, so he dug out the one he wasn't supposed to use to find an incoming call. It wasn't his lawyer, so it must be the police checking in, and he let the call expire. He hadn't bothered to set up voicemail and decided to keep it that way.

The couple arrived to do another show and tell. Mahmoud poured out half a dozen darts from his cane and made a show of their little paper sleeves, which he alleged would assure impregnation. Ceremoniously unearthing her tiny vial of ricin powder, Katrina calmly informed them "This is my extract. It's supposed to be enough for dozens of doses, but I'd feel better if we verified its potency. Anyone think of a way to do that?"

Andreas warily regarded her vial. "Are you asking for a volunteer? I might be able to locate my old landlord."

Unamused, she said, "No, seriously, we don't need a live test, just a chemical assay. You know this pharmacist dude. Maybe he could figure out how to test it."

"What am I supposed to do," Andreas implored, "say to him 'Dude, how much of this it would take to do in a grown man' after I already asked him to procure M99?"

George said the conversation was making him nervous. He wanted to know who the guy is and why Andreas had asked him to get that kind of stuff. Andreas obliged, asserting that Spyros could be trusted, and that his pharmacy school might have a lab equipped to analyze the ricin.

George demurred. "Bad idea. Suppose he tells someone there he's got poison to look at or asks for help with it. Then someone might say something. If it gets to the cops, the inquiry can wander back to you."

"Okay, okay," Andreas said, staring at the ceiling. "I guess getting an assay is out, so, it looks like we'll have to shoot someone to know if it works."

"Yeah," Katrina said, "like Schrödinger's Cat, only not a thought experiment. And you know what?"

"What?" George obliged.

"I think I know *just the cat.*"

George blinked several times. "Are you serious?"

"More than half serious. This cat is sick and should be put out of his misery."

She spoke of the neo-Nazi trolls who had been stalking and threatening her online. Could be a dude going by SuperPlato, a big fish in the ultranationalist cesspool, or one of his minions. She didn't know any real names or addresses, but surely, what with Ottovio's wares and wiles, they could finger the creeps.

Fingering his brow, Andreas said, "I don't know, Katrina. I would gladly do in that fascist, but that could be the end of the mission—if not us—if either the cops or his henchmen come after us."

Mahmoud broke his silence to say "I think it's worth trying. Katrina's in danger. If we do this, we'll know if the poison works. It will test my cover and aim. Let's think about it."

"So, are you volunteering?" George asked him.

"I would do it. I would kill this predator. To protect Katrina and for target practice."

Andreas stroked his chin. "The idea spooks me, but I must admit it has a certain macabre appeal. Mahmoud could use a live target, but this would be pretty risky. It would have to be carefully staged."

George's forty furtive years on earth instilled in him an abundance of caution along with a high tolerance for calibrated risk. Methodical and loath to improvise, by nature he was inclined to what-if. "I'm not saying you should do this, but I agree some kind of test is needed and can't think of anything better. But we need the right setup, a way to lure him out and to get away—intact and unobserved."

"Any ideas?" Katrina asked, blinking a bit more than necessary.

Twisting his pinkie in his left ear, George said, "It should happen outdoors in a quiet place, maybe at night. No bystanders. You'll need backup, in case your nationalist doesn't come alone."

"And remember," Mahmoud warned, "my dart isn't going to bring him down. Not right then anyway."

"Suppose he has a gun?" Andreas wondered aloud.

George seemed to take the men's reservations as puzzles to be solved. "All the more reason why you and I should be on hand,

Andreas. Now let's map out the setup." He envisioned Katrina loitering on a quiet if not deserted street that afforded escape options and a place for a blind man to sit, perhaps a bus stop. He and Andreas would park the scooter nearby and try to blend in. "So how will you entice your assailant to show up?"

"Email is the only way I can reach him. The address he used may be bogus but it's all I've got. I can forward his threat—the one that said 'Any day expect your throat slit bitch'—to a girlfriend, and copy him, seemingly by mistake."

"Any idea what you would say?" Mahmoud asked.

"Let's see," her fingers drummed. "How about 'Hi Eleni, Look at this adorable hate mail. Some GD GD asshole thinks enough of me to take me down. Don't worry, I can handle him. He's a gutless punk who acts tough online but won't make a move without his cretin bros to back him up. Anyway, yes, let's get together tomorrow as you suggested at the x bus stop on y street at 10 AM after my meeting to plan our next offensive. I'll hang out there until you show up. What do you say?'"

"Not bad," George said. "Who's Eleni? Not a real person I hope."

"It's supposed to be Eleni Yannatou, the activist who went on a hunger strike in Korydallos. I know her and I bet she's on that creep's shit list too. I'll fake an email address for her."

"Oh yeah," said George. "I heard about her in jail. She's kind of a legend there." He pressed his palms together under his chin, as if in prayer. "This is a long shot and there's no telling if he'll take the bait, but something tells me it's worth a try. Is everyone on board?"

Embraced by folded his arms, Andreas said, "Well, since we really need to test the stuff and it's for such a worthy cause, Mahmoud and Katrina, are you ready to conquer stage fright?"

The Iraqi didn't hesitate. "For Katrina and for you guys, I would do anything! Of course I'm in."

"Ready, Captain" gulped Katrina.

They huddled over Mahmoud's city map to choose a location, settling on a bus stop some blocks from their neighborhood, near the corner of Christomou Smirnis and Prousis. It seemed a quiet corner where the stalker might be emboldened to make a move. A bus bench would provide Mahmoud a stable vantage. As the couple departed to make ready, Andreas called out "Katrina, when you prepare the dart, be very careful. Also, you should have a knife tomorrow, just to defend yourself. Do you have one?"

"You bet. I don't go anywhere without my Swiss knife. But I also have pepper spray. I'd rather depend on that."

"Great," Andreas said, arms unfurling. "Mahmoud, spend the rest of the day practicing. Get a good night's rest and dress nicely. You should look like a gentleman out for a stroll. That day, text me before you leave. George and I will drive there and station ourselves. I'll leave the key in the scooter in case you need it. Afterward, meet back here."

"Get there a half-hour early," George told them. "Stay alert. We will have your back. Any questions?"

"Yes," Mahmoud said. "What if our target brings a friend? I will only have one dart ready to go."

"Andreas and I will handle him. But maybe you should bring a second dart. Reloading is something else you should practice."

"And if our cat doesn't show up?" asked Katrina.

"Then you will have done a field exercise under battle conditions," George allowed. "Nothing to feel disappointed about. And whether or not it works, keep your eyes out for thugs. That email is sure to inflame your stalker one way or another."

"Of course I will. After all, I'm the bait."

CHAPTER THIRTY-NINE

AROUND TWENTY PAST nine, a red motor scooter pulled up to the curb on Christomou Smirnis Street. Two men in casual attire, not young, not old, dismounted and walked in opposite directions. The taller man loitered inconspicuously in a doorway near the end of the block. His companion went around the corner to Prousis Street, where he sat on a stoop perusing a newspaper. About ten minutes later, a fair-haired woman in blue jeans and a purple pullover crossed the intersection and stood a few meters past the bus stop, idling with her phone. Shortly thereafter, a young man in black pants, light blue shirt, red tie, and white sport coat rounded the same corner. He wore dark glasses and carried a white cane, which he gingerly rapped on the pavement to detect obstacles in his path.

He tapped his way across the street to touch its curb, hesitantly stepped up, and turned right, sidestepping a small tree before continuing on. When his cane encountered the iron leg of a bench he felt his way to its far end, and took a seat there, gripping his tubular sensor between his well-dressed thighs. Were you watching closely, you might have observed the gentleman slowly untwist his cane's handle and drop it in his left coat pocket. There he sat, erect, hands folded atop his cane, humming, rhythmically rocking back and forth.

Before long, a 675 bus pulled up. No passenger got on or off. The driver hailed the man on the bench, who waved him off and resumed his meditative groove. A woman walking a small dog approached.

The dog sniffed around the man's feet and scurried on. A noisy little Fiat coup driven by a young man in a baseball cap passed by belching exhaust fumes. A girl, her midriff protruding between a constricting top and leggings pumped past on a bicycle, perhaps late for a class. An older couple emerged from a doorway halfway up the block and walked toward him, arm in arm. "*Chairetísmata*," the man said as they passed. The man in the white coat nodded in their direction as they turned left and continued down Prousis Street.

Except for the fair-haired woman's pacing with her phone and the white-coated man's rhythmic rocking, nothing stirred for the next few minutes. Then a green, rusting VW van turned off Prousis Street and slowly cruised up the block. It passed the blind man and the woman to nose to the curb opposite a garage door. The passenger door opened and a muscular man with a shaved head and a tattoo on his right bicep in jeans and a Metallica t-shirt got out and strode toward the bus stop. He passed by the woman, and then darted around a parked car to seize her right wrist from behind and wrench it behind her back. A quick motion brought a knife to her throat. She cried out as he shoved her up the sidewalk toward the van.

After pushing his recalcitrant victim a few steps, the assailant grunted and clutched at his upper back with his left hand, almost stabbing himself. The woman spun around, bit into his forearm and shook off his grip on her wrist. She ran past the blind man with her captor in pursuit, turned right onto Prousis Street and dashed up the narrow sidewalk with Metallica Man in close pursuit. As they passed, the man perched on the stoop threw down his paper, jumped up, and ran after them. At the end of the block, the woman turned right, disappearing from view. When he reached that corner, her pursuer suddenly recoiled with hands on face, cursing and crying in pain. The man who had jumped up to race after them caught up to kick him to the sidewalk and assault his rib cage before turning to run back down, toward Christomou Smirnis Street.

The van's driver, a wiry man in a black t-shirt, had jumped out to join the chase. But just beyond the bus stop, he too winced and clutched at his back. Glancing back, he saw a tall man with pulled-back hair charging toward him from halfway up the block but seemed not to notice the man sitting on the bench, who had turned in his direction and was fidgeting with his cane. The driver took the corner and ran up the hill, brushing past a man running downhill. At the next corner he found his partner writhing on the sidewalk with the woman nowhere in sight.

The two other men converged at the intersection to observe the men from the van steadying one another at the end of the block. Behind them, the man with the cane was tapping his way up Christomou Smirnis Street at a fair clip. At the van, he reached inside the open door, pocketed something, and continued up the block. Mounting the Vespa, the taller man was heard to say "You know, I'm sure the one in the black shirt is the guy who stomped me in Syntagma Square." Kicking the engine awake, the shorter man replied, "Well then, I just returned the favor." As the Vespa zoomed past the blind man, the driver raised a clenched fist and shouted "*Aferin!*" before swinging left and speeding uphill. At the corner, the man with the cane dropped a small plastic bottle into a sewer grate, turned right, crossed the street, and went tapping down the hill, softly whistling.

Metallica and his driver hobbled back to their vehicle exchanging angry words. There they yanked objects from each other's back to find they were pointed sticks embedded in cork stoppers. Still in pain, Metallica slid into his seat and instructed his partner to get going and find the woman, which of course was not about to happen.

Mahmoud entered the living room to find his comrades anxiously awaiting him and reciprocated their high fives. He nervously asked if Katrina had showed up and was reassured. She had texted Andreas that she was in a bus on her way. They congratulated him on his marksmanship and ingenious disguise and told him how impressed they were that he had fired off two darts in quick succession.

"So," George asked, "how will we know the ricin worked?"

"Do you mean whether it worked or how we will find out?" asked Andreas.

"Both, actually. We don't know who they are. If they live, we may never know what it did to them. We have to know before moving ahead."

"Well," Mahmoud told them, "ricin takes a day or two to act. You get sick after a few hours. You have trouble moving and then organs start to fail. So maybe tomorrow we should check the hospitals."

"Or the city morgue," Andreas expectantly suggested.

The buzzer sounded. Katrina had arrived at last. She embraced Mahmoud and then the other two.

"You guys saved my ass," she said breathlessly. "When I saw he had a buddy with him it petrified me. How were you able to handle them both?"

"Didn't need to," Andreas admitted. "You did. That pepper spray took out the main man and then George made sure he didn't go anywhere. Your blind friend nailed the driver as he rushed by. We watched him run up the hill to help his buddy and rode away before they could struggle back. You both were fabulous."

"I thought he was going to kill you, right there on the street," said Mahmoud grimly. "Praise Allah, you broke free and ran. But then the other one came and I had to shoot again. I dropped the second dart in my lap as I reloaded. It could have stuck into my leg."

"That's scary, love. But after all that adrenaline, we don't know what we accomplished. May never know. Bummer."

George observed that she might find out, and not in a good way. He reminded her that even if they were fatally wounded, the dudes would still have time to tell others—possibly the police—their version of the incident and frame themselves as innocent victims. It won't matter that the poison in their systems can't be identified. When the ricin started working they would connect that to being whacked in the back and tell someone.

Having witnessed both shootings, Andreas said he didn't believe the victims had any idea that the guy on the bench did it. George wasn't so sanguine. Once they start to suffer, he predicted, they will realize they were set up and they or someone else could retaliate. For her and everyone's, safety he urged Katrina to vacate her apartment as soon as possible.

Katrina remonstrated, "Why? None of those punks know where I live. Just my blog handle and email."

"Oh?" responded Mahmoud. "What about that letter threatening you? To your post office box."

"Remember," Andreas added, "your police file has your address. Also that you go by the name Katrina."

"You should assume" George warned, "that someone will track you down. How many other people have your address?"

She tried to recall who had ever visited her. "Oh gee, besides you guys, I don't know—less than half a dozen, like members of our collective who helped fix up my flat, plus my upstairs neighbor."

A discomfited Mahmoud agreed with the men. "Plus any people they told. How many suitcases do you have?"

Katrina didn't reply. Conversation gave way. George wandered over by the window. Looking down at Marias Kiouri Street, he told them, "Understand. In our revolutionary zeal, we stupidly betrayed ourselves because we forgot that only dead men tell no tales. So let's face the situation and keep moving. We have a lot to do, and it didn't just get any easier."

CHAPTER FORTY

A T THE TOP of the stairs Katrina knocked three times and then once, her code to let Penelope know who was calling. Her neighbor still asked who might be calling before unlocking the door to her cluttered kitchen. As always, Penelope seemed pleased to see her.

"Hi, neighbor. It's been a while. Careful—don't let the cat out. Please come have a cuppa and we'll chat. How have you been? What are you up to these days?"

Always questions. Katrina was used to her gregarious housemate's inquiries and usually didn't mind, but her new activities called for circumspection and artful responses, which today didn't require much crafting; she simply evaded the question. "I'm sorry Penelope, I can't hang out with you now. I just came to ask a favor."

"Sure. What can I do for you?"

"Well, I'm going home for a few weeks, maybe longer. Family matters. I have some things I'd like you to keep for me until I get back. Documents, jewelry, and a few other items. They won't take up much space. Is that all right?"

"No problemo, my friend. I'll find a closet to stuff it in. Are you worried about break-ins? There are a lot of them these days."

"Maybe a little. But here's the thing. Some twisted nationalist creep has been harassing me online, really venomous stuff. Of course, I don't respond. He probably doesn't know my real name or where I live, but just in case he decides to get personal I want to stash some stuff while I'm gone."

Penelope's eye's widened, narrowed, and pinched. "What do you think he would try to do?"

"Probably just a punk kid who hates radicals. If he got in, I don't know, he might break dishes, steal stuff, spray swastikas, maybe trash the place."

"You should take care. I would. Maybe you need someone there. Could that good-looking young man who comes and goes house-sit for you?" A man Penelope had met out back and clearly was curious about.

"Oh, you mean my friend, um, Peter? The one with dark hair and beard? He's going out of town too, or I would ask him."

"So are you two traveling together?"

Time for another evasion. "No, no, he finally got his US visa. He'll be leaving around when I do and may not come back this way."

Her explanation may have satisfied Penelope, Katrina realized, but probably didn't comfort her. If all her stalker knew about her was her politics, he might mistake one woman for the other. But if Penelope was worried, she didn't let on. "Just bring your things up here when you're ready," she told Katrina. "Oh, before you travel, you might give me a key to your place. If something did happen I would want to be able to tell you about it."

Katrina thanked Penelope for her kindness and told her she would be up with her stuff in a while. She trudged downstairs to triage her effects. A painful hour later, she toted up a box of notebooks, old snapshots, correspondence and files, and then her TV, stereo system, and jewelry box. As Penelope stowed the items, Katrina pointed out a thick envelope, which she said contained her financial records and checkbook, adding that her will, which her former employer had obliged her to prepare, was in there too.

"Why would I need your will, Katrina?"

"You won't, Penelope. There's nothing you should worry about. I'm just using you as a safe deposit box."

Katrina thanked her again and they hugged. "Here's a key to my kitchen door. My flight's tomorrow. You can grab anything from my fridge you want. And if you hear any strange noises down there, please wait a while before going down to check. If there's a break-in, best not to involve the police if possible."

Hoping Penelope wasn't concerned for her own safety and could handle whatever situation arose, Katrina traipsed back down. She dumped clothes and personal effects into a suitcase along with her air mattress, strapped her sleeping bag to her backpack, and deposited her mess kit, laptop and chargers inside.

Having done what she could to cube her four-dimensional existence into three, she wandered through its remnants and plopped into her comfy reading chair, reflecting on what had been and what might come, on the friends she would leave behind and the work she'd leave unfinished. She thought of her parents in Basel and brother in Geneva, trying to imagine how they would react if one day they saw unsettling or even horrific news stories mentioning her. And then she pictured Mahmoud, the man she was giving it all up for, still unsure why she had chosen him, of all the men she'd known. It seemed irrational, inexplicable, fateful. She had plunged into other exotic unknowns and had managed to move on. Now, thanks to serving as an assassin's assistant, here she was moving on again, this time furtively, underground, with no light at the end of the tunnel. As Andreas had warned, there was no return ticket. Tumbling into the Anatolian unknown with her man and comrades would either strengthen or kill her.

Stop tormenting yourself, girl. Kismet is calling. Hoping that her gumption and judgment would still serve her well, she pushed out of her armchair, straightened up the bedroom, and stowed away things in her kitchen. Then she shouldered her backpack, pulled her suitcase outside, and locked the door.

When Katrina arrived, George, Mahmoud, and Ottovio were huddled over the latter's laptop viewing snapshots of Bursa that Kaan had forwarded. Mahmoud broke off to let her in and embrace her. Her moist eyes widened into a stare. "You look different. Omigod—you shaved off your beard, that's what you did! Why? I thought religious guys always had to have beards."

"George convinced me that even all dressed up I still look like a terrorist and even the mustache had to go. I doubt Allah objects. Anyway, come sit down. You must be tired after all your packing. How are you doing?"

"I feel more sad than tired. Leaving my place knowing I might not come back and thinking it could get trashed was harder than I expected. But I'm so happy to be here with all of you. I'll try to stay out of everyone's way."

Instructing her to follow, Mahmoud dragged her suitcase to the master bedroom. "Andreas insisted on moving into the other bedroom so we could have this one. He'll stay there with George."

"Oh, how sweet. I was expecting to sleep on the sofa, but now we can be together. Such a *mensch*! Lucky for you he's gay or I would have grabbed him long ago." A tear drizzled her cheek and leapt to the carpet.

He took her by the waist to the balcony window overlooking the harbor, drew her to him, and found her mouth. She pressed to his chest, tightened her embrace, and then let go, whispering, "Let's go back before I lose control."

When they returned to the living room she asked the men if any reports about the shootings had surfaced. Not yet, Ottovio told her. "By now," he estimated, "they should be in hospital. But hospitals don't release patient info unless someone asks."

"Then how about the morgue? Do they make announcements?"

"Just to the cops. Sometimes coroner makes a statement. Cause and time of death, types of injuries, like that. But not today."

"I guess we can't ask about our dudes without knowing their names."

"Actually," Mahmoud said, "Andreas went to the morgue. He'll say he's looking for a homeless guy he was helping."

"I told him to visit the crime scene," George said, "to look for evidence."

"The two darts, you mean."

"Right. They could have tossed them down. Getting rid of them would help. Quite a lot."

Around four, Andreas returned from his expedition. He told them he had decided to skip the morgue, thinking it premature, and headed to Christomou Smirnis Street to look around. "And when I got there," he said, "I was surprised to see a tow truck carting the green van away. I thought it would have been long gone. A man on the curb was talking to the truck driver, but he wasn't either of our friends. When the truck pulled away he went back into his house. I deduced that he had called for a tow because the van was blocking his exit."

"Good thinking, Sherlock," George said. "So, did you happen to note the license plate as you puffed on your pipe?"

"I did, Watson." Andreas pulled out a slip of paper. "It's 7JWX309. Ottovio, would you play that number, if you please?"

Ottovio shrugged. "Never tried to hack vehicle registry. No idea how hard to do. You happen to notice what towing company? Checking on them would be better bet."

"It was a grey truck with black lettering. I think the name on the door started with Tau Epsilon." Good enough?"

"Maybe," the hacker replied, and started typing.

Katrina asked about evidence. After casing the block, he said, he found a crimson-flecked dart lying by the curb. Not wanting to touch it, he kicked it to the corner and down a storm drain.

"Only one?" she asked. "There should be two of them."

"I looked again carefully after that and I'm sure the other one wasn't there. If it wasn't picked up or dropped down a drain, the skinheads still have it. Could be in that van."

With a chuckle, Ottovio announced, "I find towing company named 'Τσουρής'. Have address and phone number."

"What's so funny, Ottovio?" Katrina asked.

"It's pronounced 'tsouris.' Jewish friend of mine told me means 'sorrow' in Yiddish. Great name for company that steals your wheels."

Andreas placed a call to the Tsouris Company. Yes, they did have a VW van with that license number in their lineup and were itching to get rid of it. For a fee of course. Andreas took down the address and told his crew he might as well scoot over there.

"You might want this," Mahmoud said, tossing him a key ring. "'It's the van's key. I took it when I left."

Motoring over to the Tsouris Company, Andreas felt his phone vibrate and pulled over to check it.

"Mr. Carnival, this is Demitrios Karras."

"Oh hi, Demitrios. What can I do for you?"

"I've been trying to reach Mister Turgut but he doesn't answer at the number you gave me. Do you know where he is?"

Andreas didn't like the sound of that. He assumed George had switched off that phone to avoid being tracked. "At the moment, no. Is there a problem?"

"The Hellenic Police called me a while ago asking about his whereabouts. Said they want him to come to headquarters to talk with them. They tried calling him too."

"Do you know what this is about, Demitrios?"

"Not really. The officer only said it was a routine investigation. My guess is that they uncovered something relevant to Mr. Bac they want to ask him about. They said they visited his address but he wasn't there."

Andreas shuddered. *Scheisse! They must have discovered his record was tampered with!*

"Umm, okay, I'll try to relay the message. Tell me, do you think they might re-arrest him?"

"I really don't know, Andreas. If you locate him, tell him to call me immediately. If he does present himself to the police, I should be with him."

Andreas thanked Karras and clicked off frowning. He kick-started the Vespa and resumed his trek to the towing company. *George won't like this. Sometimes the magic works, but not forever.*

Chapter Forty-One

THE CHAIN LINK eyesore surrounding Tsouris Towing corralled a motley bestiary of wayward vehicles, lounging like so many impounded dogs, it seemed to Andreas. The green VW microbus was chilling its wheels beside a black Mercedes-Benz that would be biting its wheels off if it could. Beyond squatted a pockmarked stucco structure housing an office and a chop shop. He presented himself within, and over the rasp of a struggling air conditioner asked a man in a grimy work shirt if anyone had spoken for the vehicle yet. The answer was no, but one guy had called. Andreas waved the key, telling him the vehicle belonged to a co-worker who was indisposed and had asked him to retrieve it. However, he added, before taking the carcass off their hands he wanted to inspect it for damage.

Outside, Andreas orbited the van with the towman in tow, opening and closing doors, peering within. Through the passenger door he popped the glove compartment. As the proprietor caught up, Andreas scowled "You know, I think that dent in the left side of the tailgate is new. I hope your driver didn't damage it."

"Unlikely," the man said, going back to take a look, as Andreas extracted a sheaf of papers from within, among them the van's registration certificate which he deftly crumpled into his pocket. Finding no cork on the floor or under seats, he was about to pull the ashtray when the towman returned to announce, "That's an old dent" and dragged Andreas around back to demonstrate. "See, it's got rust on it. Not our fault."

"I'll let it pass," Andreas replied, opening the tailgate and clunking it shut. "Can I take it away now?"

"Whatever. Just show me your driver's license so I can record it. And pay me forty-five Euros."

Andreas told him he didn't have that much on him.

"We take credit."

"I don't have any. The owner will have to come get it."

"Whenever. Our storage fee is ten euros a day."

With a shrug, Andreas mounted the Vespa. The towman shouted "Hey, let's have the key!"

"It's my friend's," Andreas responded, kick-starting. "He wants it back."

Safely away from the sleeping dogs, he pulled over to view the purloined document. It seemed the vehicle belonged to one Iannis Misallodoxía of 15 Molou Street, Piraeus. The street didn't ring a bell, but his phone disclosed it was in a barren cluster of dwellings five clicks northwest of him at the edge of town, not too far, in fact, from Korydallos Prison. He considered paying a visit, but thought *To do what, express my condolences?* Instead, he texted Ottovio the name and address, adding c what u cn find out.

As Andreas was sleuthing about, having done his homework, Kaan texted George that he had found pensions in Bursa, asking how many rooms should be reserved. Puzzled, George asked Mahmoud what he knew about it, who in turn asked Katrina to explain.

"Um, one room would be for Mahmoud and one for me. We really shouldn't stay together."

Her ensuing pitch touting her value as a field operative didn't sit well with him, insisting that the idea quite alarmed him. Mahmoud rose to her defense to describe how a third body could be useful and asked if he wanted to volunteer. Saying "Not me," he agreed to consider her fraught strategy. For no matter how harsh his judgments could be, George always tried to think things through, and thus his reply to Kaan was to await instructions.

His instinct was to steer clear of hotels altogether, and hoped one wouldn't be necessary. Especially in Bursa, where he had lived for years and probably still had a few long-lost contacts. Besides coming up with a safe house, they needed a vehicle and driver and other operational support, such as a sentry. Might be forced to steal a car and switch around some license plates. The scenario had too many unknowns. George didn't like such equations, especially ones involving his own fragile situation. Telling them he needed to be alone for a while, he downed a shot of tea in the kitchen and closeted himself in the study.

Because he now had a name and George had asked him to inquire, Ottovio did something he usually avoided and didn't much like doing—making phone calls. He started by rounding up names of hospitals and clinics in the general vicinity of the van owner's house. Of eight such establishments, only half seemed reasonable. Pretending to be a concerned relative, he proceeded to inquire if any were attending to Mister Misallodoxía. None were, it turned out, so he compiled a longer list of local mortuaries and reluctantly started dialing them, but conversing with funeral directors was even less fun. Although he got better at interrogating them as he went along, he still hated their unctuous solicitousness. Approaching saturation, he decided to only dial three more. The first had no Misallodoxías, but at the next, a Sóimple Funeral Services functionary reported that remains bearing that name had in fact recently been added to their inventory.

"Did he come to you alone?" Ottovio asked.

"We all die alone, sir," his courtly greeter replied. "But in this case, we received a pair of remains."

"Really. I hope the second one was not a relative of Mr. Misallodoxía."

"I don't know, sir. Does the name Manolis Petinos mean anything to you?"

"Not really, but I think Iannis had a friend he called Manny. I hope it's not him."

"For your sake I hope not too, sir, but you are welcome to visit our parlor to view them once we have prepared the remains."

"I'll stop by. Tell me, do you know how they died? Was there a car accident?"

"I'm afraid we don't have that information. There was no evidence of trauma when they came to us. If their families don't request autopsies we may never really know."

Ottovio thanked him, hung up, and made one last phone call, informing Andreas about the *habeus corpus* situation, and that the skinhead who had stalked Katrina was the late Manolis Petinos. The ricin had done its job, and spectacularly so, as evidenced by the rapid decline and fall of the two card-carrying creeps. Messrs. Petinos and Misallodoxía—now ex-nationalists, thwarted thugs, neutralized neo-Nazis, stiff sociopaths—were out of play. The team was good to go.

Except that, as Andreas informed him, the Hellenic Police were looking for George. Ottovio agreed that they must have decided George's profile was all too flattering. He had expected its discrepancies to be noticed, just not so soon. Not that it reflected badly on his handiwork, but it disheartened him that his technique might be less useful than anticipated. Reluctantly, he informed the mastermind that his situation remained fraught.

Ottovio's autopsy report made Katrina want to click her heels, but she refrained from any unseemly display of gratification. Proof that the substance worked mitigated her anxiety about being stalked and doubts about her cooking skills. But quickly, an inchoate unease verging on contrition, something between guilt and shame, overcame her. Almost guilt, because she was now an accessory to double homicide, however justifiable. Almost shame, because she had put the onus on her boyfriend to snuff out her nemesis. Her sensation somatized into shivers and muddied her mood when the finality of their deed hit her, except that it wasn't over for her. The bastard who had put a knife to her throat probably wasn't that prick SuperPlato, and that meant she might again be stalked.

But soon she would be traveling—that is, if her performance on Christomou Smirnis and subsequent supplication had convinced George. More than ever, she needed to persuade him she could be a critical asset, before, during and after the act. And then, if all went well, she and Mahmoud could return to Piraeus once things quieted down. And if it didn't, would she stand with him until the end? Even so, she might never see him again. But better to make history together than for her to hang back, only to go through life deprived of him, forever wondering if she might have prevented his potential martyrdom. No, nothing would stop her from being there.

Her lover was more sanguine; proud of his woman's bravery and skill, gratified that his missiles had hit two quickly moving targets, relieved that her stalker was on ice, and singularly unremorseful. He had removed a menace; it was as simple as that. And now to confront a far greater menace, a target that would likely be more distant, better protected, and with a considerably smaller bull's eye. A long shot, but one he knew he must make. It was his jihad, which if it could speak would tell him that his would be a consequential act, a historic turning point for the region and well beyond. It would certainly be for him. He was sure of that, even though he could see no farther ahead than the gates of Mihraplı Mosque. He vowed to step up practicing.

George didn't suffer moral ambiguities either, not that he could spare the time. Much remained to do, most of which wasn't possible without being on the scene. And now that his days in Piraeus seemed numbered it was probably time to go, though without his bogus passport the Turkish border was closed to him. Remembering his hometown, he recalled that several major highways converged there. Instead of holing up in Bursa, he started to think, make a run for it. Perhaps to the East on the D200 motorway and then over the Ülüdag mountains, toward Bozüyük at the edge of the vast Anatolian plateau. Or maybe take the D200 west past Izmir, where Kaan came from and still had family, on to the port of Çesme, where many ferry routes converge and illicit rubber boats stream forth. Let the others do that, not him. He was done with Greece. As long as persecution was his lot, the fatherland should have the honor.

Each of these itineraries involved commandeering a vehicle and traveling considerable distances in the midst of a nationwide manhunt. His plan to attack the G-20 meeting had presented no such issues. Mahmoud and Kaan would have had a week to scatter before their time bomb flooded the Aspendos arena with deadly fumes. He, of course, would be in Piraeus the whole time, plotting the next attack. But that was then. The prospect of starting anew back in his homeland gnawed at him along with those jugs of binary sarin he hoped were still available. Self-deportation, the only alternative he might have to forced repatriation, started to appeal.

As often was the case, Andreas too felt unsettled. Within days, they would launch the operation, and except for releasing their video, his role would come to an end. If George had other plans involving him, he hadn't signified. And next month Kosta would be released and he would have his old partner back, hopefully to rehabilitate their business and relationship. Of course, he also missed Ivan, but before long he would go back to Vienna or move on. No, his life was here, he decided, on familiar ground with a stable partner, in a place where he spoke the language and could make his own mark on the movement. Whatever befell the others, he at least could abide.

Like a fast-approaching highway sign, the words *What next?* hung over their heads. Each had their own path to follow, paths now braided together but could easily diverge as the road ahead twisted and branched. Unless it ended.

III. PARADISE NOTWITHSTANDING

Seek out your enemies relentlessly. If you have suffered, they too have suffered: but you at least hope to receive from God what they cannot hope for. God is all-seeing and wise.

The Holy Qur'an 4:103

CHAPTER FORTY-TWO

EXCEPT FOR THE bulky trash bags they shouldered, they could have been on a hiking holiday. "I hope it isn't much farther. My knees are complaining." George wasn't used to negotiating steep trails with a heavy load, and the three hikers still had more hills to traverse on their trek south.

"Patience, George." Mahmoud advised. "Could happen anywhere along here, so watch the sea." He pointed down to the littoral. "See that harbor down there? That's where I found my boat to Piraeus."

Katrina stopped and shaded her eyes with her hand to peer down the slope past vineyards and orchards to the hamlet where boats bobbed behind a protective jetty. She caught up to tell them "When they come, I hope they're rubber boats. I'm told that's what Turkish smugglers use. The Arab gangs favor leaky wooden ones that sink a lot. Let's not deal with them if we can avoid it."

"You have something against Arabs?" Mahmoud sniffed.

"Of course not, love. But these guys cut corners, charge more, and have bad safety records."

"I vote for riding in a rubber duck," proclaimed George. "I can't speak Arabic and I'm not a good swimmer. Safety first."

Mahmoud was back where he had first encountered Europe, the lovely isle of Chios, eight kilometers off the Turkish port of Çeşme two months ago, almost to the day. This day, however, Chios did not seem quite so lovely. The stiff wind that buffeted them raised whitecaps on the Steno Chiou sound. Beyond barely loomed the coast of Turkey, tantalizingly close. Perhaps the rough surf would prevent boats from running all day. If so, they were prepared to camp out.

In their do-it-yourself fashion, they had decided to bypass the protocols of ports of entry. Any formalities would take place with human traffickers instead of uniformed officials. The badge Katrina carried from her former employer would serve to identify them as humanitarians, and in fact they had come prepared to help. The sacks they carried held socks, shoes, underwear, and toiletries to distribute to incomers, her idea. In Piraeus she and Andreas had scoured the street bazaar for personal items to distribute to migrants in exchange for life preservers. Then, into the sacks would go their own articles before casting off to Çeşme with the first returning pilot who would accept their money.

Several hazy figures materialized several hundred meters ahead, approaching on foot. George stiffened in place. "They're refugees. Don't worry," Mahmoud told him, urging him forward. Three minutes later, the two groups plodded to a halt to face one another. Their counterparty numbered four, a couple shouldering backpacks and two children. The mother held the hand of a pre-school girl. A tuckered-out boy looking to be about six trailed after the father dragging a carry-on suitcase missing a wheel. Mahmoud smiled and greeted them with "*Yawm saxiid! Ahlan wa Sahlan bekum.*"

"*Ahlan beek,*" the man replied, and then a question: "*'ayn hu mukhayam lilajiiyn, min fadlik?*"—Where is the refugee camp, please? Katrina put down the sack she carried and crouched to untie it. Remembering the fenced-in tents they had skirted half an hour ago, Mahmoud manifested directions and then prompted the couple for their story. Unsurprisingly, fighting in Aleppo accounted for their plight. Destroyed or abandoned was almost everything they possessed, including the man's carpet store and his wife's accounting practice.

Katrina arose to present the family with items from her collection—two pairs of children's sneakers, socks for all, a towel, and a pouch of toiletry supplies. "Tell them we're here to help the relief workers," she said.

The couple gladly accepted her offerings. The wife tearfully thanked her. "*Ya Tibtak! Motashakr Awi!*"

Mahmoud asked the man how far they had walked. Must have been close to ten kilometers since landfall late yesterday, he was told. Had they witnessed any new arrivals, George wanted to know, and was informed none this day. Bashfully, the man asked if they had any water to spare for the children. Mahmoud handed over one of several bottles he carried and Katrina her canteen.

Profuse thanks from the Syrians as they turned to resume their trek. Mahmoud bade them to wait, tugging over his head the lanyard he wore, from which dangled a leather purse. He handed it to the husband. "I found this on a beach," he said. "A refugee must have lost it. You might as well have it. You probably will need it."

The Syrian untied the purse to find a ring, two necklaces, several gold pieces, and a roll of dinars. Over the astonished man's objections, Mahmoud insisted he accept it as an offering from Allah. "*As-salamu alaykum,*" he told them, keeping to himself its grisly provenance.

"*Wa-Alaikum-us-Salaam,*" came the husband's thankful praise with a deep bow. He took his son's hand and led the family on their way.

"They sure could use Allah's blessings," Katrina said as they grew smaller.

"Tell me about it," Mahmoud responded, silently petitioning the Deity on everyone's behalf.

For the next quarter-hour, only the crunch of gravel and rustling of leaves from the stiff onshore breeze punctured the silence, until Mahmoud pointed out a half dozen or so small craft plowing through whitecaps. They had to be refugees, he asserted; smugglers deploy swarms of boats to evade interception. Their pace quickened to a canter and then to a dash downhill under a cobalt blue sky. Breathlessly, Mahmoud confirmed his call. "Yes, that's what they are. Inflatables with at least thirty people each." He knew the game. One of those boats could have been his.

They had gotten lucky. The three travelers and the six boats converged on a rocky beach within minutes of one another. "Take off your shoes and roll up your pants," urged George, dumping out his bag of goodies on the pebbly strand. Mahmoud emptied his sack and put his backpack and cane inside it. Katrina added a zippered plastic bag with their cell phones and chargers. When a boat bottomed out a few meters offshore, George waded to it and started hauling it in as its occupants scrambled over wales into the shallows. Its pilot waved him off, yelling in Arabic "Stop that! I need to go back!"

George got the message. He waded through the departing throng to the stern. Shouting over the snarl of the outboard engine, in Turkish he declared that he had three paying passengers for the return trip. The helmsman idled the motor and demanded to know who they were. Aid workers, George replied, imploring him to help them get across quickly to respond to an emergency. "She's in charge," he said, brandishing Katrina's NGO badge, "but doesn't speak Turkish. Will you help us?"

The pilot attempted a phone call that didn't go through as George displayed six hundred euros. Pocketing his phone, the helmsman demanded two hundred more. Assenting, George clambered aboard the quivering craft, now bobbing free, and waved his comrades on as the pilot threw the engine into reverse. Stumbling madly across the pebbly shallows after the retreating vessel, Mahmoud and Katrina held high their belongings. George uttered a string of menacing profanities, pocketed his money and started to debark, prompting the driver to ease up the throttle as George urgently beckoned his comrades to splash up and slither aboard.

In hitching this ride, they had touched a tentacle of one of the human trafficking syndicates currently thriving in the greater Izmir region. As it happened, and fortunately for them, this one was not a particularly poisonous appendage and the helmsman was good for his word. As the Zodiac smacked through the chop heading East, Katrina and Mahmoud huddled amidships while at the stern George conversed with the pilot, learning that he was Syrian. In broken Turkish the young man disclosed that to make a living driving boats while awaiting his family to join him he had signed up with what he called a local aid society. He'd been making this trip almost daily for two weeks. When his relatives arrived, he would voyage to Chios one last time. The fee George handed over was an unexpected bonus, no matter that half would go to his boss, should he find out.

Partway across the strait, the sea breeze that had been slowing their progress reversed direction to push them toward the mainland. As the glow of Çeşme beckoned, George offered the pilot an extra ten Euros and their three life jackets if he could arrange transport to Izmir, ninety kilometers to the East. He had no wish to camp on some windswept strand with a throng of desperate migrants. "No problem," the Syrian responded, and made a phone call that this time did go through.

The helmsman cut the engine and crunched to a halt on a rocky beach in a small cove. His spray-soaked passengers queasily slid out to regain their bearings. To their left stood a dock piled high with life preservers and inner tubes; to the right, a thicket of shrubbery redolent of honeysuckle and bay. In between, George falling to his knees on damp gravel, uncharacteristically weepy, intoning *"Inanamıyorum, gerçek mi bu Allah'ım, çok ama çok zaman oldu."*—I cannot believe this, God. It has been so long. His piety exhausted, he followed the outlines of his companions up a bank to a roadway, where they scrambled into a boathouse stacked high with Zodiacs. The Syrian urged them to stay inside until their ride comes and slipped away. Soon a motorbike chugged to life and puttered into the gloom.

They laced their shoes and anxiously stood by until a vehicle crunched to a halt outside, followed by a hoarse "Marhaba!" On the dirt path sat They shouldered backpacks and exited to find a dusty grey van with tinted glass all around, driven by a wizened man with a greying beard wearing a *taqiyah* and a serious demeanor. Mahmoud alone was able to communicate with the taciturn Arab, who greeted Katrina with a frown as she stepped aboard. When told of their Izmir destination, the driver demanded fifty Turkish Liras from each, up front, but accepted their euros after lying about the exchange rate.

Lights off, the van jounced along twisty fog-shrouded byways, its riders uncomfortably roosting on the bare floor, clutching one another for support. Mahmoud crawled forward and steadied himself to ask how long the jolting would go on and was told that, unless the police had relocated their checkpoint, it would be smoother sailing soon. Thankfully the D300 highway soon materialized, the van's lights came on, and the ride did improve. So persuaded, Mahmoud retreated to lie beside Katrina in corrugated companionship as George took refuge in the passenger seat.

He tilted toward her. "I just realized. This is my fourth border crossing since leaving Mosul."

"You win. I'm only on my third, but that's easily enough expatriations for me."

"The only thing that keeps me going is my family. Redeeming them, I mean. What about you?

She nestled her cheek on his chest. "I already told you. It's you. And your fierce humanity. It opened me."

"To what? I don't understand."

"To what you and people like you have lost, I guess, and what it will take to make it right. It's something worth fighting for."

"But what about you? Do you have a vision worth fighting for?"

"Sure, but it's more nebulous. I want to make the world safe from tyrants, whatever it takes."

Ignoring the eyes glaring from the rear view mirror, Mahmoud pressed to her, murmuring "What it takes is us. After this one, we'll see."

The couple drifted off, hearts entwined. As they slept, George watched towns and villages flash by through half-capped eyes. In Urla, a satellite of Izmir, its substantial homes and hulking apartment blocks suggested to him that much had changed in Turkey since his hasty exile. At the agrarian outskirts of Izmir, the van turned onto a highway that hugged the long, crooked bay leading to the city center. George called Bursa to announce their arrival to a gleeful Kaan, who confirmed that, yes, his aunt Safiye was expecting them and was more than happy to put them up. In arranging the layover, he had assured

George that she was pleasant and hospitable but totally unaware of their mission and should of course remain so. George signed off, punched up a map for the driver, and clambered back. Rousing the sleepers, he reminded them that *teyze* Safiye had been told that they had met her nephew in Athens, became fast friends, and had just ferried over to join him in Bursa. From there, they would take a holiday together touring Turkey. Not much of a stretch.

The driver pulled up to Safiye's building, a modest apartment house just off of Eşrefpaşa Boulevard in the historic Kona district. George dismissed him and they gathered in the entryway. He punched 201 and announced their arrival when *kim ne, lutfen?* crackled over the intercom. "Come to the second floor." the voice advised. As they buzzed in George advised his two comrades, "Act like you aren't together. Be discreet. Sleep alone."

"Got it, said Katrina. "Just in case she's prudish. Hope she won't think you guys are boyfriends."

Chapter Forty-Three

SAFIYE DURSUN WELCOMED her guests warmly with *"Merhaba! Hoşgeldiniz! Lütfen girin!"* As they filed in George and Mahmoud accepted her outstretched hand, kissed it and touched it to their foreheads, Katrina taking their cue. Taking note of a cane protruding from Mahmoud's backpack, Safiye asked if he'd had an accident. "I twisted my ankle last week," he shrugged. "Hardly need it now."

Safiye's fifty-two years hadn't particularly plumped her figure or diminished the wavy luster of her auburn hair. Her apartment overlooking a quiet side street was comfortable and clean. Like their abode in Piraeus, it had two bedrooms and a study, but its panoply of miscellaneous furnishings made it feel less spacious. Safiye apologized for the clutter, explaining how she'd moved in with her belongings after the death of her sister.

Besides talking for a living, Safiye had the gift of Turkish *cecece*—chitchat—and soon revealed that her lectureship in Sociology at Dokuz Eylül University was paying less due to budget cuts and tenuous due to academic politics. Her reduced circumstances hadn't diminished her Turkish hospitality, which she expressed to her guests from across the Aegean through food and tea. As soon as shoes came off and introductions went around, she produced a tray of *mezze*, and of course tea, in little gold-rimmed glasses she kept refilling. Settling in, she inquired how their trip had gone. Katrina and Mahmoud let the boss relate that eleven-hour ferry ride from Piraeus had been choppy but uneventful, eliding their reverse commute from Chios. For Katrina's sake, Safiye switched to accented but fluent English and proceeded to pry out life stories. One by one they obliged with sanitized narratives focused on origins.

Prompted by Katrina, Safiye let tell that she had married and divorced childless in her late twenties, disappointing her parents, who had hoped for many grandchildren but got only one to pamper. She moved to Izmir to be near her older sister, Kaan's mother, the late Nadia. They were the only children of Russian émigrés who settled outside Antalya at the height of the cold war. Bookish but not well educated, their parents instilled in them the importance of learning and sent both sisters to college. Nadia became a social worker, Safiye a sociologist. When Nadia's Ayhan was arrested and sent to a prison near Istanbul, she was bereft. Nadia found a leftist lawyer who would dare petition the court, and went on to found a mutual aid society for families of political prisoners like Ayhan. Her yearlong efforts were thwarted at every turn. Unable to visit or even call Ayhan and now receiving hate mail and anonymous threats herself, Nadia became fearful, bitter and depressed. A few months hence she was diagnosed with cervical cancer. Safiye said she was convinced that Nadia just gave up, and believed her death radicalized Kaan right out of the army.

Their hostess clearly doted on Kaan and had missed his company during his sojourn in Athens. Why, she asked, had he moved to Bursa just after ramping up research into ancient Greek social structures? As George warily watched, Mahmoud explained that Kaan had been asked to work as a translator by an Austrian businessman he'd met in Athens who was relocating to Bursa. The prospect of an income and free lodgings convinced Kaan to take the gig for a few months and then head back to Greece. "We're taking up his offer to visit and take a quick holiday tour."

Her smooth brow furrowed. "I'm not sure how safe it is for Kaan to be running around. After he quit the Army he exposed some things the military was doing in Sanliurfa Province that the government didn't want known. Now that he's back he needs to keep a low profile."

Imitating surprise, George said Kaan had never mentioned any issues with the law, but presumed he knew what he was doing.

Safiye put down her tea. "I hope so. I don't know if you follow events in Turkey, but things are really bad here now." Katrina asked her what she meant and got an earful.

"The government jailed my brother-in-law on charges of treason, just for demanding an investigation of tainted evidence the prosecutors used in show trials that put two hundred fifty military officers behind bars over a made-up coup plot. Most of the judges were party hacks and his trial was a joke. The government even refused to parole Ayhan to attend his dying wife. And he isn't the only one. Turkey has jailed almost as many journalists as China has. It's deplorable and getting worse." Katrina didn't argue the point.

Safiye wasn't finished. "I don't want to minimize the horror you went through, Mahmoud, but we have hundreds of thousands of displaced people like you here. Our government's meddling in Syria has helped murderous jihadis to tear it apart. Paşa's theocratic rule divides Turks along religious and ethnic lines, and anyone who publicly objects is persecuted. Ataturk must be spinning in his grave."

Her soliloquy was met only by the clicking of tea glasses until Mahmoud mooted "I saw sectarian hatred and violence destroy my country twice—first thanks to the Americans and now to ISIS. In between, by favoring their own kind, the Shiite government paved the way to Sunni extremism. But it isn't an invasion that's destroying your institutions, it's more like a slow-motion religious coup. I hope it's not too late to stop it."

"It could be, Mahmoud," Safiye said, her mouth tightening. "You see, the President now has an iron grip on the affairs of state. He attacks allies who brought him to power. He has packed the legal system and the military with his cronies. He converts public schools into religious academies left and right over parents' and teachers' objections. He tried to change the constitution to make himself president for life in his sultan's palace. Do you see anyone who can stop him?"

"You never know," Katrina mused. "Empires always seed their

own destruction. They can go down in unexpected ways. The harder they strive, the bigger they fail."

George didn't sleep well that night, and not just because he and Mahmoud were consigned to couch cushions in Safiye's living room while Katrina slumbered comfortably in the guest bedroom. After Mahmoud had prayed and settled down, George lay on his back pondering his state of affairs. Here he was, stateless in his own country, his only credentials a Greek alien resident card reading Yilmaz Turgut. The law was on his tail in both countries.

Regardless, they had five days to get to Bursa, settle in somewhere, reconnoiter, work out logistics, rehearse, and then do it and get out. What kept him awake was the logistics. They hadn't scripted their entrance or exit. They needed to choreograph their movements and beware of threats lest the performance become a ballet of disaster. As little as possible should be left to improvisation. Kaan hadn't reported how access would be controlled, where police would be stationed, or what streets would be open. They needed a vehicle, but where to get, park, and run with it?

Such as it was, their plan was to take an intercity ötöbüs anonymously to Bursa. Katrina would buy their tickets. They would board and sit separately, and in four to five hours Kaan would greet them in at the terminal. He claimed to have found lodgings, but whether Hilton or hostel, George was loathe to register. He again tried to think of any old friends who might accommodate them, but no answer came. And even if there were, that would be one more person who might talk. He rolled over, punched his pillow, and willed himself into a fitful sleep.

Katrina awoke early under her feather comforter in a bedroom with Ottomanesque walnut furnishings and billowing teal draperies considering the near future and her part in it. After unproductively obsessing, she found a bathrobe in the closet and wandered down to the kitchen in search of her drug of choice. Safiye must have heard her rooting through cabinets and drawers, because soon there she was, also robed, asking Katrina what she needed. She tutored Katrina in the ways and means to brew her fix and asked an unrelated question: When were they planning to leave for Bursa and how would they get there?

Thinking that Safiye might be trying to get rid of them, Katrina replied "We should be out of your hair either today or tomorrow."

"Oh, I hope it isn't today, because I have to give an exam. After that I am free from teaching for a while and could go with you. I really miss Kaan, and this would be a wonderful excuse to go visit him."

Katrina stopped in mid-scoop. "Um, you want to take the bus with us?"

"We could, but why not take my car? That would make it simpler and more comfortable, don't you think?"

Katrina demurred, gulping. "Oh Safiye, it's very sweet of you to offer, but we can easily find our way."

"Nonsense, Katrina. I would enjoy it. It would be a lot of fun and it's an easy drive. What do you say?"

All Katrina could say was "Let me ask the guys when they get up. George may have made some arrangements I don't know about. Let's talk later."

"Whatever you decide will be fine, my dear. But now I need to get dressed and get over there to give my exam. Help yourselves to anything you see for breakfast."

"Thanks, will do."

Just what we need. A fifth wheel. No thank you.

CHAPTER FORTY-FOUR

"SHE SAID *WHAT*?"

George did not take well Safiye's offer to drive them to Bursa. The news literally stopped his breath.

Katrina refilled his tea glass. "She kept insisting she wanted to see Kaan and it would be no trouble. I didn't know what to say, so I just told her we would consider it."

"Impossible!" George exhaled. "Tell her we have plans to stop along the way. Maybe visit my sister in Balikesir for a few days. Something like that."

Mahmoud regarded his cheese *börek*. "Wait, think about it. We need someplace to stay. We don't have credit cards or IDs to show. Safiye can sign for rooms and we can give her money. This could help us."

"I'm still opposed," George said. "She'll want to be with Kaan. We couldn't talk in her presence. We need every minute to prepare. We can't have her there."

"I see your point," Katrina responded. "She'd be like a ball and chain . . . unless, that is, she became one of us."

"What did you say?" George spat, along with some tea.

"You know, that car of hers could come in handy. And given what she and Kaan have been through, can you imagine her turning us in?"

"Not intentionally. My gut feeling is that she'd be just as happy to see Paşa come to an early demise, but knowing her nephew was involved would scare her stiff."

"And," she submitted, "besides having a car, wouldn't she be just the sort of cover we need?"

"Good point," Mahmoud interjected. "George, we still have no mobility there, unless you set up something we don't know about."

"Sure, the car. The cover. But even if she doesn't balk, odds are she'll squawk."

"How so, George?" Katrina asked.

"Any of us could be identified. If Kaan is, the police will find her and pressure her to talk. She might turn on us to save his skin. Or hers."

"That could happen whether she's with us or not, you know," objected Katrina. "Look, she's already worried her nephew might be popped for blowing the whistle. Wouldn't telling her not to come make her even more anxious?"

Mahmoud agreed. "Whether she's involved or not, we've got to prepare her. Once the news breaks, she could start talking. We need to control the situation."

Once again, George faced the injection of a new accomplice, similarly female, into an operation that he hadn't planned but was nominally running. Morosely massaging his temples, he plaintively uttered "Are you saying the only way to manage her is to bring her in?"

"I think it's either that or we lace her tea with ricin," Katrina said. "What other choices do we have?"

"Get serious," George said. "I agree, we don't have a lot of options. But how much does she need to know?"

Katrina drew in her breath. "Why don't we tell her this: 'We know how much you want to see Kaan, but if you go to Bursa now, you could get in over your head. It won't just be a social visit. You will be regarded as an accomplice to a crime against the state whether you are or not. It could mean never seeing your nephew again. You will know things you don't need to know. Think about it. If . . .'"

George cut her off. "Something like that. But who's gonna tell her? You?"

"If you want my opinion," Mahmoud said, "It was her dear nephew's stupid idea to come here anyway. We should tell him what we're thinking and let him decide what to do."

"Okay, I'll call him," George said grimly. "Once he understands that she'll connect us to the operation at some point, hopefully he can talk her out of coming."

Safiye came home around three with bags of groceries. George slipped into the guest room, telling them "I'll be busy for a while." After the couple helped put the food away, Mahmoud repaired to the living room to watch TV while Katrina helped Safiye get dinner going.

"That's a wonderful young man," Safiye said, eyeing Mahmoud on the sofa. "He's smart, well-mannered, and quite handsome, don't you think?"

"Yes, Safiye, he really is a great guy."

"I think he likes you. If you asked me, he'd be a great catch if you could get him. That is, if you're looking . . ."

"Believe me, Safiye, I've thought about it. But it would never work. We come from different worlds."

"Don't be so sure, my dear. After all, Kaan's father is a Muslim from Istanbul who married a Jew from Antalya whose parents came from Russia. They had a very good marriage up until the day my sister died."

"So Kaan is Jewish? Who knew?"

"You wouldn't know. Most of our family is secular, like me. But Kaan's parents didn't reject tradition. They celebrated Jewish high holidays and fasted for Ramadan. I'm not sure if they believed in God. They always said they put their faith in the people of Turkey."

"Well, from what I know, I think Kaan does too, and would agree with you about how bad things are here."

"Oh, I know he does. Before he left, he told me he wants to take his country back."

"Back from what? Back to where?"

"Back from state fundamentalism, I assume. Back to the secular nation built by Atatürk."

"Did he say how?"

"No, I don't think he had a plan, but I got the feeling that he would take action if he had the chance."

"Does that worry you?"

"I care for his safety, but I wouldn't condemn him if he got involved with a militia or something. I just don't want him to."

Taking a deep breath, Katrina ventured "What if I told you he might have done that?"

"It wouldn't surprise me, Katrina. I can't imagine him joining a fighting unit, but I wouldn't put it past him. So what do you know about it?"

Katrina was spared elucidation thanks to George wandering into the kitchen with his phone. "Safiye, excuse me. This is Kaan. He wants to speak with you." With a big smile she took the phone to say "Kaan, is that you? We haven't talked in so long. How are you?" Phone pasted to ear, she entered her bedroom and closed the door.

Mahmoud cautioned, "George, I hope you didn't tell Kaan that she wants to come."

"Not really. I told him to say he's heard there could be trouble in Bursa and this isn't a good time to visit."

"And then, if she still wants to go?"

"I guess we could poison her and take her car."

"Right," Katrina responded. "And end up booked for homicide? Anyway, there's no time to do her in and bury her remains."

A few minutes hence, a somewhat glassy-eyed Safiye shuffled in and slumped at the breakfast table. Katrina broke the awkward silence. "So, how did you find your nephew?"

"He's in way over his head," she managed to say. "It petrifies me. I couldn't convince him to call it off. What did you do to him?"

"Wait," Mahmoud said. "What did he tell you?"

Expelling a sigh, she voiced "At first he said I shouldn't come because of rumors there would be a terrorist act. When I told him whatever it is, I wasn't afraid, he said it would be a very big deal. I asked him what was supposed to happen and how he knew about it."

Stretching taut a kitchen towel, George prompted "And he said?"

"Nothing at first. But I kept digging until he told me what would happen. Asked me not to interfere." Leveling reproachful eyes at George, she asked "Did you put him up to this?"

"No," George replied, letting the towel fall limp, "This is something he chose to do. It was his idea, his jihad. We worked together to make it happen. You would piece it together anyway sooner or later, so best you know now."

Touching her shoulder, Katrina said "I'm sorry you're upset, Safiye, but you already suspected he might be involved in something militant. At least now you know what not to say if the police ever come calling."

Another sigh. "It's just too much. First they took Ayhan. Then I lost my sister. Now Kaan is throwing his life away."

"It's not like that," George said. "First of all, he isn't going to kill anyone. Second, nobody will suspect he's involved, and no one besides his roommate knows he's in Bursa, and he knows nothing of it. And from what you said last night, it seems you wouldn't mind if someone knocked off Paşa. Am I right?"

"Yes, about killing him," Safiye admitted. "I would dance in the street."

A chortle from Katrina. "Hopefully without security cameras looking on."

Mahmoud said "You said you wanted something to be done. If not now, when?"

Safiye had picked up a pencil and was fidgeting with it. "All I can say is this thing damn well better work or it would be a total loss."

"So then," George inquired. "Are you at peace with the idea?"

"I can't say I'm at peace with it, but there it is. So, when will we go?"

"Tomorrow if possible. Did you tell Kaan you were taking us there?"

Safiye continued petting the pencil as if it were a cat. "No. I wasn't sure about it myself."

George drilled down. "So, have you decided?"

She put down the pencil and looked up to George. "Yes, I'm sure. I want to be with Kaan and see the tyrant die before my eyes." Her posture stiffened. Right arm raised, she proclaimed "Mustafa Kemal Atatürk, we are coming to avenge you!"

Bracing himself on the tabletop, George fixed his eyes on hers. "Please keep that worthy sentiment to yourself, Safiye. In fact, you must say nothing about this to anyone, ever. Once we set out, you will be under my command. You must follow every order and be ready for any of us to die, including yourself. Can you handle that?"

Katrina and Mahmoud exchanged blinks. Safiye extended her hand to cup George's knuckles, saying "I'm ready. Let me tell you a story. A few years ago one of my students, a lovely young man, graduated and went to serve in the military. He was a great guy who loved everyone and couldn't understand sectarian or any other kind of hatred. The Army put him in a unit in the east that went after Kurdish partisans. They weren't even PKK, just militias defending their homeland. A mortar fell near him and he bled to death. It was probably friendly fire. He had nothing against Kurds. They had nothing against him. It was the government who killed him. Someone should pay for that."

"And to avenge him, your brother-in-law, and the many other victims of the state in a big way," George inquired, "would you pay whatever price you had to?"

Safiye released his hand and leaned back. "I'm no suicide bomber. I just want to be with Kaan. He's all I have. So yes, I want to go. There must be things I can do."

"You don't have to decide this minute," Katrina said. "Let's get dinner started. Your comrades are hungry for more than revenge."

Chapter Forty-Five

T HE LITTLE BEIGE Fiat sedan with four occupants entered the E881 motorway under overcast December skies. Their chariot had seen better days, better decades even, but Safiye's *araba tamircisi* had changed the oil and told her it was good to go. Safiye's leisurely below-the-speed-limit pace would get them to Bursa within two hours. George rode next to her. Katrina and Mahmoud occupied the back discreetly holding hands. Soon splatters of rain dotted the dust on the windshield. The forecast was for two days of rain across western Anatolia, followed by clearing and unseasonably warm weather, portending a perfect day to make history.

From his shotgun perch, George wearily briefed their driver in Turkish. It had been a long night for all; bringing Safiye up to speed without jarring acceleration, clarifying everyone's special role, inquiring after lodgings, and preparing suitcases. Now he described Kaan's living arrangement, underscoring that roommate Ivan must remain unaware of their intent or even their presence, avoiding speculating about what Ivan might do if Kaan went missing.

A stretch of construction restricted the roadway, slowing their progress as they joined a queue of cars parading behind a tractor hauling hay. "Tell me again what I'll do at the mosque," Safiye said. "I know what kind of scene I'm supposed to make, but how will I know when to do it?"

Patiently George explained "It will go like this. You'll enter the courtyard with the crowd, find where Kaan is, and stand somewhere behind him. He'll be recording a video on his phone and can't be disturbed. Katrina should be to your left, closer to the front. She'll be Mahmoud's lookout."

"Will she give me a signal?"

"No. Locate Mahmoud and pay attention to him. He'll briefly raise up his cane. That's your signal to scream that a thief took your purse—so remember to leave yours behind. Paşa will probably pause at the commotion. That's when our friend will strike. Assuming it's a hit, things may get weird. Keep calm, go with the crowd, and try to exit the compound where you came in."

"And you'll be waiting in my car somewhere nearby?"

"Right, but I don't know where yet. I'll decide when we see what the security setup is. I'll pick you and Kaan up first and then the other two. We'll have our stuff in the trunk and can head in whatever direction seems safest."

Safiye pondered her instructions. "Something just occurred to me."

"What's that?"

"Kaan won't be the only person using a camera. There might be news crews inside, and spectators will take pictures. Any of us could be recorded. Don't you think that can cause problems?"

"That's been on my mind too." He switched to English and cast a glance to the couple in the back seat. "That's why none of us should be seen together. Safiye's disturbance should take eyes off Mahmoud, but he still could be spotted or photographed. It will be up to you, Katrina, to get him our quickly. Run interference but don't escort him. Keep him from being dragged off, whatever it takes."

"I'm not sure how I could stop that," she answered, squeezing boyfriend's hand, "but yes, whatever it takes."

The rain had tapered to drizzle by the time Bursa's outer limits loomed. Even under threatening skies they decided it made sense to stretch their legs at the Mihraplı mosque. She left the E881, proceeding south on Akpınar Street until minarets loomed above.

Kaan's snapshots and their street surfing had made the area familiar enough to note that something new had been added—disorderly stacks of yellow barricades in a corner of the parking lot.

Safiye squeezed into a spot on a side street and they leisurely crossed Dikkaldırım Street to the main gate, where before splitting up George tasked Safiye with inquiring what traffic restrictions might be imposed. A groundsman trimming roses directed her to the visitors' kiosk just inside the main entrance. From behind a gleaming ornate mahogany desk, a dour bearded man in a nicely tailored suit informed her that on the day of the event no parking would be allowed within the complex. Although street parking would be available, the *memur* advised that Bent Street along the west side of the complex would be closed off to accommodate press and security, and there would be no parking on the Avenue. When she asked if tickets were required, he said that the ceremony was primarily for the families of the honored children, but a limited number of spectators would be admitted through the main gate, first come, first served. Arrive early, he cautioned. There was sure to be a line, and a slow one at that, because everyone entering needed to be scanned.

While Safiye was chatting up the official, the others reconnoitered, separately circling the grounds, each ascending a different set of steps to a plaza that might accommodate three hundred people or so. One by one they inspected the ablution fountain where workmen were setting up a speaker's platform, just as Kaan had expected. Mahmoud walked the colonnade that ringed the courtyard to identify the best vantage points, estimating how much shelter the pillars, seemingly slimmer than in Kaan's photos, might afford. Katrina surveyed means of egress, noting three sets of broad steps down to the driveway and the massive oak doors leading into the mosque. It might, she observed, be possible to leap from the railing three meters to the pavement, but it would be a rough landing.

Back from her encounter in the foyer, Safiye approached George to brief him, but he turned and walked away with a *tssk* and a nod toward the main gate. The team exited one by one to trail after George across busy Dikkaldırım Street to a storefront labeled *Eczane*.

When they had assembled, he said "If I can, I'll pick you up near this pharmacy. If I can't, I'll be idling somewhere up this parallel street or around the corner on this side street."

"Hold on," Mahmoud said, looking back. "Suppose they block the gate? They might keep everyone inside so they can identify suspects. What then?"

"Just act confused and wait it out," George told him. "Find a kind soul to escort you into the mosque and out the front. Of course, if you're spotted, there's not much anyone can do. But as a blind man, you should be the last person anyone would suspect."

Mahmoud stood and gazed at the gate, hands stuffed in pockets. Kicking a small stone into the street, he replied "Right, George. The last one."

Late the night before, Katrina and Safiye had perused small hotels and pensions online to settle on the inexpensive and somewhat inappropriately named VIP Apartments, on a residential street with easy access to the D200 motorway. The clerk Safiye had spoken with affirmed that they had space for her family and yes, she could pay in cash if she put down a deposit.

In the cramped, subdued lobby, the desk clerk had less interest in who would be sharing the space with her than in the three hundred Turkish Liras Safiye handed over as a deposit. Using cash had been George's urgent suggestion when she had offered to book their room with her credit card, precipitating a lecture on how not to leave paper or electronic trails.

A claustrophobic ascent in a creaky elevator brought them to a third-floor suite redolent of ammonia and air freshener, featuring two double beds in one room, a living room with a day bed, a dining area, and a kitchenette.

"Maybe we should buy some food," Katrina urged. "If we take meals here we'll save money and avoid being seen together in public."

Safiye, suffering from intense immersion and keen to see Kaan more than anything, wasn't interested in shopping or eating in.

At her urging, George rang him up and arranged a rendezvous, not letting on where they were staying or that his aunt was with them. Kaan suggested patronizing a dimly lit *lokanta* on the fringe of downtown that George said would have to do and received its coordinates.

It excited Kaan to be reuniting with Mahmoud and especially George, not so much Katrina. He made haste to leave, telling Ivan he wanted to get out of the house to hang out downtown and maybe see a movie. Swaying his way on the Metro, he reviewed his agenda: Tonight they would catch up and go over the plan. Tomorrow they would congregate to rehearse their movements in the performance space he'd prepared to give Mahmoud and the others one last chance to practice their moves. And the next afternoon, at 2 PM precisely, it would be show time.

When the travelers drifted into the restaurant he'd picked, Kaan already occupied a table for four, happily waving them in. Hand poised in midair, his eyes widened in confused recognition. Instead of a Turkish kiss, George got a glower, the couple simple *merhabas*, and for Safiye a somewhat formal "*Merhaba teyze Safiye . . . Hoş geldiniz . . . Nasilsiniz?*"

"*Çok iyimim, siz nasil?*" came her formality and then her hug. "You look good, nephew. I've missed you!"

A fifth chair was produced along with platters of *mezze*. Ignoring the dolma, stuffed olives, baba ganoush, and other delights before him, Kaan respectfully inquired "To what do we owe this honor, teyze Safiye?"

Hand on Kaan's shoulder, George explained. "Here's the deal. After you indicated to Safiye what we're up to, she went from being upset to demanding to take part. We begged her not to, we explained the risks but she insisted on being with you and driving us here. Her car will be essential to us. She'll take the role of distracting the audience. You'll still serve as cameraman. Neither of you should come under suspicion."

Still not mollified, Kaan lamented the risk to her and the operation. What had they been thinking, if not drinking?

Somewhat icily, the first woman to insert herself into the group spoke up. "Kaan, it was your idea that we stay with her that led to this. Her love for her country and for you did the rest. So here we are and, speaking for myself, I am glad she's with us. She's a great lady."

The man who had objected to that woman emitted a sigh and leaned back in his chair, avoiding her imploring gaze as George distractedly bit into an olive and Mahmoud twirled a dolma on a toothpick. Safiye dabbed her eyes with her napkin. "All right," he averred, "I know when I'm outgunned. If this is what you guys want, let's do this and make it work!"

"Well," Safiye sniffed, "I was half hoping you would refuse, . . ." but noticing Katrina's glare, continued ". . . just kidding. Now bring us up to date, *sevgili yeğenim*. We need to know everything you do."

Chapter Forty-Six

ANDREAS STOOD AT the balcony door staring meditatively at the shipping harbor, his wistfulness illuminated by an orange sunset skipping across its dark blue chop, one hand clutching a black sock. The sock, which he had come across cleaning their bedroom, belonged to Ivan. Vacuuming the floor, he had paused, thinking of the others. Since seeing them off on the ferry, just one brief text from George saying they had safely arrived. He had refrained from reaching out, telling himself they were fine, just preoccupied or neglectful. Still, he knew himself well enough to expect anxious musings before long. But there was no reason, he decided, not to say hello to his lover, and so rang up Ivan.

As usual, Ivan was delighted to hear from his inamorato. He had been fixing supper before finishing up some paperwork, he said, after which he would watch a Turkish sitcom for camp entertainment and language education, but tonight his television host had gone out. To the cinema, he'd said.

Trusting that Kaan wasn't available for good reason, Andreas got Ivan to recount what he'd been up to. Mostly work, essentially unrewarding, was the flat reply. Ivan threw back the question. Mostly housekeeping, Andreas said, admitting to boredom and horniness since they parted. The feeling was mutual, Ivan responded. Perhaps he hadn't met the right ones, but Turkish men seemed so . . . unapproachable. So, he urged, why not zip over to visit him? For a rollick. On him.

Entertaining Ivan's generous proposition, sporting a grin, Andreas said "That's quite irresistible." But quickly he realized that wouldn't do. Not on *this,* of all weekends, when his team was in action and he would have to edit footage. Thinking of Ivan there in the thick of things, he flipped the proposition. "Even though it would be great to see Bursa, I'm getting my salon ready to reopen next week. So how about you take a long weekend to visit here. Like after work tomorrow."

Ivan proved amenable. Upon arrival the next evening, they would meet at the Metro terminus and charge off to some dance clubs. After they signed off, Andreas congratulated himself on removing his friend from the fray. It would provide his team a temporary safe house and shield Ivan from newscasts—assuming his people were on track. To allay that anxiety, he decided to check in with Kaan and was gratified when he picked up the call.

"Andreas? Say hey! Great to hear your voice! Good timing too. The gang's all here!"

Kaan's cheery affect hinted that alcohol might also be present. "Where's here? What's going on?"

Kaan was, in fact, on his second Efes beer. "At a restaurant. Shall I introduce you? To my left is George, and to my right are Mahmoud and Katrina." Facing him sat someone he didn't mention.

Andreas wanted to be in the room, to hear about their journey, to know how they were feeling about things. Kaan passed the phone to George, who said both the voyage to Izmir and the trip to Bursa had gone smoothly, and that they occupied "anonymous lodgings." He handed off to Katrina, who gave Andreas a virtual tour of the performance venue. Mahmoud mentioned they would do a dress rehearsal tomorrow and asked Andreas how he was doing before activating the phone's speaker and laying it on the table.

Drolly, Andreas announced "There have been reports of two mysterious deaths that police believe may be homicides. Systemic poisoning is suspected. They are looking for witnesses who may have seen the victims' attackers, who are described as a tall man with a sandy ponytail and a man of medium build with long black hair, oh, and a woman with wavy blond hair. Can any of you recall seeing any such persons?"

When the chorus of chuckles dissipated, he admonished, "So why haven't you communicated? You know how I worry." Katrina immediately apologized. We had a lot going on, she explained. Our bad.

Suddenly a new voice: "Blame it on me for monopolizing their time. But we are all fine and pumped up, as they say."

"And who might you be?" asked the table.

"Oh hello. I'm Safiye, Kaan's aunt. On his mother's side. Very pleased to meet you."

The table's voice turned edgy. "Hey, what's going on?"

At which point George snatched up the phone and drifted to the back of the restaurant as Kaan's finger wagged. "Safiye *teyze*, you shouldn't have said that. He doesn't need to know about you." Like radicalism, loose lips seemed to run in his family, an inauspicious conjunction.

Safiye lowered her gaze in contrition. "I'm very sorry, *yeğenim*. I will be more careful."

George returned and handed Kaan his phone. "I told him the situation. He said he's okay with it. But listen to this: He convinced your roommate to visit him this weekend. He may be able to keep him there until Monday. That means your apartment is available for a day or two. We may not need it, but it gives us an option. What's your address."

Kaan scribbled on a napkin and passed it over. "It's a five-story concrete building with shops underneath, several blocks east of the Demirtaşpaşa Metro stop. Our flat is 502, five flights up. I also wrote down the code for the door locks. Where are you staying?"

"In a hotel," George tactfully replied. "You know how to reach us."

Throughout dinner Kaan struggled with the concept that his aunt was about to become his accomplice. Several times, he asked her to hang back, but she wouldn't hear of it. When he suggested that she drive the getaway car, George had other ideas. "I'll drive. She'll provide the distraction to free up Katrina, whom he advised to station herself near Mahmoud. "Assuming he isn't ID'ed as the shooter, try to block or distract anyone who might approach him." Addressing Mahmoud, "You mustn't break character. Take someone's arm as you leave, but not hers."

"And if he's spotted?" Katrina hesitantly asked.

"Try to misdirect their attention. You could pretend to panic and rush around like a clumsy fool. Stumble over chairs. Get in the way of pursuers. Buy him time, even if it means you get left behind."

"Fine, but suppose that isn't working. Then what?"

George cleared his throat and said "Look, if Mahmoud is caught, he—if not all of us—will be as good as dead. You already knew that. You must not allow him to be taken alive."

Mahmoud interrupted. "Wait a minute, George. There's not much she could do if they're after me. But I don't expect that."

"If your aim is true, he'll look to see where it came from. Before anyone knows what's going on, officers could pour into your area. What will you do?"

"I-I would ask what happened, because I can't see. And sit still."

"Sure, sharpshooter, but they might have their own ideas about you. If they try to take you away, it's Katrina's job to make sure you don't live to tell tales."

Through clenched teeth, Katrina inquired. "What do you mean?"

"How many darts did you bring?"

She glanced at Mahmoud. "Um, a bunch, including his two favorites. Why?"

"And enough of your substance to charge them?"

"Sure. More than enough. What about it?"

"Then carry an extra one that's ready to go. Wrap it up and keep it in your purse."

A plaintive glance to Mahmoud. "And do what with it?"

George's eyes flashed around the table. "It's obvious, isn't it?"

Safiye's mouth hung open. Kaan's tea glass levitated in midair. Mahmoud put his down and settled back in his chair. Katrina knit her eyes as George went on. "You need to get to him. If he's been shot or cornered use all your strength to stick him through his trousers. Pull it out and toss it away. Whisper goodbye and walk away."

He turned to Mahmoud. "You'll be interrogated but will say nothing except to demand a lawyer. Soon you'll be too weak to speak. Let's hope Paşa is in the same condition."

He deposited his tea and stared into his empty glass.

"I-if Mahmoud misses his shot," Safiye asked, "should she still do that?"

George looked up at her. "Hopefully not. If no one saw him shoot, he'll be okay. But if anyone did they could still go after him."

Mahmoud's eyes darted to Katrina and back to George. Leaning in, he hissed "I'm willing to die, but I won't allow Katrina to do that. If she's seen stabbing me she could be taken too. No, I'll just run for it. Let them gun me down and get it over with."

"Yes, do that, but I think she should still be prepared. In case you can't break free. As a last resort."

Safiye paid the tab in cash and a subdued five-some filed out to greet the urban evening. Dismissing the depressing subject, Safiye suggested finding a market to buy food for the next couple of days. On the next block Katrina noticed Mahmoud had lagged behind and circled back to find him gazing into a shop window that displayed men's clothing. "You know," he said, pointing to a fedora with a narrow brim, like ones retired men and hipsters affect, "I would like a hat, a gentleman's hat like that white one there. It would complement my disguise, don't you think?"

"Ooh, definitely," she replied. "Let's go in and try it on."

Inside, he asked the clerk to show it to him and found that it fit nicely. "Very smart," Katrina told him admiringly. "You'll be dressed to kill." It was closing time, and the clerk was eager to complete the sale and go home. Taking advantage of his impatience, Mahmoud bargained the price down by a quarter.

Hat in bag, they took after the group, now out of sight. Rather than blindly search, Katrina called George to find them filling a basket in a *bakkal* nearby. "Buy a lemon, please," she instructed. "I'll need that. Oh, and some strong coffee. Tea doesn't quite do it for me."

They loitered by the haberdashery as the shopkeeper locked up and dashed off, taking note of passersby, savoring their moment of solitude. "Suppose we could go anywhere we wanted after this is over," he said, draping his arm upon her shoulders, "where would it be?"

She cast her eyes upward in thought past amber streetlights to the charcoal haze above. "Back to Piraeus, I guess, at least for a while. Then I'd like to visit my family, like I told Penelope I was doing."

"With or without me?"

"Oh, with you of course. I was taking that for granted. Wouldn't you like to see Switzerland?"

"Sure, if they'll let me in."

"We'll have to see, but I want so much for you to meet my parents, my brother, and the rest of our little clan. My parents are in Basel, but I have an aunt and uncle who live in the mountains. It's beautiful up there. I'll bet they already have snow."

Noting a man with a beard and *taqiyah* approaching, Mahmoud slipped his arm off her shoulders. "I would like that," he said. "if George doesn't have other plans for me."

"Would that interest you?"

"I don't know. I'm not sure I want to be a career assassin."

"You told me you believed Allah wanted you to do this. Did that change?"

"I did think that. I thought it every step I took away from Mosul. But not any more. After all, who am I to say what Allah wants besides devotion and obedience?"

"Is that all? All you want?"

"The only other thing I want right now is you. And to find a place for us. A place where we can build something. But I have no idea what or where that would be."

George and Safiye emerged from the darkness laden with grocery sacks. Kaan had slipped into the Metro. The four of them piled into the Fiat and George threaded it back to the hotel. They would arise before dawn and devote the day to rehearsing their moves—but not at the mosque, full of workers and watchers. They would use the space that Kaan had found, which he had said was very large.

Before retiring—Safiye and Katrina to share the bedroom, the two men the daybed—they decided to put on a fashion show. George, whose only change of clothes consisted of a shirt, jacket, socks and underwear, declined to participate. He asked to borrow Safiye's car key and Katrina's pocket knife, saying he had something to do outside and not to wait up for him.

Soon, was Safiye modeling an ankle-length purple dress and a plain black headscarf. From Safiye's wardrobe Katrina had picked out a black dress of modest length with sleeves, dark stockings and tan flats, and a forest green silk scarf to cloak her blondness. Mahmoud in his white coat and shirt, red tie, and black trousers was pronounced elegant, save for his sensible running shoes. Raking his new hat and donning dark glasses, he giddily showed off by hoisting his cane and tapping about the room, clumsily avoiding a chair here and a person there.

"You will be a big hit, Mister Assassin," Katrina cooed. "So here's an accessory for your wardrobe." From her handbag she extracted a little prayer cap, a traditional men's *taqiyah,* embroidered in black and gold. "Wear it under your hat," she said, handing it over. "After you shoot, leave the hat behind. You'll be harder to pick out in the crowd."

"Not a bad idea," he said, running the cap through his fingers. "Where did you get this?"

"I pinched it from that men's shop while you were closing the deal," she said. "Took another for Kaan to wear and then take off when he takes off. It's red or course. Probably shouldn't have, but I just couldn't help myself."

"Thanks. God is great. I hope he forgives you."

She gazed into his dark eyes. "Go with God, love. Just not all the way to paradise. Not yet."

Chapter Forty-Seven

IN THE DAMP of a misty dawn, a pair of athletic shoes slipped over a windowsill as four chilly figures loitered in the gloom. Presently a door opened and they filed into a cavernous space littered with dim objects. The shoes' owner switched on a bank of fluorescent lights that revealed the objects to be a forklift, two small earthmovers, metal drums, and scattered stacks of building materials.

"Believe it or not, this room is bigger than the plaza behind the mosque," Kaan told them. Pointing out chalk marks he'd scratched on the cement floor, he said with a sweeping flourish, "This is a full-size outline of the plaza." His rough rectangle nearly filled the room, interrupted where it intersected the occasional immovable object. "I marked the three stairways with these rounded rectangles. The garage doors represent the rear entrance to the mosque. The octagon shape over there is the fountain kiosk, and the square in front of it is the speaker's stand." He'd also marked the inner extent of the colonnade by spotting X's more or less where its pillars stood.

He sprinted to a back corner and returned with an oblong cardboard box about two meters long by half a meter square and stood it on the chalk square. Near the top each side of the box was a circle of chalk about twenty centimeters wide. Capping it with a block of wood for stability, he said "There's your target, Mahmoud. Try to hit it from a few different places."

George's voice echoed at them. "I don't like this. What if someone comes in?"

"Don't worry," asserted their impresario. "Nobody uses this place. There's been a lull in construction. I've been here four or five times and nobody was ever around. So places, everybody." He herded them to the far front corner. George hung back, gripping a length of copper pipe he'd picked up, but when it started to chill his hands he decided it wouldn't be of much use and laid it down.

"Walk up the steps next to you," Kaan told Mahmoud. "Cross over to the colonnade on the other side and sit on that wooden crate I put there. Katrina, come in and station yourself near Mahmoud. You need a good view and access to him afterward. Next, I enter and stand on that triangle near the front. Safiye, you're last. Go to that little circle behind me. George, of course, is parked somewhere across Dikkaldırım Street." George was currently parked by the doorway, anxiety fueling his motor.

"Wait," Mahmoud said. "Safiye, before we start, tell us again the program."

Safiye took from her purse notes she'd scribbled summarizing the order of events: Participants are scanned at the mosque's front door and the adults proceed to the courtyard to seats in front. Dignitaries, including the President, enter and take their seats. The children file in and stand before the spectators. Someone will rise to welcome all and introduce the Imam, who'll introduce the mayor, who'll make remarks and welcome the President, his entourage, and local officials. After the Imam offers prayers, the President will speak and present a Qur'an embossed with a presidential seal and a certificate to each child as his or her name is called out.

"Everyone got that?" importuned the master of ceremonies. "On your marks! Get Ready! *Gelsiniz*!" Mahmoud entered the chalk rectangle, tapped his way to his crate of honor and settled down. As the other three took their places, Mahmoud twisted the cane's handle off and dropped it in his jacket pocket. Laying the cane on his lap, he pulled and pocketed the stopper from the rubber tip, and sat at the ready.

"Mahmoud," Kaan instructed, "you'll cue Safiye by slowly lifting your cane straight up. Safiye, immediately scream that your purse is gone. Make a fuss looking for it but don't stand up. This is when Mahmoud must shoot. As soon as he does, Katrina, call George so he knows what is going on."

George's voice ricocheted at them. "Hold on! Katrina, do not phone or text me. The police will later read call logs. The whole time, except for Kaan's, phones stay in the car, all shut down."

"You're right, George," Kaan agreed, "and before tomorrow, let's kill all our call and text records."

"Good idea," came the echo, despite George's uncertainty about whether that could help.

"So, Kaan continued, "Mahmoud, sit tight if you can. If a spectator wants to escort you out, accept the offer. Don't tap when someone is guiding you. Okay? Then get ready . . . GO!"

As echoes of Safiye's scream died away, Mahmoud propelled a dart into the box just outside the target circle. They regrouped for two more takes, but Mahmoud missed his third shot and wanted to keep practicing. For the next ten minutes he went through his motions from different locations, as Katrina dashed about collecting spent ammunition. Though still not satisfied, he said his aim was as good as it was going to get and announced he was ready to go. They followed Kaan to the side door to head over to his apartment for breakfast. Ivan was by now at work, and at day's end would head directly for Athens and Andreas.

Kaan had just clicked the shed's door closed when a gruff voice announced "*Durun! Kimsiniz?*" He turned to see a security guard, demanding to know what they were doing in his building. Kaan cheerfully explained that they were an amateur theater group who had been using the big space to rehearse a production of Shakespeare's *Julius Caesar*. "The acoustics in there are great," he bubbled. "I hope you don't mind. We didn't disturb anything."

"You can't use this building," the guard barked. "It's private property." From the look of them, he must have concluded they were a harmless bunch, because he simply ordered them away and not to return.

They traipsed through the muddy construction site with George muttering "I told you so. You better go back later and erase those chalk marks." Withholding consent, Kaan showed them to his building's back door that he'd propped open and led them up fire stairs to his flat.

Over tea, toasts, black olives, slices of tomato, and white cheese they gave voice to concerns about tomorrow. Aside, of course, from getting Mahmoud out alive they all agreed the loosest end was where to drive to. Kaan suggested that if no one pursued them they could come back to his place where they could monitor TV news. Once they knew what the authorities were up to they could plan their travels accordingly. George preferred to head toward Izmir as directly and soon as possible.

"What if my car is identified?" Safiye asked. "If they have the numbers, we're kaput."

"Taken care of," George said, idly rotating his fork in his stubby fingers. "Your license plates are in the trunk."

"Why did you do that, George? I can't drive around without plates."

"You're not. Last night I went out and got you new ones. Found a car a few blocks away and took off its plates. Then I pulled the plates from another car and replaced them with the first set and put its plates on your car. Later, I'll put yours back on and ditch the stolen ones. Standard procedure."

Mahmoud's main concern was whether all of them could gain entrance. "If it comes to that, I'm sort of dispensable," Katrina offered.

"Not so fast," said George. Aren't you forgetting something?"

She glanced at Mahmoud and lowered her eyes. "Oh yeah, that." That which they hadn't rehearsed. The unthinkable that. "Sorry. Of course I need to be there."

"We all need to be there," Mahmoud said. "But I definitely must get in, so let's go down there when we're done talking."

"I hope you know what you're doing," George said. "The less attention you call to yourself, the better."

"Understood, but if my idea works out, fewer people will notice me. Let me tell you . . ."

The man with dark glasses and a white cane stepped gingerly across the threshold of the Mihraplı Mosque and stopped to orient himself. He hesitantly tapped toward a voice that greeted him until his cane blundered into a claw foot of an ornate desk. "*Afedersiniz bayim memuru,*" he replied. "Can you please tell me how I might attend the Qu'ranic ceremony tomorrow?"

The official lifted his eyes from the book he was reading and peered over his glasses at the neatly dressed stranger to ask "Perhaps. Are you a family member or a spectator?"

"*Hiyer, bayim memuru,* I am neither of those things. I am a scholar of comparative religion from Baghdad visiting your fine city to attend a symposium. When I heard of tomorrow's proceedings, I knew I must come." Before his interlocutor could reply, he continued. "President Paşa will officiate, I am told. I have come to greatly admire this man. He is, I believe, a bold and wise leader, if not a world-historic figure. To witness him here tomorrow would most gratify me, and so I ask for your kind assistance. Would you allow me to enter early? You see, I don't do well in crowds."

"*Effendim, ben görüyorum,*" the *memur* acknowledged. "Well, I don't suppose one more body would be a problem. I will add you to the list of guests who will enter through the main door. What did you say your name was?"

Trying not to move his eyes while thinking, Mahmoud replied "My name is Hassan, Doktor Akhmed Hassan." He was honoring his brother and his mother by using his first and her maiden name.

"*Çok iyi, bayim Hassan,* I will list you. Please be at the gate to the park no later than one PM. After you announce yourself to the officials out front, you will pass through security and through these doors. I will have someone escort you to the courtyard."

"*Çok teşekkür ederim, bayim memuru,*" Mahmoud effused. "You are most kind. I do not wish to be in the way and prefer to sit to the side, where I'll feel safer."

"The six rows in front are all reserved but not those in the colonnade. Just tell whoever attends you that you wish to sit in the colonnade. Can you see at all?"

"Outdoors, I can see dim blobs, and with a magnifier can make out print if the light is strong enough." Touching his black glasses, he added "My cataracts make me very sensitive to glare."

"Very well, then. We will look for you tomorrow."

Thanking the official again, Mahmoud turned and followed his cane outside, past barricades and magnetometers already being put in place and out the main gate to stand at the curb, where shortly a voice asked "May I help you to cross the street, sir?" He assented with a nod and Katrina took his arm to pilot him to the far shore of the broad avenue. "I'm in," he whispered unnecessarily. "Add to my list of names one Akhmed Hassan."

CHAPTER FORTY-EIGHT

MAHMOUD AWOKE BEFORE first light to slip from the bed as George slept and showered in hot lather with a cold rinse. He chose not to shave, having decided regrowing a beard was an idea whose time had come. His ablution refreshed but failed to wash away his grim unease. Wrapped in a bathrobe, he took the bath mat into the kitchenette and knelt in prayer. After reciting his *rak'ahs*, he rinsed yesterday's mud off his shoes, donned his costume, placed a neatly folded white handkerchief in the breast pocket of his jacket, took up his cane, and took to the street for an early morning constitutional.

A little later, also robed, Katrina made the kitchenette her workshop. Accompanied by snores from the daybed, she wiggled her digits into surgical gloves. From a canister of tea she had imported, she extricated a rubber stopper and a glassine packet of rolled-up strips of paper. From a pack of Marlboros, she withdrew two cigarettes and ripped them open over the sink to extract a sharpened bamboo stick from each, over which she fitted snug paper collars. She worked one of the bamboo shafts into a hole in the top of the stopper, which had been smoothly abraded to resemble a bullet, and held it up for inspection. She then drew about fifty cc's of water into a juice glass. With her pocket knife, she quartered the lemon she'd asked for, juiced one piece into a saucer, scraped away seeds and bits of pulp, and added the juice to the water. Removing the lid of a small amber jar, she withdrew a small vial from its cotton-ball nest and emptied its contents into the glass. With a plastic spoon, she gingerly swirled the whitish granules until she couldn't see them any more. Gently, she lowered her dart, tip first, into the cloudy liquid and set the glass aside. *I apologize if the lemon stings, Mister President. I had to use it to dissolve your medicine.*

From her handbag came a tube of Mentos. Carefully unfolding the foil wrapper on one end, she gently squeezed out all but four of the candy disks onto the counter, and neatly stacked three of them. Bottom first, she pressed the second bamboo shaft into her little tower, fitted it with a collar, and with mordant eyes gently lowered the business end of her assembly into the soaking glass. As the miniature missiles absorbed their payload she blotted her eyes with her sleeve, suddenly aware that she was hyperventilating. *Madam, if you could find out but a man to bear a poison, I would temper it; that Romeo should, upon receipt thereof soon sleep in quiet.*

After a decent interval, she removed the rubber dart from the glass and set it on a paper towel inside the cupboard under the sink. Plucking up the minty missile, she slowly worked it into the candy wrapper, taking care not to crush the foil, coaxing it down until its sharp tip was out of sight. Sniffling, she twisted shut the wrapper and gently angled her ultimate refreshment down into the inside pocket of her handbag. *Come, gentle night, come, loving, black-brow'd night, Give me my Romeo; and, when he shall die, take him and cut him out in little stars, and he will make the face of heaven so fine that all the world will be in love with night and pay no worship to the garish sun.*

Her preparations complete, she emptied the glass into the sink drain and meticulously washed it, wiped down the kitchen, and bagged her little vial, spoon, and gloves. In the bathroom, she scrubbed her hands, washed dried tears from her face, and went to dress for Pyrrhic success, leaving the kitchenette to Safiye to rustle up a Turkish breakfast with tea brewed from Katrina's stash and coffee for the Swiss.

George was taking tea by the time Mahmoud returned from his stroll. The Iraqi seemed rattled, relating how a police patrol car had passed by as he tapped along the sidewalk practicing his gait, spooking him sufficiently to pretend an apartment complex was his destination. After the car moved on, he tapped back as fast as he dared. The minor incident concerned George. He worried that if later Mahmoud's description were to be broadcast, the policeman might remember him and connect him to this neighborhood. As company commander, he ordered them to clear out from the hotel that morning, and without argument after breakfast they dressed and packed up.

Mahmoud told them to sit tight while he armed his weapon. With a damp washcloth, he wiped down his cane, pulled off its rubber tip, removed its rubber stopper and wiped down both items. Protruding two centimeters from the stopper was a roofing nail he had stuck clean through it. His spectators might not have noted a small loop of monofilament dangling from the head of nail that would serve to yank it out. After reinserting the stopper and setting the ferrule on its base, he twisted and pulled off the cane's wooden grip and wiped it down. Sighting down the empty pipe, he inserted a ramrod improvised from a straightened coat hanger bulked up with layers of dampened toilet tissue and reamed out the dried spittle and debris left from shooting practice, swabbing it again with fresh tissue to dry it.

After snugging the stopper with the nail into the cane's hollowed-out ferrule, he donned rubber gloves and retrieved Katrina's armed dart from its lair. Centering the hole in the base of the dart over the nail, he made an assembly that he wiggled into the cane. He reattached the handle, inverted the cane, and shook it to assure himself that his missile was well secured. Bending his ramrod into a bundle, he deposited it and his gloves in Katrina's garbage bag and tied it up. "Okay," he told them, "we can go now."

Safiye checked them out at eleven. They packed their things into the trunk and George piloted the Fiat through a confusion of one-way streets and congestion that congealed as they neared the mosque. Forty minutes after they'd set forth came a lucky parking spot several blocks from the complex. Nobody broke the edgy silence as Mahmoud steeled himself to be on his own. In the awkward manner of a boy being sent off on his first train trip, he hugged everyone, adjusted the *taqiyah* Katrina had presented, and got out with hat and cane.

"The next time we are together," he said, donning his fedora, "the world will have turned toward the sun."

They watched him tap down the street. *"Başaracaksın, İnşallah!"* Safiye cried from her window.

Shortly after he faded from view, the others exited the car and walked to the avenue to encounter a great murmur of people clustered around the main entrance, spilling out into the street and down the sidewalk directly across from them. Looking for Kaan, Katrina jumped up on low wall to get a better view. She picked him out near the back of the disorderly queue, looking one way and the next.

"This is bad," Kaan said when they came up to him. "Almost two hours to go, and there must be hundreds of people before us. They all can't get in."

"I knew we should have left earlier," moaned Safiye.

"No, this is better," George replied. "Less exposure this way. Less chance we'll get eyeballed hanging around."

To their left, they saw that Mahmoud in the line of happy families clustered at the VIP security gate. They watched him inch forward, converse with a man sitting at a table, get wanded, and tap his way into the grounds.

George had been observing traffic patterns and told them what to expect. "I think we can still meet at corner by that apothecary. Look up the streets that meet there for the car. Jump in and we'll head toward the D200. Be there with nobody in pursuit. I don't want to go looking for anyone. And by the way, Safiye, aren't you planning to make a scene about your purse being snatched?"

"Why, yes. Should I not?"

He touched the handbag she had absent-mindedly brought with her. "No, do it by all means, but unless you actually plan to lose it, maybe you should let me put it in the trunk with our sleeping phones." A sheepish Safiye handed it over.

George grimly surveyed the milling throng near the entrance. "All three of you have to make your way closer if your going to get in. Do what it takes." Adding he would come back if he found out anything they needed to know, he stuffed Safiye's handbag under his jacket and went off to reconnoiter.

Kaan had a strategy. He told the ladies he would edge through the crowd, excusing himself while discreetly calling out a woman's name, and dubbed Katrina Fatma. When she heard *"Neredesin* Fatma?" she was to work her way toward him tugging Safiye, who would pretend to be disoriented and in need of minding. Along the way, Katrina should respond here I am; I am coming with *"Buradayım! Geliyorum!"*

After Kaan plunged in, Katrina chanted "boo-ra-die-yim, gel-ee-yor-um" under her breath twenty times, then ducked into the crowd clutching Safiye's wrist. Just two calls and three responses did the trick. Almost half way through the throng the women spotted Kaan. With a final "Michael, boo-ra-die-yim," Katrina touched Kaan's arm, adding to his dismay the unnecessary "gel-ee-yor-um." Ignoring her faux pas, he motioned them to stay put and slowly edged forward to melt into the flock of the faithful. With a hand squeeze and a "See you later," Katrina followed suit. Watching her trail away, for the first time in quite a while Safiye mouthed a prayer.

Chapter Forty-Nine

POLICE OFFICIALS STARTED admitting spectators at ten minutes after one. As Turks tend to queue in a clump, everyone immediately surged forward, compressing those in front. Ten minutes later Kaan was being wanded, holding up his phone. Halfway up the grand staircase he peered back to see Katrina being admitted. The human tide wafted him onto the plaza and down the aisle to note the phalanx of well-groomed families occupying the first few rows. He secured a seat near the aisle four rows behind them that he deemed sufficient for his purposes, and stood by his chair to scan the scene. Directly in front of the fountain, a raised lectern with a single step on both sides, a dozen or so empty chairs arcing before it. To its right, under the colonnade, two rows of empty chairs awaited officiants. To his left, he spied the sleeve of a white coat, the rest of it obscured by a pillar. *Must be.*

Holding his phone high, he panned through a full circle, narrating for the benefit of his editors abroad. Donning earbuds and taking his seat, he replayed the take and judged it good enough. A flash of white in his peripheral vision alerted him to Mahmoud in his dark glasses and white hat leaning past his pillar, his head turned toward him. Kaan gave a nod and looked for the Swiss miss. There she was, sitting in the colonnade next to the filigreed railing, three or four meters from Mahmoud. *Places everybody.*

Wishing he's brought a handkerchief, he wiped his sweating brow with his sleeve while hyperventilating, just as a portly man with a red fez and billowy Ottoman tunic and pants strode past and stood to the right of the podium behind two tall drums. Another man, this one in a grey business suit, emerged from the mosque, walked briskly down the aisle, and gestured to the Ottoman, who then commenced to drum in a slow, syncopated beat. The procession began, headed by an Imam attired in a brown gold-trimmed robe and a white cylindrical hat. Men in sober suits and several similarly subdued women followed, now and then nodding to audience members as they paraded down the aisle to establish themselves in the reserved seats opposite Mahmoud. The last one to file past walked alone. It was the only man he recognized, and it made his heart shiver. *I see thee before me, for the first and last time!* Kaan followed his progress camera arm upraised, unwilling to stand while all others were seated.

Mahmoud had discreetly slid his folding chair back to keep anyone from standing behind him. He now edged it ahead to the scant shelter of his pillar. Tilting forward, hands on knees, cane between them, he surreptitiously scanned the audience. He couldn't make out Safiye, but noted Kaan holding up his camera. Had he dared to peek to the side he would have seen Katrina sitting well to his right and become anxiously aware of the gendarme in fatigues standing behind her, a semi-automatic slung across his back, surveying the audience.

To diminished drumbeats, a man with glasses, beard, and *taqiyah* atop his bald head, came from the mosque shepherding a double file of well-scrubbed children, youngest first. They paced forward chanting in Turkish: "We are the future, the hope of the Turkish Republic. With the blessing of Allah, we will serve its people," to array themselves before the podium. The man with glasses ascended to the podium to welcome them, their families, the distinguished guests, the spectators, and made a flourish of introducing the Mullah. The holy man whisked through a prayer, blessed the students, and thanked the dignitaries for gracing his historic *cami*. The bald man, apparently head of religious education, retook the podium to say a few words about his program and then introduced the Mayor of

Bursa, who effused over the mosque's role in the community. Then he was introducing the main man, praising him with more words than necessary for his prodigious promotion of religious education. To enthusiastic applause, the President ascended the dais, unfolded some notes, and drank from a sea of adulation.

As the clapping subsided, the children standing before him burst into screechy song—not the Turkish National Anthem, but a heroically melodic ode to the President that he personally had commissioned the previous year. As they chorused, Mahmoud twisted off his cane's handle, palming it into his jacket pocket. Extracting the retaining plug from the mouthpiece, he dropped it in the other pocket and folded his hands over the tube. The youths soldiered through two choruses and stood at attention. As applause again rang out, the president smiled, raised his hands for quiet and looked down at his notes.

Mahmoud stiffened his spine and ventilated his chest cavity, wiped his clammy palms on his trousers, and gazed darkly toward the podium, struck by how much smaller his bull's-eye seemed than he'd envisioned. If he aimed for the neck, the dart might hit skull or starched collar and bounce off. He decided to aim for shoulder. If the dart came in low it could still enter the bicep. And if those sleeves were armored? A sudden breeze from behind that fluttered his hat blew away the thought, a tailwind that might possibly help. He seated his fedora just as the President began to orate.

His plan was to signal Safiye when the President was in full throat, but scarcely thirty seconds had passed when a cry of *"Dursin! Dursin!"* echoed through the colonnade, followed by *"Çantam nerede? Hırsızı durdur!"* Evidently, Safiye had jumped the gun. The President paused and looked toward the disturbance, which continued quite audibly with *"Benim param! Benim telefonum! Heyhat!"* Mahmoud filled his lungs, telling himself *Take it easy. Make it smooth.*

His cane rested at an acute angle between his legs. Fluidly raising it to his lips, he leveled it just above the President's shoulder. Then a slight pop as his missile launched on its ten-meter journey. By the time it reached its final destination he was tucking the tube between his legs, head down, armpits trickling, brow glistening. *How could anyone not have seen that?*

He looked up to see the President's left hand touching his right coat sleeve. Through his shades he couldn't be sure if anything protruded, but it seemed a definite hit. The President shot a glance in his direction, then looked left, saying something indistinct before blundering down to the floor. Mahmoud could see him gesturing as murmurs echoed through the colonnade, and resolved to sit still in feigned ignorance. Suddenly he remembered that his cane was topless. Hoping all eyes were fixed on the President, he plucked its handgrip from his pocket and nestling it in his palms, worked it in.

Several spectators rose to their feet in curiosity. At someone's request, the bald man in the taqiyah addressed the children and started shooing them back down the aisle. Men in suits were gathering around the president, one of them gesturing in Mahmoud's general direction. The gendarme on his right started edging along the railing toward him. Unaware of his approach, Mahmoud leaned to the bearded man to his left and in Turkish asked "What just happened? Why did he stop talking?" As the gentleman started to reply, a commotion. Reaching for his weapon while boosting himself onto the balustrade, the gendarme seemed to lose his footing. He pitched backward, toppled three meters down to the driveway, and fell on his rifle, discharging it. Mahmoud startled and instinctively swiveled toward the sound to see Katrina on her knees peering down through the balustrade before remembering to correct his demeanor.

Hardly anyone in the plaza had witnessed the officer's mishap, but they all heard the report and did not take comfort. Half the audience was now on its feet, gestating rumors, preparing to bolt. Chairs were shoved aside as people scurried for exits, some doing duck walks. Others crouched in their seats as passengers on a plummeting plane. Mahmoud could see men clearing barricades from the rear staircase as a knot of security agents and gendarmes proceeded to escort the President him toward it. In the midst of mounting hysteria stood Kaan on a chair, capturing it on video.

Bending down, Mahmoud removed his fedora to reveal his black taqiyah. He tossed the hat under his seat just as a hand touched his shoulder and a soft voice said "Time to go, sir." There was Katrina, wide-eyed, grimacing. "Stay low and follow me." He hunkered down and shuffled after her, wishing his cane were a witch's broom. Katrina was being absorbed by a milling mob attempting to crowd into the mosque. Mahmoud followed her, hobbling along under the colonnade. Just after he passed the west staircase, a half dozen police in riot gear charged up it and fanned into the plaza. As Mahmoud duck walked, someone grabbed his arm. Heart racing, he stiffened with dread.

"Here, sir, let me take you," said a voice in Turkish. Mahmoud recognized him as the man he had sat near and gave thanks. "I believe this belongs to you," the man said, seating the hat that he'd left behind on his head, slightly askew.

"Çok teşekkürler," was Mahmoud's thankful reply, and with lowered head he allowed the man to guide him forward, through the massive doors to the sanctum within, buzzing with attendees wading forward. For better or worse, Katrina seemed not to be among them. Ushering him to the main entrance and past its now memur-less desk, the gentleman held open the door. Mahmoud delicately stepped over its high threshold onto the sun-swept porch. Pressed from behind, they proceeded down the stone stairway to the grassy park, from whence a murmuring crowd spilled into the street.

"We are out in front," his shepherd informed him. Where do you need to go?"

As Mahmoud struggled to compose a response, Katrina tripped up to seize his other arm, exclaiming "Merhaba Akhmed! geliyorum!" in her best Turkish.

Mahmoud returned the pleasantry, praised Allah, and told his escort that this person was his helper and would guide him from here. With profuse thanks he wished him good fortune as he was towed away.

"When I saw you with an escort I hung back and followed," she said *sotto voce.* "I worried that someone would come after you. Luckily, nobody did, but let's get the hell out of here."

Pressing forward, Katrina, dust marks on her dress, and Mahmoud, hat in hand, took in the scene. At the main gate, officers were profiling and pulling people aside for interviews. Before them was the VIP gate, manned by a pair of guards. Mahmoud released himself from her grip and tapped forward. He brushed one of them, excusing himself with "*Afedersiniz*," and inquired as to the way out. Giving him a cursory look-over, the officer set him off toward it as if releasing a wind-up toy.

Mahmoud passed through the portal and slipped into the crowd. He turned to see Katrina being let out and stood quietly in wait. A milling multitude blocked their view of the assigned meeting point across the intersection. Katrina guided him toward a less densely populated spot, whereupon a scarfed woman thrust a microphone at him, inquiring in Turkish "Here we have a blind gentleman coming out. Sir, what was it like for you in there?" Mahmoud froze in place for a good five seconds before Katrina yanked him away, whispering "*Scheisse!* You could be on national TV?"

To connect with George they had to cross the street clotted with evacuees and onlookers. At the median strip they saw no sign of him or the Fiat. Upon reaching the parallel street, Katrina spotted the car in the parking lot of an apartment house. Somewhat more rapidly than they should have, they paced to the sedan and clambered into the back seat, almost squashing Kaan.

"C'mon, let's get out of here!" she urged.

"Wait. Safiye's missing!" Kaan said. "Did you see her?"

They hadn't. Across the avenue, the remaining spectators were still queued to be metered through the gate. "I'll try to find her," Kaan said, jumping out before George could stop him. He yelled out his window "Hurry! Don't talk to cops!" as Kaan jogged away. The street they were on was unobstructed, but that avenue of escape might not last for long.

"I saw her when she yelled," Katrina said. "After, I saw a cop heading her way, but then things happened fast and I lost track."

"Do you think they detained her?" asked Mahmoud.

"What for? Losing her stuff?"

George turned around to face them. "Worst case, they take her for questioning if they suspect she was a plant."

"What kind of plant?" Mahmoud asked, thinking of trees.

"You know, someone used to distract or disrupt. Exactly what she was. As we say, *suç ortağı.*"

A helmeted motorcycle policeman bristling with cop gear pulled up to the curb about five meters away. He glanced in their direction, dismounted, and then leaned against his steed to survey the scene across the street.

"*Bok!*" George cursed. "I'm moving us away."

"Wait," Mahmoud said. "How are they gonna find us?"

"I'll take a chance and text him. Get your heads down!"

His passengers awkwardly slumped onto the seat cushion. George put the car in gear and crept onto the street. The cop regarded their departure over his shoulder, and in the mirror George observed him jotting something down. "Don't look now, but I think he copied our license tags," he said with a sly smirk. "Lot of good that will do him."

George eased the car up the narrow street cordoned off from the avenue by a broad, vegetated median, halting in a muddy parking lot two blocks away. "Keep down. Take a nap," he told the couple and then dispatched a text message.

Kaan stood near the main gate watching people dribble out. She might yet be forthcoming, but the compound was by now primarily populated by men in paramilitary and other uniforms. He moved on. Approaching the VIP entrance, still flanked by two policemen, his phone tingled to signify George's whereabouts, which he noted but chose not to acknowledge. Some people were gathered in the walled park and the portico above it, but not her. After loitering nervously for what seemed eons, his impatience was

Geoffrey Dutton

rewarded when one of the front doors opened to emit a somewhat fazed Safiye. She appeared not to notice his wave as she descended the steps and approached the gate. He retreated into the shelter of bystanders as she spoke to the guards, who let her pass. "*Neredesin Fatma!*" he softly called, "Fatma *neredesin!*"

Chapter Fifty

A T THE END of the block George turned left and took Hayran Street to a confluence of roadways and headed north as Safiye cowered in the passenger seat, her handbag firmly pressed between her legs. "I went through so much over losing it, and now I'm so happy to have it," she whimpered, fondling her phone. "My whole life is in there."

Kaan leaned forward. "What exactly did you go through, Teyze Safiye."

"A-a gendarme came over after I shouted, wanting to help. Then all hell broke loose and he ran away. But on my way out he stopped me and asked if I wanted to file a report."

"Great," Katrina said. "Just what you wanted. And then?"

"He asked for my name, address, and phone number in case my purse turned up. It put me on the spot. I wasn't ready with an answer."

George's eyes flicked right. "So what did you say?"

"I made something up. Said I was from out of town. Gave my parents' old address in Antalya."

"Bad idea, he responded. "What about your name?"

"I just made up one—Aysel Balci I think I said, oh, and I told him I can never remember my cell phone number."

"Good girl."

"How come you didn't leave right then?" asked Mahmoud.

"I wanted to, but the crowd was thick. The policeman insisted I'd had enough stress and escorted me into the mosque so I could go out the VIP gate."

"So nice of him," George sighed.

"But in the front lobby were two more policeman and a detective."

"They question you?"

"Oh yes. Asked me the same questions. I think I was able to give the same answers."

"You think."

"I must have. And they asked why I had come there."

George sucked in air. "And you said . . ."

"Said I was on holiday, which I sort of am, and the usual nonsense about wanting to see the Great One. After that they let me go."

He exhaled. "You had us worried. Except for the real address, you did well."

At the D-200 highway George blended into traffic heading west. Safiye asked Mahmoud what it had been like for him.

"It all happened so fast. I must have hit him, but I don't know if it penetrated. I thought they'd spotted me and wanted to run. Then that gunshot, maybe at me. It was all I could do to sit still. What was that?"

"I don't know," Kaan said. "I was hoping one of you could tell me."

"Blame me," Katrina said, removing her headscarf.

"What do you mean?" Mahmoud asked.

"It came from down on the driveway. From an assault rifle that belonged to a guy I bumped into."

"What guy?"

"A gendarme in a combat gear. He had stood behind me, rifle slung across his back."

"Oh, yes, I saw him there," Kaan observed.

"So after you plugged the President and things got weird, he started moving toward you, along the railing. It worried me, so I stalked him. Then he started to get up on the railing, so I thought I should help him."

"Help him up?"

"No, down. I pretended to stumble, rolled over, pushed on his leg, and over he went. I think he landed on his gun and it went off. Didn't expect that. I just wanted him out of there."

"How were you able to do that?" Safiye asked. "To a gendarme, even."

"I'm out of practice, but the move came naturally. My sport used to be martial arts."

"Did he die?"

"Hope not. I guess we'll find out."

Kaan was staring at his phone, replaying his movie. "I didn't catch you boosting that gendarme," he said, "not that we'd want to show that. But I did get Paşa getting stung. You can't see what hit him, only his reaction."

"And then what?" Mahmoud asked. "Let me see."

He replayed the scene for the couple. "That's Safiye calling out. Paşa looks up. Now she yells again and he looks toward her. One, two, three, four—there: he grabs his arm, looks confused. Turns to his right. A couple people look that way, not many. He turns back, mumbles, and stumbles down to the floor. There's the Mayor trying to steady him. Then they huddle."

"What were people around you saying?" Mahmoud asked. "Did they think something hit him?"

"Nothing like that. You hear a woman near me ask what's going on, and a man tells her that maybe he had a heart attack."

"There's the gunshot," said Katrina. The video wobbled about in a blur of motion.

"It startled me," Kaan said. "I looked around and forgot what I was doing. When I remembered, I turned around to show the audience reacting. Some people duck down, others get up to leave,"

The view panned back to the podium. Mahmoud narrated. "Men come from behind Paşa. They surround him and then lead him out the back. Gendarmes charge up the steps."

Katrina said "You don't see anything Mahmoud does. That's good."

George wasn't so sure. "Maybe. Who knows how many other pictures were taken there? Our assassin may be in any number of them. Girlfriend too."

Katrina glanced at Mahmoud. "You should change your clothes."

"All of you should," said George. "I'll get off the highway so you can dump what you're wearing. We need petrol too."

"Then where, George?" Kaan asked. "To my place?"

"I don't know," George said. "Before I decide, I want to know what's being reported. Safiye, find some news on the radio."

George pulled over to the side of a Petrol Ofisi station and unlatched the trunk. Mahmoud and the women took to the rest rooms with their traveling clothes, swiftly returning with their costumes stuffed into plastic bags. They found the Fiat at a gas pump and Kaan purchasing drinks inside the station for their parched palates. He scrambled back in, imploring "Get us out of here, George. They're looking for Mahmoud!"

"How do you know?" George said. "All the radio said was that there was a possible attack on the President."

"It's worse than that," Kaan said. "On the TV in there they showed clips of the ceremony, the scene outside, even pictures from a news helicopter."

"Did you see me?" Mahmoud asked.

"Not inside, Mahmoud. Outside, being interviewed!"

Safiye gasped. George shouted "Seriously? Explain that, mister stealth assassin!"

"W-when I got out a reporter shoved a mic in my face asking what it was like for me there. I got away as fast as I could."

"Because I dragged you away," Katrina added. "It paralyzed you."

Accelerating onto the highway, George inquired "If that's all it was, why is it on the air?"

"They said that authorities are interested in locating this man,"

Kaan told them, "who may or may not be blind. Didn't say why but we have to assume that he's a suspect."

"There could be other pictures too. We have to get out of here," cried George, moving into the fast lane. "Kaan, what do you want to do?"

"Go home. Ship my movie to Piraeus and act normal when Ivan returns. So drop me off at a Metro station. The last one's coming up at Ülüdağ University."

"What about the rest of us," Katrina asked. "Go back to Safiye's?"

"We should split up. Safiye should take you two with her and go back to work as if nothing happened. Then head back to Piraeus as soon as you can. Swim if you have to."

Katrina shivered. "But what about you, George?"

"Watch, wait, and try to make whatever happens work for us. Whether Paşa survives or not, I'm sure they'll tighten the screws. That will stir up discontent we can organize."

"So, in Turkey then?" Kaan inquired.

"No point going back to Greece and a manhunt. Best for me to lie low is Balıkesir, at my sister's house. Probably not much is happening there politically, but she has kids I've never met. My introduction to being an uncle."

As scenery blurred by, Mahmoud chewed on George's words. The job was over and now the team was breaking up. Ever since escaping from Mosul he'd been depending on leaders, followed orders. Wondering if his battalion was still together somewhere he asked George if he knew what had become of Commander TigerPaw.

"No idea. Might still be in Turkey or have returned to IFB headquarters in Rojava. Why do you ask?"

"I was just wondering if the unit was still together, how it was doing."

Katrina cast a doubtful glance at him. "Where is Rojava?" she asked. "What's IFB?"

"In northwestern Syria, south of Gaziantep," George informed her. "IFB is the International Freedom Brigade, your friend's military unit."

"Oh sure, his battalion. I just didn't know the initials." Her brow furrowed. Peering over her glasses, she said "We have to talk."

Safiye smiled. "You both are welcome to go home with me and stay as long as you want while you figure out what to do. I would enjoy your company. And frankly, I'd rather not be alone right now."

As twilight melted into evening, George took the university exit and followed the Metro tracks to the station. He halted a hundred meters from the terminal, saying he wanted to avoid surveillance cameras. As her nephew got out, Safiye kissed his cheeks and sniffled "I hate leaving you like this. Please call me so I know you're okay and come to see me when you can."

He returned her kiss and said "Even though I didn't want you here and may still regret getting you into this, it might not have happened without you. Take care getting home and well after. I love you and I'll visit when I can."

George tersely advised Kaan to be discreet when he contacted Piraeus. "Just text. Say we found our mark, we're all okay and I'll be in touch soon. With you too. Stay tuned."

They bumped fists. Kaan opened the rear door and reached in to hug Mahmoud, telling him "You were incredible today with your pea shooter. You had full control and total coolness. Brother, I hope this isn't the end for us." He took Katrina's hand and squeezed. "Sister, you really came through. I'm sorry I misjudged you. I think you guys are good for each other. Take care."

With a wave and a "güle güle", he turned and walked off. They watched him fade away into the terminal as George got out and reinstalled Safiye's license plates. A few exits on, he pulled up to a construction site and tossed the stolen tags in a dumpster. Back on the road he said "Next we find another trash bin for your clothing and that cane, and then on to Balıkesir. I hope I can remember where my sister lives and she'll have me. She was never very happy about my career path, but so it goes."

Chapter Fifty-One

THE FIAT MOTORED westward as dusk slid toward evening, past the turnoff to Istanbul, past big box stores and supermarkets, industrial parks and car dealerships, into flatlands with bare orchards, fallow fields and small towns. The weather, as were its four occupants, was unsettled. George continued to drive, Safiye next to him, the couple slumped behind. When the news bulletins kept repeating themselves, Safiye hunted for music, as soothing as possible. When chamber music filled the cabin, she sighed. "My sister loved music. This was one of favorites. We played this movement at her memorial service. Everyone cried. Listen!"

"That's so haunting," Katrina said. Makes me want to cry. What is it?"

"Beethoven. A slow movement from a middle string quartet. To me, it evokes plodding along an endless journey through trackless lands."

"Like us, right now," Katrina agreed.

George, no classical music buff, yawned. "Let's hope it doesn't put me to sleep."

Head nestled on Mahmoud's shoulder, Katrina murmured "I love you. Really do."

Mahmoud rested his hand on her thigh. "I love you too. I'm sure of it. Just don't know why."

"Me neither. It isn't because you're brave and fight for freedom. And it isn't that you're good looking, though that got me going.

Maybe it's your purity of spirit and steadiness of purpose. Never met anyone like you, and just knew I had to have you in my life."

"Someone once said 'Life happens while you're busy making other plans.' That's how I feel now."

She lifted her head to meet his eyes. "Say more."

"Ever since my parents were murdered, I've been on the warpath. My jihad was my own, nobody else's."

Her hand moved to his chest, feeling it rise and fall. "And now it's not?"

"Like I said the other night, it's changing. Working as a team, especially with you, gave me courage and maybe even my life today."

"And yet," she said, tracing a heart on his breastbone, "I was prepared to take it from you. How crazy is that? Don't answer."

He embraced her shoulder. "I will answer. Yes, totally crazy. It only would have traded my misery for yours."

"The thought of killing you made me ache. I even thought about carrying two darts, you know, Romeo and Juliet style."

"You did? Now that's even crazier."

The adagio being broadcast ended. She sucked in air and let it out with a sigh. "I'm ready to stop killing people if you are." His response was to clasp her closer.

Another news bulletin. When it ended, George cried "We did it!" rousing Safiye from her Beethoven-induced trance.

"What? What did he say?" Katrina cried.

George recapped. "Paşa was hospitalized several hours ago in Ankara for observation, following what some allege was a failed assassination attempt at a ceremony the President was attending in Bursa, but his spokesperson said there was no connection. His condition is reported as stable."

"No connection, my foot!" Safiye yowled. "Ever heard of cause and effect?"

Katrina was more subdued. "It just hit me. I really, really hope he doesn't die."

"Why?" Mahmoud asked.

Pounding Safiye's headrest, she elucidated. "Because then he'll be a fucking martyr. Thousands of brainwashed idiots will rally to his party and his successor will double down in his name. Screw that. I want him to suffer—no, just to linger and fade away. The uncertainty will energize Turks to take charge of their destiny."

"I see your point," he answered. "Neutralizing him might be better than killing him."

"And didn't you say blaming this on ISIS would rally Turks to restore democracy? Somehow, I can't see that happening."

"So who should we say did this," Mahmoud asked, "the MLKP?"

George snorted. "Hardly. We're an outlawed, marginalized revolutionary party that few Turks even know about. Taking credit for ourselves might recruit some new cadres, but it won't rally the masses."

Safiye turned to him. "Then make people think the so-called Parallel State did it. You know, the Davacists. The ones who have been trying to take over from within. They'll surely exploit the situation."

"I remember Kaan describing them," Mahmoud said. "But wouldn't the ruling party simply crack down on them?"

George nodded. "I would certainly expect that. But they're well entrenched and would fight back. I expect the power struggle to go on for a while."

Katrina put in her two cents. "Anarchists should use this moment to build a third way. Educate people that this infighting is no good for them and move them to be more self-reliant."

They had rolled into a small town. George stopped in front of a shuttered store. He turned off the lights, cut the engine and turned to face them. "I don't think Turks would take to anarchy, but yes, it's time to organize. Safiye just convinced me our video needs a new script. Instead of ISIS, it should be Mehmed Davacı taking responsibility for toppling a tyrant and calling on Turks to revolt."

"Saying . . . ?" Safiye asked.

George cupped his face in thought before responding in Turkish: "Something like 'Citizens of Turkey, this is your last chance to throw off the yoke of tyranny. Your leaders have corrupted the fatherland grasping for absolute power. Think: Do you want to submit to a caliph ruling by decree from a palace? Do you want freedom of belief and freedom of speech? For democracy and freedom rise up and drive the traitors from power! Do not fear! We will support you at every turn. Long live the fatherland and the greatness of the Turkish people!'"

"*Taman,*" concurred Safiye. She summarized for Katrina, who asked if Davacı should claim responsibility for attacking Paşa.

"No need," George said. "People will simply assume that."

"So if that's what you want to say," Mahmoud said, "you should let the others know."

George plucked his phone from his pocket. "I'm calling Kaan. He needs to make it sound right. He's good with words."

Still processing the events of the day, a weary Kaan Sultanoğlu shed his shoes in his hallway. His stomach growled, but eating and sleeping would have to wait. First, he needed to dispatch footage to Piraeus. His phone, he discovered, was dead, but thankfully, connecting his charger revived it. A discreet beep signaled a missed call, from George, less than twenty minutes ago. Hoping it didn't signify trouble he hesitantly rang back.

The good news, George told him, was that the President was in hospital. Before he could ask for details, George started talking about the movie. For the next ten minutes, George pressed his fatigued and skeptical comrade to rewrite the script to finger a Davacist conspiracy and narrate it himself.

Kaan initially resisted the sideways move, but George's proposal pumped his conspiratorial juices, and soon he was suggesting new angles for the narrative. How about, he suggested, we montage in a clip of Mehmed Davacı with children? An image of Paşa's palace? Shots of police attacking demonstrators in Taksim Square or of scandal-ridden construction projects? Keep it simple, George replied. Text Ottovio to alert him the video and new script were coming soon. Compose a new narration based on what they'd discussed as a voice memo in Turkish, and upload it for a soundtrack.

After ringing off, Kaan texted Ottovio: our team won. we r ok.

pictures + sound soon. Then he popped open a bottle of beer, perched with it at the kitchen table, and started scribbling. By the time he'd emptied the bottle he had a decent draft. Thinking it needed a kicker, he paced the living room, cogitating in circles until words came: *This is a revolution. Some call it the second Turkish Revolution, but we say the first one still is not finished. Join the resistance, and together we will overthrow tyranny!* He read it aloud. Sounded good, so he recorded it. Replaying, he felt his delivery didn't have enough gravitas. Again he recited, in a more gravelly tone, pausing for effect where he thought images should go.

More or less satisfied, for his comrades' benefit he recorded an English version, and then another memo relating what had gone down and what they needed to do. Apologizing for a last-minute surprise, he explained why their story had changed and how they might visualize it. His eyes grew heavy as his content beamed up. Piraeus would have to take it from there.

All afternoon, Andreas watched TV in his flat, surfing through channels he could get over the air. On the other side of the room, the Greek geek was coaxing news feeds from the maw of the Web into his laptop.

"This cellular modem is so freaking slow," Ottovio complained. "Remind me why we aren't working at the condo where there's cable."

"I told you. Ivan's staying there. He mustn't see what we're doing."

"Whatever. It doesn't make it any easier."

A few hours into their vigil came news that something strange and unexpected involving the President of Turkey had gone down in Bursa at some mosque, but details were scant. The Andalou Agency feed wasn't showing anything. That no arrests or suspects were mentioned gave them optimism, but not enough to relax. A streaming newscast stuttered across Ottovio's screen. They couldn't understand the words but fuzzy pictures showed police corralling an anxious mob trying to exit the mosque.

Still no communication from their comrades. Where were they?

How were they? Had Kaan made a movie? If things had gone badly, there might not be a video—or one really painful to view.

It looked like it might be a long evening and they both felt a need for sustenance. Ottovio ordered out a large pizza with Greek sausage, anchovies, olives, and Feta on his half and Margherita toppings on his friend's side. Andreas went to get it and a bottle of wine. As they chowed down Ottovio's phone tingled with Kaan's hopeful message. At the speed of cell, Kaan's upload could take at least half an hour and just as long to download, he told Andreas and repaired to the couch, wine glass in hand.

When Kaan's files finally materialized they viewed the video first and were impressed by its clarity and what it disclosed. Just a brief hint of Mahmoud that they could easily cut out, then a narrated sweep of the audience. After some tedious preliminaries, a woman cries out—in Turkish, so it wasn't Katrina—and the Great Leader grabs his arm and stumbles off stage right. Police and his retinue react. Wait, was that a gunshot? A wobbly blur followed by milling panic. Confused but impatient to move on, the Greek started editing with the Austrian kibitzing about overlaying titles and splicing in Mahmoud's pre-recorded narration with ominous drum music.

He was deep into it when Andreas reminded him that Kaan had also sent three audio files. He broke off to play them. First came the Turkish narration that they couldn't understand, but the English version only added to their bewilderment. A message from the secretive power broker Mehmed Davacı? What about ISIS? Only after sitting through Kaan's voice memo did they get his drift: The putative perps had changed and in their haste they'd wasted precious time.

"Kaan says George wants it this way," Ottovio said, downing a cold salty slice of pie. "So that's what we do. We start over."

"Sorry," said Andreas, getting up. "I'm afraid you're on your own now. I gotta go."

"Where to?"

"To see Ivan. We were supposed to eat down at the microlimani but I punted that to work here. We have a date to go to a club downtown. I can't blow that off too."

"You picked a funny time to have him come and party. We have work to do."

"It's for the sake of the mission. We needed him out of there. And my social life has been null and void since he left. Give me a break."

Ottovio emptied the bottle of red into his goblet. "Maybe I should start charging you guys. It's always Ottovio do this, Ottovio do that. Fix up phones. Fix up police records. Make a video. You know, I could make good money doing that kind of *skàta*."

"But you say you enjoy it. That you *like* learning new things."

"Like how to talk to morticians—just what I needed to know. And cracking into servers is nothing new. I like the puzzling, but it takes time and after a while it gets old."

Andreas stiffened pouting. "Do you think I'm in it for the money? Hell, I'm losing money. Did anyone pay me to take over for George and keep us together or get him out of jail? What happened to your sense of solidarity, Mister Rent-a-Geek?"

"Take it easy. You don't know how to do this, so leave me alone. Go party. But keep your phone open in case I need you."

Ottovio scribbled something and handed it over. "When I upload video I text you and Kaan and George to take a look. This will be web address and password to get in."

After Andreas trudged off, Ottovio settled down with his laptop and wine, scanning the Web for breaking news from Turkey, eventually discovering that the President was hospitalized. That looked promising. A terse, guarded release from the Andalou Agency noted that there had been a "security incident" in Bursa, but the only casualties were a couple of trodden-upon spectators and a gendarme who was in poor condition after suffering a fall. Police were investigating and looking for witnesses.

Before starting over he searched for other news mentioning Bursa and then he saw it: a photo of Mahmoud in a white hat and dark glasses with a mic shoved at his puss. It didn't look good. They saw him do it and are looking for him. But at least he still seems to be at large. Anyway, he had a story to tell. He swigged his wine and got on with it.

Less than two hours had passed when he heard a door slam and someone clumping up the stairs. His body tensed. The door opened. It was Andreas.

"Why are you here? I thought you would be dancing your ass off by now?"

Andreas looked tired, seemed dispirited. "I decided not to party. Came back to help" was all he said. Ottovio let it slide. Whatever the reason, it worked for him.

The two of them edited, sequenced, argued over what visuals to use, wipes versus dissolves, and whether to dub in the Turkish national anthem. Ottovio even processed the soundtrack to disguise Kaan's voice. As their production compiled, Andreas asked "Do you think they're hunting for him?"

"Looks like it."

"Not good. He'll have to be very careful from now on. Like George."

"Reminds me of a joke I heard," Ottovio said, sitting back. "Wanna hear it?"

"Sure. I could use one."

"Okay. How many martyrs does it take to change a light bulb?"

"I give up."

"Just one, the guy who sticks his finger in the socket."

By 2 AM Andreas was dozing and two productions sat on the geek's server, one in Turkish and the other in English. He texted Kaan and George how to access the content but did not expect reviews to come in anytime soon. Just one task remained, something he hadn't reckoned on. In his memo, Kaan had urged him to hack the videos into the front pages of multiple news sites. He knew several techniques for doing that but had never tried any of them. Simultaneously defacing a bunch of web servers was a motherboard of a task, and he repaired to the couch to chew on it. He hadn't come up with anything by the time he drifted away until the morn.

Chapter Fifty-Two

A MISTY RAIN INGESTED the beams of the headlamps and trickled up the windshield. Classical music still whispered from the radio, now a romantic symphony by another one of those Germans. The rhythm of the wipers syncopating with passing street lamps had lulled his passengers and put George in a reflective mood, wondering how he would find Irmak and how many kids she might have now, when a blue flashing light behind him snapped his eyes to the mirror. Palpitating, he eased up on the gas and sidled into the breakdown lane as the vehicle gained on him and then sprayed past going at least a hundred thirty, an ambulance, not a police car. He exhaled.

Back to Irmak. He had long ago lost track of her phone number and address. The last time he had visited her and Guray, he had just gone on the lam and only stayed one night, telling them he would be in touch but never was. Not that he and Irmak didn't get along; they usually did, at least before. But with a price on his head, it wouldn't have served either of them well to keep her posted. He wondered if Guray was still around. That last visit, he'd picked up on sparks of tension between them. A child, who must be ten by now, had been on the way. Guray seemed a little too happy-go-lucky to transmogrify into a *baba*, and Irmak was complaining about his slacker ways, badgering him to bring home more money. Knowing she had a fuse as short as his, he figured there was at least a seventy percent chance she'd kicked him out by now.

It was almost ten when he veered onto the D230 on the outskirts of Balıkesir. He dimly recalled where his sister's neighborhood had been—south of the highway, not too far from a park with a stadium. Twenty minutes of blundering through rain-slick streets brought him to the park, but it seemed to have been transplanted, surrounded by buildings he was sure hadn't been there a decade ago. Rather than curse the darkness, he parked by a construction site on a side street, zippered his jacket, and reclined to find solidarity with the sleepers.

Daybreak came with fog in place of rain. Mahmoud's eyes fluttered open and he sat up, feeling chilled, stiff, and disoriented. All he could discern though the clouded windows was that they were in a city, where men were assembling at a worksite across the street. Tilted back in the driver's seat, George was softly snoring. Katrina and Safiye were gone. He checked his phone. Seven-thirty-five. He got out to escape the humid cabin's stale air and stretch his legs. Assuming that the women were taking a walk, he stood by until they precipitated at the end of the block bearing paper cups. Tea, he supposed, or coffee. It was both; tea for the Turks, coffee for the foreigners.

"*Gunaydin*, Mahmoud," Katrina smiled, proud to have picked up "good morning," and then "*Nasilsin*?" asking how he was.

He told her he felt cold and gladly accepted a cup of pre-sweetened coffee. They got back in the car to find George rubbing sleep from his face. Katrina passed him tea and inquired of their whereabouts. "My sister lives over there somewhere," he said, gesturing with his cup. "I didn't want to wander around at night to find the house or make her feel obliged to put us up. In fact, I don't want her to even see you people. She'll ask a lot of questions. You don't want her interrogating you."

"How will you explain showing up after so many years?" Mahmoud asked, "where you've been and what you were doing?"

"I worked that out when I was driving. I'll tell her I got tired of exile. That I missed the homeland. Missed my comrades. Missed her and wanted to spend time with her kids. Came by bus from Izmir after hitching a ride from one of the islands."

"She'll probably want to know more than that," Safiye said.

"Irmak knows I've done stuff I can't talk about. She'll understand."

"But suppose she's not here anymore?" Katrina asked. "What will you do?"

"Probably take a bus back to Bursa. Nobody's looking for me there and some people I know must still be around. I'll stay with Kaan for a while until I can make connections."

"What about Ivan? He'll be back by then," Mahmoud said.

"We've never met. I'll just be an old friend who blew into town and needs a place to stay. But let's try to find Irmak now."

Safiye took the wheel. "Her house was on a little street that ended in front of some kind of school, I remember, Let's head that way," he said, pointing southeast.

Several fruitless meanders later, Safiye rolled down her window at a bus stop to ask a woman if there was a school nearby. There's a technical academy over there she told them, pointing to their right. A few zigzags brought them to a small campus. George told her to circumnavigate as he peered down side streets. "*Harika!* There it is, Orbay Sokak. Now I remember. Just one block long. She's at the other end. Yes, it's this dingy little house. Park around the corner, away from it."

He retrieved his backpack from the trunk. "Wait here ten minutes," he instructed. "If she's still here and will have me, I won't come back. Find your way to the E881 and head south." Reaching through the rear window to grip Mahmoud's shoulder, he told him "I will miss you, my fearless friend. So, what's your plan from there?"

Mahmoud shrugged. "Wait in Izmir to see what develops, I guess. After my beard grows back we'll probably ferry back to Piraeus."

"Let it get nice and bushy," Safiye allowed. "I'd rather not be alone for a while."

"You would need a Greek visa to board a ferry," noted George. "You might have to float across again."

Mahmoud stared blankly at the ground. "I suppose. Depends if they're looking for me."

Katrina asked, "George, are you sure about being on your own here?"

"It's a chance to consider next moves, reach out to old cadres, build a network, continue the struggle. But this time, I'll do it differently."

"How so?"

He leaned on the door, staring into the middle distance. "In exile, I thought I had to control everything—work out a plan and make everyone stick to it like good soldiers. This operation made me more—as military strategists say—'situationally aware' and willing to improvise."

"So, are you happy with how it worked out?"

"Sure. It could have gone much, much worse. Whether Paşa makes it or not, what we did was a big deal that'll change the power equation. It'll push the government off balance. We need to keep pushing. You guys may needed again. Stay tuned."

"Sure," Mahmoud said noncommittally. His voice dropped. "But tell me one thing. We're pretty sure Yilmaz Turgut isn't your real name. You're really Gurcan Bac, aren't you."

Shrugging a *tssk*, George shouldered his backpack. "No, I'm not, but just between us, he was a good friend of mine."

After he rounded the corner they fell to inconclusively conjecturing about what might devolve and what their next moves ought to be. When it seemed their comrade had found his safe house, Safiye started the car. As they pulled away, Mahmoud texted him: **good luck. we go now. be in touch.**

On the D330, Mahmoud kept twiddling the radio for news. The airwaves kept reiterating that the President was still in hospital, only now it was food poisoning. Strangely, official sources weren't talking terrorism. Why, Mahmoud wondered aloud. Could they be laying a trap? Safiye suggested that in the absence of public evidence that an attack took place, the regime might be cooking up a story and an adversary of convenience to pin it on. After all, she added, they had plenty of enemies—PKK and communist militants, ISIS, and Mehmed Davacı. Or they might finger a foreign power—Syria, Russia, Israel, or even America. Or, offered Katrina, should Paşa recover, the regime would have no need to explain its embarrassing lapse of security. But no such fabrication would hold water once Kaan's movie hit the internets.

Izmir at last. The three travelers unloaded belongings and traipsed up to Safiye's flat. Shoes were shed, tea was made, TV switched on. When no new developments displayed, Safiye took to the kitchen. Flopped on the couch, hungry for news she could understand, Katrina clicked to a German news channel. Mahmoud stood by and commenced to stab at his phone.

"I want to call Andreas," he said, "to let him know we're all okay. Can I use your phone? Mine isn't turning on."

"Sure. My Ottovio Special is in my handbag. I think it's in the guest room."

Katrina turned back to the TV and pictures of restive refugees, these in Germany. Suddenly recalling what else the purse contained, she shouted "Mahmoud! Be careful! I just remembered I left that . . ."

From the hallway another shout. "Ow! What was that?"

Blanching, Katrina sprang to her feet and ran to find him sitting on the bed, pulling a crumpled tube of mints from his right palm.

"It stabbed me when I reached into the purse. Is this what I think it is?" he asked, eyes wide.

"Omigod! Omigod!" she cried. "I forgot it was still in there. *Scheisse!*"

He let the wrapper tumble onto the bed. A droplet of blood oozed from his palm.

"What should I do?" he asked her.

"We gotta drain that out," she said breathlessly. "Come to the bathroom."

She pulled her pocket knife from her jeans. "Sit on the toilet with your hand on the sink," she told him. "I'm gonna open that up. Just a little gash, but it's gonna hurt, I'm afraid."

Mahmoud sat down and put his arm out. She grasped his fingers and lanced his palm as he gripped her leg, grimacing. Then she was bent over, sucking, spitting into the sink. Three times she did that until crimson smeared her lips, then put his hand under the tap as she scooped water into her mouth and spat it out.

"What was that doing there?" Mahmoud gasped as water swirled pink.

"That dart was for you, Romeo, but it wasn't supposed to happen this way. You remember George putting me up to it, saying it was a last resort if they were to take you. Oh love, I should have listened to you when you told me you would rather be gunned down than have me do that. Makes me want to do it to myself."

"Stop saying that! I'll be fine. It was just a little prick and it must be gone now. Go see if Safiye has any bandages."

Katrina entered the kitchen, ashen-faced. Safiye said "I heard shouts. What happened?"

"Mahmoud had an accident. With a poison dart. I tried to flush it out. Now he needs first aid."

Safiye rushed to the bathroom to see Mahmoud still rinsing his hand, seemingly calm. She found some gauze and tape and threw him a towel. "Dry yourself," she said.

Mahmoud complied and winced as Safiye dabbed rubbing alcohol on the cut. Katrina positioned pads as Safiye crisscrossed gauze around his hand and bound it with white tape.

"I think you should lie down," Safiye told him. "How do you feel?"

"My hand hurts, that's all," he said. "Thank you. You did all you could. Now it's in Allah's hands."

"I hope Allah's immune," Katrina said. "Go lie on the couch like a good boy."

Katrina steered him to the living room and gave him the remote so he could watch TV. He searched for news in Arabic as the women went into the kitchen. "What's the worse that could happen?" asked Safiye, nervously wiping her hands on her apron.

Katrina shuddered. "Get sick overnight. Die within a day or two. Don't want to think about it."

"What's the next worse thing?"

"I dunno. Never looked into what ricin might do if it doesn't kill you. Then there's blood poisoning. I'm sure my knife wasn't too sterile."

They assembled a salad and heated leftover cheese böreks in the oven. Mahmoud came in to join them at the table. Except for the clink of tableware, sounds of chewing, and him averring that he'd be all right, they ate in silence. The women cleaned up and everyone retired early. Safiye urged Katrina to sleep with Mahmoud lest he need help during the night and met no objection.

She snuggled next to him, stroking him, kissing him. Mahmoud responded, kissing her mouth, moving down her neck to lick her stiffening nipples before pulling her to him. Swept away by ardor, they made passionate love, she biting her lip to suppress moans of pleasure, and then spent, fell into sleep tenderly clamped in a delirious embrace.

Chapter Fifty-Three

MAHMOUD AWOKE JUST before dawn, bilious, his joints aching, in a sweat, flesh smarting as if rubbed with sandpaper. Trying not to wake Katrina, he swung his feet to the floor, pushed himself upright and shuffled to the bathroom to vomit into the toilet. His wounded hand throbbed, sending prickly sensations up to his shoulder. Purchasing his way back clutching the walls, he tumbled into bed, stirring Katrina, who rolled over to hug his torso.

"That hurts," he said, lifting her arms from his chest. "This isn't good."

She withdrew her hand to caress his brow and said "You're hot. How are you feeling?"

"Not so great. My body aches and burns like I had just run a race in blazing hot sun."

She hugged him again, tentatively. He kissed her. "Even my lips hurt. Is there anything we can do?"

"After you slept, Safiye and I surfed for treatments. Seems you should take lots of fluids and something to settle the stomach. Stimulants might help. I'll make tea for you."

She disengaged herself and shortly was back with a big mug of black tea laced with honey. She propped him up and fed it to him, saying "When I was doing the Ebola thing in Senegal I found a village healer with a very sick patient. He fed her some nasty potion and made her repeat a chant. 'EE-yo-ma-ma,' I think it went, 'EE-yo-ma-MA.' Let's try it."

"EE-yo-ma-ma, EE-yo-ma-MA," she intoned.

"EE-yo-ma-ma, EE-yo-ma-MA," he repeated.

"EE-yo-ma-ma, EE-yo-ma-MA."

"EE-yo-ma-ma, EE-yo-ma-MA."

Soon Mahmoud slept again. As light filtered into the room, Katrina recalled that patient hadn't survived, but then few of them did. She pondered whether to take him to a medical center. What she knew about ricin told her hospital care would be palliative at best. Painkillers, drips and transfusions might help, but there was no cure. Anyway, if she told them what was wrong with him and certain inferences were made, the trail might sooner or later lead to Safiye.

She lifted the comforter and gazed at him in his Boston Red Sox t-shirt, the one from the Piraeus flea market. On his arms and legs, dark veins pulsed under translucent cyanic skin. His breathing was regular, but shallow and raspy. Spittle dappled his lips. A lachrymose wave of fatigue seized her. Wondering if she'd absorbed poison from suctioning his blood, she curled up next to him and wept herself to sleep.

Awaking at seven, Safiye showered and dressed. On her way to the kitchen, she looked into the guest room to find the couple asleep. She pulled back the covers to inspect his wound for signs of infection. His hand and arm were all but colorless. His breath came in short rasps.

She prodded Katrina, still curled in fetal withdrawal. "Katrina, wake up. Is he all right?"

Katrina's eyes fluttered. She stretched and crouched over him. "He's really sick. It hit him before dawn."

She slid off the bed, covered him, and they went to the kitchen exchanging worries. "I need coffee," Katrina said. "I want to give him some too. Make it strong."

"Would that be good for him?"

"I read that ricin causes low blood pressure that stimulants can help."

A steaming carafe was prepared. Katrina sugared and delivered a mug of it. She lifted his head and wafted the liquid under his nose, cooing to him to wake up. When he didn't respond, she cupped his chin and chucked it side to side saying "Hello, anybody home?" His skin felt cold.

He stirred. Through slitted eyes, he murmured something. She asked if he could sit up. When he struggled to sit up, Safiye tugged him forward as Katrina stuffed pillows behind his back and put the mug to his lips. "Coffee. Nice and fresh. Swallow please." After a couple of sips Safiye asked how he was feeling. Weak, he replied. Earlier he had sweated. Now he felt chill, but his overall discomfort was a bit less and the nausea and shooting pains had subsided.

A little later, nature called. After struggling to get up, he called to them to help him to the bathroom. He passed loose stool and said he wanted to go to the living room. They guided him there and helped him to kneel on the carpet to recite *fajr ṣalāh*, after which they draped him on the couch and covered him with a blanket to watch TV.

Over breakfast in the kitchen the women discussed hospitalization, which Safiye concurred would be inadvisable and unproductive. Soon Mahmoud hoarsely summoned them to say he was hungry, altogether a good thing. Safiye boiled soft "apricot" eggs. Katrina sliced an apple and spread fig jam on toasts. After eating most of it and ingesting more coffee, he reported feeling better.

Safiye said she had a ten o'clock class to teach that she didn't want to blow off, and left the couple to their devices, urging Katrina to call her if she needed help with nursing, the locals, or anything. Katrina joined him on the couch and massaged his legs, which he said still ached, but at least rubbing them no longer hurt.

"Let's assume you make it and we can move on," she said. "Do you still want to go back to Piraeus?"

"I might, but I'd rather go back to Iraq."

"What, to fight ISIS again?"

"If I had to, but no. I want to help their victims."

Katrina pensively took that in. "Not what I expected to hear. Say more."

"So here I am, half-dead from a dose of my own medicine."

"Actually, it's mine. But go on."

"So far, our operation hasn't changed anything. It still might, but maybe for the worse. I'm not sure I want to risk my life and not accomplish anything useful. But if you help people in need, you know it's useful."

She frowned. "Umm, yes, that's what I thought I was doing in Africa. I'm sure I helped some people somehow, but I hardly saw any results. Mostly I just felt jammed between a bunch of rackets. But don't let that discourage you. Is there something in particular you want to do in Iraq?"

He coughed several times, raising purple blotches on his face. "Excuse me," he gasped. "Yes. A lot of Iraqis have fled ISIS to Baghdad. They need housing and work. The government isn't doing much for them. There might be a way I could help."

"Which would be . . . ?"

"A space where they could live, work, and reconnect. I see it as a large building. Baghdad has many empty ones. Some are damaged and looted, but not all. Part of the building would be living spaces made from shipping containers or built with scavenged materials. It would be a squatter village, but indoors and organized."

"With air conditioning, I hope."

"Maybe, but electricity still isn't very reliable. A roof garden might make it cooler."

"And the other part?"

"Workshops and small factories, little *cough* businesses like appliance and phone repair, making clothing, little clinics, food pantries *cough*."

"Sounds like you're planning a town. Where did you get this idea?"

"Two years ago I took a course in systems design. Not designing computers, modeling human ecosystems. *cough* My professor was amazing, so insightful and holistic—one of his favorite words. He was from Iran and had studied in America. When ISIS took over my school, they executed him and most other Shiites."

"I'm really sorry to hear that."

"So now, instead of avenging him I want to honor him by implementing his vision."

She got up and went to the window, looked down on the street. People were going about their morning business. It struck her how much his idea resembled the self-reliant communities she and her anarchist cohorts had been trying to establish. *I hope he makes it. I'd really like to be part of something like that. Even in Iraq.* She turned to see he'd fallen asleep, so she pulled up his blanket and went back to searching for remedies.

Mid-afternoon Safiye returned from school laden with a bag full of fruit—peaches, bananas, pomegranates—and another she said was from an apothecary.

"How's our patient?" she asked.

"He's sleeping, coughing now and then," Katrina replied. "No worse, it seems. What's all this stuff?"

A colleague in the History Department, a Chinese man who had studied traditional Asian medicine, had put her on to an elixir. When she told him she had a friend with a serious, mysterious illness he inquired about his symptoms and suggested giving the patient a lot of fruit. He also wrote her a recipe for herbal tea, and on the other side printed some Chinese characters.

"He sent me to this Chinese herbalist over in Alsancak to get the ingredients. It was quite an experience. I gave the list to this old man and he made a package for me."

"Do you know how to use these things?"

"The old man hardly knew Turkish so couldn't explain anything, but my colleague already had. Here's what we have." She dumped out a chunk of ginger, a ruddy, woody shelf mushroom, and a twisted, forked root. "We just have to cut up these things and simmer it all for an hour, strain out the solids, and serve it as tea."

Katrina read the recipe. "He called this mushroom *ling zhe*," she said. "That's ginger, and this gnarly thing is a ginseng root. So let's brew some up. What do we have to lose?"

They hacked up the woody fungus and the ginseng, sliced the ginger, and dumped the pieces into a pot with two liters of water to boil.

"Oh, yes," Safiye said. "We're supposed to add this, for congestion," opening a packet of dried chrysanthemums." She sprinkled them into the pot and watched them unfurl like water lilies.

Katrina gently roused Mahmoud and helped him up to nibble at the fruit. When she judged the mystery tea had sufficiently steeped, Safiye strained it and took a sip. "Ach!" she said, wrinkling her nose. "It's quite earthy, very bitter." She poured a cup and swirled in teaspoons of honey to make the potion almost palatable.

Katrina brought an odiferous mug of brown liquid to the couch. Mahmoud pulled on it, suppressed a gag and coughed some out. Wiping his mouth, he said "Ugh, what is this stuff?"

"An elixir," Katrina told him. "Drink up, honey. It's good for what ails you."

Sipping under protest, he asked "So what's going on? Any news about Paşa?"

"Oh yes!" Safiye called from the kitchen. "Look at this!" She brought in a tabloid newspaper she'd picked up with a photo of the President, walking with a metal cane, his wife by his side. "It says he left hospital last night, but Prime Minister is still fulfilling his duties."

From Katrina came an ambivalent "Oh well, we tried."

"He doesn't look well, does he?" Safiye said. "He seems pretty pale and sort of bent over. Must have caught it from you, Mahmoud."

Mahmoud perused, unimpressed. "Very short. Says nothing about what might be wrong with him."

Katrina checked her phone to see if there was an official story on the Andalou site. "Hmm. That's interesting. 'The government issued a statement that, contrary to false claims on the Internet, no attack on

President Paşa took place in Bursa. He was treated for food poisoning, has been released from hospital, and is recovering quickly.'"

"The video must have come out!" Mahmoud said excitedly, then coughed. "See if you can find it!"

Safiye brought in her laptop and they poked around. A promising link led to a YouTube video that had since been removed. A story in a German newspaper described the video, attributing it to Davacısts.

"Yes," said Katrina. "It says that a video said to be from Mehmed Davacı's organization appeared on the home pages of several Turkish news sites, including Zaman and Andalou Agency. It featured pictures of Davacı himself and footage from a ceremony in Bursa where the President is seen clutching his shoulder before being escorted away. It goes on to say 'The narrator of the video, which has now been removed, claimed that President Paşa is a dictator and a traitor to the Turkish Republic, against whom they have urged the people to rebel to restore democracy.'"

On Turkish media sites Safiye found a rising tide of speculation about what had gone down and muted murmurings about Davacıst stratagems. She found a picture that included Kaan's backside shooting his movie, and then Mahmoud's face as seen on TV, still being referred to as a "person of interest," She said she wanted to call her nephew.

"I guess that would be okay," said Mahmoud. "Use my phone." He got up to find it and walked slowly to the guest room before the women could stop him. On his return he remarked "You know, I couldn't have made that walk a few hours ago. My legs still hurt but the pain is much less. Give me more of that ugly tea. "EE-yo-ma-ma, EE-yo-ma-MA!"

Chapter Fifty-Four

KAAN WAS ABSORBING a Turkish TV talk show when his phone sounded. The call came from Mahmoud, but he answered it to find his aunt on the other end with things to ask and things to tell. She asked what he knew about his video and reactions to it.

"My friends released it early this morning, while Paşa was still in hospital. I saw the preview. It was pretty well done, if you ask me. But they didn't tell me which sites they were able to post it on. Did you see it?"

Safiye told him no, it seemed to have vanished, but she'd read it got on at least two sites plus YouTube briefly.

"Yeah, I can't find it now either. Bummer. But it's had an impact."

She asked him what the impact was, could, will be.

"It started arguments. Some people believe it was from Davacı or his allies. Others say it's a government set-up so they can purge of Davacist officials. There's talk that PKK, other Kurdish groups, ISIS, and assorted leftists, including MLKP might have done it. Not everyone believes the official story about food poisoning, so they argue about that too. For me, it's great fun."

Safiye said she wasn't sure how much fun it was and wanted to know what he thought would happen next.

"Well, it looks like Paşa won't die, but he seems weak. If he doesn't get well it will set off a power struggle in his party, and retributions against Davacı's people. The military could take sides or split apart. I'm still hoping it all will unleash animosities, but it's too soon to tell. We should be out organizing the masses to storm the palace."

That wasn't in her current plan, Safiye replied, and then said she was concerned about Mahmoud.

"What's wrong with him?"

She described the accident, his symptoms, and his suffering. He was fighting for his life it seemed.

"What? That's terrible! Let me speak with him."

Mahmoud got on the line and croaked hello to his comrade. Joked that now that he knows what Paşa has been going through, maybe he should be giving interviews.

"You seem to be in good spirits, considering. Do you feel better now?"

Mahmoud said he did, a little. The shooting pains were gone, but he still ached all over and no energy.

"Hey man, you got to beat this thing. Keep telling yourself that. Let them pamper you. Is George with you?"

Mahmoud told of spending the night on the street in Balıkesir and dropping George at his sister's place. Then he asked Kaan what he'd been up to.

"Scripting the video. Sorry you didn't get to see it but it might come around again. I expect Ivan any minute. Don't know what his mood will be. Andreas told me they broke up."

Mahmoud said he was sorry for them and asked how it had happened.

"It seems that Ivan called it off when Andreas didn't show up to meet him at a club. Andreas said he was on his way but decided helping Ottovio finish the video was more important and turned around. He's depressed about it, but I think he made the right call. I'll get Ivan's take soon enough, I suppose."

He would call Andreas when he was feeling better, Mahmoud said. No need to give him another thing to be depressed about. Then he asked Kaan what was next for him.

"Since I could be on a hit list for revealing state secrets, I gotta keep a low profile. No plan except work with Ivan and keep in touch with George in case he hatches a new project."

Any idea what might that be, Mahmoud inquired.

"Not really, but somewhere there's a stash of sarin that he might find a use for. So what about you? What will you do? Go back to Piraeus?"

Mahmoud surprised him by saying after recovering his strength he wanted to go home—well, to Baghdad, not Mosul—to do humanitarian work.

"Reee-ly? What about your girlfriend?"

All his comrade could say was they were working it out. He wanted his next project to involve helping rather than hurting.

"You want to quit the movement? But we need you, man. What about the revolution, your jihad?"

It was hard to explain, Mahmoud said, adding he was tired now and wanted to take a nap.

"OK, get some sleep, my friend. I'm sure you'll get better. Talk to you soon. *Allahaısmarladık*"

After an uncomfortable night the invalid's condition seemed to have improved. His aches and pains diminished, but strength and stamina ebbed and flowed. He would awaken from naps feeling refreshed, only to relapse later on. The females mothered him with fruit, bread, fish, and elixir, but his appetite remained depressed. Safiye had found a cane for him, a real one this time, made out of wood, which he refused to use when Katrina took him for a constitutional in the neighborhood park, only to return exhausted.

The invalid in Ankara was rarely seen in public. Officially, his unsteady gait was laid to a fall that had injured his hip. He gave no speeches and proclaimed via spokesmen and news releases. Of course, his abnormally low profile and appearance gestated rumors that he was losing his grip on power, perhaps fading away, speculations that the captive press kept tamping down.

That afternoon, while watching TV as they sipped antitoxin

tea—both women had taken a liking to Mahmoud's elixir—news came that the Prime Minister, a fixture of the government for over a decade, had unexpectedly resigned after undisclosed differences with the President. The prospect of new elections put the nation on edge. Would the President hit the campaign trail, as always? Would he be seen as damaged goods or would sympathy for him buoy his party's fortunes? Would any opposition parties ally with the Davacists, and what would they do if they achieved power?

Mahmoud, dozing with his head in Katrina's lap, had nothing to say about that, but Safiye did. "Paşa pushed the PM out, I'm sure. If he wins the election he'll revise the constitution to consolidate power. Think of that; here we were, five nobodies . . ."

"Six nobodies and a notorious fugitive from justice, actually, but whatever," put in Katrina.

". . . who may have changed the course of history. How much of what happens next will we have been responsible for? It gives me the shivers."

Katrina stroked Mahmoud's hair and studied the stubble sprouting on his cheeks. "But this is the man who changed history. The rest of us are just supporting players."

Mahmoud opened one eye. "I heard that. Don't let yourself off so easily." He struggled up from her lap. "Do you think this operation was my idea? Did I plan it alone? Where did the poison that's in me come from?"

"Umm, no, no, and me."

"So you agree, we all had our roles and responsibilities, all equally important."

"Sure. You could say we all pointed the gun and you just pulled the trigger."

"Right. You could also say I'm the suicide bomber and you're the bomb maker.

"Anyway, your point would be . . ."

"That we made something consequential happen by working together, all of us." He locked onto her eyes. "Isn't that what you anarchists try to do?"

"Sure. It's my mission, in fact."

"Well, isn't 'mission' just another word for 'jihad'?"

"I guess, if you put it that way. It's your soul telling you what you gotta do."

"See, I made George's operation my jihad without even knowing what it would be. What it turned into was very different, but it was still my jihad. I believed in it, even more than the original mission—because I and the people around me were making it happen. And now, just like you, I want people everywhere to realize they have power to affect events."

Wiping a tear from her cheek, she bent to embrace him, kissed him, said "I love you. Wherever you want to go, take me with you."

He fixed his eyes on her misted glasses. "Even to Iraq?"

"Love, if that's your jihad, it's mine too."

Saying he felt cold and wanted to retire, Mahmoud struggled up. He kissed her forehead and asked for privacy while he prayed. Safiye wrapped him in a shawl and the women withdrew to the kitchen. Washing and tidying up, they speculated about how serious he was about moving to Baghdad. Whatever he might do next, they agreed something about him had changed.

Katrina threw off the blanket that was making her hot. Next to her, Mahmoud slept on his back emitting shallow wheezes. She curled on her side ruminating about Iraq, thinking it wasn't like her to make rash decisions, but that's what she'd done when she made a life in Greece and then again after she met and soon adored him. All of that still felt right, but Iraq?

The blurry green numerals of the nightstand clock glowed 4:37. She pivoted out of bed, found her glasses, and went to the hallway. At the kitchen table, her fingers turning crimson from picking pomegranate seeds from a glass dish, she contemplated her options. Something was telling her to take it slow. Even if it was only her inner child talking, she felt she should listen. It felt abrupt and would surely worry her family. Saying she was off to another war zone wouldn't surprise them, but sooner or later she would have to tell them about Mahmoud. Her parents were pretty tolerant but that might stretch it, especially if she were to convert to Islam, voluntarily or not. As a devout agnostic, that too gave her pause.

No, they should, she decided, return to Piraeus, her adopted city, also overflowing with castaways of the same senseless conflict. Why not build his dream there, where there were comrades and resources they could mobilize? She would haul him back there as soon as he was ready to travel, in a wheelchair if need be.

She got up, rinsed the red from her fingers, downed a glass of water, and then went back to snuggle with him. In bed, she embraced his chest. He had stopped wheezing and under the blanket his skin felt cold. Her ear to his chest detected no rising and falling. She circled to his side and jiggled his shoulders. "Mahmoud! Mahmoud! Wake up!" When he didn't stir, she shook harder. "Come on, Mahmoud! No! Don't do this to me!"

On her way to the bathroom Safiye heard muffled sobbing. She cracked open the guest room door to listen. Katrina was on her knees at the side of the bed, her head on Mahmoud's chest, shoulders quivering. "*Alma Allah!*" she cried, taking to her knees to embrace them both. At last they lifted their heads from his pale torso, their faces streaked with tears. Grey light filtered through the bedroom window that looked out on a stucco wall pierced by an open window with a drawn-down shade. On its sill, a rock dove paced, softly cooing. It stopped its bobbing, seeming to regard them, until a puff of wind gyrated the window shade and the bird took flight.

Safiye wiped her eyes with her nightgown. "I'm not sure I can bear this."

Katrina looked down on Mahmoud's face. It looked peaceful, mouth slightly agape, almost smiling. She gently touched his cheek, pressed fingers to his lips and let them slip away. "I'm afraid we have to. It was his jihad and, at least for now, it's ours."

Chapter Fifty-Five

THE TEMPERATURE IN the passenger cabin approached thirty and was rising. "If only they would close the damn door and run some cool air in here," Katrina told Safiye over her phone, "we wouldn't feel like fish in a canning factory." Izmir was unseasonably warm, but she'd been told temperatures were more normal in Athens, only an hour away once they close the damn door.

She fanned her face with her safety card. "The memorial service was very moving, don't you think?" Safiye asked, not waiting for an answer. "Except for Mihraplı I haven't been in a mosque for years. I thought the Imam did a very good job. Everyone was so helpful and kind."

"I felt welcomed there, and even though I didn't understand a word, it moved me to tears. And having Kaan there really comforted me, not just by translating but also by being so supportive and not blaming me for anything. We cried together."

An announcement crackled through the cabin. "Looks like we'll be leaving soon," Katrina said. "I have to go. Thank you for making all those arrangements. It would have been double hell without you."

"I hope that's the last passing I'll need to attend to," Safiye said. "Please let me know you got home safely and keep in touch. I want to know how you are doing. *Allahaısmarladık*, my dear."

Katrina had picked up a bit more Turkish. "*Güle güle*, Safiye. I owe you. *Teşekkür ederim.*"

She buckled up and tried to make herself comfortable as the plane backed off. The man in the window seat bumped her arm fishing for his seat belt and excused himself with *"Afedersiniz."* He looked to be about sixty, with receding black hair streaked with grey. Unlike most other men on board, he wore a business suit, with a red and blue tie hanging loose around his neck.

"No problem," she sniffed. "I'm glad to be on our way."

He smiled, settled in his seat, and opened his Turkish newspaper. As the plane taxied, Katrina reached down to take a moleskin journal from her handbag, and on a fresh page started writing: *12 December: On my way home on Aegean Airlines from Izmir. I'm happy for that but it bums me out that I changed my whole life to be with him and now he's gone. I have no idea what it all means. What would Rumi say?*

A tear from her eye fell to the page, bleeding the word *gone* into a purple halo. She pulled off her bandanna and blotted at it.

"You cry," her companion said with a strong accent. "Sad to leave Turkey?"

"Sad to leave like this," she answered. "It's a wonderful country, especially its people."

"You come on holiday? Been here before?"

"My first time. Came to visit with my boyfriend."

"Oh, is he here? I can change seats with him."

"Thank you, but no need. He's up there," she said, nodding upwards with a sniff. Without comment, her seat mate glanced at the overhead bins and then resumed reading. The engines revved and the airplane throttled down the runway, gathering speed, nosing up from the tarmac. She gripped her armrests as she sank into the cushions.

The plane climbed sharply and vectored west. Sunlight spun through the cabin, then the clunk of wheels being stowed away. Katrina loosened the seatbelt, reclined, and closed her eyes. The gentleman folded his newspaper and said "Terrible what's going on. Turkey has a lot of troubles. But they didn't have to suspend the constitution because of them."

Katrina's eyes winked open. "I wish I knew more about it, but it's hard for me to follow news there. Do you know what's going on?"

He slapped the newspaper on his palm. "First Paşa took ill, then the Prime Minister resigned. Then the generals took over, promising new elections but didn't set a date. Things don't look good."

Katrina nodded. "What do people say? Have you heard of any protests?"

"A mass demonstration in Istanbul was broken up yesterday. Some other cities had them too. But the press is censored. You only get the official line now. Most information is from foreign media. Hard to know what to believe."

"Isn't it," she said, thinking of George's predictions, which unbottled her anger at him for her pointless sacrifice. *Is this what you expected, Mister Mastermind? Got a plan to deal with it?*

She managed to reply "But at least people can express themselves on social media. Unless that's censored too."

"Yes, some of it is, like Twitter. And my company has to play along. We have no choice."

Katrina asked what his company does that the government wants to control. He explained that it's a major Turkish Internet service provider that sometimes is ordered to block social media traffic. At times the government has requested their server logs, but they were able to block that in court. But now, with martial law, it looks like they will have to comply.

The cabin attendant came by with beverages and little packages of butter cookies. She took one with a pale cup of coffee. He took tea and they sipped in silence for a while. He lowered his tray, deposited his cup, and inquired "So, what do you do?"

She moved to Piraeus year before last, Katrina explained, to work as a community organizer after a tough stint in Senegal. He said he knew how miserable life in Greece had become. "And not just there. In many countries people are being left on their own to struggle. It's good that you are helping them project their voices."

She asked what brings him to Athens. To finalize a partnership agreement, he said, with a Greek telecom company. "I don't know what it's about," she told him, "but it's great to see Greek and Turkish companies working together. Cooperation beats competition any day. And we do project our voices, every chance we get. Isn't that what your company is for?"

"Oh yes. We offer our users free Web sites and tools to set them up with no coding. Many are blogs that discuss serious matters, not just music, food, gossip and selfies. We have more than twenty thousand sites now."

"Wow, that's a lot of voices. Would be nice if they were listening to one another."

They stopped talking. He gazed out the window. Katrina closed her eyes again.

Soon he said "What did you mean, about listening?"

"Not really sure, but couldn't there be channels between them or something? You know, kind of like Reddit. Channels where they can, like, barter, loan money, organize collective projects, move them along. Real activism, not just mouthing off."

He pressed to recline and stared at the cabin roof. "Our apps let them discuss and act on serious matters. We can supply the oxygen, but they must breathe."

He reopened his newspaper. She reclined and was half asleep when he said "You know, I like your ideas. You say you organize people for a living?"

"You mean getting them to cooperate? Sure, but mostly in real life, on the street, face to face, also with our phones, of course. Can't say I make a living at it, though." Her African sojourn, she said, had taught her what people could do for themselves acting together. She didn't use the A-word to describe her movement philosophy. Instead, she said she tries to encourage "collective autonomy."

"Interesting," he said, shifting in his seat. "Another mobile app we have uses our Web services to provide a flexible payments system enabling customers to trade with one another. You made me realize that they could use it for a lot more than commerce."

"Like what? Bartering?"

"That and maybe more. They could also hold auctions to match what people need to what others have to offer—not just goods, but labor and expertise too."

"Such as?"

"Oh, like providing building materials, transporting goods, or meeting up to help out. Our app could do all of that."

"Would you take a cut of the action?"

"We'd charge fees after the first ten transactions each month, but they would be quite small. Once we recover development costs it won't take much to run the service. We already have the hardware."

She pressed her fingertips together under her chin. "Will this deal you're doing make the app available in Greece too?"

"We hope so. We just need to harmonize with EU practices. Why do you ask? Would you want to use it?"

"I would love to. If enough people over there got into it, could be a very useful tool."

He extracted a small wallet from his breast pocket. "Here's my card. You seem to be a very bright woman active in your community. I'd like to stay in touch. Perhaps you could help us set up a field test in Athens. I would be happy to pay you for your work."

She read the card. *Olympos InterConnect, Orhan Demirci, President & CEO.* He asked for it back and took out his pen. "This is my cell phone number and my email address. Feel free to contact me if you want to do something. Do you have a card?"

"Not on me. But give me one of yours." She wrote down the number of her old flip phone that she'd left in Piraeus.

"And your name too, please, Miss . . . ?"

"Burmeister. Anna Burmeister." She offered her hand. "Very nice to meet you, Mister Demirci."

"It's pronounced De-meer-gee" he said, taking it. "Turkish 'c' sounds like 'g'."

"Right, sorry. And Turkish 'g' is pronounced like nothing, I've noticed."

With an indulgent smile, he said "That's almost right. We have two g's. The one with a mark over it isn't pronounced. It just extends the sound it comes after. And if that isn't enough, we have two c's, s's, o's and u's. Makes up for not having q and x."

She laughed. It was the first time she'd done that in days.

The plane throttled down to make its final approach. Orhan straightened his tie. Katrina slipped on her shoes. Tilting up, she said, "Just thought of something. I know a Greek guy who could help you get your app up and running over there, if you wanted. He does magic with computers and cell phones and lives in Piraeus. Always looking for new technologies to conquer."

"That's good to know. Can you give me his name? I might want to talk with him."

"Don't really know it, actually. Everyone just calls him The Greek Geek."

Orhan chuckled. "Well, then, tell him about our conversation and ask him to contact me."

"Be glad to, Mister De-meer-gee."

"Much better, Anna. But just call me Orhan, please."

"Will do."

The plane pulled up at the terminal. At the chime she got up and from the overhead and removed a backpack and a decorative cloth bag that held Mahmoud's shirt, phone, wallet and passport. "It was very, very nice to meet you," she said. "Mustn't forget my boyfriend's effects."

Orhan blanched and grasped her arm, saying "Oh dear, does that mean what I think it does? I'm so sorry. I thought you were making a joke when you said he was up there, but I didn't want to pry. Forgive me."

"Not to worry. Anyway, it's hard for me to talk about. I'll be all right."

"No, wait. Come with me. Our partner company is sending a driver to pick me up. After he drops me at their office he can take you home. Don't protest. I insist. It's the least I can do."

"That's so kind. All right, if you insist, I'll accept. *Teşekkür ederim!*"

When the first limousine ever to stop in front of her house braked to a halt, the driver wouldn't accept any gratuity, telling her it had been taken care of. She went around back and warily let herself in, not sure of what she'd find. Her bicycle was still tethered Her outside door showed no sign of forced entry. She unlocked the kitchen and peered in. A quick tour of both rooms satisfied her that they were as she'd left them, and so she shed her backpack, extracted Mahmoud's effects from the pretty sack Safiye had given her, and arranged them on the table. It occurred to her that his passport held the only picture she had of him.

She flung open the windows to air the place out. Penelope apparently had emptied her fridge, but the freezer still contained a package of coffee. She set up the espresso maker, pulled her Ottovio Special from her backpack and called Andreas, who picked up on the second ring.

"*Grüzi*, Andreas. Katrina. I just got home."

"Katrina, *Willkommen zuhause!* How are you?"

"I'm a bit sick to my stomach, but I had a pretty good trip. It's great to be home."

"Kaan told me everything. It devastated me. I can't even imagine how you must feel."

She got up to pour her coffee. "Sad as hell. Guilty as hell. And mad as hell. That I let George talk me into setting that death trap. Mahmoud was right when he said it would be throwing two lives away for no good reason. Look what we got."

"What you got right now are good friends and many years ahead of you. To cap off the first day of the rest of your life, let me take you to dinner. Anywhere you want, name it."

"That's so sweet, Andreas. Sure. I'm a bit queasy now but it will pass."

"I'm sorry you're not feeling well. Do you have a bug?"

"Who knows. It's definitely not poison unless it was those cookies I had on the plane. I hope I'm not pregnant."

"Hmm. That would be dreadfully ironic. Anyway, why don't we go down to the *Microlimani*. We can amuse ourselves looking at rich people on their yachts and eat seafood. I'll borrow the Vespa and pick you up at six-thirty. Okay?"

She chugged the rest of her espresso. "Sure. Sounds lovely. But one more thing."

"What's that?"

"I know he won't fit on the scooter, but can you get Ottovio to join us?"

"I can ask. But why?"

"I miss him. Plus there's something I want to tell him."

"Okay, I'll ask. But speaking of him, you should know something. The other day I asked him to check the current police database for each of us. George's record was full of fresh annotations. Nothing for Mahmoud or Kaan, the usual for me, but your record had a recent note that you were currently in Switzerland. Why would that be?"

"Gosh. Let's see, I did tell that to one person as a cover story."

"Who was that?"

"Penelope, my house mate, when I gave her some things for safekeeping. I told her I was off to visit my parents. Do you think . . . ?"

"*Scheisse!* An informant?"

"No! Can't be. We've done too much together." A pause. "*Scheisse* is right! She has my journal!"

"We'll get to the bottom of this," he said. "I'll have Ottovio check *her* record. Try to act normal when you see her. Make up stories about Switzerland. Maintain cover until we know more."

"Will do. Anyway, I found out something today that I think will ring Ottovio's chimes. It's a little complicated. Let's just say it could be that geek's big break."

"I can't believe I'm hearing this from someone in your situation."

"What am I supposed to do, cry for a month and wear black the rest of my life? Not that I don't look good in black."

"Well, no, but . . ."

"Let me tell you something the Imam said at Mahmoud's service. Hold on." She took a slip of paper from her billfold. "It's from the prophet Muhammad. Kaan translated and wrote it down for me: '*How wonderful are the days of the believer, for his affairs are all good.*

If something good happens to him, he is thankful for it and that is good for him. If something bad happens to him, he bears it with patience and that is also good for him.' And that's what he did."

"I think I'm going to cry now."

A passing cloud moved on to flood her kitchen with sunlight. The curtains fluttered, bathing her face in flickers of sunlight. Twin stars cast from her glasses onto the ceiling. "I take it to mean," she said, "have faith, calmly adapt to whatever comes. And don't just mourn. Believe in something worthwhile and organize like hell."

"So what do you believe is worthwhile?"

"Collective autonomy, for one thing. I also believe I'll take a long, hot shower and then a nap. See you later."

Acknowledgments

NO AUTHOR IS an island and no book floats to shore unsupported. The village that it took to midwife *Turkey Shoot* is full of perceptive, patient, and kind characters to whom I am truly indebted for making it as good as it is. While I didn't run with every edit or suggestion proffered, over the course of nine full revisions my correspondents' earnest feedback utterly affected how I fashioned the plot, voiced my characters, expressed their uniqueness and interactions, chose words, modulated phrases, wove in facts about places I've never been to, and expressed sentiments in tongues foreign to me.

Let's start at the beginning: Enduring thanks to author and editor Gary Nilsen, whose developmental edit on my first draft pained me to read but was all true, for sifting through my trash. To physician and author Alexa Fleckenstein, my heartfelt gratitude for chewing through the early chapters I thrust at her over many months and for her insightful European perspective.

Then there were my generous beta readers: Ultra-responsive literary maven Jay Alexander; author, playwright, professor, and filmmaker Daniel Gover; esteemed poet Laura Bernard, the well-travelled and well-read Nick Chrisman; all-around wordsmith San Cassimally; the able Dr. Arnold Kamis and members of his writing group; and the redoubtable Debra Kraus for her staunch encouragement and soulful edits to love scenes.

I owe authors Matthew Amster-Burton, Elliott Colla, Hilton

Obenzinger, and John Weber of Welcome Rain Publishers and Emily and Christopher Bell of Atthis Arts for helping me understand and weather the vicissitudes of the book industry as I queried countless agents and publishers in four countries. It's now up to me to make a go of it.

When I fancied a film adaptation, script consultant Amanda Nelligan, screenwriter Jean-Marie Mazaleyrat, director Ahmet Boyacioglu, and producer Nikos Moustakas vetted drafts and synopses. Their helpful feedback kindled hope that Turkey Shoot may yet find its way to filmdom.

I particularly owe Kelly Santaguida of Gatekeeper Press for shepherding the novel and I through the inscrutable processes of publication and distribution. I commend that enterprise to the attention of anyone in search of a co-publisher.

Most especially, I thank my radiant Aygül, who has lovingly forborn my self-confinement and patiently corrected ungrammatical Turkish dialog over three years of drafts and revisions. Thank you, one and all, for supporting me in this quixotic project that corporate publishing establishment seems to have found irredeemable.

About the Author

A FORMER ACADEMIC WIDELY recognized for innovations in digital mapping, Geoffrey Dutton repaired to industry as a developer, analyst and consultant, eventually settling down as a technical communicator telling computer users what they should and shouldn't do. A gnawing unease over where tech was taking us led him to quit the biz, whereupon he unlearned expository style to deconstruct the digital mindset. Over the last six years he's variously posted over 400 articles, essays, stories, and memoirs at Progressive Pilgrim Review, CounterPunch, Medium and, in the Atthis Arts anthology *As Told by Things,* a short story narrated by a grumpy malware-infested PC. Having said all that, he has no special qualifications as a novelist beyond sweating through nine editorial revisions of this, his first.

Kismet willing, his next book will be nonfiction, an exploration of how electronic gadgets and digital communications are altering our identities and relationships to other people, objects, and the environment, and whether technology is an occult force of nature bent on obsoleting us, a corporate strategy to enslave us, or both.

Geoff lives in the Boston burbs with his spouse, daughter, and two overfed and under-exercised pussycats. He enjoys cooking for his family, especially with wild mushrooms that he carts home from tramps in the woods. All are quite well, thank you.